# IN PURSUIT
# OF HIS WIFE

BY
KRISTI GOLD

MILLS
BOON®

First Published in Great Britain 2016
By Mills & Boon, an imprint of HarperCollins*Publishers*
1 London Bridge Street, London, SE1 9GF

© 2016 by Harlequin Books S.A.

Special thanks and acknowledgement are given to Kristi Gold for her contribution to the Texas Cattleman's Club: Lies and Lullabies miniseries.

ISBN: 978-0-263-91860-1

51-0516

Our policy is to use papers that are natural, renewable and recyclable products and made from wood grown in sustainable forests. The logging and manufacturing processes conform to the legal environmental regulations of the country of origin.

Printed and bound in Spain
by CPI, Barcelona

**Kristi Gold** has a fondness for beaches, baseball and bridal reality shows. She firmly believes that love has remarkable healing powers, and she feels very fortunate to be able to weave stories of love and commitment. As a bestselling author, a National Readers' Choice Award winner and a three-time Romance Writers of America RITA® Award finalist, Kristi has learned that although accolades are wonderful, the most cherished rewards come from networking with readers. She can be reached through her website at www.kristigold.com or through Facebook.

# One

Seated in a wicker glider on the mansion's stately porch, Nasira Edwards admired the beauty of the Wild Aces, the ranch her brother, Rafiq, had bought his beloved bride-to-be, Violet. Nasira appreciated the way landscaped lawns gave way to green pastureland. She relished the warm May breeze, the climate so different from London this time of year. When she had originally traveled to Royal, Texas—home to the legendary Texas Cattleman's Club—she had done so to prevent Rafe from exacting revenge on his friend, Mac, for a mistake she had made over a decade ago. She had come to clear the air, right past wrongs, and fortunately she had succeeded. Yet that had not been the only reason behind the journey. She yearned for the peace this place could provide, yet peace had not come. The lingering pain of loss was simply too overwhelming.

In response to the memories, she withdrew the bracelet from the pocket of her dress and studied the tiny silver rattle charm she had received upon confirming her pregnancy. A surprising gift from a husband who had not embraced fatherhood. Still, she had viewed the welcome gesture as a symbol of hope for a bright future, until the day all hope had been splintered like shards of fragile glass.

Her palm automatically came to rest on her abdomen, now as barren as her life had been for a while. The baby she had so desperately wanted, and tragically miscarried, had changed her completely. Odd how she could miss someone she had known for such a brief time. And strange how badly she missed Sebastian, though he had been emotionally absent for the past six months. She had had no choice but to continue to put physical distance between them in an effort to reassess their future.

When the door opened to her left, Nasira expected to find her brother, Rafiq, checking on her welfare. Instead, Rafe's friend, Mac McCallum, stepped outside and gave her a pleasant smile. "Are you doing okay?"

She did not deserve his good humor or respect after what she had done to him in the distant past. "I've been enjoying the Texas sunset."

"Looks to me like that old sun has been gone a while," he said. "My sister sent me out here to tell you dinner will be ready in a few."

Food held little appeal in recent days. "I appreciate Violet's hospitality, but I am not very hungry."

"Suit yourself, but if you keep going this way, you'll be blown to New Mexico if the wind picks up steam."

She smiled reluctantly and stood. "I suppose if that is a possibility, I should attempt to eat something. Are you staying for dinner?"

"Not tonight. I'm meeting up with Andrea."

Nasira suspected Mac had feelings for his personal assistant that went beyond the boardroom, even if he could not admit it to himself, according to her future sister-in-law, Violet. "Is this business or pleasure?"

He frowned. "Business, of course."

"It's rather late in the day for that, is it not?"

"Unfortunately it comes with the territory of McCallum Enterprises."

When the discussion lulled, Nasira saw her chance to verbally make amends for past mistakes. She studied the wooden planks beneath her feet for a moment before regarding him again. "I wanted to extend another apology for what I did to you all those years ago. The guilt has been unbearable."

Mac lifted his shoulders in a shrug. "Hey, you were young. We were both young. You were just trying to get out of an arranged marriage to a man twice your age."

That ill-fated visit to the university to stay with her brother had set a horrible course that had led to Rafe's need for revenge. "Yet I was wrong to use you to achieve that goal, especially when I climbed into your bed for the sole purpose of having my father discover us. And because our father blamed Rafe for not looking after me, that led to his determination to seek revenge on you. I shudder to think what might have happened had I not come here to intervene."

"It all turned out okay," Mac said. "He's no longer trying to buy up the town to get back at me, he's going to marry my sister, and we're going to be one big happy family."

Nasira was happy for them all, but still… "Even after Rafe's torture and confinement for years due to my errors in judgment, he has forgiven me. I suppose I need to know if you will forgive me as well, though I would understand if you would not."

"Consider it done, Nasira. That's old water under the bridge now that Rafe knows I didn't really sleep with you. And since he's marrying my sister, I consider us all one big happy family."

Relief washed over her, though she couldn't claim to be happy over the state of her own marriage. "I so appreciate your understanding."

"No problem. Mind if I ask you something?"

"Not at all."

He raked a hand through his dark blond hair. "Don't take this wrong, but I'm wondering what the hell your husband was thinking when he let you get away?"

The course of the conversation made her somewhat uncomfortable. "It is rather complicated. Sebastian is complicated. After ten years of marriage, at times I wonder if I know him at all."

"One thing I do know. When a man doesn't realize the value of his wife, that's borrowing trouble. I just hope he comes around soon and realizes what he'd be giving up."

If only she could believe Sebastian had the capacity to be transformed into someone who would fight for their relationship. "I truly appreciate your concern and understanding, Mac."

"You're welcome. Guess I'll be heading home to the Double M now." He started toward the steps but paused and faced her again. "Before I leave, I'd just like to say it's fairly clear you don't need another big brother, but if you ever want a sounding board, you know where to find me."

How nice to come upon such a benevolent man. She certainly had not received so much compassion from her own husband in quite some time. "Thank you."

Mac returned to her and rested his palms on her shoulders. "Keep your chin up and keep standing your ground. You deserve the best."

Until six months ago, she had believed she had been blessed with the best of everything. Almost. "For the sake of clarification, Sebastian is not mean or cruel. He is simply too controlled and at times, distant. I have often wished he would lower his guard and demonstrate some sort of emotion, but I've accepted that it will most likely never happen—"

"Unhand my wife, you bloody bastard!"

Nasira barely had time to comprehend what she had heard before her estranged husband rushed onto the porch, drew back his fist and hit Mac in the chin, knocking the rancher backward against the brick wall.

When Mac gave Sebastian a menacing look, Nasira returned to reality in time to step between the men. "What are you doing, Sebastian?"

He pointed at Mac and sent him a menacing glare. "I'll not allow another man to grope my wife."

Never had she'd seen Sebastian act this way, and as much as she deplored violence, and despite her shock over his sudden appearance, she was pleasantly surprised, albeit somewhat mortified. "Oh, for goodness' sake. He is only a friend and he was not groping me."

Mac pushed away from the wall, rubbed his chin and glared at Sebastian. "If I didn't think so highly of your wife and her brother, I'd invite you to take this out into the yard and finish it, you jackass."

Sebastian balled his fists at his sides. "I would be glad to finish this."

Nasira spun on her husband. "Stop this right now, Sebastian. No one will be fighting if I have any say in the matter, and I do." She turned back to her friend and sent him an apologetic look. "Mac, I am so very sorry for my husband's behavior. I assure you he's not normally so impulsive with total strangers. And if you would not mind, I would like a few moments alone with him."

"No problem," Mac said before turning an acrid look on Sebastian. "I'm going to give you a pass, Edwards, and only because you're Nasira's husband. But don't push your luck by trying something like that again."

Sebastian straightened his tie and smirked. "If I find you touching Nasira again, I cannot promise there won't be a repeat performance."

"Just take better care of your wife and you won't have to worry about me."

After Mac disappeared into the darkness, Nasira prepared for a confrontation. "What were you thinking, and why on earth are you here?"

Sebastian opened and closed his fist. "I wasn't thinking, only reacting to a man with his hands on my wife. A man from her past, no less. And I have come to escort that wife back to London."

Her fury began to escalate. "First of all, nothing ever existed between myself and Mac, other than he was attempting to assist me in fooling my father into believing I'd been compromised."

"He looked as if he would like to compromise you in earnest a few moments ago."

She refused to give credence to his suspicions. "Your imagination is evidently running wild. And most important, I am not your property, Sebastian. I will return when I decide to return. *If* I decide to return."

"You're my wife. You belong with me."

At least he hadn't said she belonged *to* him, as if that were any consolation. "I came here to gain some perspective and I am going to stay until that is accomplished. You might as well climb back on the jet and wait at home for word from me."

"I refuse to go until this issue is resolved."

Despite his stubborn attitude, Nasira began to notice how handsome he looked and knew immediately she would lose her determination if he stayed. Too much time had passed since they had made love—the one thing that had always been right with their convenient marriage. Yet that had been his decision, not hers. "At the very least I will be here until Rafe and Violet's wedding at the end of the month."

"I'll wait as long as it takes."

She brought out the best argument to convince him to go—the shipping business he owned and ran. "I cannot believe you would ignore your duties and abandon the company for any length of time."

"I own the company. I can do what I please."

Such a frustrating man. "Do you have an answer for everything?"

He sent her a slow, easy smile. The smile he had given her all those years ago from across a very crowded ballroom, as if they had been thrust into a storybook scene. The smile that had convinced her to enter into an arrangement to escape her father's clutches. "Have you had dinner?"

No, and she had begun to feel the effects. "I have not, although Violet has prepared a meal."

"I'm certain she will understand if you would rather dine with your husband. We could continue our discussion then."

While Nasira took a moment to consider her options, the door swung open again and out walked Rafe, her tall, dark, handsome overly-protective brother.

He immediately eyed Sebastian with disapproval. "I see you did not follow my advice and remain in London, brother-in-law."

Sebastian looked equally miffed. "And when we spoke by phone two days ago, I made it quite clear I would make that decision without your interference."

Nasira stared at her husband before returning her attention to her sibling. "Rafiq bin Saleed, why did you not tell me you spoke with Sebastian?"

Rafe did not appear the least bit contrite. "You mentioned on numerous occasions you did not want to be disturbed by him."

"And he refused to allow me to speak with you when you ignored my calls to your cell," Sebastian added.

She despised it when men insisted she could not look after herself. "You had no right to take the choice out of my hands, Rafe."

"It makes little difference now," Sebastian said. "I'm here and I intend to make the best of the situation."

She only wished she knew what else he intended. That information would only be gained if she accepted his invitation to dine with him tonight. "I'm going to accompany Sebastian to dinner. I will be gone an hour or so."

"Do you believe that is wise, Nasira?" Rafe asked.

"We bloody believe that is none—"

"I can speak for myself, Sebastian. I am no longer your charge, Rafe. I can take care of myself. Tell Violet I truly appreciate her hospitality. We should go now, Sebastian, before I change my mind."

With that, Nasira followed Sebastian down the porch steps and when she didn't immediately spot a sedan, she paused on the pavement. "How did you arrive here?"

He nodded toward a shiny black truck at the end of the drive. "This is all they had available to rent at the airport."

Nasira covered her mouth to keep from laughing. "Oh, my. Can you handle that?"

He looked somewhat incensed over what he apparently considered an insult to his masculinity. "Of course I can handle it. I made it here, did I not?"

"All right," she said, and then continued toward the monstrosity.

Once there, Sebastian opened the passenger door and held out his hand. "Your cowboy chariot, madam. Let me assist you."

"I am almost six feet tall, Sebastian. I can manage climbing into a truck by myself."

"Only trying to be a gentleman, Sira."

The sound of his pet name for her stopped Nasira in her tracks. "Do you know how long it has been since you called me that?"

He winked. "Perhaps too long."

She had no clue where all the charm and machismo had been hiding. Following the miscarriage, he had spent long hours at work and little time with her. Perhaps he had turned a corner that would lead to change. Only time would tell. In the interim, Nasira would remain cautiously optimistic.

As they sat in the red booth in the Royal Diner, Sebastian found his wife to be predictably cool. And as always, very beautiful. The white cotton dress fit her to perfection, contrasting with her long, dark hair draped over her slender shoulders. Since her departure, he'd spent many a night in their bed, longing for her company. Since the loss of their child, he'd spent most of his time avoiding her out of fear. Not fear of her. Fear of losing her. Yet that was exactly what he had done by pushing her away. A bloody self-fulfilling prophecy that he couldn't explain without baring raw emotions.

Pushing the thoughts away, he turned his attention to the plastic-covered menu and scanned the unpalatable selections. "What do you recommend, Sira? The double cheeseburger or the fried catfish plate?"

That earned him her smile. "I realize this place isn't exactly your cup of tea, but I find it charming."

"I find it overly quaint and a heart attack waiting to happen."

"They do have salads and I hear the grilled chicken is very good."

He closed the menu and set it aside. "I will make do with the limited choices."

"What are you having?"

A tremendous urge to kiss her. "I'm going to sample the steak. And you?"

She laid the red-checkered napkin in her lap. "Definitely a salad."

"You should eat something a bit heartier. You're too thin."

"I am the same weight as I was before I left London."

"I'm only concerned about you, Sira."

She sent him a skeptical look. "Oh really? Where was all this concern over the past six months?"

He didn't feel this was the time or the place to get into such a serious subject, and thankfully a waitress arrived to interrupt their conversation.

She patted her rather large blond hair, pulled a pencil from behind her ear and a notepad from the pocket of the red apron. "Howdy. I'm Darla. What can I get the two of you darlin's to drink? Maybe some sweet tea?"

He couldn't quite fathom these strange Texas customs. "I prefer to sweeten my tea myself. With sugar and milk."

"She means cold tea," Nasira said. "I will take a glass with lemon."

He needed something much stronger to make it through this evening. "Bring me ale."

The woman raised a painted eyebrow. "Ginger ale?"

Bloody hell. "Beer."

"Sebastian, I cannot drive that truck," Nasira said. "For that reason, I suggest you forego the ale."

She did have a point and in accordance with his plan, he needed to prove himself worthy of her company. "Water will be fine."

"With lemon?" Darla asked.

"Why not? If that is fine with my wife."

Nasira frowned. "Of course it is. And I would like a salad with the dressing on the side."

"She would also like the grilled chicken," Sebastian added despite Nasira's disapproving look. "I'll have the rib eye. Make certain it's cooked through."

Darla looked somewhat appalled. "You mean well done?"

"Precisely."

The waitress jotted down the order then gathered the menus. "You two aren't from around here, are you?"

Sebastian sent her a mock grin. "What gave us away?"

"The men around here order their meat rare." With that, Darla waddled away, muttering under her breath.

Nasira immediately turned a sharp gaze on him. "Why do you insist on doing that?"

He opted to play ignorant. "Doing what?"

"Ordering my meals for me. I am quite capable of deciding what and how much I eat."

"I've always ordered for you, Sira."

"I know and I do not care for it."

"And you waited ten years to tell me?"

"It seemed simpler not to make waves and avoid conflict."

Did she think so little of him? "I'm not your father, Nasira. If you want something from me, you need only ask."

She stared at him a few moments. "I want another baby."

The one thing he felt he could not give her. "Impossible."

"Why, Sebastian?"

He could only offer her a partial truth. "You had a devil of a time when you miscarried. The doctor said—"

"That I am quite capable of conceiving again and carrying to full term. The risk is not any greater than any woman who has lost a child in the first trimester."

He imagined his own mother had believed that very thing. "Look, this is not the time or the place to discuss this."

She lifted her chin and leveled a determined glare on him. "Unless we discuss it, I will not be returning to London with you in the foreseeable future."

Sebastian swallowed around his shock. Not once during their time together had she issued threats. "We will talk about this some other time."

The waitress returned with their drinks, and they waited in silence for their order to arrive. All conversation ceased as they ate food that was surprisingly palatable. He spent a good deal of time watching the patrons, when he wasn't watching his wife pick at her meal.

Unfortunately, she only afforded him a glance when he asked, "How do you find the fare?"

"Adequate," she said and then took another bite.

He wondered if he would spend the next few days dealing with one-word answers while attempting to convince her to come home. Would she rebuff his advances, or eventually return to what they once had? He longed for the latter. He longed for her. All of her. First, he had to regain her trust and respect, if at this juncture, and in light of his mistakes, that were even possible.

By the time he had paid the bill, Sebastian worried he had ruined his chances at reconciliation.

Not yet. Not until he convinced her they belonged together, with or without children. How exactly he would achieve that goal remained to be seen. He knew only one way to do this—by using a tried and true technique that had never failed to turn her into clay in his hands.

"Sebastian, what are you doing?"

"Finding a private place to talk."

He had definitely found it, Nasira realized when he continued past the Wild Aces and took a dirt road that forked to the right. Once he reached the fence line, he backed the truck up beneath some low-hanging tree branches.

Before Nasira could voice a protest, Sebastian slid out of the seat, rounded the hood and opened her door. "Now if you will come with me please."

Clearly he had taken leave of his senses. "I refuse to traipse around in the dark, Sebastian."

"We're not going to traipse. We're going to sit in the back of this truck."

She felt certain that might not be in her best interests. "Why can we not remain in the front seat?"

"Because it's a beautiful night that should be spent beneath the stars and the moon."

She started to say they could barely see the stars but the opportunity to respond was lost when he reached in, took her by the waist, and lifted her out and onto her feet. "First that dreadful fight with Mac, and now you are manhandling me like some Neanderthal. What has come over you?"

"My behavior isn't necessarily so out-of-character for me, though it's been quite a few years since I've engaged in it."

Nasira released a cynical laugh. "You will have a difficult time convincing me that you ever behaved in that manner. In all the years I've known you, I have never seen you raise your voice, much less your hand."

He smiled. "Oh, you would be surprised what a scrapper I was in my formative years. I managed to get tossed out of three boarding schools before I finally settled down in my final year before university."

She could barely make out his smile, but she could

hear the pride in his voice. "That is definitely news to me and frankly somewhat appalling."

He leaned over and brushed a kiss across her cheek. "Are you certain you're appalled, or did it perhaps impress you?"

It had both surprised and in some ways set her senses on fire, not that she would dare make that admission. "It served to remind me what ridiculously volatile creatures men can be."

"Let's find a place to sit before we continue this conversation."

As long as they remained upright, she should be safe from giving in to his sensual charms. Then again, he had not attempted to touch her in so long, she could not even imagine that would be his goal. "Fine. But I only wish to stay for a while. I am fatigued from all the drama tonight."

"No more drama," he said as he took her by the hand and led her to the rear of the vehicle. "Now to ascertain how this bloody thing opens."

Before Sebastian could make a move to investigate, Nasira pulled the latch and lowered the tailgate. "It is really quite simple."

"How did you learn to do that?" he asked, sheer awe in his tone.

She shrugged. "I've seen Rafiq open one."

Sebastian reached out and brushed her hair away from her shoulder. "You are truly an amazing woman."

"Why? Because I can trip a release on a truck?"

"Because you are so observant and incredibly beautiful."

As much as she appreciated the compliment, she also recognized he had never paid her many, except about her physical attributes. "Thank you. I suppose we should get this over with so I can get a good night's sleep."

Without warning, he hoisted her up on the edge of the gate, causing her dress's hem to ride up her thighs. And while she made the appropriate adjustments, he climbed into the truck bed and had the nerve to position himself behind her, his long legs dangling on either side of hers. "Are you comfortable?" he asked as he circled his arms around her middle.

Uncomfortable would be more accurate; she didn't—or shouldn't—welcome the close contact. "No, I am not. I cannot have a decent conversation when I cannot see your face."

"You only have to listen to my voice."

Oh, that voice. That low, grainy bedroom voice that had enticed her on so many nights. And days. No matter how deep their conflicts had run, he had always been able to seduce her into submission. Granted, she had done her share of seducing as well, including the night she had conceived their child—without telling him she had stopped taking her birth control pills, which was information she had concealed until she had confirmed the pregnancy. Somehow he had forgiven the deception, or so he had said, yet she believed he had never forgotten it.

Nasira found herself leaning back against him, and turning her thoughts to the danger of succumbing to his power when he moved her hair aside and feathered kisses on her neck. "This is wrong, Sebastian," she said with little conviction.

"Remember that night in the carriage?" he said, proving he was bent on ignoring her concerns.

"Yes, I remember." How could she forget? On their honeymoon, he had arranged for a horse-drawn tour of Bath, which had led to taboo touching beneath the blanket, all leading up to a night she would never forget. The night she had lost her virginity and in some ways, her heart.

He slid one palm down her throat and traveled beneath the bodice where he cupped her breast through the lace bra. "I recall you were trembling, as you are now."

She hadn't noticed that at all. Her attention remained drawn to his fingertip circling her nipple now bound in a tight knot. "I was somewhat nervous."

"You were hot," he whispered. "I imagine you're hot now."

Before Nasira could prepare, Sebastian parted her legs with his free hand while sliding his other underneath the bra. "Pull your dress up to your waist."

The request was both startling and highly erotic. "Why?"

"So you might see what I'm doing to you."

As badly as she wanted his attention, she did not wish to make another grave mistake by giving in too soon. "This behavior will solve nothing, Sebastian."

He continued to fondle her breast without missing a beat. "I disagree. It will solve our need for each other. It will serve to remind us how we've always needed each other."

So caught up in his seduction, she clung to the last thread of sanity, relying on bitter memories to maintain her composure. "You haven't been concerned about my needs for months."

He kissed her cheek. "I know, and I'm bent on making up for my neglect. Can we for once stop thinking and allow ourselves only pleasure for a while?"

"But—"

He brought her head around and kissed her soundly. "Let me make love to you, Sira. Please."

She should issue a protest, she should be more resistant, yet she had become too caught up in the anticipation of how she knew he could—and would—make her feel. Too sexually charged over witnessing a side of him she had never seen before this evening—the jealous side, willing to defend her honor.

After she complied, he whispered, "Take off your panties."

This time she didn't hesitate to follow his directive, and after she lifted her hips and slid the lace down to her thighs, she no longer questioned the wisdom in allowing this to happen. After all, he was not a stranger. He was her husband, and she had been without intimacy for much too long.

While Nasira watched, Sebastian moved to the apex of her thighs and began to stroke her. A flood of heat and dampness caused her breath to catch in her chest. He knew how much pressure to apply. How to tease her into oblivion. The moments seemed so surreal—both of them in the back of a truck out in the wide open spaces of Texas, a warm breeze blowing across her face, her husband's hand between her legs bringing her closer and closer to the threshold of orgasm. She wanted badly to keep it at bay, to keep her eyes open, but all to no avail. When Sebastian slid a finger inside her, whispered a few words some might find crude, the climax crashed into her, bringing with it a series of strong spasms.

Nasira was barely aware that Sebastian had taken his hand away, but very aware when he moved beside her. When she heard the rasp of a zipper, she opened her eyes to see that he had shoved his slacks down his hips, revealing what the spontaneous foreplay had physically done to him.

"I need you, sweetheart," he whispered. "Come here."

She needed him as well. Much more than she should. "You want us to lie down in the back of this truck? I question the comfort in that." She also questioned her own sanity.

He grinned. "Who said anything about lying down? I am relinquishing control to you and hoping for a memorable ride."

Awareness over what he had intimated sent Nasira's pulse on a sprint. Every word he uttered seemed to be a jolt to her libido. Every suggestion added fuel to the building fire. Realizing the fit of the dress might not allow for enough room, she hopped to her feet to face her husband. She boldly unzipped the dress, pulled it over her head, tossed it and the bra into the bed of the truck and then pushed the panties down where they fell to the ground. She was totally, unabashedly naked and remarkably ready to finish this interlude immediately.

With that in mind, she climbed back into the truck on her knees to straddle Sebastian's thighs. Yet he thwarted that immediate plan when he said, "Wait."

She didn't want to delay another moment. "Why?"

"Birth control," he grated out.

Of course that would be his primary focus, and it should be hers as well. She lowered from her knees and sat on the gate, hugging her arms to her breasts. "I have not resumed taking the pills. I had no reason to do that."

She saw dismay in his expression before he stood and pulled up his slacks. "And you should have informed me immediately."

She suddenly felt very exposed, both physically and emotionally. She also sensed a hint of accusation in his tone. "If you are intimating I planned this so you could impregnate me, I was not the one who drove here for the purposes of seduction."

He released a rough sigh. "You're right, and my apologies for doubting your motives. However, if you consider our past, you certainly shouldn't blame me for my concerns."

Furious, Nasira came to her feet and grabbed her discarded clothing. "Obviously allowing this interlude under the circumstances has been a colossal mistake."

She glimpsed anger in his expression before she pulled the dress over her head, heard it in his voice when he said, "The sounds you made alone indicated you certainly enjoyed it."

"Evidently I am not immune to your charms," she said. "But mark my words, this will not happen again until we come to terms with our issues. And we have several, including your lack of trust in me and your resistance to having another child."

He slid out of the truck to tuck in his shirt. "We have a month to work out our differences and reach a compromise."

*If* they could work anything out. Nasira was not certain they could. "Presently I need to return to the house and you need to return to wherever you are staying for the duration."

He streaked a palm over his nape. "Actually, I haven't a place to stay at this point in time. It appears there are no rooms in the inns due to some rodeo event in the area."

Of all the irresponsible, ridiculous excuses. "You did not make arrangements before you decided to travel here?"

"It was a spontaneous plan."

An illogical plan in her opinion. "I can't very well have you in my room under my brother's roof. He is well aware we're having problems, and I prefer we not sleep in the same bed until we've had more time to work on our issues."

"I will take whatever room they have available if you don't wish me in your bed."

"There isn't another room, Sebastian. The house is still undergoing renovations and I have the only accommodations left."

"Then I suppose I shall sleep in the truck until other arrangements can be made."

Oh, for heaven's sake. "All right. You may stay in my room as long as you have no expectations and you leave before first light. I truly do not wish to explain your presence to Rafiq or to have him assume we've been…you know."

"I'm certain Rafe has engaged in…you know, since his intended is living with him."

"She is also pregnant," she added, curious to see how he might react.

"Really?" he said with little enthusiasm. "I didn't know the old boy had it in him."

"He does, and he is very protective of Violet, as well as me. On the other hand, he is not particularly fond of you at the moment. He assumes you have done something to wound me."

"And clearly you have allowed him to have those assumptions."

"Like it or not, Sebastian, your behavior for the past few months has been very hurtful to me."

He sighed. "And that is why I'm here now, to atone for my transgressions. Regardless, I promise to remain on my side of the bed until you are ready for me to fully atone."

When he suggestively winked, Nasira realized having Sebastian in her bed would not be wise for many reasons. "I will make a place for you on the floor."

He had the nerve to kiss her hand. "Whatever you wish, fair lady."

She wanted not to be so attracted him. She wanted not to want him, yet sadly she still did. "It is late," she said as she wrenched from his grasp. "And one more thing. When we arrive, be quiet. I prefer not to wake the household."

# Two

"What is he doing here?"

Sebastian had barely entered the two-story foyer before being verbally accosted by his brother-in-law. "I'm accompanying my wife to the bedroom."

With her hand on the banister, Nasira sent a sheepish glance in Rafe's direction. "He does not have a hotel room for the night. However, he has promised to leave first thing tomorrow morning."

Rafe gestured toward a formal floral settee. "The sofa is available."

Angry over the suggestion, Sebastian dropped his bags on the ground. "I won't fit on the bloody sofa. And if you recall, I'm still married to your sister and I have every right to sleep with her. Once you're married, you'll soon learn that problems can and will arise in every union."

Rafiq took a step toward the stairs. "She does not want you here."

"I invited him, Rafe," Nasira said. "But only for the night. Now if you will excuse us, we are both exhausted from the evening's events."

"Quite memorable events," Sebastian added knowing he would probably incur his wife's wrath.

Rafe pointed at him. "I do not wish to see you here when I awaken."

Sebastian saluted. "Yes, sir, commander sheikh."

Without looking back, Nasira hurried up the stairs and paused at the landing before regarding Sebastian again. "Are you coming?"

He suddenly realized he should attempt to turn Rafe into an ally, not an enemy. "In a moment. I'd like to have a word with your brother."

He saw a fleeting look of panic in her eyes. "All right, if you two promise to remain civil."

A promise Sebastian hoped he could keep. "I have no problem with that."

She glanced past him toward her brother. "Rafiq?"

"I will maintain my calm," Rafe said.

"I am counting on that," Nasira said before she climbed the remaining stairs and disappeared.

Sebastian decided he could use a bit of a pick-me-up and with that in mind, he grabbed up the smaller bag, set it on the sofa, unzipped it and withdrew a bottle of mediocre scotch, the only thing he had been able to find at the lone liquor store in town. "Would you care to join me in a drink?"

"No, I would not," Rafe said.

"Then would you mind providing a glass. I find it somewhat uncouth to drink from the bottle."

Without speaking, Rafe left through a door at the back of the parlor. He returned a few moments later with a crystal tumbler he set on the white coffee table before taking a seat in a club chair across from the sofa. Sebastian poured himself a glass of the amber liquid. Though he preferred ice, he thought it best not to press his luck.

After taking a long drink, Sebastian settled in on the settee as the low-quality scotch burned down his throat. At this rate, the combination of booze and jet lag could very well land him on his arse. Of course, he could rest assured he would sleep well…on the bedroom floor.

"Where is your lovely fiancée?" he began when Rafe failed to speak.

"She is sleeping," he replied. "The pregnancy has fatigued her greatly."

Sebastian remembered that all too well from the time when Sira was carrying their child. He also remembered the sound of her mournful cries when she had lost that child. "I'm sure the wedding plans have also contributed to that fatigue. How are you faring with that, by the way?"

Rafe crossed one leg over the other. "I have left the preparation up to the women. I only require knowing where I need to be and when I should be there."

Sebastian doubted he would escape that easily. "I suppose that is probably best."

Rafe inclined his head and studied him. "I suspect you did not detain me so you could speak about wedding plans."

Sebastian finished off the scotch with a grimace and poured another glass. "No. I felt it necessary to outline my intentions toward your sister. Has she mentioned me at all?"

"She only intimated your marriage is in shambles and hinted the breakdown is due to your inattentiveness."

As hard as it was to hear, he couldn't debate that assessment. "I've only had her welfare in mind since the miscarriage. I wanted to give her as much space as she needed. I realize now that was probably a bloody bad idea to show up, unannounced."

"Yes, and it has created a problem that will not be easy to rectify."

It occurred to Sebastian that he could possibly elevate Rafe's opinion of him if he appealed to his ego by asking for advice. "You seem to be a man who knows the workings of a woman's mind. Do you have a suggestion on how I could get back in Nasira's good graces?"

Rafe didn't seem to be flattered, though. "Perhaps you should return to London and allow her to decide if she wants to resume the marriage."

Not the answer he'd hoped for. "Look, Rafe, we've invested ten years in this union—"

"Convenient union, not a love match," Rafe added.

Point reluctantly taken. "Nevertheless, I care greatly for your sister and I'm not willing to give up what we've had for a decade without a fight. But I need assistance in order to win her back. Who better to help me than her brother, who knows her better than most?"

When Rafe remained silent, Sebastian almost gave up until his brother-in-law said, "Shower her with small tokens of your affection."

"You mean flowers and jewelry?"

Rafe looked at him as if he were a total dimwit. "Not only material gifts. And do not concentrate solely on sexual matters."

No sex or hearts and flowers. What was left? "I'm afraid I am still at a loss."

"I have learned women appreciate gestures that might seem insignificant to most men," Rafe said. "They greatly enjoy breakfast in bed. Massages. Having their hair washed."

Sebastian could handle any and all of those things, as long as he had some privacy to do them. "I now understand what you're saying, but I do have another problem. If I am going to woo her, I bloody can't do it in a hotel."

"And I do not wish to witness this wooing." Rafe came to his feet. "I have a possible solution to your lodging issues."

Sebastian finished his second drink and stood, realizing all too well that he should have stopped with the first scotch. He'd always been able to hold his liquor but at the moment he felt as if he could fly without the benefit of his corporate jet. "What do you have in mind?"

"A private residence where you could reside during the duration of your stay. The owners are friends of a friend and they will be leaving for a trip out of the country for two months. I will call tomorrow and let you know if they are amenable to the request. It will be up to you to convince Nasira, without coercion, to join you."

Sebastian had no intention of coercing her. Not when he had other ways to convince her. "I'll try to persuade her."

"If you are unsuccessful, will you agree to return to London?"

Only if and when he had exhausted every option. "That seems fair enough."

"Good. I am going to retire now. I will inform you in the morning if I have secured the accommodations."

"Thank you, Rafe. I certainly value your opinions and your willingness to assist me."

The man seemed unimpressed with Sebastian's gratitude. "I am doing this for Nasira. Her happiness is paramount. I will not tolerate anyone who does not respect her wishes. Keep that in mind as you move forward with your goal."

Before Sebastian could respond, Rafe turned and started up the stairs without looking back. Sebastian dropped down on the settee and rubbed both hands over his face. If he didn't get up soon, he could end up sleeping on the sardine-can sofa.

On that thought, he trudged up the stairs and made his way to his reluctant bride's boudoir. He rapped on the door and when he didn't get a response, entered the room to the sounds of running water.

He had one of two options—leave and let her have her privacy, or shower her with affection in the shower. Option two earned his vote. As long as he proceeded with caution.

He stripped off his shirt, inadvertently popping a button, then sat on the edge of the mattress to toe out of his shoes. He carelessly kicked them off, barely missing the French doors leading to a balcony. In an effort to compose himself, he removed his slacks and underwear with more patience, then tossed them aside on the window seat to his right. When he rose from the bed, he realized he would have to keep a tight hold on his libido. He also realized he wasn't the only one standing.

"Down, old chap," he muttered when he walked to the door, then paused to take a deep breath to regain some semblance of control.

If he played his cards correctly, this could be the first step in demonstrating that he could be the kind husband his wife needed.

Nasira needed a shower and a good night's sleep. She also needed to know exactly what Sebastian was saying to her brother, but that could wait until morning.

Standing beneath the spray, she closed her eyes, bent on washing away the memories of those intimate moments under the stars in the rear—of all things— a Texas truck. Still, her mind whirled back to the interlude and the way Sebastian had so easily unearthed sensations she had greatly missed. Sensations she still experienced with a succession of tremors and tingling. Her husband had so masterfully manipulated her into oblivion with only a few strokes, and once more the heat began to make itself known....

Nasira shook off the images, stepped to the side of the spray and opened her eyes, determined to regain some perspective without undue influence from her spouse until she was forced to face him again.

The plan went awry the moment the glass door opened, Sebastian walked into the shower and moved behind her, as if he had a standing invitation.

His audacity momentarily stunned her into silence. Yet when he reached around her and grasped the bottle of shampoo from the mosaic tile shelf, she spun on him, putting herself in close proximity to a very naked, very virile, very *stimulated* man. "Do you mind?"

He took a quick sniff before placing some of the liquid in his palm. "I do not mind at all. In fact, I like the lavender. Now turn around."

She gathered all the reasons to resist him. Reasons that had ironically kept him from her over the past few months. "You may turn around and leave."

"Not until I wash your hair."

That would qualify as an unusual request. "Why?"

"Could you humor me, please?"

She caught the faint scent of alcohol. "Are you intoxicated?"

"Only with your beauty."

Clearly the liquor was speaking for him. "I smell scotch."

"I might have had a drink. Or two."

"I consider that inadvisable in light of your fatigue."

"I'm not too exhausted or too mashed to wash your hair. In fact, it would be an honor to do it. And I promise you will enjoy it."

Granted, she would, though she wondered who had kidnapped her stoic husband and replaced him with this considerate clone. She mulled the offer over a few minutes and surrendered to the prospect of pleasure—with one concession. "Oh, all right. But only if you will leave after you are finished."

"Agreed."

Nasira faced the tiled wall again and attempted to feign indifference. Yet when Sebastian slid his hands into her hair and began to massage her scalp, she practically melted against him. "That feels exquisite," she murmured.

Sebastian brushed a kiss across her cheek. "You deserve to feel that way. I recognize I've neglected my duties and haven't exactly been a doting husband."

She had never expected him to be doting, yet she did approve of this version of Sebastian. Then suddenly his hands drifted from her hair to her shoulders and came to rest on her breasts. Odd how he had not touched her in six months and now, as if someone had snapped on a sexual light switch, the former version of her husband had returned.

"You are exquisite," he murmured as he pressed against her bottom.

"You are a cad."

"Henry is the cad. I have no control over him."

Nasira stifled a laugh. "I have always wondered what would possess a man to name a cherished part of his anatomy after his prized horse."

He winked. "It's quite logical because that horse is a premiere stallion."

She elbowed him in the ribs. "Since you are finished

washing my hair, I need to rinse out the shampoo and you need to vacate the premises."

Against her better judgment, she turned her back to him, stepped beneath the flowing water and soaked her hair, giving Sebastian complete access to her body. He took supreme advantage of her vulnerable position by running his palms down her torso, over the bend of her waist and on to her hips.

Regardless of her nagging need for him, Nasira side-stepped Sebastian and sent him a frustrated look. "You agreed that when you were finished, you would leave."

He took the blue washcloth folded on the shelf and added a small dollop of gel. "I'm not finished yet."

Unable to move, Nasira watched as Sebastian washed her body, beginning with her shoulders and arms before he moved down to her breasts, and then her belly. He knelt and bathed each of her legs gently, all the while smiling up at her until he straightened. His crystal blue eyes seemed to darken as he shifted his attention to between her thighs. He lingered there for a time, teasing slightly, setting her on edge before he stepped back and draped the washcloth over the chrome rack to his left.

"There you go," he said. "Clean as a whistle."

"Why are you doing this, Sebastian?"

His eyes looked a bit hazy now. "Because I want you to relax. I'm certain you will sleep much better now."

Not very likely. Not when she still wanted him in every way. "I am onto you, Sebastian."

He attempted an innocent expression. "I'm sure I do not know what you mean."

"Yes, you do. However, you can attempt to seduce

me from dawn to dusk but we will still remain at an impasse."

"I was simply trying to be considerate." He grabbed the bottle of gel and began lathering his body. "Granted, a dawn-to-dusk seduction sounds interesting. Perhaps we shall try that in the near future."

"I'm going to bed now," she said as she quickly rinsed off without looking at him.

"I will join you shortly."

"I'll make you a nice place on the rug."

"I so cherish being treated like the family hound."

She sent him a quelling look as she opened the glass door. "We agreed on that arrangement."

He gave her a half smile. "Spoilsport."

As usual, he glossed over the seriousness of their situation with wit and sarcasm. Angry with him, and herself, Nasira left the shower, dried off, wrapped the towel around her and tucked it closed between her breasts. She then twisted her hair into a braid, brushed her teeth and returned to the bedroom, leaving Sebastian alone to finish his shower.

In the past, she would have crawled into bed without clothes but decided with her husband in the house, it would be best to dress in a short blue gown, as if donning silk armor. Of course, if Sebastian sneaked beneath the sheets in the middle of the night, the negligee wouldn't provide any real protection.

Protection. He would not attempt consummation without any form of birth control. He had made that quite clear earlier. In that case, she supposed she could be benevolent and allow him into the bed.

She questioned the wisdom of that reasoning when Sebastian entered the room, a thick white towel slung low on his hips. Even after all their years together, even after seeing him completely nude in the shower a few minutes ago, the sight of his lean swimmer's physique still took her breath away. Many nights she had explored all the masculine planes and valleys, at first under his tutelage, until she had learned exactly how to touch him and kiss him. She had possessed a certain power over him during those times. She dearly wanted to experience that now...

"Sira, are you all right?"

Startled into reality, Nasira averted her eyes and shook off the recollections, though she could not shake the heat. "I am tired."

"As am I," he said as he approached the bed. "So exhausted I could sleep on the floor. Oh, that's right. I'm supposed to do that very thing."

Nasira pulled back the comforter and pointed to the opposite side of the mattress. "I am willing to take pity on you as long as you maintain a wide berth between us."

He grinned. "You are most generous, my lady. And I promise I will be the perfect gentleman."

If only she could believe that. "I will hold you to that promise."

As Nasira slid beneath the covers, her husband returned to the bathroom then came back without the towel or any clothes whatsoever. "Could you possibly put something on, Sebastian?"

He frowned as he climbed into bed beside her.

"Sweetheart, you know I prefer to have nothing on when I sleep. So do you."

"We are guests in this house."

He rolled onto his back and stacked his hands behind his head. "I highly doubt Rafe or Violet will do a bed check to make certain we're appropriately dressed."

That led Nasira to another question. "What did you and my brother discuss tonight?"

He continued to stare at the ceiling. "The strange ways of women and the complete ignorance of men."

"Be serious."

"I am."

"Then please explain."

"At times women say one thing, then do another, while most men are painfully honest. You'd rather spend a day shopping and men would rather engage in sports. Women want to discuss their feelings. Men would rather discuss something as dull as the weather to avoid that at all costs."

"The last part is definitely accurate," she muttered.

"Perhaps that's because we don't necessarily have deep feelings."

"Or at least those you care to share."

Too weary to continue the conversation, Nasira turned off the lamp and turned her back to her spouse. "Good night, Sebastian."

"Sleep well, Sira."

If only she could. For at least an hour, maybe more, Nasira tossed and turned, well aware that her naked husband was very near…and deep in throes of slumber, as evidenced by his steady breathing.

Little by little Nasira began to drift off and soon found herself immersed in an erotic state when Sebastian's hand drifted to her breast. She reveled in the intimate stroking between her thighs. Once more she was captive to his skill and to her own sexuality. Another orgasm—the second one tonight—claimed her with remarkable force. Before the climax had completely calmed, Sebastian moved atop her then eased inside her. Steady thrusts, ragged breaths, undeniable mutual desire…

He whispered her name and she stroked his hair, as if nothing bad had ever transpired between them.

Then suddenly awareness dawned of what they were doing, and what they hadn't done. "Sebastian," she said in a harsh whisper. "We have to stop."

When Sebastian tensed and shuddered, she recognized she had been too late with the warning.

After he finally rolled away, Nasira waited for his reaction and wondered if he was even aware of what had transpired. She received her answer when he sighed, sat up and muttered, "Bloody hell, what have we done?"

She snapped the light on and studied his profile. "Apparently we had unprotected sex."

He shot her a borderline distressed look. "Apparently."

"This is not all my fault, Sebastian. I told you to sleep on the rug."

"You offered me the bed."

"You did not have to accept."

"You shouldn't be so sexy."

"You should have foregone the liquor."

He raked a hand through his tousled hair. "It's clearly futile to blame each other or concern ourselves with the consequences. What's done is done."

"If you are concerned about pregnancy, I was off the pill for almost a year before I conceived the last time. It is highly unlikely that would happen again after only one time."

He appeared skeptical. "Unlikely but not impossible."

Normally Nasira would be happy to know she might finally have a baby, but not with such serious problems still looming over them. "Would it be so horrible if I happened to be pregnant?"

After punching his pillow twice, Sebastian shifted onto his side, keeping his back to her. "That's a discussion for another day."

"A discussion we need to have very soon, Sebastian."

"Would you prefer I move to the floor?" he asked after a few seconds of silence, reverting back to the man who refused to have any semblance of a meaningful conversation.

She preferred he stop clamming up. "It's too late to concern ourselves about that now."

"Then good night, Sira."

"Good night, Sebastian."

As she stared at the ceiling, Nasira wondered how she could feel so bereft after making love with her husband. It was as if they'd returned to the days before she had left London—she was suspended in a state of emotional gridlock with a spouse who constantly erected emotional walls. Could they get past the standoff? In the morning she would decide once and for all if finding out would be worth the potential heartache.

# Three

Nasira awoke to an empty space beside her and a strong sense of regret. She could only imagine what Sebastian was thinking. She wouldn't be surprised if he had already summoned the pilot of his posh corporate jet and flown back to London.

After showering and seeing to her morning routine, she dressed in white slacks and a sleeveless blue blouse, slid her feet into silver sandals and started downstairs to see if he had indeed left. When she heard the sound of two familiar male voices, she acknowledged she had been wrong in her assumptions, at least for the moment.

She reached the bottom landing, crossed the parlor and headed into the kitchen to find her husband and brother seated at the built-in banquette, having coffee together. They both quickly stood, looking as if they were errant schoolboys caught in a prank.

"Good morning, darling," Sebastian said, taking her aback with his friendly tone. "Sleep well?"

She didn't know if he was playing at being clueless or he didn't remember what had happened between them. "I slept well enough."

"Good because we have a busy day planned, thanks to Rafe."

Nasira leveled her gaze on her brother. "What does that mean?"

"I will let Sebastian explain," Rafe said as he started toward the parlor. "At the moment, I have to accompany Violet to speak with the caterer."

With that, he rushed away, leaving Nasira alone with her husband. "I find it difficult to believe my brother would involve you in the wedding plans, so I assume we're not expected to meet with the caterer."

"You would be correct. I asked Rafe to find us suitable lodging and he has the perfect place."

"Us?"

"Yes."

"I never agreed to that."

He gestured toward the chair Rafe had vacated. "Please sit so we can discuss this."

"Yes, let's." She settled in to the seat and waited for him to continue.

"Would you like coffee? Or perhaps tea?" he asked.

"I would like orange juice." And an explanation for why he clearly believed she would want to cohabitate with him, especially after his attitude last night.

He rose from the chair and walked to the refrigerator to retrieve the orange juice, poured her a glass and set it on the wooden table. He then took the chair opposite her and folded his hands before him. "I realize you left London to escape me, or perhaps our problems, but I am not willing to toss in the towel until we have explored all alternatives to remaining apart indefinitely."

Neither was she, though she understood they might never be able to compromise on the issue of having children. They never would unless he decided to actually discuss it. "You believe the only way we can do that would be to live under the same roof?"

"Yes, I do."

She had her doubts. "I know you, Sebastian. You will not tolerate a simple hotel room, and I do not believe you'll find a penthouse suite anywhere near Royal. If I decide to do this, I refuse to reside too far away from Rafiq and Violet."

"You're right, but there are houses available."

She suffered the second shock of the morning. "You purchased a house?"

He shook his head. "No. Rafe knows a man who is willing to open his home to us while he and the family travel abroad."

Living in a stranger's house did not seem like a favorable option. "What man?"

"His name is Sheikh Darin Shakir. I believe he hails from a country close to your homeland."

She had heard the name bandied about by Mac. "I know of him. In fact, his reputation precedes him."

Sebastian frowned. "In what way?"

"He killed a man several years ago."

"He's a bloody murderer?"

She gained some satisfaction from shocking her husband this time. "Actually, it is my understanding his love interest was being held captive by this criminal, forcing him to shoot the evildoer to save her life. Although I despise violence, I find the concept of coming to a woman's rescue somewhat romantic."

"I find resorting to murder somewhat disturbing." Sebastian sat back and sighed. "Perhaps we should explore other avenues."

"It's past history, Sebastian. He is very well respected and in fact married to the woman he saved. They have several children."

"Are you absolutely certain the man is safe? I refuse to put you in harm's way."

"As I've said, he is a hero in the town's eyes. I also know my brother would never send me into a dangerous situation."

Sebastian slapped his palms on the table and stood. "Then it's settled. We shall go meet this knight in tainted armor and see if the house passes muster. We need to hurry since they will be leaving shortly after lunch for the trip."

She refused to rush into the decision to join him. "I still have qualms about living together at this point in time."

"What qualms?"

"First of all, although I came here to confront Rafe, I also intended to have time away from you to think."

"On the contrary, last night you wanted to talk."

He did present a valid point. "Yes, but I'm not certain you would be willing to do that."

He rested his hand on the back of her chair. "If we decide the accommodations are suitable, I will strike a bargain with you."

Always the negotiator. "Go on."

"If you will give me one week and the arrangement doesn't suit you, or if I don't meet your expectations, then you are free to leave and I will return to the UK."

She mulled the proposition over a moment and decided that it did seem fair. After all, she truly wanted to attempt to mend the relationship if at all possible. "All right. I will agree to your terms."

"Great. Our chariot awaits."

She pushed back from the table and came to her feet. "I wouldn't consider that truck a chariot."

"I had another vehicle delivered this morning from Dallas. One that is more suitable. You'll see when I bring it around."

"Believe it or not, I find that somewhat disappointing."

He pushed a lock of hair behind her ear, a habit he had established from the first night they had met. "Why is that?"

"Sedans do not have beds."

Noting the look of sheer surprise on Sebastian's handsome face, she turned to retrieve her purse and sunglasses, smiling all the way upstairs and back down again. Perhaps she should not be encouraging her husband in a sexual sense, yet she could not seem to resist the desire his presence had resurrected. The ever present need.

If they had to exist in close quarters, she should make the best of their time together for however long it might last. If they jointly decided their marriage was over, she would make more memories to carry with her to override the bad.

If luck prevailed, the Shakirs' family home would be a happy place perfect for new beginnings.

"This isn't a house, it's a fortress."

Nasira tore her gaze away from the massive white stone structure to glance at Sebastian. "And this veritable limousine you've leased goes quite well with it."

He sent her a half smile. "It's a Jaguar, Sira. Only the best for my bride."

She didn't bother to ask how he had acquired it simply because she did not care. She only cared about meeting the mysterious man who resided in the residence. And of course, the woman who had been worthy of his rescue.

As soon as Sebastian pulled to a stop beneath the portico, a dark-haired, dark-skinned man dressed in black shirt and slacks emerged from the double iron doors. Nasira recognized him from the photograph she had seen at the Texas Cattleman's Club—Darin Shakir, sheikh extraordinaire.

He opened her door and greeted her with an intense look and a guarded smile. "Mrs. Edwards."

"Sheikh Shakir," she said as she slid out of the luxury sedan. "It is a pleasure to finally meet you."

"The pleasure is mine," he said with a nod.

Sebastian rounded the hood and offered his hand to Darin. "I truly appreciate your offer, Sheikh Shakir."

"You may call me Darin," he replied. "I have never embraced my royal status."

Nasira had also learned that about him, which could explain how he had settled in a place like Texas. Then again, so had her brother.

Darin showed them into the house where they were met by an attractive woman with red spiraling curls and bright green eyes. "Welcome to our home, you two. I'm Fiona Shakir."

"I am Nasira Edwards, and this is my husband, Sebastian," she said, beating her spouse to the punch.

At that moment, three dark-haired little boys entered the room and stood between the Shakirs like miniature soldiers. "These are our sons," Darin said. "Halim, Kalib and Samir."

Fiona rested her palm on the youngest one's head. "Otherwise known as Hal, who's ten, Kal, eight, and Sam, five."

The pitter-patter of footsteps echoed in the marble entryway, drawing everyone's attention to the little girl dashing into the foyer, her auburn-tinted curls bouncing in time with her gait. She immediately threw her arms around Darin's legs, leading him to sweep her up. "And this is Liana, our youngest," Darin said. "She will be three years old in three months."

When the little girl touched her father's face, and the stoic sheikh gave his daughter the softest look, Nasira's heart melted. "You have a beautiful family."

Fiona patted her belly. "Thank you, and in about five months, we'll be expanding it with another boy."

Nasira experienced a sense of awe and a slight sting of envy. "Four boys should be interesting."

"Very interesting," Sebastian said. "How do you manage caring for so many children?"

Fiona slid her arm around Darin's waist. "With a lot of love and sharing."

"And our nanny, Amelia," Darin added.

"A part-time nanny," Fiona amended. "When Amelia isn't here, I've learned to be extremely organized out of self-defense. Otherwise the house will be utter chaos and I'll be a raving maniac."

Darin pointed behind him. "Boys, return to the play-room." No sooner than he commanded it, the Shakir sons departed.

Fiona gestured toward the hall beyond the foyer. "Come inside and I'll show you around."

"I would enjoy seeing the livestock," Sebastian said to Darin. "We can leave the wives to tour the house and talk about us when we're out of earshot."

Darin finally smiled. "I would be glad to show you the stables."

"Take Liana with you," Fiona said. "She'll throw a fit if you walk outside without her."

Sebastian looked somewhat alarmed. "Is it wise to take a child around the horses?"

Fiona smiled. "She's fine as long as she's super-vised."

Darin shifted Liana from one hip to the other. "We

have several Arabians if you and your wife would like to ride."

"It would be a pleasure," Sebastian began, "yet I'm afraid my wife would probably balk at the idea."

But Sebastian was wrong. "I would love nothing more than to go for a ride. I spent much of my youth on the back of a horse."

Sebastian frowned. "You've never told me that in our ten years together."

"You never asked."

"Ten years?" Fiona interjected as if she sensed the tension. "Darin and I have been married that long. Do you two have children?"

Nasira swallowed around the nagging lump in her throat. "Not yet."

"We have a very busy life in London," Sebastian added. "And we both enjoy traveling. Nasira is involved in charity work and my shipping business requires quite a bit of time."

Fiona shrugged. "Children are definitely time-consuming."

"And wonderful," Nasira said, determined to get her point across to her husband. "I definitely want at least one or perhaps two."

Sebastian regarded Darin. "Shall we begin the tour of the stables? We wouldn't want to detain you in light of your upcoming vacation."

Leave it to her husband to avoid the topic of children. And that gave Nasira pause. "I am very much looking forward to seeing the rest of the house."

"Right this way," Fiona said as she gestured Nasira forward.

They made their way through a large formal lounge with gleaming dark wood floors and several seating areas containing multicolored leather furniture and assorted club chairs.

She already felt at home surrounded by such opulence. "This is very grand but comfortable."

"Thank you, Nasira." Fiona nodded toward the sweeping staircase. "We have five bedrooms upstairs and our other family room, which is always a mess. So I'll concentrate on the downstairs for now. But feel free to explore when you're here."

Provided they decided to stay there, though she had to admit she would love it. "We so appreciate your hospitality."

"You are so welcome," Fiona said as she took off at a fast clip. "The two guest bedrooms are down here."

Nasira admired the luxury of the first bedroom Fiona showed her. It was accented in whites and grays with a plush king bed and gorgeous en suite bath. The second was equally remarkable though the color palette featured differing shades of blue. Nasira welcomed the fact that if serious conflicts arose during their time her, she could have one room and Sebastian could have the other.

"Amelia usually stays in one these rooms when she spends the night," Fiona began, "but we're taking her with us. Darin and I could use a little alone time, if you catch my drift."

Nasira was not familiar with the term, yet she did understand the meaning behind it. "I have no doubt enjoying private moments with your husband must be difficult in light of the children's needs."

The redhead grinned and winked. "We women have needs too."

Something Nasira had realized all too well last night. "Yes, we do."

Fiona led her out into the corridor and waved her forward. "The housekeeper, Annie, will be in every day if you decide to stay with us. And she prepares wonderful meals."

"That would not be necessary."

"I insist," Fiona said as she stopped in the great room. "Besides, Annie would be lost if she didn't have something to do. I promise she won't be in the way. In fact, you won't even know she's here most of the time."

A phantom maid was quite a novel idea. "Well I would not want her to feel unwanted."

"I can show you our bedroom if you'd like," Fiona began, "or we can take a look at the kitchen."

"I would love to see the nursery," Nasira blurted without thought.

"Then follow me."

They crossed to the opposite end of the house and walked down another long hall until Fiona paused at a door with a keypad. "This is the elevator to the upper floor. I'll leave the code in case you need it."

She could not imagine why they would. "Did I not see a staircase?"

"Yes, you did." Fiona smiled as they continued on side by side at a much slower pace. "We use it to get to the second floor fast if one of the kids needs us during the night. Darin is usually the one who hops out of bed first. He's a very light sleeper."

"How did the two of you meet?" Nasira asked, overcome with curiosity.

"In a Vegas lounge," Fiona said. "I happened to be bartending when he walked in and he thought I was someone else."

"Someone else?"

"Yes. An FBI agent. It's a long story but let's just say that particular night started a harrowing adventure that led to this wonderful life full of love and chaos and beautiful children. And speaking of children, this is where the babies stay."

Fiona opened the double doors to a large nursery that Nasira could only describe as a children's wonderland. A majestic white canopy crib draped in sheer pale green netting to complement the gender-neutral decor had been positioned between two windows. Stuffed animals of all shapes and sizes dotted built-in shelves that also held trinkets and framed photos of the Shakir children at various points of their life. It was a remarkable place that indicated a very happy family lived here.

Fiona pointed to a small bed to their right. "Liana still sleeps there for the time being. We'll move her upstairs to the big girl room right before the baby comes. At least that's the plan. I'm not sure how well her daddy is going to take not having her nearby."

Nasira could see where that might be an issue. "They seem to be very close."

"She's definitely a daddy's girl. You'll figure that one out if you and Sebastian have a daughter."

Regret and memories washed over Nasira as she walked to the crib and ran her hand over the soft coral blanket folded at the end of the mattress. How many times had she imagined her own baby in such a precious bed? How many times had she cried over the end of that dream? Her hand automatically came to rest on her abdomen, and then the familiar tears arrived as sudden as a summer rain. Unwelcome tears that she could not seem to control.

She felt a hand on her shoulder. "Nasira, are you okay?"

Not in the least. She turned around and sniffed. "I had a miscarriage six months ago. It was early in the pregnancy but still no less devastating."

Fiona snapped a tissue from the box on the changing table and handed it to her. "I'm so sorry, Nasira, and I can relate."

She dabbed at her eyes. "You can?"

"Like you, I had a first trimester miscarriage between Kal and Sam. It broke my heart."

Finally, someone who could understand and perhaps provide insight. "How did Darin react to the loss?"

Fiona shrugged. "He was extremely supportive even though he didn't touch me for a couple of months. I think he worried I might break."

"Sebastian avoided me for six months."

Fiona's green eyes went wide. "You haven't made love since you lost the baby?"

Nasira felt the urge to confess, yet thought it best not to reveal too much. "That was the case until last night, although I am still in a quandary over how it happened. In fact, the whole evening was rather odd."

"I'd think you would be relieved," Fiona said. "Six months is a long time without making whoopee."

"True, but Sebastian's behavior was completely out of character. First of all, he arrived at Rafiq's house uninvited and punched Mac McCallum because he believed we were having some sort of tryst, which is absolutely absurd."

Fiona gasped. "He did not!"

"He did. I was completely shocked by his behavior yet admittedly somewhat attracted to his sudden show of machismo. Sebastian is usually so controlled."

Fiona chuckled. "I know exactly what you mean because Darin is like that, too. But there's no shame in wanting to jump his bones after he defended your honor, even if he mistakenly thought you were fooling around."

Nasira had definitely wanted him, yet she had never been the aggressor in the relationship. "For the sake of accuracy, I was not exactly looking to rekindle our love life at that moment. Yet he convinced me to have dinner with him and then he virtually seduced me in the ridiculously large pickup truck he rented."

"Welcome to Texas, girlfriend. Sex in a pickup truck is practically a sport."

Nasira couldn't contain her smile. "That actually came later, in the middle of the night, after Sebastian had two toddies on top of his jet lag." She sighed. "You must think I am a complete dolt, telling you all the sordid details."

Fiona folded her arms across her middle. "Hey, I'm

a good listener, and it's sure not stupid to want to make love to your husband."

Then why did she feel so foolish? "I should not want him after what he has done. Or what he has not done. Not only did he avoid lovemaking, any serious communication between us has been at a complete standstill. He refuses to talk about our loss or how he feels about it."

"Darin isn't a great communicator, either," Fiona said. "But I can't imagine him completely shutting down and if he does try that, I have ways to make him talk."

"Sebastian has not only shut down, he acts as if he no longer wants children. Maybe he never has. In fact, I had to stop taking…" She had already revealed too much. Said too much. "Again, I do apologize for burdening you with my problems."

"Burden away, Nasira. We're members of the miscarriage club and it's not a good club to join."

"No, it is not."

Fiona's face took on a serious expression. "If you don't mind me asking, do you know why your husband suddenly changed his mind about being a father?"

This would be the most difficult part to explain. "Actually, we met and married very quickly and we never actually discussed it at length. I did know that his father and stepmother were adamant that he produce an heir because he is an only child, so I mistakenly assumed we would eventually have children. Yet it took years before we finally conceived." With some regrettable deception on her part.

"If he doesn't change his mind, what are you going to do?"

"I have no clue at this point in time." And she really didn't.

Fiona patted her cheek. "Stick to your guns, Nasira. It's one thing if both parties don't want a baby, but it's another thing if one does and one doesn't. Regardless, I hope you both work it out."

So did Nasira. "That's why we are here. I initially came to Royal to check up on my brother and gain some space, yet Sebastian insisted on following me. We have both agreed to try to compromise. Hopefully, opening your home to us will aid in that goal."

"It's a magical place," Fiona said with a grin. "But just another bit of friendly advice. If he has sex on his mind, don't make it easy for him until you know you're both on the same page when it comes to the future. If he doesn't want to talk, then give him a little nudge."

If only she had mastered that tack. "What do you suggest?"

"Be a seductress, but play hard to get to get what you need. Eventually you'll have him eating out of your hand."

"Would that not make me a tease?"

"Sometimes we have to resort to desperate measures, Nasira. Playing cat and mouse always drives Darin insane, and I guess that's why we have so many kids."

They shared in a laugh and a surprising embrace before Fiona said, "Let's go see if the men have come in from the stables."

Nasira felt she should express her gratitude again.

"Let's. And please know how much I appreciate your candor and comradeship. You have bolstered my optimism."

"No problem, Nasira. We girls have just got to stick together."

The sound of feminine laughter filtered into the chef's kitchen, leading Sebastian to believe the two wives must be getting along famously. He couldn't exactly say the same when it came to his connection to Darin Shakir. The man spoke in brief sentences and appeared to be incapable of smiling, unless it was directed at his daughter. However, he had been a polite host during their tour of the stables, right down to pointing out where Sebastian should step to prevent ruining his Italian loafers.

As Nasira moved into the room, chatter went on around him but he tuned it out and focused on watching his wife. Even after all the years they'd spent together, Sebastian still found her grace and beauty breathtaking. He liked the way she kept her slender hands in motion when she spoke. He liked the way her dark eyes lit up when she laughed. He truly relished her breasts that were unfortunately concealed by her black hair falling in soft waves, crimped from the braid she'd worn to bed last night. He imagined those silken locks on his chest, along with her soft lips, moving down his belly and lower....

"Can I get you anything, Sebastian?"

He brought his attention to Fiona to find her sporting an odd look. "I could use a glass of water." Mainly to pour down his shorts to preserve his dignity.

"Would you like one too, Nasira?" she asked.

His wife frowned at him as if she had channeled his dirty thoughts. "No, thank you. I suppose Sebastian and I should take our leave so we can discuss your wonderful offer for us to stay in your home."

Darin stepped forward, the toddler still on his hip. "We will give you your privacy while we return to our packing. If you decide to stay, we will provide you with the key and the gate code so you may return at your leisure."

Fiona set a glass of water on the marble island next to Sebastian. "Liana, tell Mr. and Mrs. Edwards goodbye."

After Darin set the little girl on her feet, she immediately rushed to Sebastian and wrapped her arms around his legs. "Bye, bye, Mr. Man."

Seeing the grin on the child's face sent a spear of regret through Sebastian. He ruffled her dark hair and returned her smile. "Goodbye, Princess Liana. I am grateful to have met you and your noble steed, Puddles."

Her grin widened as she moved to Nasira and took her hand. "Bye, bye, pretty lady."

Nasira knelt at her level and touched the girl's face. "Goodbye, little princess. Have a wonderful time on your trip."

Fiona stepped forward and took Liana's hand. "Take your time, you two. When you're ready, just press the button that says *family room* on the wall by the stove and we'll come running."

After the couple disappeared around the corner, Sebastian faced Sira again. "Well, what do you think of the place?"

"I think it is very lovely."

"Not too shabby, I suppose."

"I also think your reaction to Liana was lovely as well."

He should have seen that coming. "She's a very interesting child though somewhat chatty. She is quite enamored of her pony."

"She seemed somewhat enamored of you."

"She is simply friendly." And he simply needed to divert Nasira's attention from the topic before she forced him to revisit his decision not to have a child. "By the way, there's a spa on the deck next to the pool. That alone would persuade me to stay."

"I cannot recall if Elsa packed my swimsuit."

"Elsa never forgets a thing. And on the off chance she did, we will swim in the nude."

She averted her eyes. "Keep your voice down, Sebastian."

Her innocence had come out of hiding. "Why? I assume this couple knows about all things sexual considering they are well on their way to creating an entire rugby team."

That earned him her smile and a wistful look. "You are so amusing. They have a wonderful family. They are quite lucky to have each other."

He realized how strongly his wife had been affected by the children. Children he could not offer her at the moment. Nevertheless, he hoped to come up with a plan that he would present later. Much later. "Are you still willing to reside here with me until the end of the week?"

"Yes, with a few conditions," she said.

He should have seen that coming. "And what would those be?"

"First, we stay in separate suites."

Bloody hell. "Why?"

"Because we need to concentrate on our relationship without any complications that will cloud our judgment."

Double bloody hell. "If you are referring to sex, you must admit that has always worked well between us. Why would we want to exclude that from our time together?"

She barked out a cynical laugh. "I find that somewhat ironic considering that until last night, you refused to sleep with me in every sense of the word for the past six months."

He couldn't provide an explanation without baring his soul completely. He had been taught by his father early in life that men did not give in to emotions. "I was simply allowing you to recover completely."

"Have you forgotten what happened last night when you were in my bed?"

"Actually, I barely remember it." Unfortunately.

"You do remember the birth control issue, correct?"

He had attempted to forget that, yet the possible consequences still haunted him. "Yes, I remember."

"Well, nothing has changed in that regard. We still do not have any protection against pregnancy."

Not yet, but he intended to rectify that with a trip

to the market. And perhaps he would pick up a box of chocolates along with the condoms. "I see your point, and I agree to your terms." For the time being.

"Second condition," she continued. "You must promise you will engage in meaningful conversations and answer my questions with candor without any comedy."

That would be somewhat difficult. "I promise I will try, as long as you promise to be patient."

"I will agree to those terms."

Simple enough. "Then I suppose we should tell the Shakirs we will be accepting their hospitable invitation."

Sebastian could only hope that agreeing to her terms would not prove to be his downfall.

# Four

Later that afternoon, when they returned to the Shakirs' house, luggage in hand, they found a note on the door from the owners inviting them to enjoy their home, and lunch awaiting them.

After Sebastian keyed in the code to allow them entry, Nasira started for the guest wing with her husband trailing behind her. She paused in the hallway to turn and almost ran into a wall of masculine chest. "Which room do you prefer?"

"The one where you'll be staying."

She sighed and stepped back. "We've already discussed this, Sebastian. Until we have our issues settled, I insist we adhere to our initial plan."

"I am only being honest at your request."

And infuriating. "I will take the suite on the right

and you can take the one across the hall. I assure you, they are both very nice. I will meet you in the kitchen after I have settled in."

"Yes, dear."

Relieved her husband had not put up much of a fight, Nasira entered the blue suite and set her suitcase and garment bag on the bench at the end of the bed. She quickly hung her dresses in the huge closet and put away her other clothes in the bureau, then returned to the corridor to find it deserted. Without waiting for Sebastian, she immediately left for the great room, all the while reflecting on his interaction with little Liana. He seemed quite charmed by the toddler, and perhaps that meant there could still be hope for their marriage yet. Or perhaps it had only been a show for the proud parents.

When she reached the kitchen, Nasira found a spread of luscious salads, cheeses, breads and cold cuts laid out on the informal dinette set against a large picture window that revealed a remarkable view of the countryside.

"It certainly looks appetizing."

She turned to find her husband standing close by, hands in pockets. "It looks wonderful. All of it. The food. The pastureland. The pool and the spa. We might as well be staying at a resort."

He raked back a chair, sat and then rubbed his hands together. "Personally I could consume most of this."

She claimed the seat across from him. "Please let me have a bit before you take it all."

He winked. "Sweetheart, although I would like it all, I will take what you will give me."

She could so easily walk into his lair but remembered

Fiona's advice. She would play along for now before she would play hard to get. "I promise I will give you enough to keep you sated."

He appeared pleasantly surprised by her response. "I look forward to it."

As they dined, a heavy fog of tension hung over them. A palpable tension long absent from their lives. Nasira held tight to her goal to persuade him to talk about issues he had always suppressed. During this time together, she vowed to learn as much as she could about the man she had lived with for a decade, and she would do whatever that required.

"I found Fiona Shakir to be quite friendly," she said, breaking the silence.

"And clearly quite fertile."

"Would you please stop deriding her for choosing to have children?"

He pushed aside his empty plate. "I'm not deriding her. I'm simply stating the obvious."

Nasira opted for a change of subject. "What should we do this afternoon?"

His smile arrived as slowly as the sunrise. "I know what I would like to do for the remainder of the day."

*Stay strong, Nasira.* "I would like to hear your plans, as long as they involve remaining vertical."

"I'd say that's altogether possible and in my opinion, preferable during a lengthy ride."

Images of being taken against a wall plagued her. "Need I remind you of our agreement?"

He rubbed his chin. "I do not readily recall any clause prohibiting horseback riding."

She tossed her napkin at him and he caught it in one hand. "You cad."

"Cad? What did you think I meant?"

She pushed back from the table and stood. "Do not play ignorant, Sebastian. Since you've arrived, every time you open your mouth, innuendo spills out."

He had the gall to grin. "Perhaps you only assume that because you're having naughty sex thoughts."

That only heightened her irritation. "If that were the case, could you blame me?"

He released a rough sigh. "No, I suppose I couldn't. You have been greatly deprived, with the exception of last night. However, I would like to make up for that now if you will allow it."

She refused to give in so easily. "I appreciate the gesture, but you will have to make up for my deprivation without any expectations in regard to lovemaking."

He pushed the chair back, came to his feet and executed a bow. "My lady, I would be honored if you would join me for an equestrian adventure, and I promise no clothes will be shed."

She could not help but smile. "Yes, I will join you. And speaking of clothes, I will need to change into something more suitable."

He slapped his forehead with his palm. "I didn't bring anything but slacks and loafers."

"Then perhaps we should find something else to do."

"No, I'll travel into town to purchase appropriate clothing. Or perhaps I should say I'll mosey into town."

"Is it worth that much effort?"

He walked up to her and kissed her cheek. "*You* are

worth the effort. And I need to pick up a few more items that will benefit us both."

Before Nasira could respond, Sebastian strode out of the kitchen, leaving her standing there, pondering what he had up his sleeve. She would simply have to wait and see.

Nasira waited for what seemed to be infinity for Sebastian to return, until her patience began to wane. Dressed in designer jeans and fashionable boots, she located the path that led to the pasture and made her way to the stable. She soon came upon a large white rock structure surrounded by paddocks that held grazing mares and a few precious foals. It appeared everything about the ranch fostered new life and that only fed her melancholy.

When she entered the barn, Nasira found a lengthy aisle lined with stalls, mostly empty until she reached the end of the line where a beautiful bay stuck its head out of the top of the door.

She cautiously approached to measure the horse's reaction to her appearance. When she held out her hand and began stroking the thin white blaze between its eyes, she immediately received a soft nicker.

"Can I help you, ma'am?"

In response the unfamiliar voice, she turned her head to the right and spotted an older man with white-streaked hair peeking out from beneath his black baseball cap, whiskers scattered about his careworn face. She offered a smile and her hand. "I am Nasira Edwards, the Shakirs' houseguest."

His face relaxed as he gave her hand a hearty shake. "Oh, yeah. I met your husband earlier. He told me the two of you might be wantin' to take a ride today."

"And you are?"

He raked off his cap and grinned. "I forgot my manners. I'm Hadley Monroe but most people call me Cappy. I prefer that."

An odd name but a very cheerful man. "It is a pleasure to meet you, Cappy. I assume you work for the Shakirs."

He settled the cap back on his head. "Yes, ma'am. I take care of the livestock and my missus, Annie, keeps the house. That gelding you're scratchin' is Gus, or that's what I call him. He has some fancy name that's about a mile long."

She glanced at the mesmerized horse and smiled. "Do you live nearby?"

Cappy hooked a thumb over his shoulder. "If you go up those stairs back there, that leads to our place."

"Over the barn?"

He chuckled. "It's nicer than most people's houses. The nicest place I've ever lived in. Mr. Darin and Mrs. Fiona are good people."

"Yes they are."

The sound of footsteps drew Nasira's attention to the stable's entry to see a tall man striding down the aisle. She recognized the confident gait, the lean, toned body, the charming smile and handsome face. She did not recognize the chambray shirt rolled up at the sleeves, the jeans encasing those long legs or the cowboy boots covering his feet.

"Well, well," she said as he stopped before her. "Has there been a British invasion in the western store?"

Her husband's smile expanded. "As they say, when in Rome."

"Or Royal."

"I'm attempting to blend in. Do you not approve?"

She took a visual journey down his body and back up again. "Actually, I approve very much."

"I would think so since you seem to have an affinity for cowboys of late."

"Excuse me?"

"Your *friend*, Mac, the manhandling rancher."

The jealousy apparently had not abated, and that somewhat shocked Nasira, as well as aggravated her. "Oh, nonsense, Sebastian. Please get over that."

Without offering a rejoinder, Sebastian reached around her and stuck out his hand for a shake. "Nice to see you again, Cappy."

"Good to see you, too, Buck."

That turned Nasira around to face the grinning graying ranch hand. "Buck?"

"Cappy gives everyone a nickname," Sebastian said. "Isn't that right, Cappy?"

The older man touched the bill of his cap. "Yesiree, Buck. I call 'em like I see 'em."

Sebastian slid his arm around Nasira's waist. "What would you suggest for my wife?"

Cappy rubbed his chin for a few moments. "I can only think of one thing that fits. Beauty."

Sebastian laughed. "That would definitely fit."

Nasira felt heat rise from her throat to her face.

"Surely you can come up with something a bit more creative, Cappy."

The man grinned again. "Like I said, I call 'em like I see 'em. If you folks will excuse me, I'll go get Studly and bring him in so I can get back to work."

After Cappy left, Nasira faced her husband again. "Who is Studly?"

"Darin's stallion," Sebastian said. "His proper name is Knight something."

She had entered the land of strange names. "I would definitely prefer that to Studly."

"I'd prefer Studly to Buck."

Nasira could not help but smile. "Studly Edwards. It has a nice ring to it. Perhaps if we have a son we could use it."

Sebastian looked as if she had told him he had to sell the shipping business. "Darin told me to explore the path outside the back paddock. It leads to a nice creek," he said, changing the subject.

Of course he would avoid the topic of children. But as far as Nasira was concerned, they would be broaching that subject soon enough, and the discussion could determine their future.

Cappy returned leading a beautiful black Arabian with a large tooled saddle dotted with elaborate silver on his back. "Here ya go, Buck. He's ready to ride."

Sebastian frowned. "No English tack, I see."

"Nope," Cappy said. "But those prissy saddles aren't much different. This is just a bigger seat with a horn to hang on to. There's no need to bounce up and down unless you wanna do that."

The larger seat did not appear to be able to accommodate two people, which led Nasira to ask a question. "Will I have my own horse?"

"That fellow you've been scratchin' is all yours," Cappy said. "Gus will take good care of you. I'll get him tacked up and then you all can take off."

Nasira stood by as the ranch hand led Gus out of the stall and toward the rear of the barn. While she and Sebastian remained in the aisle, the stallion began to grow restless. "He appears to be rather spirited," she said. "Are you certain you can handle him?"

Sebastian scratched the horse's neck and that seemed to calm him somewhat. "If I can handle chasing a three-inch ball with mallet in hand on the back of a racing beast during a game of polo, I can manage one spirited stallion."

She had clearly dealt a blow to his ego. "Of course. How foolish of me to question your manhood."

"My manhood is never in question, sweetheart. You should know that after ten years."

"It is understandable I would have forgotten since I have had very limited exposure to your *manhood* for the past six months."

"Touché. Yet I do recall your manhood drought ending last night."

"Unfortunately I do not recall much about that at all, and neither do you, considering we were both half-asleep."

Cappy returned with the gelding, interrupting the banter and greatly embarrassing Nasira when she considered that he might have overheard. "They're all yours," he said. "Just go out the front, take a right and follow the trail past the back of the barn. Once you reach water, you're all out of path."

"Would we be allowed to explore the rest of the acreage, Cappy?" Sebastian asked.

The man chuckled. "Well, that would be close to two thousand acres, but if you want adventure, be my guest. Just take care not to get lost."

Nasira could imagine wandering around for days and days. "I believe we will stay on the path. My husband does not have the best sense of direction."

Sebastian sent her a quelling look. "Might I remind you that you have been known to become lost looking for the tube?"

"I have not."

"Yes, you have."

She suddenly remembered one incident from long ago. "For heaven's sake, Sebastian, that happened once right after we married and I barely knew my way around London."

Cappy cleared his throat. "I hate to interrupt, but I need to muck these stalls while you're gone. I'd like be done before midnight."

"Of course," Sebastian said. "Do you need assistance mounting your steed, Sira?"

She answered by putting her boot in the stirrup and hoisting herself onto the saddle. "No, I do not."

Sebastian laid a dramatic hand over his heart. "You wound me by not allowing me to make any show of chivalry."

She clasped the reins in one hand. "Knowing you

as well as I do, you only wanted an excuse to put your hand on my bum."

He frowned and mounted the stallion with ease. "Darling, you are going to lead our friend here to believe that I'm a scoundrel."

"If the moniker fits, *darling*."

Cappy narrowed his eyes and studied them both. "How long have the two of you been hitched?"

"Ten years," they responded simultaneously.

"Well, that explains it," Cappy said. "Just some friendly advice. The missus and me have been married nearly forty years. In that time we figured out when you find yourself bickering a lot, the best way to cool down is taking a nekkid swim together in the crick. You should try it."

"Crick?" Sebastian asked.

Cappy scowled. "That's Texan for creek. See y'all when you get back."

With that, the man disappeared, leaving Nasira and Sebastian sitting atop the horses, staring at each other. And when her husband presented her with a slow, knowing grin, Nasira pointed at him despite the seductive images flashing in her mind. "Do not even think we will be engaging in that behavior."

He shrugged. "I can see some merit in the man's suggestion."

So could she. Bent on ignoring him and her own questionable thoughts, Nasira nudged the gelding forward with her heels, not bothering to look back.

When she guided Gus through the stable doors into the bright sunshine, Sebastian rode up to her side. "Perhaps you should lead the way since I have such a *terrible* sense of direction."

She turned right on the path without giving him a passing glance. "Could we call a truce and concentrate on having a pleasant ride?"

"I suppose I could do that. Will I be allowed to speak?"

She sent him a sideways glance. "I highly doubt I could prevent that if I tried."

"Your request is my command."

Whether he could be quiet for any real length of time remained to be seen, Nasira thought as they rode down the path at an easy pace.

As they traveled on, she relished the feel of the sun on her shoulders, the scent of freshly cut grass, the wide expanse of open land before them where livestock grazed nearby. "Oh, look," she said, breaking the silence. "A baby cow."

"I believe the proper term would be calf," Sebastian began," although that does conjure images of a disjointed leg frolicking in the field."

It took great effort to contain her laughter. "Always the witty one."

Another span of silence passed before Sebastian addressed her again. "When did you last communicate with your mother?"

The question came as a surprise to Nasira. "When I became pregnant."

She could feel his gaze boring into her. "Are you saying she doesn't know—"

"About the miscarriage? No."

"Why haven't you told her?"

"She did not share in my excitement over the pregnancy. She has never been concerned about my life."

He released a rough sigh. "I've never understood your hesitancy to reconnect with her."

"She does not welcome that, Sebastian. I remind her of my father."

"You are still her child."

"Perhaps, but I was raised by the palace staff. She only gave birth to me out of obligation."

"In a manner of speaking, I can relate. I'm certain that was the reasoning behind my birth. And that insistence on producing heirs is no bloody reason to bring a baby into this world. Nothing good can come of it."

"We are both good people, Sebastian."

"Good people whose mothers were forced to bring us into being."

Nasira saw an opportunity to encourage him to expand on his feelings. "Yet your mother loved you, did she not?"

"Yes, she did, until her untimely death."

A death that he had never discussed in detail in Nasira's presence, despite the fact she had asked numerous times during the beginning of her marriage. Eventually she had given up. "What exactly happened to her, Sebastian?"

His jaw tightened, a positive sign of anxiety. "She became ill."

That much she knew. "What did that illness involve?"

Sebastian shaded his eyes and focused on the horizon. "I believe I see the creek ahead."

Sebastian's behavior was a certain sign of emotional avoidance as far as Nasira was concerned. "I assume it must be painful to discuss the particulars, but I would like to know."

"It doesn't matter how or why. It only matters that she left her only son orphaned."

The comment gave Nasira pause. "Is that why you've avoided having a child of your own? Do you fear you will somehow desert them?"

"No. I've spent a lifetime having the importance of an heir crammed down my bloody throat."

Denial or not, Nasira sensed she had touched on the crux of his reluctance. "Have you ever considered the absolute joy fatherhood brings?"

He continued to stare straight ahead. "Most people I know pawn their children off on the nanny for the sake of their sanity."

Her husband was either terribly misguided or overly cynical. "Not the Shakirs. You would have realized that if you noticed the way Darin looked at his daughter."

"I noticed." Sebastian's tone was oddly laced with sadness.

Nasira wanted so badly to reach him. To uncover the secrets he harbored in his soul. "And you have no desire to experience that love?"

He attempted a smile that did not quite reach his eyes. "I desire to find out if Studly can fly."

When Sebastian and the stallion took off, Nasira remained behind for a few moments, pondering his need to escape. The behavior was so unlike Sebastian the businessman. As long as she had known him, he had always been a take-charge man. A man who had never avoided any challenges. A man who had been inclined to run from all things emotional.

Before her husband put too much physical distance between them, Nasira spurred the gelding into a gallop. She did not catch up to Sebastian until she reached the tree-lined ribbon of water where he had dismounted. She found him standing on the bank, the stallion's reins secured to a low-hanging limb. She climbed off Gus, tied him to the tree opposite Studly and went to Sebastian's side.

"Why do you always do that?" she asked when he didn't acknowledge her.

He picked up a stone and tossed it into the muddy green water. "I find speed exhilarating."

Her frustration over his evasion began to escalate. "That is not what I meant, Sebastian."

"I know."

The acknowledgment surprised her. "You promised me you would make an effort to be open about your feelings."

He finally faced her. "I would prefer to have a nice, relaxing afternoon with my wife, not to dredge up past history and events that cannot be changed. Could we possibly do that and leave the serious talk for a later time in a place that is not quite so serene?"

She recognized that her husband responded better with gentle persuasion. "All right. We shall postpone the conversation for the time being."

"I'm glad you see it my way."

When Sebastian took a seat on a large stump and

began to remove his boots and socks, Nasira worried he had other activities in mind. "Surely you are not going to take Cappy's suggestion about going swimming naked in the creek."

He glanced at her and winked. "I will if you will."

"I will not." Though admittedly she would under better circumstances.

"I thought as much," he said as he rolled up his pants legs. "Never fear, my dear. I'm only going to put my feet in the water. Would you care to join me?"

Nasira eyed the muddy green stream and wondered what lurked beneath. "Should we be afraid of reptiles and man-eating fish?"

Sebastian stood and shed his shirt, revealing all the wonderful planes and angles of his chest that Nasira had always appreciated. "Reptiles and fish would be more afraid of us."

"I thought you were only removing your boots."

He hung the shirt on a tree limb and swiped a palm over his nape. "It's rather warm out. Feel free to take yours off, too."

She claimed the spot on the stump Sebastian had vacated but only bared her feet. "You are so amusing."

"You are so gorgeous."

She rolled up her pants legs and stood to find the grassy earth remarkably soothing beneath her soles. "You are such a flatterer."

"I'm sincere in my compliments." He held out his hand. "Let me assist you as we explore the murky depths of an uncharted Texas *crick*."

As much as she wanted to assert her independence,

Nasira thought it best to hold on to her husband for support in the event something unknown attacked her toes. She clasped his hand and allowed him to guide her down the sloping bank and into the water. "It is much cooler than I expected," she said, her words followed by a slight shiver.

"I think it's rather nice," he replied without releasing her. "And not a sea creature in sight."

"Not any we can see. We have no idea what might be lurking beneath the surface."

"I shall protect you, fair maiden."

No sooner than he had said it, Nasira lost her footing and began to fall backward, inadvertently wrenching her hand from Sebastian's grasp. She landed on her bottom in the shallow water, sending a spray of moisture into her face.

She sputtered and wiped her eyes then looked up to find her husband standing over her. When he offered his hand, she swatted it away. "What were you saying about protecting me?"

He executed a bow. "My sincerest apologies, but you took me by surprise. You are normally very coordinated."

She came to her feet and slicked back her hair. "The bottom is as slippery as glass. And heavens, the smell."

"How can I make this up to you?"

She glared at him. "Help me out of this awful creek."

"I have a much better idea." Apparently, it included Sebastian immersing himself in the water and surfacing with a smile. "Now we are both wet and smelly."

"Lovely."

He surveyed the area a moment. "Do you know what this reminds me of?"

"I haven't a clue."

"Our trip to Tahiti."

Her mind whirled back to that grand adventure during a time when they could not get enough of each other. "If I recall, that involved a secluded cove with a waterfall, not a narrow cesspool."

"The scent isn't that foul. It's the moss."

"It has to be the cod."

"I could be mistaken, but I believe cod is a saltwater fish."

"You and your trivial facts."

When she playfully pushed at his shoulder, he swept his hand through the water and splashed her again. The battle then commenced, each trying to best the other with liquid bombs until they were both winded with laughter.

Nasira could not recall how much time had passed since they had acted with such wild abandon. How long it had been since they had shared so much laughter. She felt so connected with him, yet somewhat cautious. They still had quite a bit to resolve.

"I believe it is time to retreat," she said, but before she could evade Sebastian, he reached out and pulled her to him.

"Isn't this much better than arguing?" he asked as he guided them farther into the creek until the water lapped at her waistline.

Unable to resist her sexy, damp, shirtless husband,

she draped her arms around his neck. "I suppose it is somewhat better." And welcome. And wonderful.

He feathered a kiss across her cheek. "This is the part I remember about Tahiti."

"Only we were not fully dressed, although at least you had the foresight to remove your shirt today. I highly doubt I will ever be able to get the swampy scent out of my blouse."

"We could simply remove your blouse now."

When he reached for the buttons, she wagged a finger at him. "Now, now. We have an agreement. Conversation first."

He managed to slip open the first button and parted the placket. "What would you like to discuss?" he asked as he traced the top of her bra with a fingertip.

A topic that would ruin the mood. "Nothing at the moment. We should return to the stable with the horses since your mount seems rather restless."

He glanced at the stallion now pawing the ground. "Could I at least kiss you before we leave?"

"You usually do not ask permission."

"I'm only following the rules, per your request."

That alone should earn him a reward. "I suppose a small kiss would be all right."

Clearly her husband did not know the meaning of *small,* as if she expected him to give her anything less than a thorough kiss. Yet when he lowered his lips to hers, she found the gesture to be more tender than deep. Soft and somewhat restrained...in the beginning. And then the passion took hold. A passion she could not fight. Yet if she did not stop him now, she might not be able to stop at all.

As unwise as it seemed, at that moment she simply did not care to resist him.

# Five

Before Nasira could prepare, Sebastian opened her blouse completely, unfastened her bra and lowered it enough to pay attention to her breasts. He knew precisely how to use his tongue to bring her to the point of no return. He used the pull of his mouth to great effect, causing her to tremble slightly. She clasped his head to follow his movements as he shifted from one breast to the other and closed her eyes to immerse herself in the feelings. In spite of the voice telling her to resist, she felt needy and powerless and completely under his control as he worked the clasp on her jeans, slid the zipper down and slipped his hand into her panties. And suddenly her no-sex vow went the way of the prairie wind.

Somewhere in the recesses of her mind, she knew she should tell him to stop and regain control. "Sebastian," was all she could manage in a winded voice that she barely recognized.

He raised his head and whispered in her ear, "Remember Tahiti."

She could barely remember her name in light of Sebastian's intemperate strokes between her thighs. Yet Sebastian seemed bent on teasing her into oblivion, slowing his sensual caressing as if he wanted to prolong the process. She wanted to hold off the release, and oh how she tried, but her body would no longer allow it.

In a matter of moments, she feared her legs would no longer support her as she bordered on a climax. As if her husband could sense her predicament, he tightened his grasp on her, yet he did not let up until the orgasm began to build and build. He simply told her in a low, sensual tone how she felt, what he wished to do to her. What he *would* do to her when the time was right.

Nasira stopped thinking, practically stopped breathing as she let the heady sensations take over. She rode the release wave after wave until it had subsided. And then came the regret and remorse.

"You promised me," she said as soon as she recovered her voice.

He redid her jeans and bra then buttoned her blouse. "I apologize but I could not help myself. You're very alluring when you're wet. In every sense of the word. And you have to take into account that I presently require nothing in return, therefore it's not exactly sex."

"Good grief, Sebastian, that is semantics. We were not playing tiddlywinks."

"Definitely not. No squidgers were involved."

A litany of choice words ran through her brain, yet she could only think of one ridiculous provincial phrase. "Bite me, Buck."

He had the gall to grin. "We will explore that after dinner, Beauty."

"You are…you are…such a—"

"Skilled lover?"

"Plank," she said, repeating the slang she had learned in London.

"I've been called worse than a jackass," he said as he took her by the shoulders, turned her around and patted her bottom. "Let's go, old girl, before Cappy labels us horse thieves and sends out the guard."

She trudged out of the creek, squeezed the water from the bottom of her blouse and twisted her hair into a braid. After they had donned their boots and Sebastian had put on his shirt, they mounted the horses and started back to the stable in silence.

"Are you angry with me, Sira?"

Was she? "I am not happy that I've been so weak."

"You're not weak, sweetheart. You're a woman and you have needs."

She thought back to Fiona's declaration earlier. "You are correct. I do have needs. I simply do not care for you using that as a distraction from our real problems."

"First, you're miffed because I haven't paid enough attention to you, as you pointed out so succinctly before you left London. Now that I am attempting to make up for lost time, you no longer want my consideration. Which is it, Sira? Hands on or hands off?"

She wanted to scream from frustration. "Ignoring me isn't only about withholding lovemaking, Sebastian."

"Forgive me for facilitating your orgasm. All three of them, if my memory serves me correctly. Should you require another, you'll have to ask."

Nasira glanced at Sebastian to see if he appeared as angry as he sounded. "I will not be asking until I am assured we are on the right path to mending our marriage."

"That is your call."

Without warning, Sebastian took off again and this time, she immediately followed. Yet the gelding was not as fast as the stallion and her husband arrived a few paces ahead of her. After Sebastian dismounted and headed into the barn, she soon followed suit and led the Gus inside.

When Sebastian did not afford her a glance, Nasira tied the gelding to the stall's railing and faced him. "I know you are upset with me, but—"

"Upset?" He loosened the girth strap, pulled the saddled off and turned toward her. "Why would I be upset when my wife seems bent on rejecting my attempts to recapture some intimacy?"

She bristled at his hypocrisy. "Now you understand how I have felt the past six months."

He set the saddle on the nearby stand a bit harder than necessary. "I see. Your actions and words are based on retribution."

Something about his observation rang true. "As I have said several times, I refuse to have my libido cloud my judgment."

He released a cynical laugh. "I do not recall any refusal when I had my hand down your pants earlier."

The comment brought about a searing heat between her thighs, causing her to shift from one leg to the other. Before she could retort, Cappy came down the stairs and when he reached the aisle, gave them both a long once-over. "Did you two not understand the nekkid swimming part?"

The heat shifted to Nasira's face. "Actually, we were wading in the water and I slipped."

"I had to rescue her from the creek's clutches," Sebastian added. "My wife can be quite clumsy at times."

Cappy sported a skeptical look as he loosened the girth strap on Gus's saddle. "In case you're hungry, the missus put a roast in the oven for the two of you. She said it should be ready in about an hour and she'll be back later to clean up."

"I can do the dishes," Nasira began, "although I would like to meet her and tell her thank you."

"Annie's a stickler for giving people their privacy, and I'm thinkin' that's exactly what you two need, so I'll tell her you'll handle the cleanup."

Nasira didn't want the man getting the wrong idea. "We truly do not require privacy, Cappy. She is welcome anytime."

"If you say so." He pulled the saddle off Gus's back and grinned. "By the way, ma'am, you missed a couple of buttons."

Too mortified to offer an explanation, Nasira turned to retreat to the house without looking back, the sound of the men's laughter following her for the next few meters.

She was so angry, she practically stomped up the path. If her husband thought he would escape her ire, he was sorely mistaken. As soon as she took a shower, she planned to confront Sebastian over his amusement at her expense. Until that point, she would simply avoid him.

"Sira, wait up."

Nasira quickened her gait in response to the directive. "I am not speaking to you."

"Actually, darling, you just did."

Infuriating man. "Go away, Sebastian."

"Not until you give me the opportunity to apologize."

"I am not in a benevolent mood."

The comment seemed to encourage Sebastian's silence, or that was what she thought until she heard, "Damn my leg."

Only then did she turn around to discover her husband bent at the waist, both palms resting on his thighs. She could leave him standing on the path in pain, or she could see about his injury.

Nasira turned around, strode to him and hovered above him. "Did you suffer a wound?"

"Only to my pride."

Then he raised his gaze to her, grinned, grabbed her around the waist and tossed her over his shoulder caveman-style. "Let me down, you brute!" she said, to no avail.

"Not until we arrive at our destination."

"I cannot believe you lied to me about your leg."

"Actually, I did have a slight twitch of momentary pain."

"I have trouble believing that. Granted, you will have several pains if you continue to carry me like a bag of grain."

"Sira, you are many things. Weighty is not one of them."

She supposed she should consider that a compliment.

Once they reached the deck, Sebastian climbed the stairs and put Nasira down, yet kept her hand clasped in his. "I beg your forgiveness for my inconsiderate laughter in the stable. However, I did defend your honor after your departure."

She folded her arms around her middle. "Was that before or after you morphed into a Neanderthal?"

"I believe that was after I beat my chest and declared you my woman."

"You are such a comedian, Sebastian."

"I am a man quite enamored of his gorgeous wife, and I do hope she will forgive me."

She wanted so badly to remain angry at him, but he possessed the power of persuasion usually reserved for practiced barristers. "You are forgiven. Can I please bathe now?"

He winked. "Do you require assistance?"

"No, I do not."

Without awaiting a reply, Nasira turned and entered the house to wash away the remnants of murky river water—and the mistake she had made by believing she could distance herself from her husband, physically and emotionally. The more she was with him, the more she realized how good the majority of their marriage had been. Worse still, she recognized how much she truly loved him.

And as she walked into the bedroom and spotted the bracelet on the bureau, the reminder of their loss, she questioned whether he would be willing to give her the one thing she wanted most from him.

Only time would tell.

Sebastian sat alone at the dining room table, staring at the familiar number splashed across his cell phone screen. He needed to answer the call but dreaded it all the same.

After one more ring, Sebastian swiped the screen and said, "Hello, Stella."

"For pity's sake, Sebastian, where are you?"

His stepmother was nothing if not direct. "Texas."

"You went after her even after I advised against it."

"Yes, but before you go off on the virtue of patience, she is my wife and I have every right to seek her out."

"Yes, you do, yet it could make matters much worse."

"We're getting along famously."

"I hope that is the case," she said skeptically.

"It is. How is Father?"

The slight hesitation had him bracing for bad news. "Actually, he's had a cheery day. He played chess with the butler this morning."

Odd that his patriarch could remember how to play a board game yet at times forgot his own son's name. "That's good. He's a tough old guy."

"Yes, but might I remind you, the last time you spoke

to the physician, he told you he's going to continue to fade away, little by little, until we won't recognize the man he used to be, and he quite possibly will not recognize us."

Sebastian didn't need to be reminded of that. "I know, Stella. That's why it's imperative I work out my problems with Nasira and return to London as soon as feasible."

"And that is why you must consider having a child as soon as possible. I would like your father to go to the hereafter knowing he has an heir."

As if Sebastian needed more pressure in the procreation department. After all, his father had been partially responsible for his reluctance to try again with Nasira and wholly responsible for Sebastian's mother's death. "There is no guarantee that will happen before his demise."

"The doctor believes he still has a few years left in him."

But would they be good years?

Sebastian looked up to see Nasira standing in the open doorway, giving him a good excuse to cut the conversation short. "I will take your request under advisement. In the meantime, I'm going to have dinner with my wife. Tell Father hello from both of us."

Stella barely had time to say goodbye before Sebastian ended the call. He pushed the phone aside and studied Nasira. Her long, silky black hair cascaded over her shoulders. She wore a pink sleeveless blouse that complemented her golden skin and white loose-fitting slacks that hid her best attributes. Not an issue. He knew exactly what the cotton fabric concealed.

"You look very pretty tonight."

She pulled back the chair across from him and sat. "Thank you. I see you've gone from cowboy to corporate billionaire. If I had known you were going to wear a suit and tie I would have donned an evening gown."

"Force of habit," he said as he shrugged out of his jacket and laid it on the seat next to him. "Better?"

"A bit more casual." She bent her elbow on the table and supported her cheek with her palm. "Did you do all this?"

"Will I score a few points if I said yes?"

"You will score points if you tell me the truth."

"Actually, the table was already set. I did remove the food from the oven."

"It smells wonderful," she said as she unfolded the white napkin and laid it in her lap, prompting Sebastian to follow suit.

"That it does."

When he reached for her plate, she waved him away. "I am quite capable of helping myself."

"Far be it for me to tread on your independence."

She took a less-than-generous helping of the roast beef and vegetables. "You have a habit of doing that."

"I do?"

"Yes, you do. I suppose I cannot fault you considering I was rather helpless when we married."

She had been the picture of innocence. "You've grown quite a bit, Sira."

"I would hope so after ten years." She took a bite

then a drink of water from the cut-crystal glass. "Evidently Annie is fond of salt."

Sebastian took a much bigger bite of the fare and found it to his liking. But he thought it best to be as agreeable as possible. "Perhaps a bit. I just spoke with Stella. She told me to give you her regards."

"How is James?"

"She said he had a good day, right after she lectured me on leaving without giving her notice."

Nasira's brown eyes widened. "You didn't tell her you were coming here?"

"I left word through the servants. It was very much a spontaneous decision."

"I am certain she was worried."

"Possibly, but she was more concerned about other issues."

"What issues?"

He was hoping she wouldn't ask. "You know Stella. She is a broken record when it comes to producing an heir."

"That is understandable, Sebastian. She knows how badly your father would like to see that happen."

He had suddenly lost his appetite. "My father has no right to dictate my future after what he did…" He refused to go there for if he did, he would have to offer an explanation.

"What did he do, Sebastian?"

He took another bite that now tasted bitter as brine. "I'd prefer not to discuss it."

Nasira wadded the napkin and tossed it on the table.

"This is exactly the reason we are having problems. Your inability to communicate drives me batty."

"It's complicated, Sira. I see no point in dredging up the past."

"Perhaps you should since it's apparently affecting our future."

He shoved back from the table and began to pace. "You are asking too much of me."

"I am only asking for honesty, Sebastian. My intent is not to cause you pain. Does this have something to do with your mother?"

He turned midstride and faced her. "It has everything do with her."

"Please, come sit and tell me about her. Surely you have good memories."

More than she would ever know, unless he finally told her. Then he could gradually move into the bad, if he dared.

He reclaimed his seat and stared at the food now growing cold on his plate. "I have no idea how to begin to tell you about Martha Ella Edwards."

Nasira set her plate aside and folded her arms atop the table. "I know you were ten when she passed, so I suppose you can begin by telling me what you do remember."

He smiled at the recollections, the special moments that he had never shared. The painful times he couldn't share, at least not now. "She was extremely devoted to my father and to me. She used to call me her little drummer boy because I had a penchant for stealing wooden spoons from the kitchen and banging them on anything stationary."

"Clearly you were destined to be in a rock band."

"I thought that too after Mother bought me a real set of drums on my eighth birthday. But of course James could not endure the noise and had the servants toss them two days later."

Nasira laid her palm on his hand, which was now resting on the tabletop. "I am so sorry, Sebastian. I know you and your father have always seemed to be at odds, but I assumed that had to do with the two of you butting horns over business like two battering rams."

If she only knew the reason behind Sebastian's well-hidden resentment. If he let down his guard, she would. "I never approved of the way he treated my mother, as if she were no more than a concubine put on this earth for his pleasure."

"How could you believe that at such a young age? Was he inappropriate in your presence?"

"No. I only learned some facts later and drew my own conclusions."

"You are going to have to be less vague in order for me to help you move past this."

"I don't need your help, Sira, or your pity."

"I would never pity you, Sebastian, but I do believe you need to have someone as a sounding board. And I would hope after ten years together you could trust me enough to fill that role."

He pondered her words a moment and realized she was probably right. He also knew that by being totally transparent, he would be inviting a measure of pain. Yet he couldn't think of one soul he trusted more than his wife, and he had done her a disservice by not revealing his secrets. Only after doing so would she understand why he could not in good conscience go forward with their plans to have a child.

"I will tell you what you believe you want to know, but I assure you it's not pretty."

"I am stronger than you think, Sebastian."

He would not debate that. At times he wondered if she possessed more strength than him. "This secret, the one no one speaks of, has to do with my mother's demise."

Nasira leaned forward and sent him a concerned look. "Please tell me and end this suspense."

He drew in a deep breath and prepared to lower the boom. "My father killed her."

# Six

Nasira placed a hand over her mouth to stifle a gasp. Myriad questions whirled through her mind like a crazed carousel. "Why? How?"

Sebastian disappeared into the kitchen and returned with a tumbler half full of his favorite scotch. "Why? Because he's a selfish bastard who only cares about his desires. *How* involves… "

When he hesitated, Nasira's anxiety escalated. "Go on."

Sebastian streaked a hand over his shadowed jaw. "He knew she was ill and didn't lift a finger to help her."

She sat back, her shoulders sagging from mild relief. "I truly thought you were going to mention knives or guns or perhaps poison."

He settled back into the chair and took a sip of the

drink. "He might as well have put a gun to her head by not seeking medical attention when she clearly needed it. I knew something was wrong that morning."

Nasira realized he was perched on the precipice of deep emotional pain. "The morning she passed away?"

He shook his head. "No. The last morning I saw her alive." He stared at some unknown focal point, as if he had mentally returned to that day, before he spoke again. "I had been on summer break from boarding school and it was time for me to return. Of course, I happened to be running late when Mother summoned me into her quarters. She was propped up in bed and she looked very pale. She told me she loved me and hugged me as if she didn't want to let me go. As if she knew it would be the final time. And I wrenched out of her grasp because I knew if I didn't leave at that moment, I would earn my father's wrath for making the driver wait. I never expressed my love for her, and I have lived with that regret for almost three decades."

Her heart ached for him. "You were only a child, Sebastian. You could not have foreseen the future."

He released a weary sigh. "Perhaps, and I would not have predicted what I would learn when I was called into the headmaster's office two days later. My father did not bother to personally retrieve me. He sent one of the bloody staff members to tell me my mother was dead. He did not shed one tear at the wake. Worse still, he admonished me for crying."

Nasira had always been fond of her father-in-law, who seemed nothing at all like the tyrant Sebastian had described. "I am stunned at his behavior. James has always treated me with kindness and affection."

Sebastian leveled his gaze on her. "You've never disappointed him, and I have never lived up to his standards."

"You are a brilliant businessman. I cannot imagine he would hand over the company to you if he did not truly believe that."

"He did so because he had no choice since I failed to produce an heir. I refuse to relinquish that control to him."

Had this been the reason behind his reluctance to have another child? A vendetta against an unfeeling patriarch?

She would not know the reason behind his resistance unless she asked, yet she sensed this might not be the time or place to do so. She did have another important question. "I understand James treated you poorly, but do you truly believe he neglected your mother's health issues? I've heard the staff speaking highly of their relationship."

Sebastian tightened his grip on the glass in his hand. "I heard the servants discussing a few details when they didn't realize I was eavesdropping. As we both know, they are the eyes and ears of the household."

"And did you confront your father over this idle chit-chat?"

He pushed the scotch aside as if it held no appeal. "At ten years old, I didn't dare try. Since that time, he has never been one to discuss personal affairs. Had I inquired, he would have dismissed me, as he did whenever I asked anything about my mother."

Her husband had based his conclusions on rumors, not fact, and that bothered Nasira. "Have you considered talking to Stella to verify what you heard all those years ago?"

"Yes, and she stated she wasn't at liberty to provide the details. Then she advised me to stop living in the past."

Stella's reluctance to clear the air was unacceptable as far as Nasira was concerned, albeit an indication of her devotion to James. But she did not feel she had the right to intervene…yet. Right now, she was thankful Sebastian had begun to open up for the first time during their union. She did not want to push her luck by applying too much pressure. "I am really very sorry about what you've endured, Sebastian. I wish there was more I could do or say to ease your distress."

"I'm not distressed," he said as he pushed back from the table and stood. "But there is something you could do."

She could only imagine what he had in mind. "Yes?"

"Accompany me to the festival downtown."

The request totally took her by surprise. "What festival?"

"I'm not certain. I believe it involves street vendors and a carnival. I thought it might be a good way to soak in the culture."

Quite possibly a good way to temporarily erase the past, Nasira thought. Understandable he would want to do that, and this time she would allow it. Still, she certainly would not refuse the opportunity to spend some quality time with her husband. She came to her feet and attempted a smile. "That sounds wonderful. I suppose I should change."

He stood, rounded the table and then touched her face. "You're a beautiful, remarkable woman, Sira. Never think you should change for me."

The sheer emotion in his eyes, the absolute sincerity in his voice, sent Nasira's spirits soaring. Perhaps they had reached a turning point, the prospect of a new beginning. Yet she acknowledged they would not obtain that goal until her husband was willing to tell her the unabridged truth.

Sebastian had avoided the whole truth like a practiced coward. He hadn't told his wife that rejecting parenthood had more to do with his fear for her safety and not his determination to avoid his father's interference. Someday he would reveal the bitter details behind his mother's death, but right now he wanted to leave the past behind and concentrate on the present.

With that in mind, he took Nasira's hand into his as they strolled the streets of Royal crowded with cowboys and kids, two of whom sprinted past them on the sidewalk.

"This place is certainly full of children," he said. "I'd expect to see the Pied Piper coming around the corner at any moment."

Nasira sent him a frown. "This is a festival, Sebastian. What else would you expect?"

Better manners. "True. The town appears to treat

procreation as a sport as revered as their Friday night Texas football."

As they continued on, one particular display caught his curiosity and caused him to pause. "What in the bloody hell is cow patty bingo?"

Nasira's gaze traveled to the group gathered around the exhibition. "Well, it clearly involves a cow and some sort of game board and... I believe it is best we keep walking."

He couldn't contain his laughter. "I could not agree more."

They continued on past several artisans with tables full of their wares. As they approached one fresh-faced young woman with baskets of multicolored flowers, Sebastian halted, released his wife's hand and selected a single red rose. "How much is this?"

"Two dollars," the blonde replied. "Or six for ten dollars."

"One will do." He withdrew his wallet from his rear pocket and pulled out a twenty-dollar bill. "Here you go. Keep the proceeds."

The teen appeared awestruck. "Thanks bunches. It's for a good cause."

"What cause would that be?"

"A new football stadium."

He started to argue that an orphanage would constitute a better cause, but thought better of it. "Best of luck on your venture," he said, then turned to Nasira. "For my lovely bride."

She took the rose and smiled as if he had offered the

moon and stars, not a simple posy. "To what do I owe this wonderful gift?"

He kissed her cheek. "For agreeing to wed the likes of me."

"Most of the time, I happen to like being wed to the likes of you."

She might rescind her half compliment if she knew of the lies he still harbored. "Shall we take our chances on the games up ahead?"

"As long as they do not involve cow patties."

"I believe they are games of skill involving tossing rings."

She hooked her arm through his. "Then by all means, let us test your skills."

Unable to help himself, Sebastian leaned over and whispered, "I'm definitely up for testing all my skills when we return to the ranch."

He expected his spouse to deliver a derisive glare over the innuendo. Instead, he received a surprisingly sultry look. "That is altogether possible if you are a good boy tonight."

Perhaps Rafe had been correct—simple gestures could pay off in spades.

When they traveled on toward the brightly-lit gaming booths, Sebastian spotted a young boy dressed in jeans and miniature cowboy boots, turning in circles in the middle of the sidewalk, swiping the tears furiously from his face. A group of boisterous teens approached him, seemingly oblivious to the distressed child.

Sensing disaster, Sebastian immediately removed Nasira's hand from his arm, swept the boy up and away

from the danger of getting run over by unconcerned ad-
olescents, then set him down near a street light, away
from the crowd. "Are you lost, young man?"

He turned his misty brown eyes on him and sniffed.
"My dad told me not to talk to strangers."

Sebastian took a step back so the boy wouldn't feel
threatened. "That is banner advice under normal circumstances. I only want to help you locate your parents
and return you safely to them."

The child seemed to mull that over a minute before
he spoke again. "A girl was chasing me and I lost my
dad."

"What does your father look like?" Nasira asked
from behind Sebastian.

When the boy turned his gaze on Nasira, he seemed
to relax and smiled as if he were quite smitten. "He's got
on a cowboy hat and boots and jeans and I think a blue
shirt. Where'd you get it?" he asked, looking at the rose.

"Sebastian gave it to me." She pointed behind her.
"We bought it at a booth not far from here."

"I might want to get one of those for my…" He
lowered his eyes and kicked a pebble into the street.
"Mom."

After exchanging a knowing look with Sebastian,
Nasira offered him the flower. "I am certain my husband would not mind if you give her this one."

"Not at all." He did mind that the description of the
missing parent didn't provide much hope of immediately finding him. "Is your father tall like me?"

He nodded. "Uh huh. But he doesn't talk funny like
you. Are you from Dallas?"

Nasira laughed. "We are from London, far across the ocean."

The child's expression brightened. "We learned about that place in school. I'm in the second grade and I like to ride horses and... Dad!"

Clutching the rose, the boy ran straight into the arms of a man sporting a suspicious look as he headed toward them. As soon as he arrived, Sebastian thought it best to offer an explanation before the presumed father jumped to the wrong conclusion. "We found your son quite distressed and lost. It seems you've arrived just in the nick of time."

"Looks that way," the cowboy said as he eyed the flower before regarding his child. "You know better than to run off without me, Brady. Your mother's going to skin my hide for not watching you better."

"I didn't mean to do it," Brady said. "Angie was chasing me and I ran too far, I guess. And then this man picked me up before I got run over by kids and the lady gave me her flower so I could give it to Mom."

"Mom, huh?" the father asked.

Brady shrugged and muttered, "Maybe Angie," then turned his attention back to Nasira and Sebastian. "They're from London. Do you know about London, Dad?"

"Yep, I do," he replied. "I also know that I told you to stay away from people you don't know."

Sebastian offered his hand for a shake in an effort to reassure the man. "I'm Sebastian Edwards."

The cowboy hesitantly accepted the gesture. "I'm Gavin McNeal, former sheriff."

No wonder he had looked at Sebastian as if he were a deviant. "You're no longer in law enforcement?"

His features went from rock hard to only slightly stony. "I gave that up to spend more time with this kiddo, and the one we have on the way. I'm a full-time rancher now, although I do pull deputy duty now and again if the department's shorthanded."

A clear message to Sebastian the cowboy could still hold his own around unwelcome strangers. "I'm certain your service to the community is very much appreciated. And to put your mind at ease, Brady did mention he wasn't allowed to talk to strangers. Of course, I assure you our intentions were perfectly honorable."

"Yes, they were." Nasira moved to Sebastian's side. "However, my husband has forgotten his manners as he has failed to introduce me."

That could be a rather large strike against him. "My apologies. This is my wife, Nasira."

"I am Rafiq bin Saleed's sister," Nasira added. "You might know him."

"Only by reputation," Gavin said. "I did hear something about some folks from England staying at the Shakirs' place, so I assume that's you. My ranch isn't too far from there and my wife, Valerie, and Fiona are fairly good friends."

Apparently news traveled at warp speed in this dusty Texas town. "We're only going to be here for a few weeks. Do you have any suggestions on sights we should see while we're here?"

"You should have dinner at the Texas Cattleman's Club," he said. "And when you do, be sure to check out the statue of Jessamine Golden. That's my wife's great-great-grandmother."

"I have seen the statue," Nasira said. "But I am sure my husband will find it quite interesting."

Brady began tugging on his father's hand to garner his attention. "Can we go ride the roller coaster now?"

"Sure thing, bud, as soon as I find your mama, who was hanging out near the arts and crafts last time I looked." Gavin regarded them again. "Nice to meet you folks, and thanks for corralling the kid. What do you say to Mr. and Mrs. Edwards, Brady?"

"Thank you for getting me not lost and for giving me the flower."

"You are quite welcome," Sebastian said.

"Goodbye, Brady," Nasira added. "I hope you have a wonderful time this evening, and I am certain Angie will appreciate the rose."

Gavin took Brady's hand and touched the brim of his hat. "Have a good night, folks."

Watching father and son walked away, Sebastian experienced a good deal of regret as he remembered a time in the distant past when he'd had the same relationship with his own father. The relationship that at one time he'd hoped to have with his own son, until he realized the lack of wisdom in that. He was amused as Brady started chattering about the funny-talking man being a superhero, and did they have those in London?

The comment caused Sebastian to chuckle. "From shipping magnate to superhero. Quite a leap."

Nasira tucked her arm into his again as they started

down the sidewalk. "I would thoroughly disagree. You are a natural-born rescuer."

He frowned. "I wouldn't go that far."

She tipped her head against his shoulder. "I would. In a sense you rescued me."

He had never looked at his marriage offer in that way, but he understood why she might. "Perhaps I saved you from a life of misery with a forced marriage to a man chosen for you, but you would have found a way out of the predicament without my assistance."

"I suppose that is possible," she said. "But I am glad that I met you that night at the gala."

"I'm grateful you gave me a second glance considering all those potential suitors surrounding you."

"Yes, but not one offered to whisk me away in their Bentley."

They exchanged a smile and walked on in silence, but one question nagged at Sebastian. "Have you enjoyed our life together, Sira?"

She paused a moment before answering. "We have had wonderful adventures and amazing travel. You have introduced me to many new experiences."

"No regrets?"

"Only one."

"What would that be?" he asked though he already knew the answer.

"We have no children."

He had strolled right into that one. "I understand you're still mourning the loss, yet I can't understand why you would want to risk your health after you had such a difficult pregnancy."

She stopped and faced him. "Life is not without risk, Sebastian. And at times risk comes with precious rewards."

He didn't know how to answer to satisfy her needs. He didn't know if he would ever want to enter that territory again. "Speaking of risks, would you care to climb on that giant Ferris wheel and take it for a spin?"

Nasira glanced over her shoulder then regarded him with a frown. "You know I am afraid of heights."

"You have no need to be afraid while in the presence of a superhero."

She smiled. "This is true. If I agree, will you promise to hold on to me?"

"You may count on my undivided attention."

"Then yes, I will join you on that contraption, and hope I do live long enough to regret it."

Sebastian led Nasira to the line of people awaiting their turn on the ride. When their time came, he approached the elderly gentleman in charge of the ride and withdrew his wallet. "How much, kind sir?"

"Three tickets."

Tickets? "I wasn't aware we needed those." He pulled a twenty out of his pocket. "Will this do?"

"I don't make change, mister."

"No change necessary."

The attendant grinned, displaying a remarkable lack of teeth. "I guess it'll do at that."

"Amazing how money opens doors," Sebastian said as they climbed into the car.

Nasira grabbed the railing and sat, looking somewhat fearful. "Amazing how rickety this ride seems."

He lowered next to her and wrapped his arm around her shoulder. "Just hold tight to your knight."

She surprised him with a soft kiss. "Happily, kind sir."

When the wheel began to move, sending them up toward the night sky, Nasira closed her eyes and tensed against him. He held her tighter, stroked her arm and rested his lips against her temple. He experienced such a fierce need to keep her sheltered from harm, and a secret fear that he could not be the man she would want in the future if he couldn't give her the child she desired.

But tonight, he could give her all his consideration and forget the chasm that still existed between them.

When they reached the top, the ride jolted to a stop, causing the car to slightly sway and his wife to clutch his thigh in a death grip. Stifling a wince, Sebastian lifted her hand and kissed her palm. "Open your eyes, sweetheart."

"Must I?"

"No, but you're missing an extraordinary view."

After a few seconds ticked off, she finally lifted her lids and looked around. "I must admit, all the lights are beautiful. They remind me of our holiday together two years ago."

While she must have been struck by sentimentality, he was hit by some rather sexual memories. "Ah, yes. Rome. We barely left the room."

"That is not true. We had several meals on the veranda."

He brushed a kiss across her lips. "That's not all we did on that veranda."

Her smile arrived slowly. "True. You have always been quite devilish when we travel."

"And you are always quite willing to dance with the devil."

"Evidently I cannot resist your charms."

He pushed her hair away from her shoulder. "Would you be willing to dance with me later tonight?"

Without giving him a verbal response, Nasira wrapped her hand around his nape and pulled his mouth to hers, taking Sebastian by surprise. As the ride began to move again, picking up speed, they continued to kiss as if they were youngsters in the throes of first love. But they weren't youngsters. They were husband and wife in the midst of a troubled marriage, yet he felt as if this could be the path to healing.

When the ride bumped to a stop, they finally ended the kiss only to be met by applause, whistles and cat-calls. Sebastian helped Nasira out of the car and they rushed away, then paused and shared in a few laughs.

Nasira wrapped her arms around his waist. "I do believe you have ruined my reputation."

He pressed a kiss on her forehead. "If you agree to return to the ranch now, I will endeavor to ruin it more."

She studied his eyes for a few moments, as if searching for something unknown there. "Sebastian, I...."

"What, sweetheart?"

"I think that is a marvelous idea."

Saying what she had wanted to say would have been a horrible idea.

Still, Nasira had come very close to voicing an emotion she had never admitted to him, or to herself, during their decade together. She loved him, and most likely had for many years. Love had not been a goal in their marriage. A marriage based on convenience and mutual need. Yet somehow she had introduced the emotion into the union when she had allowed Sebastian into her life, and into her heart.

That did not change the fact that her husband might not feel more than fondness for her. That did not negate that they wanted to journey down different paths and if he had his way, their future would not include having a child.

Yet as she rode back to the ranch, her hand resting lightly in Sebastian's, she did not care about compromise or doubts. She only wanted to enjoy this night with her husband in the event these memorable moments might be their last.

She leaned back against the headrest and sighed. "I realized something tonight that I have never considered before."

"You are not so afraid of heights?"

"No. I enjoy country living."

"That's why we have the country home in Bath to escape the hectic pace in London proper."

"I know, yet I feel a certain freedom here. It does sound odd, I suppose."

He pulled beneath the portico and shut off the ignition. "This place does afford quite a bit of privacy, which reminds me." He reached into the back of the car, retrieved a silver bag full of pink tissue and handed it to her.

"What is this?"

"Open it and you'll see."

She rummaged around and withdrew a bathing suit that was little more than a labyrinth of turquoise strings. "I have never flown a kite in the dark."

"Very amusing. We both need to relax, and what better way to do that than to swim."

"Isn't it too cool to swim?"

"The spa and pool are both heated."

She could imagine they would generate their own heat, yet she worried about the privacy issue. "I would still have to get out of the spa or pool." She shook the swimsuit at him. "This barely covers anything at all. What if someone happens upon us?"

"You have a robe, do you not?"

"Yes."

"Besides, you have a remarkable body. Why not show it off?"

"I do not think it is wise to show off my body this much when two other people reside on the property."

"Two people who've been instructed to give us complete solitude."

He had supported his arguments much too well, drat him. "All right. I will join you in a swim." She pointed at him. "But only for a swim. Heaven knows I wouldn't want to be caught doing anything else."

He gave her a winning grin, the one that had always won her over. Patently sensual, and slightly wicked. "Yes, dear. Only a swim."

As much as she would like to trust him, Nasira was not sure she should. Trouble was, could she trust herself?

# Seven

The moment Nasira stepped onto the deck and slipped off the robe, swimming was the last thing on Sebastian's mind. The suit fit her to perfection, from the low cut of the bodice to the bottoms secured by two ribbons at her rounded hips that accentuated her long torso. Her hair flowed freely, straight and sleek, begging for his touch. When he honed in on the diamond hoop at her navel, her attempt at rebellion during her brief university days, he had fond memories of playing with the bauble with his tongue…as well as other more intimate places now covered by a small fabric triangle. That alone caused him to move down one stair to conceal the result of his sinful thoughts.

He had to remember to take it slowly, let the evening progress with no expectations in terms of lovemaking.

He needed to concentrate on making his wife feel appreciated and respected, even if it meant using his tongue solely to talk for the time being.

Unfortunately his randy libido seemed to be speaking much louder than his honor. He would simply have to quiet the urges and not appear as impatient as a lustful schoolboy.

*Down, Henry.*

When Nasira stuck her toe in the deep end of the pool to test the water, even that seemed overtly sexy to Sebastian. And when she executed a perfect dive, surfaced not far from him and slicked her hair back from her gorgeous face, he gritted his teeth to keep from going after her like a lion and a gazelle.

"Bravo," he said as she waded toward him. "You're a regular little mermaid."

She lifted her hair to secure the tie at her neck. "I almost had equipment failure when I dove in. Could you have not found something a bit more modest?"

At the moment he realized that might have worked better in light of his burgeoning erection. But then again, probably not. She could be wearing a heavy trench coat and he would still want her, especially if she were nude beneath it. He would like very much for her to be nude beneath him. Or perhaps on top of him. Standing up against the deck would also work to his satisfaction…

"Have you been rendered mute, Sebastian?"

For the most part, yes. "I'm sorry. Did you ask me something?"

"Never mind." She joined him on the step, keeping

a relatively safe distance between them. "The housekeeper turned down my bed. Did you notice if she is still here?"

No, but he did notice that if the bikini were a bit lower, he could possibly see her nipples. "I'm almost certain she performed those tasks while we were away."

Sira leaned forward, causing the top to gape and allowing him the view again. "It would probably behoove us to check."

"That might be breast." *Dammit.* "I mean *best*."

She sent him a mock scolding look. "I have barely been in here five minutes and you are already misbehaving."

Guilty. "It was only a verbal faux pas, Sira."

"Then take care to mind your mouth."

And he did…by planting it on her mouth, disregarding his earlier cautions about going slowly. He expected she might shove him away, or perhaps push him into the water, yet she joined in as if she needed this as badly as he did.

After they parted, she tipped her head against his forehead. "I hate that I am so helpless around you."

He lifted her chin and forced her to look at him. "You are not helpless in the least, and you are not an innocent. You are as drawn to the devil in me as I am the vixen in you."

"So you think."

"So I know."

He loosened the ties at her neck but paused before he went further. "Tell me you do not want me and I'll stop."

"I…cannot."

Which was all the encouragement Sebastian needed to continue. He removed her top, tossed it aside and then toyed with the band riding low on her hips. "Stop now?"

She released a ragged sigh. "No."

After he slid her bottoms away and draped them on the chrome railing, he led her into waist-deep water and kissed her, his hands roving over her breasts. She soon pulled away, moved back and smiled. "The vixen says take off your bathing suit."

"Far be it for me to argue with her," he said as he shoved down his trunks, stepped out of them with effort, and hurled them onto the deck.

She crooked her finger at him. "Come here, devil."

They came together in another blast of heat, of that passion they'd known from the beginning. She scraped her nails down his back, while he attacked her neck with kisses and brought her legs up around his waist. It would be so easy to take her here, take her now, yet the nagging concerns over pregnancy prevented him from doing so. He should have brought the blasted condoms with him.

"Do it," she whispered with desperation as she reached beneath the water, took his erection in hand, and guided it inside her.

Driven by pure lust and need, he thrust into her, twice, before he gathered every ounce of strength and pulled out. "The bedroom," he managed around his labored respiration.

She looked at him and blinked twice. "Why?"

"More privacy." A lame excuse but the only one he could provide without completely destroying the mood.

"All right," she said as she lowered to her feet. "But hurry."

That request he could categorically fulfill, and he did as he took her by the hand and led her to the chaise on the pool deck. They wrapped up in the towels he'd brought, periodically kissing and intimately touching as they headed into the house. Once they reached the corridor leading to the guest suite, he paused and backed her against the wall immediately outside the door to his quarters.

He wanted her to remember this, to know how badly he wanted her, to make her want him as much. He parted the towel and suckled her breasts, first one, then the other, before sliding his lips down her torso.

Then he went to his knees, nudged her legs apart and sent his mouth on a mission between her thighs. He used his tongue to divide her warm flesh, tracing circles around and around that intimate spot, intent on driving her wild.

She bowed over him, running her hands over his scalp, her breaths coming in short pants. She dug her nails into his back so deeply, he thought she might have drawn blood. He didn't care. Giving her pleasure was well worth the pain.

"Sebastian." His name came out of her mouth in a harsh whisper as he stroked her with his tongue softly, then harder as he covered her completely with his mouth and suckled that sweet spot.

Her legs began to tremble and a low, sexual sound filtered out of her as she began to orgasm. He didn't let up until he had ridden out every pulse of the climax, then he kissed his way back up her beautiful body.

She reached for him again and demanded, "Now."

"Not yet," he said as he clasped her wrist to still her hand. Otherwise the act would be over in short order.

Without protesting, Nasira followed him into his bedroom. While she turned down the comforter, he opened the nightstand drawer and retrieved the silver packets. He turned and found her stretched out on her back on the bed, her damp hair a sexy, tangled mess, her knees bent in preparation for him. Yet when she spied the condoms in his grasp, she suddenly sat up on the edge of the mattress and lowered her eyes.

After laying the packets on the side table, he claimed the space beside her and rested a hand on her bare leg. "I realize this isn't what you want, but under the circumstance, it's a necessity."

Her gaze snapped to his, the haze of desire completely gone. "Is it?"

"We still have much to discuss in regard to that issue, by your own admission."

She pushed her hair back from her face. "Yes, you're right, but the reminder of our impasse took me aback for a moment. I suppose I simply wanted to forget our dilemma this evening. I wish you could have held off with the condoms a bit longer."

Frustration brought him to his feet to face her. "This wouldn't have been a bloody issue if you'd started taking the pill again."

"As I've said, I had no reason to do that when you were so bent on ignoring me." She pinched the bridge of her nose and momentarily closed her eyes. "I am so angry."

"At me?"

"At myself. I have walked into the same trap, succumbing to your charisma and allowing you to lead me away from our problems."

Now he was angry. "I did nothing of the sort. We are husband and wife and we should thank our lucky stars we still want each other so fiercely after ten years of marriage."

She let loose with a cynical laugh. "Of course you would see it that way. But sex is not a cure-all for serious marital problems."

If she only realized that was the only way he knew how to communicate his true feelings for her. The right words had never come easily for him. Neither had acknowledging his emotions. "Why can you not be happy with what we have? Why do you see the need to change everything?"

She pulled the sheet up to cover herself. "Because we cannot be truly happy unless we fix what is broken. Only until you open up to me completely can we move past our problems."

He knew where she was going, and he didn't want to bloody go there. "I've told you more about my mother's death than I've ever told another soul."

"Yet you have not told me everything, Sebastian. Aside from your father's careless disregard and your guilt over your last moments with your mother, there is something else keeping you from committing to fatherhood."

He clenched his jaw against the litany of curses threatening to spill out. "You have no idea what I went through."

She stood and leveled her gaze on him. "Then tell me all of it. Make me understand."

He didn't dare. "I am going to take a shower."

He turned to retire to the bath, only to have her call him back. "When will you stop running away, Sebastian?" she asked. "When it is too late for us?"

The words impaled him like a knife to his heart. "You're asking too much of me tonight, Sira. If it's too difficult for you to be intimate with me, then by all means, retire to your blessed bed and I'll stay in mine alone. If you happen to change your mind, then it will be up to you to come to me. In the meantime, I'll not bother you again."

And this time, he vowed to stay true to his word.

He had not spoken to her for two days. In fact, Nasira had barely seen her husband except in passing. He had spent much of his time in his quarters, sequestered away with his laptop.

Today that would come to an end, if she had any say in the matter. She had given him a wide berth to think about what she had said, but they had come to a crossroads. His time was up.

She opened the door to his bedroom without knocking, only to find him packing. A blinding fear overcame her, then resignation that perhaps she had pushed him too hard.

He afforded her only a glance while he placed a suit in the garment bag without speaking.

"Are you returning to London?" she asked, expecting an affirmative answer.

"No. I'm going to Dallas," he said, shattering her expectations, and filling her with relief.

She moved closer to the bed, but not too close. "Why Dallas?"

He dropped a few toiletries into a small carry-on bag. "I've managed to secure an invitation to an importers conference."

She folded her arms around her middle. "How long do you intend to be gone?"

He zipped the case and placed it on a bench at the end of the footboard. "I'll return tomorrow afternoon."

"Did it occur to you to invite me along?"

He sent her a sideways glance. "You'd be bored."

"I have attended these functions with you before."

He zipped the garment bag and turned. "Yes, you have, but that was before I knew you considered me a closed-off bastard who runs at the first sign of trouble."

"You ran from me the other night. You ran after I lost the baby."

He dropped onto the edge of the mattress and forked his hands through his hair. "Perhaps you're right."

It was an admission she thought she would never hear. She sat down beside him on the bed. "I am not willing to give up on us yet, Sebastian. I would like to accompany you on this trip and we will go from there."

"Well, I've always enjoyed having a beautiful wife at my side."

That ruffled her feminine feathers. "I do not want to go as your arm ornament. I want to be there as your equal. You have never viewed me as that."

He appeared extremely confused. "Where is this coming from?"

"Well, if we want to sincerely work on our marriage, then I think it's best to be honest. Many times I have asked about the company, and you brushed me off."

"I never thought you were interested in that part of my life."

"It should be part of my life as well. After all, my father was just as immersed in the shipping world. I might not have finished my degree, but I observed all aspects of the operation. I possibly know as much about it as you do."

Now Sebastian looked skeptical. "You mean that riveting world of routes, imports and exports, and shipping containers?"

"Yes, and the importance of making connections. I am quite capable of doing that. In fact, I'll wager I will make at least two this evening if I go with you."

"I've always enjoyed a good wager. And if you succeed, I will give you whatever you desire."

"Anything?"

"Within reason."

That probably eliminated her request for a child. "And if I do not succeed?"

"I will only ask that you be patient with me. I'm not good at all this sharing-my-feelings rubbish."

An odd facet of their relationship suddenly struck

Nasira. "Do you realize that up until six months ago, we rarely ever argued?"

He seemed to mull that over for a minute. "You are absolutely right. Perhaps that is because you are perfect."

He sounded strangely sincere. "Of course that is a fallacy."

"Not to me."

"Sebastian, I know I have some habits that must drive you batty."

He rubbed his chin. "It is rather disconcerting when you rearrange my bureau drawers."

"Guilty as charged. Can you not do better than that?"

"You laugh at all my randy jokes."

"How is that an imperfection?"

"Because no one else bothers. That possibly indicates a severe lack of judgment, or perhaps bad taste."

That made her smile. "What else?"

"You bring me a drink when I'm harried after a long day."

"Again, I do not see the problem with that."

"Perhaps I prefer to fetch my own drink."

"Do you?"

He grinned. "No. The truth of the matter is, Sira, nothing you do drives me to complete distraction. Actually, that's not the truth. I'm very distracted when you walk into the room, wearing nothing but a smile, and when you wake up beside me with your hair tousled and a sleepy look on that gorgeous face. You distracted me the other night from my goal."

"Yes, I realized I ruined that goal, yet you have to

know that was not my intent. I feel horrible we did not make love."

He took her hand in his. "I meant my goal to convince you I care beyond making love to you. I want another opportunity to prove that."

"I want that as well." And she did. "And I truly want to go with you to Dallas."

"All right, as long as you understand I only have a one-bedroom suite with a king-size bed. Of course, I suppose I could see if they have another room for you."

She shook her head. "That isn't necessary."

Looking extremely pleased, he patted her thigh and stood. "The jet is waiting so you should pack. Do you have a cocktail dress for the reception?"

She came to her feet and frowned. "Do birds fly?"

He softly touched her face. "Yes, they do, and I look forward to watching you fly tonight."

But Nasira feared that by hanging on to the marriage, she might eventually fall.

Sebastian spotted her standing across the crowded room. She wore a formfitting sleeveless black silk gown with matching heels, her wrists bedecked with diamond bracelets and her sleek hair flowing down her back. Her slender hands moved gracefully as she spoke with an older gentleman who appeared completely enthralled by the conversation, and her.

Sebastian couldn't recall the last time Nasira looked so very beautiful. Correction. He could. The first night he'd seen her at an event much like the one tonight. Also on their wedding day when she had been dressed in white satin and looked like the exotic princess she was, albeit a somewhat wary princess due to their spontaneous decision to marry. Perhaps he had rescued her that day from the clutches of her father's idea of a suitable spouse, but she had saved him from a life of loneliness.

"That's one looker right there."

Sebastian turned to his right to find a portly man with thinning hair clutching a martini and staring at Nasira with lust. "That happens to be my wife."

"I know," the miscreant said. "I just spent the last thirty minutes listening to her singing your praises. By the way, I'm Milt Appleton with M.A. Imports."

Sebastian downed the rest of his scotch then eyed the man's offered hand and reluctantly shook it. "Pleasure, I'm sure." Or not.

"Anyway," Milt said. "I'm looking for a shipping company that can handle my European routes. Your girl convinced me I should consider going with you." He pulled a business card from the inside of his coat pocket. "Here's my information. Give me a shout in the next day or two."

Sebastian took the card and pocketed it. "I will be in touch soon."

Milt pointed at Nasira and narrowed his eyes. "And take care of that one. She's one in a million."

Sebastian had begun to realize the absolute accuracy of that statement. She was graceful, intelligent, resolute and reliable to a fault. She had always been there when he needed her, and he had repaid her by not being there when she had needed him. Now that he finally got it, he had to figure out what to do about it. One idea came to mind, a simple gesture that would demonstrate how much she meant to him, even if he felt he could not give her the child she still desired.

On that thought, he crossed the massive room and came to her side. "I lost track of you for a moment, darling."

She presented a smile. "I have been conversing with this lovely gentleman. Sebastian, this is Mr. Walker. Mr. Walker, my husband, Sebastian Edwards, owner and CEO of the shipping company I mentioned. Darling, Mr. Walker is quite interested in the services you have to offer."

At least this one didn't seem to be interested in the services his wife could provide. "A pleasure to meet you, Mr. Walker," he said as he stuck out his hand.

"The pleasure is all mine," the man replied. "I've given my information to your wife and we'll discuss the particulars later. Speaking of wives, I should find mine. Have a good evening, you two."

After the aged businessman hobbled away, Sebastian slid his arm around Nasira's waist. "Clearly I have lost our two-contacts wager since I was recently confronted by your first contact, the lecherous Milt."

"He's harmless," Nasira said.

"And flirtatious, I gather."

"Slightly, yet nothing I could not handle."

Sebastian glanced to his right. "Would you care to dance?"

She looked at him as if he had lost all reason. "This is not a cotillion, Sebastian. It's a cocktail party."

"I hear music coming through the speakers and I believe I spy a dance floor."

She followed his gaze toward the bar before bringing her attention back to him. "Yes, that seems to be a dance floor. With no one using it."

He clasped her hand. "Then perhaps it's time to get this dance party started." When she began to protest, he pressed her lips with a fingertip. "Let's be bold for a change. Let's show them the portrait of two people who do not give a tinker's damn what anyone thinks."

Her grin came out of hiding. "Let's."


After Sebastian guided her onto the modest wooden dance floor, Nasira walked into his arms. Yet when she noticed several people staring, she immediately went rigid.

"Relax," Sebastian whispered.

"How can I when we are making a spectacle of ourselves?"

"If anyone takes exception, it's only because they're jealous."

She reared back and leveled her gaze on him. "Jealous of two people who are clearly wacko?"

"Jealous of me for having such a remarkable wife. Jealous of you because you are the most beautiful woman in the room. In the world, in my opinion."

"If you put it that way…"

Deciding to ignore the attention, Nasira rested her cheek against Sebastian's shoulder and swayed in time to the soft sounds of a bluesy instrumental. She relished the feel of his strong arms holding her close, the aromatic scent of his cologne, his skill. She had learned that he was a great dancer the first night they had met, when he had asked her to dance at the gala, much to her father's chagrin, whose cautions had gone unheeded. When she took inventory of her life and the decision she had made, only one regret remained. A dream she might have to disregard to keep her marriage intact.

Sebastian suddenly stopped moving and only then did she realize the music had stopped, and they were now surrounded by several other couples who had taken to the floor.

Her husband presented a proud smile. "See? We have started a trend."

She laughed with pure joy. "Yes, we have."

"Shall we dance again, fair lady?"

She had something else in mind. "Actually, unless you care to stay, I would rather return to our room."

He made a show of checking his watch. "It's still early. We could have a late dinner."

Obviously he did not approve of her plan for some unknown reason. "I have had enough appetizers to last for several days."

"I have not."

"Room service is still available."

"True. I will gladly accompany you to our quarters, as long as this does not entail heavy conversation."

That would come later. Much later. "Agreed."

Reclaiming her hand, Sebastian led her through the lobby to the glass elevator that would take them to the executive floor. They entered the deserted car and took in the plethora of city lights dotting the Dallas skyline as they ascended. Unfortunately the view left Nasira breathless, and not in a welcome way.

As if he sensed her trepidation, Sebastian wrapped his arms around her from behind and held her close. "I'm right here, sweetheart."

She leaned back against him. "I know, and admittedly it is a nice panorama."

He brushed her hair aside and kissed her cheek. "At least this time you're keeping your eyes open to enjoy it."

"You take good care of me, Sebastian."

"You deserve it, Sira. You deserve everything your heart desires."

If only he could agree to give her the most important of her heart's desires. Nevertheless, she wanted to spend the evening in a lighthearted mood with no old recriminations to intrude on their time together. She also intended to bask in the glory of winning the wager about making connections at tonight's party, and if good fortune prevailed, convince him to allow her to take an active role in the business. If she could not immediately become a mother, she could certainly establish a career beyond charity work.

Those plans began to fully form as they entered the penthouse suite a few moments later. She immediately crossed the suite and walked into the bedroom with Sebastian trailing behind her. Once there, she removed her jewelry then fished through her pocket and withdrew the best part of her plan.

She turned to find her husband seated in the club chair next to the sliding glass doors leading to the veranda, his hands draped on the chair arms as if he were the king of the castle.

She approached and offered him a handful of business cards. "Here are a few more contacts."

He took the stack and looked through them before regarding her again. "You are amazing."

She smiled. "Yes. Yes I am."

He set the cards aside and returned her smile. "I'm glad you have finally come to that conclusion."

She perched on the edge of the mattress opposite him. "I am teasing. I simply struck up a few conversations and that led to mentioning the company and what we have to offer."

"We?"

She prepared to plead her case. "Yes. I assume that since I made the effort, I should be rewarded with a measure of involvement. Also, three of the contacts are women and it would only be natural that I would be the best candidate to communicate with them. Of course, I would have to be allowed access to the contracts and the shipping routes…"

He effectively cut off her thoughts when he reached over, clasped her arms, pulled her up and brought her into his lap. "You have done a superb job," he began. "And you definitely deserve to be rewarded."

She could not resist rolling her eyes. "Exactly what do you have in mind?"

He pressed a kiss on her cheek and suddenly looked very serious. "I want to give you what you want most."

She clung to hope and prepared to be disappointed.

"You know what I want most, yet you have been adamant about not giving it to me."

"I've had a change of heart."

Did she dare utter the word? No. She had learned not to assume. "Please end the suspense and say it."

"I want to give you a child."

This almost seemed too good to be true. "Are you certain?"

"Yes. As long as we adopt."

# Eight

In a matter of moments, Nasira went from euphoric to disappointed. "Why is that necessary when we know we can conceive?"

"Because there are many children out there who need homes. We have that home, two in fact, and enough money to provide a solid future."

She pushed out of his lap and turned to look at him. "I truly want a baby who is a part of both of us."

Frustration clouded his expression. "You're a humanitarian, Sira. I thought the idea of giving an orphan a home would appeal to you. There are plenty in Eastern Europe."

"It does appeal to me in the future, yet I want to know how it feels to carry our child to term. As a man, perhaps you find that difficult to understand."

"I do understand, but I'm only considering your health. Why put you through the risks of another pregnancy if it's not necessary?"

She worried he would never understand. "The doctor said—"

"I know what the doctor said." Sebastian shot to his feet and began to pace. "I'm certain they said the same thing to my mother, and we know how that turned out."

Now she was completely confused. "I do not understand."

He paused to face her again. "No, you don't, because I didn't tell you the entire set of circumstances behind her death. She was pregnant because my father insisted she go against medical advice and have another child."

Shock rendered Nasira momentarily silent. "When did you learn this?"

"At the same time I learned how he was neglecting her health issues right before she died."

"More hearsay from the staff?"

He glanced away. "Yes, but I'm sure they spoke the truth."

"How can you be sure, Sebastian? You were a child yourself. Perhaps you misunderstood."

"I didn't misunderstand," he said, his tone full of anger. "I heard a reliable source say she'd had several miscarriages and each one took its toll on her. My father apparently ignored the danger and impregnated her once again. I will not put you through that."

At some point in time in the near future, Nasira vowed to find out all the details, no matter what it took. "I am not your mother, Sebastian. I have had one miscarriage and only one. I have no reason to believe I could not see the next pregnancy to term. I am willing to take that chance, and I hope you are as well."

He walked to her and clasped both her hands. "Please don't ask that of me, Sira. The thought of something happening to you is unbearable. And to know I would be responsible is inexcusable."

When she saw the vulnerability in his eyes, Nasira realized she might never break through his fear. A fear she had never witnessed in him before. She still hung on to a shred of hope that maybe with time, and more medical intervention, he would come to realize that childbirth wouldn't detrimental to her health.

She felt compelled to hold him, to tell him all would be well, yet she felt as though he had erected an invisible wall around himself. "All right. We will stray from this topic for now and attempt to enjoy the rest of our evening."

He released a rough sigh. "I'm not certain that is possible."

"It can be. Perhaps we should take a walk."

"I would prefer to stay in for the remainder of the evening."

Normally she would expect an invitation into bed. But this was not a normal situation, as evidenced by the fatigue in his tone. "If that is what you wish."

"It is."

She struggled to come up with a plan that might buoy his spirits. She returned to their mutual past and better days for inspiration. "I have a proposition."

His smile arrived slowly. "I've always enjoyed a good proposition."

The bad boy billionaire had come back to life. "This involves dessert."

"Interesting you should use that term."

The real Sebastian had arrived, and she felt a modicum of relief. "I meant dessert as in cake, on the veranda. We have not done that in a very long time."

He turned her hands over and kissed both her wrists. "Perhaps it's time we begin to recapture what we've lost."

Nasira chose to interpret Sebastian's statement as reclaiming the routines that had once given them pleasure, aside from lovemaking. She gently wrested her hands away and walked into the living area to retrieve the menu.

While she flipped through the selections, Sebastian came up behind her and peered over her shoulder. "The raspberry truffle cheesecake looks good," he said. "Shall I order that for us?"

She closed the menu, laid it aside on the desk and then turned, which placed her in extremely close proximity to him. So close she could barely catch her breath. "Actually, I would prefer to order for myself."

"My apologies. I've already forgotten one important lesson—let Sira make her own culinary decisions."

In light of the sexy gleam in his eye, she would forgive him this slight slipup. "Apology accepted. And I would like the sampler that includes several choices."

He frowned. "Are you certain you can handle that much food?"

"I can because I am suddenly starving."

Oddly, her appetite had increased over the past two days. In fact, the last time she had been this hungry...

That was not possible, not after only one time. Not so soon. She was being silly. Optimism over resolving their issues was simply driving her cravings. That had to be the case.

Seated at the small table on the hotel's veranda, Sebastian watched his wife eat with total abandon and couldn't quite believe his eyes. "In all our years together, I have never seen you entirely clean your plate."

Nasira dabbed at her mouth with the napkin and set it aside. "It was very tasty."

"Apparently. Should I order you more?"

That earned him a frown. "I could not eat another bite. I believe the country air is making me very hungry."

"Sira, we're in the city."

"True." She shifted in the chair and studied the horizon. "I had no idea Dallas would be so metropolitan."

"Did you believe you'd find people riding around the city streets on horseback?"

"Of course not. However, I did see a horse-drawn carriage downstairs."

"Perhaps we should make use of one."

She brought her attention back to him. "It is rather late."

"Not too late to enjoy the sights."

"I thought you wanted to stay in."

Sebastian was so restless, he wasn't certain what

he wanted, except to be close to his wife. "It will be a nice diversion," he said as he pushed back from the table and stood.

"All right." Nasira came to her feet and pointed at him. "No funny business."

Damn. "I only wish to have the honor of your company." And that was a colossal lie, though he vowed to respect her wishes.

By the time they reached the hotel lobby and walked out the revolving doors, the sidewalks weren't as crowded as Sebastian had expected. Fortunately he spotted a carriage stopped near the curb only a few meters away. He approached the gentleman dressed in Western garb positioned in the driver's seat. "Good evening, sir. Are you currently for hire?"

The man stared down at him. "Actually, I was just about to head to the house."

Sebastian withdrew his wallet and offered the man two hundred-dollar bills. "Will this make it worth your while?"

The driver eyed the money for a moment. "My wife's got dinner waiting."

He pulled out another hundred. "Now you can buy your wife dinner."

"I s'pose I could take you a few blocks."

Greedy scoundrel. "I would think that amount would buy us a few kilometers."

Nasira elbowed him in the side. "*Darling*, the poor man wants to go home to his wife."

Her compassion had him looking like a pitiless cad.

"Of course. My apologies. I only want to show my brand-new bride a memorable evening."

The driver grabbed the reins and sneered. "Then let's get this show on the road so you can get on with the honeymoon. Just don't get it on in my carriage."

"For three hundred dollars, I should be allowed to prance naked in a parade," Sebastian muttered as he helped Nasira up into the seat.

After they settled in, he draped an arm around her shoulder. "Was that jab to my ribs necessary?"

"Were your derisive comments necessary?"

"The reprobate seemed determined to stiff me."

"He clearly holds his wife above work. And what compelled you to claim we've recently married?"

His faults had been laid bare. "Well, in a way I feel as if we are newlyweds. We've discovered quite a bit about each other over the past few weeks."

She mulled that over for a moment. "It is odd to think that two people who have spent so many years together would still have the capacity to learn more about each other."

He had told her things he had never uttered to another soul. Details he had planned to take to his grave. Yet he did feel less burdened knowing she now understood why he did not want her risking carrying his child after her previous miscarriage. "Let's promise that we'll continue this unusual pattern in the upcoming weeks."

She laid her head on his shoulder. "A stellar plan."

As they rode through the streets of Dallas, serenaded by the clip-clop of horse hooves, Sebastian tugged Nasira closer to him. Without a blanket to conceal them, she was not in danger of any funny business, as she had so aptly put it. That did little to quash his desire for her. That did not stop him from rubbing her shoulder with one hand and tracing slow circles on her thigh. She responded by making small sounds that served to heighten his need for her, and drove him to kiss her thoroughly. And she kissed him back with enough passion to make him want to say to hell with propriety, pull her panties down and take right there in front of the entire town…

The sound of applause forced them apart. There was a crowd gathered at the corner where they had stopped for a traffic light. Sebastian did what any good Brit would do—stood, executed a bow and gave them a royal wave.

When he settled back in the seat, Nasira began to laugh and he followed suit. Once they recovered, he leaned and nuzzled her neck. "You smell like lavender. Is it a new perfume?"

"You gave it to me for my birthday."

Unfortunately that purchase had been made three months ago by Stella when he had forgotten. "Ah yes. Now I remember."

She swatted his arm. "You do not, but you are forgiven."

"For everything?"

"For now."

He refused to ruin the mood by asking her to elaborate. Instead, he decided to put all his cards on the table at the risk of rejection. "Would you mind if I take you back to the room and ravish you?"

"Not in the least."

That had been much too easy, in his opinion. "Really?"

"Yes."

"Should I perhaps define ravish?"

"I assume you mean you wish to remove my clothes, take me to bed and have your wicked way with me."

"Precisely."

"My answer is still yes."

Shifting against the building pressure in his groin, Sebastian tapped the driver on the shoulder to garner his attention. "Kind sir, please return us to the hotel as quickly as possible and you will earn a sizeable tip."

The man glanced over his shoulder. "We've barely been three blocks."

Sebastian had no desire to argue the point. "Unless you want your bloody carriage serving as a boudoir, you will do as I say."

The jerk had the gall to grin. "You got it."

Sebastian settled back against the seat and smiled. "Let the faux honeymoon commence."

Nasira worried they might not make it past the elevator before clothes began to come off. Her resolute husband somehow maintained enough control to refrain from disrobing until they reached the suite. On the way to the bedroom, they began shedding attire and shoes and by the time they fell back on the mattress, they were entirely naked and completely entangled.

Sebastian suddenly stilled and rose up. "I want to slow this down. I want this to last and if we keep going, it will be over in a matter of minutes."

She pushed a wayward lock of hair from his forehead. "You will receive no objections from me."

He rolled her onto her side so that she was facing the glass doors and moved against her back.

"Do you recall our first night?" he asked as he ran his palm over the curve of her hip.

"How could I forget? I was so very nervous, and you were so gentle."

"You were also a virgin, something you didn't tell me until right before that pivotal moment."

"I wanted to seem worldly. I did not want you to know I was so inexperienced."

"You also didn't want me to know you'd never had an orgasm. You told me the morning after. I've always been curious why you had never pleasured yourself."

"That would have been considered forbidden."

"And have you experimented since we've been married?"

"Never."

"Not even over the past few months?"

She sensed his sudden bout of guilt. "No. I only wanted you."

He slid his hand to the inside of her thigh. "And I made you wait for months."

"Having you touch me was worth the wait."

As they lay there in silence, Sebastian plying her with gentle strokes, the lights of the city illuminated the darkened room, making the atmosphere seem highly sensual and romantic. Nasira closed her eyes, taking in the ambience and willing the climax to remain at bay. Yet her efforts proved futile, and she again gave in to nature's course and her husband's skill as she experienced blessed relief.

So deep was the blissful aftermath that Nasira wasn't aware Sebastian had left her until she heard the sound of him tearing a condom wrapper, a reminder that he still was not willing to conceive a child. She shifted to her back and wrenched the negative thoughts from her mind. And when he returned, she welcomed him into her arms and her body. Feeling the play of his muscles beneath her palms, she held on tightly as he moved inside her, deeper and deeper, faster and faster. She listened to the sound of his ragged breaths and knew the exact moment when his own orgasm took over. Then he whispered her name.

After a time, he rolled to his back and took her with him, their bodies fitting together like a perfect human puzzle. During the next span of silence, she expected to hear his steady breathing, indicating he had fallen asleep. Instead, he played with her hair and showered her face with gentle kisses.

She was beginning to give in to the lull of sleep herself when he sighed and rested his lips against her ear. "I love you, Sira."

Never in her wildest dreams had she ever believed she would hear those words, though she had secretly hoped that someday she would. Even now she believed she might be dreaming. She said the only thing she could manage to say. The words she had kept harbored in her heart for fear that if she voiced them, she would be lost to this enigmatic man forever.

"I love you, too."

While Sebastian continued to hold her close, Nasira felt as if all her wishes had come true. All but one. Yet now that she knew her husband truly loved her, would she be foolish to believe she might be granted the child she had always wanted? Perhaps that would be too much to ask, yet as she recalled both Violet's and Fiona's claim that Royal, Texas, was a place bestowed with magic, she desperately wanted to believe she could have some magic of her own.

Time had passed quickly since their return to the Shakirs' ranch. Sebastian and Nasira had shared three wonderful and blissful weeks full of meaningful conversation and memorable moments. She had never felt so cherished, or so loved, by her husband.

Sebastian had showered her with small gifts, had made love to her often and had barely tended to business. Following Violet and Rafe's wedding in two days, she planned to return to London with her husband and continue their marriage with an eye toward a bright future, even though he had given her no indication he wanted to work on having a baby. Yet she believed that with a bit more gentle persuasion, he would eventually come around, and hopefully she was not giving way to false optimism. If not, she would have to decide if she would be willing to adopt and give up the dream of feeling her own child growing inside her.

After finishing her morning tea in the kitchen, Nasira took the cup to the sink, and immediately felt two strong arms encircling her from behind. "How dare you leave me alone in bed?" Sebastian asked in a teasing tone.

She turned and kissed his unshaven chin. "If you recall, I am meeting Violet for breakfast."

He slid his hand beneath her blue tailored blouse and cupped her breast through her lace bra. "Do you need a ride?"

"I thought I would drive myself."

He rimmed the shell of her ear with his tongue. "That wasn't the ride I had in mind."

Of course not. "I do not want to keep Violet waiting. She is anxious enough with all the wedding chaos."

Sebastian slid his hands over Nasira's hips and pressed against her. "What time do you expect to return?"

She saw afternoon delight in her near future. "I assume in few hours. We have to go over the final details and that could take some time."

He scowled. "The blasted wedding is spoiling my fun."

She patted his pajama-covered bottom and stepped aside. "You have had more than your share of fun of late."

He leaned back against the counter, bringing his bare torso into full view and sparking Nasira's imagination. "If I can interest you in more fun, let me know. In the meantime, while you ladies are discussing catering and flowers, I shall be making a few calls to prospective American clients."

Before she forgot her duties and caved in to her own cravings, Nasira grabbed her bag from the counter and kissed her husband squarely on the mouth. "I should be back before lunch. Be naked and waiting in the bed."

He grinned and winked. "If you give me advance warning, I'll be waiting naked in the foyer. Or if you allow me to drive you, we could have a quick roll in the car."

"Definitely a cad," she said as she headed to the entry, plagued with visions of Sebastian taking her down on the plush rug or in the sedan. Or both.

Nasira fished the keys from the pocket of her dress and slid into the driver's seat, thankful Sebastian had encouraged her to learn to drive on the correct side of the road for when they returned for visits. She liked the thought of coming back to Texas to see her brother's baby and perhaps by then she would be carrying one of her own. Or perhaps it was much too soon to hope for that blessing.

Setting those nagging concerns aside, she navigated the country road with relative ease and arrived at the Royal Diner to find Violet's new Jaguar—a wedding gift from Rafe—parked in the lot near the street. Nasira selected the empty space beside the sedan, turned off the ignition and regarded her watch. The fact she was fifteen minutes late flew in the face of her usual punctual self.

After she entered the restaurant, Nasira caught sight of Violet and Mac's assistant, Andrea Beaumont, seated at a small table in the corner. She strode across the room at a fast clip, until a bout of dizziness caused her to slow her pace. Clearly she was in need of sustenance, yet the scents emanating from the kitchen served to make her a bit queasy.

"I am so sorry for my tardiness," she said as she settled into the chair across from Violet and set her purse at her feet. "I awoke a bit later than planned."

"I hope you had a good reason," Violet said with a teasing smile.

"I do too," Andrea chimed in. "Did your handsome husband detain you?"

Nasira felt heat rise to her face. "Actually no, but that is only because I climbed out of bed before he roused."

"In that case, you should have hung around a little longer," Violet said. "I take it you and Sebastian are mending fences and maybe making a baby in the process?"

If only the last part were true. "We are making very good progress. Now what have I missed in regard to the wedding plans?"

Violet studied the notepad before her. "Actually, I'm fairly sure everything is in place. The menu has been finalized and the flowers have arrived from Hawaii. The cake is going to be gorgeous and the tent should be set up by two. Andrea arranged for a quartet to play during the ceremony and she's confirmed Rafe and Mac's tuxedos are ready to go."

"Now we only have to make sure the groom arrives on time," Andrea added.

With the arrangements already taken care of, Nasira wondered why she had been invited to the lunch today. "What can I do?" she asked.

Violet grinned. "Make sure the groom arrives on time."

Nasira returned her smile. "I can certainly do that, although I believe my brother will be there early, anxiously waiting to claim his bride. What time would you like us to arrive?"

"I'll be getting dressed at the house around noon," Violet said. "I could definitely use your help zipping my dress, if I can get it zipped."

Andrea laid a hand on Violet's arm. "Stop it. You're barely showing."

Violet patted her slightly distended belly. "My baby bump is much bigger, and I'm sure the breakfast I'm planning to eat isn't going to help." She slid a menu in front of Nasira. "I highly recommend the buttermilk pancakes with a side of bacon."

Nasira's stomach lurched at the thought. "I believe I will have toast and tea."

Andrea pushed away from the table and stood. "You girls enjoy your meal. Unfortunately Mac has a full schedule today so I'm going to have to settle for coffee and a granola bar I have stashed in my desk."

Violet frowned. "Tell my brother to stop being such a slave driver."

Andrea released a cynical laugh. "That would be like telling a cowboy to give up his spurs," she said as she headed out.

As soon as Andrea left, Violet shook her head and sighed. "I'll be so glad when those two finally admit they want a relationship beyond business. Mac is so stubborn he can't see the forest for the trees. I really want to shake some sense into him."

"Most men are stubborn," Nasira said. "My husband included."

"But he's coming around, right?" Violet asked.

"Yes, he is." Nasira wanted to delve into more detail but decided not to burden her brother's bride with her problems. "How have you been feeling with all the wedding stress?"

Violet took a sip of water and leaned back in the chair. "Better than I expected. The morning, noon and night sickness has subsided for the most part. I could still fall asleep on my feet at times, which I've learned is typical."

Nasira recalled the fatigue, along with the overwhelming sadness after her loss. "It is normal."

"I'm so sorry for being insensitive, Nasira," Violet said, her tone laced with sympathy. "I know how difficult it's been since your miscarriage."

"It's all right, Violet. Enough time has passed where I no longer fall apart around pregnant women."

"Are you sure?"

"I am sure. I would never want you to feel you have to be guarded around me when it comes to your pregnancy. In fact, I am thrilled to have a new niece or nephew. And I would enjoy living vicariously through you until I have my own child. After all, you can give me advice when that happens." *If* that happened.

"I'm personally looking forward to the next phase," Violet continued. "I have a friend who claims she couldn't get enough sex, and I know that will thrill

Rafe. Of course, the best part about being pregnant is…" She leaned forward and whispered, "No period."

*No period…*

The comment prompted Nasira to grab her cell phone from her bag and retrieve the calendar app. After she scanned the dates and did a mental countdown, she was overcome with panic when she should have been overcome with joy.

"Are you all right, Nasira?"

She raised her gaze to Violet. "I… I think…"

"You think what?"

"I might be pregnant."

And if that were true, she could only imagine what that possibility would entail. Perhaps stress had been the cause of her missing her period. Perhaps it would be best to wait a bit longer to find out the truth.

# Nine

"You're definitely pregnant, Nasira."

A short while later, Nasira found herself at Rafe and Violet's home, holding the second of two positive pregnancy tests in one hand, steeped in shock. "I cannot believe this."

Violet wrested the plastic stick from her grip and set it on the vanity. "Believe it. I think taking a third is a bit of overkill."

Nasira pinched the bridge of her nose and closed her eyes. "How am I to tell Sebastian?"

"Easy. 'Sebastian, you're going to be a daddy.'"

If only it were that simple. If only he would embrace fatherhood. If only... "He will not be happy about this."

"What makes you believe that?"

Nasira opened her eyes to Violet's concerned expression. "It is very complicated. My husband is complicated."

"I can do complicated, Nasira. Now let's go into the living room and you can explain."

Nasira aimlessly followed her future sister-in-law into the parlor and settled in beside her on the sofa. After taking a cleansing breath, she began the arduous explanation by recounting Sebastian's concerns for her safety, his bittersweet memories of his mother, his reluctance to be like his father. She ended her explanation in a haze of tears, saying, "I am worried he will never accept the news at this point."

"He has no choice," Violet said with certainty. "It might take some time, but after he sees you're totally healthy and happy, he'll get used to the idea. And as soon as he holds your baby the first time, he'll wonder why he wasted so much energy worrying over nothing."

Nasira wished she could be so confident. "I hope you are right, Violet."

"And on the off chance I'm not, what are you going to do?"

Nasira had yet to make any solid decisions in that regard. "I suppose I will wait and see how Sebastian reacts when I deliver the news."

Violet took her hand. "I know it's tempting to put it off as long as possible, but the sooner you tell him, the sooner you'll know how to prepare for the future."

"I would rather hop a plane to Bermuda and bask on the beach."

"And I wish I could wear normal jeans again."

They exchanged a smile and a quick embrace before

Nasira came to her feet. "I so very much appreciate your counsel. Please wish me luck."

"Good luck." Violet stood and drew her into another embrace. "That's what family is for. And if your husband acts like a jerk, you know you always have a place here with us."

"I would never want to impose."

"You wouldn't be imposing. I'm sure Rafe would be thrilled to have his pregnant little sister and wife hanging around, driving him insane with sporadic hormonal outbursts."

Nasira tried to laugh yet it sounded hollow. "That would be the last thing my brother would want, having his younger sibling residing under the same roof while he is in the honeymoon phase with his new bride."

Violet's expression went suddenly serious. "He's very protective of you, Nasira. I'd hate to think what he might do if he knew about Sebastian's attitude toward fatherhood."

The thought made Nasira even more anxious. "Promise me you will not tell him."

"I promise," Violet said. "And you promise me you'll call as soon as Sebastian knows. If he throws a fit, get in the car and come here so he can cool down."

Nasira sincerely wanted to believe that would not be necessary, yet she found comfort in the offer. At least she would not be alone should Sebastian decide to walk out on their marriage. "I will, and thank you for being such a grand friend. I suppose I should go now and face the music."

"Nasira, in my heart of hearts," Violet began, "I believe everything will work out well. Sebastian might be snake-bit in the baby department, but it's obvious he loves you very much."

Nasira wanted to have faith in that as well, but her concerns only increased as they walked out the door into the warm May night.

"One more thing, Nasira," Violet said when they reached the sedan. "Every child is a gift and if Sebastian can't see that, then he's a fool. Don't let him allow you to think this is all your fault."

Nasira touched the place that housed her unborn child. "You are right. This baby is all I have ever wanted." And could be all she would have if her love for Sebastian, and his love for her, proved not to be enough to overcome their differences.

As she drove toward the ranch, Nasira recognized she would need a good dose of courage, and perhaps ammunition, for the upcoming debate she would surely have with her husband. On that thought, she pulled the sedan to the side of the road to make a call that could provide her with the information she needed. A fact-finding mission that could possibly hold the key to the past, and perhaps the fate of her future.

She withdrew the cell to input the number and waited. When she heard the familiar voice, she drew in a deep breath and exhaled slowly. "Stella, this is Nasira. I am in dire need of your help."

"What ever is wrong, dear?"

Everything. "Nothing really. I simply need to know all the details of Sebastian's mother's death."

She was met with momentary silence before Stella spoke again. "I am not at liberty—"

"Please, Stella. This is of the utmost importance. I need to know. Sebastian needs to know."

"Then you will need to speak to James about it."

That posed a grave dilemma. "Do you believe he's able to tell me?"

"Oh yes. He often leaves the present, yet he is very much suspended in the past."

"I do not want this to upset him."

"I assure you, it will. It does every time he goes back to that time, and he does so often."

"I would never want to cause James any distress, but this is very important." Even though going behind Sebastian's back could incur his wrath, and only make matters worse. Still, she had to take that chance in light of learning she was pregnant.

A span of silence passed before Stella spoke again. "All right, but be quick about it, and if he becomes too upset, I implore you to end the conversation."

"I promise I will."

"Then wait a moment and I will bring the phone to him."

Nasira heard indistinguishable sounds then James's careworn voice saying, "Hello, Nasira. Stella tells me you want to talk about my Martha. She was a jewel of a woman…."

She listened patiently as her father-in-law extolled the virtues of his late wife, and with great interest when he finally arrived at the fateful day in question. The information was both stunning and troubling. By the time the conversation ended, Nasira was no less clear on what she should tell Sebastian. The truth could truly set him free, or sever their marriage once and for all.

She had no choice but to reveal everything, every last dreadful detail, and prepare for the predictable fallout after she confessed to him she was pregnant.

Sebastian was beside himself. Nasira hadn't called to say why she had been detained, and her phone was going directly to voice mail. That caused him great concern. He should have given her a ride to the diner. He should have rented a second car. What if she had been in an accident, or at the very least, found herself lost on some dilapidated Texas back road? If she didn't arrive soon, he would contact the law and organize a search party.

After he heard the front door open a few minutes later, though, he finally relaxed…until he noticed the distressed look on Nasira's face when she entered the great room. He shot off the sofa, his nerves on edge. "What happened to you?"

She tossed her bag on the coffee table and collapsed in the club chair across from him. "The meeting with Violet went longer than planned."

It was so unlike his wife to blatantly lie, but she had. "I called Violet. She said you left the diner an hour ago."

Nasira averted her gaze. "I suppose I did at that. I was on the phone and lost track of time."

He was plagued by an immediate surge of jealousy. "Were you talking to that McCallum fellow?"

She nailed him with a glare. "Do not be absurd, Sebastian. I haven't spoken with Mac since the night you arrived."

Only minimally relieved, Sebastian lowered onto the sofa and leaned forward to look for any sign of deception in her eyes. "Who else in town would you be talking to if not him?"

She kicked off her sandals and curled her legs beneath her. "I never said I spoke to anyone from Royal. For your information, I was in touch with London."

He couldn't seem to contain his sarcasm. "It's no wonder the call took so long if you talked to the entire city. Could you possibly be more specific?"

"If you must know, I spoke with Stella."

He worried the news might involve his father, and it might not be good. "What did she want?"

"Actually, I called her."

"To check in on our status?"

"To gather the details of your mother's death, which I did."

He waffled between resentment over the intrusion to borderline anger. "Forgive me if I'm feeling somewhat betrayed. The least you could have done was tell me your plans to contact her."

"I understand, but I felt it was of the utmost importance you know the whole truth."

"I don't see why any of it should matter now."

"It does, Sebastian, and you'll realize why as soon as I tell you what I've learned with your stepmother's assistance."

For some reason, he experienced trepidation over the possible contents of the conversation. "I'm quite surprised Stella would tell you what she knows, if she really knows anything pertinent beyond what I've heard."

"I learned the facts from your father, not Stella."

The revelation took Sebastian aback. "My father doesn't remember what he had for dinner."

"He does still remember the past, and quite well."

Sebastian couldn't argue with that observation. "I'm not certain I care to hear his version of the truth."

"You are going to hear it," she said almost forcefully. "And I believe you will be glad you did."

He believed she would be sorely disappointed. "I'll be the judge of that, but please, continue. I enjoy a good fairy tale now and then."

She shifted her weight slightly, a certain sign of her uneasiness. "First of all, your mother was not pregnant at the time of her death."

"Of course he would say that—"

"She *was* pregnant not long before her death," Nasira proclaimed before he could finish his sentence, then added, "A fact unbeknownst to everyone, including your father."

Sebastian allowed the astonishment to subside and logic to come into the picture. "I have a difficult time believing a straightforward woman like my mother would conceal a pregnancy from anyone, let alone her husband."

A strange look passed over Nasira's face. "She had her reasons, Sebastian. Some might say good reasons under the circumstances."

He saw no excuse for blatant dishonesty, and he had a difficult time believing his own mother—the one he remembered—would engage in serious subterfuge. "And what would those reasons be?"

"She kept the pregnancy hidden because your father was adamant she not have another child due to her multiple miscarriages. He sided with the physicians, not your mother, although he claimed that was agony. He loved her so much he hated not giving her a baby."

He had never known his father to agonize over anything other than the state of the global economy. "Clearly James was not without fault in the matter since I assume he was present when she conceived."

"Yes, but she lied about using birth control because she wanted another baby that badly."

Exactly what Nasira had initially done to him, as if history were bent on repeating itself. "Did the pregnancy directly cause her demise?"

"Indirectly. She apparently had another miscarriage and chose not to tell anyone, including her physician. That led to a lethal infection and subsequently, her untimely death."

He took a few moments to digest the information, then summarily rejected it. "It would be just like my father to twist the truth to relieve himself of all culpability."

"He has no reason to lie, Sebastian. Stella told me he has lived with horrible guilt since the day your mother passed away. He blames himself for her decision to keep quiet about the baby. He believes if he had not been so set against her conceiving, she would have told him about the pregnancy and he could have prevented her death."

He acknowledged the scenario made sense, yet he had trouble trusting the source. "I'm still having a great deal of difficulty believing my father remained totally in the dark."

"Stella suspected you would, so she offered to give you the official certification."

"That only confirms the cause of death, not my father's claims."

Nasira impaled him with a glare the likes of which he'd never witnessed. "If you will stop being such a buffoon and search your soul, you might finally realize that your mother was not a saint, and your father is not Satan."

He suddenly felt extremely drained. "I'll attempt to come to terms with the information, but I cannot promise I will feel any differently."

He could tell by the lift of her chin and the defiance in her eyes she wasn't quite finished with the lecture. "It is high time you call an end to your suspicions and resentment. If you don't, you will possibly regret the decision after it is too late to make amends with James. Believe me, that is a burden you will not want to bear."

Sebastian wanted to debate the pros and cons of forgiveness, but his emotions were too tangled in turmoil. He rested against the sofa and feigned a calm demeanor. "Did you enjoy your time with Violet?"

Nasira's dark eyes widened with disbelief. "You wish to know about my day after what I revealed?"

"I see no point in dwelling on the past."

"I do if it relates to our future, and our present situation."

"This information has no bearing on us, Sira, aside from the fact it does reinforce why it's not wise for you to become pregnant again."

"As I have said before, I am not your mother. I am healthy and able to bear more children. Women have babies every day without incident. Life holds no guarantees and comes with a certain amount of—"

"Risk," he finished for her. "I understand that, but it's a risk I don't care to take with your well-being. And if you don't mind, I would like to move off this subject for now."

She lowered her eyes and clasped her hands tightly in her lap. "I cannot discard my worries, Sebastian. Not after what I discovered today."

Concern came crashing down on him as he braced for confirmation of what he suspected she was about to say. "Please tell me you're not pregnant."

She centered her gaze on his. "I am pregnant, and I am thrilled. I hope you will put aside your fears and celebrate the news."

Celebrate? He came off the couch, laced his hands behind his neck and began to pace like a caged cougar. "How can you expect me to be happy after what you've told me about my mother?"

"I knew I was taking a chance by unveiling the truth, yet I had to be forthright."

He spun around to confront her. "That truth only cements my apprehension."

"Your mother chose to become pregnant against medical advice and your father's protests. She also chose not to seek appropriate treatment after she lost the baby, and in turn inadvertently caused her own death due to her deception. In a way I understand—"

"Of course you would," he said, noticeable anger in his tone. "I imagine you would do the same."

Fury turned her features to stone. "I would not do the same, and I cannot fathom why you would believe I would risk my life to have a baby if I had been told the cost would be so high. But I have not been told that, Sebastian. On the contrary, the doctor said I have every reason to believe this time will be different."

"And what if it's not? What if you lose another child? Worse still, what if you lose your life?"

She finally rose from the sofa. "I refuse to buy into your pessimism and fears. I choose to be optimistic and hopeful. If you cannot join me in that optimism, then there is no hope for us at all."

He experienced a different fear. "What are you saying?"

"I am saying go back to London, Sebastian. If you do not want this child, and clearly you do not, then I cannot be with a man who will not support me during my pregnancy. I would prefer to be surrounded by people who will be happy to provide that support. I have that here with Rafe and Violet."

"I need time to think." Time to assess the possibilities.

She picked up her purse, withdrew the bracelet with the rattle charm he had given her all those months ago and laid it on the table before him, as if she was bent on wounding him further. "Then think, but I warn you not to take too long. In the meantime, I am going to stay with Rafe until you decide what you want. I respectfully request you not attempt to contact me until you've made up your mind. I will have someone return the car later this evening."

As he watched his wife walk away, Sebastian experienced a strong sense of déjà vu. Her departure from London a brief month ago had come with the same demand not to contact her. Then, too, he had suffered an emotional pain that stole his breath and his resolve. With his overriding fear of losing Nasira, he had definitely cemented that self-fulfilling prophecy he'd been so concerned about.

He wasn't the kind of man who would abandon his child, provided that child came to be, yet he worried his wife had already abandoned any expectations of salvaging their marriage.

If he did not come to terms with impending fatherhood, and learn to embrace it, he risked saying goodbye to his beautiful Nasira for good.

He had too much to consider, and too little time.

"Have you heard from your worthless husband?"

Seated in the chair next to the window, Nasira glanced up from the book she was pretending to read, steeling herself against her brother's consternation. "Have I?"

He moved from the doorway and perched on the bench at the end of the bed. "If I knew, I would not have asked."

"If my memory serves me correctly, you failed to tell me Sebastian called when I arrived here. How can

I trust that you have not thwarted his attempts to contact me this time?"

"I assure you he has not called and if he had, I would have informed you immediately. I have learned my lesson in that regard."

She highly doubted that. "I truly do not want you to worry about my situation during what should be a joyous time for you and Violet. Are you looking forward to the wedding tomorrow?"

"I am looking forward to having Violet back in my bed. I do not understand the tradition involving withholding the bride from the groom before the wedding."

"It is believed that sleeping with the bride the night before the wedding will invite bad luck."

"It only invites sexual frustration."

Spoken like a man. "Has she left yet?"

"No. She is still packing her suitcases while Mac remains downstairs, growing increasingly impatient. What will you do if Sebastian returns to London without contacting you?"

Nasira refused to give up on him yet. "I am trying not to entertain that possibility."

"Regardless, I will contact Nolan Dane after Violet and I return from our honeymoon. He's a lawyer here in Royal who used to work for me."

"I do not need a barrister." At least not presently.

"You might in the future. He will provide a reference for a family law attorney should you decide to pursue a divorce. Preferably a high-profile attorney to ensure you will receive an equitable share of your husband's assets. One who has experience dealing with international divorce."

She tossed her book onto the side table and sighed. "I do not need Sebastian's money, Rafe. I have more than enough left of my inheritance."

"That is your decision."

"Yes, it is."

"At the very least he should be required to support the child."

She should not be surprised that Violet had told Rafe about the baby. Somewhat disappointed, yes, but not at all shocked. "I see you have been talking to your fiancée."

"Do not blame Violet, Nasira. I pressed her for information when you arrived on our doorstep, looking as though you had lost your dearest friend. She had no choice but to reveal the details to put my mind at ease, although she did not accomplish that goal."

"You need not worry, brother," Nasira said. "I will manage on my own if necessary."

Rafe took on an angry guise. "I would like to seek out Sebastian and tell him—"

"You will not say a word, Rafiq. This is not your concern."

"You have always been my concern, my petite pearl."

She smiled at the brotherly term of endearment. "I am no longer your life, Rafe. Violet is. Your unborn child is."

He rose from the bench, crossed the space between them and pressed a kiss to her forehead. "You will al-

ways be a part of my life. I will always be there to protect you if your husband refuses to do so."

She had to learn to accept that Sebastian could be
absent from her world forever. That she might never
converse with him again. Hold him again. Make love
with him again...

The shrill of the doorbell thrust her thoughts back to
the present. The sound of the deep, endearing voice demanding he see her sent her shattered heart on a sprint.

Had he come to tell her he intended to stay, or to say
farewell for all eternity?

# Ten

As his brother-in-law descended the staircase, stood in the opening to the parlor Sebastian prepared to be thrown out on his arse. Yet when Nasira followed not far behind, sporting a plain cotton blouse, light blue slacks and a champion scowl, he sensed she would prefer to do the honors herself. He would accept that fate. He deserved it.

He glanced to his right to see Violet and her brother, Mac, Sebastian's former nemesis, seated on the sofa as if they planned to preside over a kangaroo court with him playing the defendant. Rafe brushed past him and claimed the overstuffed chair adjacent to the settee, not bothering to hide his disdain for his sister's spouse.

Nasira remained in the foyer, her arms folded beneath her breasts, looking every bit the hanging judge. "Well?"

"May I speak with you in private, Sira?" he asked with forced civility. "It's extremely important."

She regarded the curious onlookers before bringing her attention back to him. "Whatever you need to say, you may say it in front of my family and friends."

She had turned his privacy plan on its proverbial ear, and he would have to accept it, even if it meant an unwelcome audience. "You're absolutely right. Your friends and family are most welcome to witness what I have to say. I only hope they support my decision."

Her shoulders immediately tensed. "I assume that decision involves your return to London."

Wrong. He took both her hands in his. "I'm not going anywhere without you. I'm here to humbly ask you to forgive all my faults."

"Such as?"

He'd compiled a laundry list that was too long to recite now, so he would concentrate on those which would matter most to her. "Forgive me for periodically leaving my towel on the floor after I shower. Forgive me for leading you to believe that I think you're not capable of being involved in the business, because you are, and I welcome your input. Above all, I beg you to forgive me for being such a bloody, controlling coward."

"I have never said you are a coward."

A point in his favor. "Perhaps not, but I wouldn't blame you if you thought it." He paused to draw a breath. "The truth of the matter is, I have fought with men twice my size—"

"Seriously?" Violet interjected.

"I'd believe it," Mac added.

Rafe cleared his throat. "Let the man continue. Violet needs her rest and at this rate, we will be here until midnight."

Violet leaned over and patted her husband's cheek. "Thank you, honey."

"As I was saying," Sebastian continued, "I've been in several situations that required bravery, but the thought of being responsible for a tiny, helpless creature frankly scares the hell out of me."

He studied Nasira's eyes and saw a glimpse of understanding, or so he assumed. "Sebastian, you are in charge of a major corporation. I am confident you can handle fatherhood with the same aplomb."

"Except for the dirty diapers maybe," Mac said, earning him a look from Rafe.

"I can only promise I will try," Sebastian said sincerely. "But what I lack in skill, I will make up in the willingness to learn."

Instead of falling into his arms, she frowned. "Why the sudden turnaround, Sebastian?"

He should have realized she wouldn't make this easy on him. "I spent hours thinking about what you said. Life isn't without risk, but I'm willing to take that risk with you in light of the reward. I've also spoken with Stella and my father. I've come to the conclusion that I've wasted many years resenting a man without just cause, and I will never know true peace unless I learn to forgive his faults. And I hope you forgive mine. In reality, I'm very much like him, and only part of that is learned behavior. The other part is genetic."

He couldn't seem to even coax a slight smile from her. "Will you be able to love our baby?"

More than she would know. More than he could express. "I vow to love our child as much as I love our child's mother."

When he pulled the bracelet from his pocket in an effort to confirm his commitment, and placed it on Nasira's wrist, his wife finally smiled. "That is all I needed to know. And I love you, too. I forgive you all your faults, if you will forgive mine as well."

His spirits soared like a hawk. "You're perfect, Sira. But I need to warn you, you'll have to be patient with me. I'm going to worry about you every moment of every day during your pregnancy. I'm definitely going to be ridiculously overprotective and I'll be gauging your every move—"

"Shut up and kiss me, Sebastian."

She would get no argument from him. As he took her in his arms and kissed her soundly, for the first time in many years, he felt entirely at peace. Once they parted, he realized the room had cleared out as though he was a randy rock star giving a bad performance. "Would you care to accompany me back to our rented ranch?"

She hid a yawn behind her hand. "Gladly. I am so exhausted. I could not sleep without you by my side."

Neither could he. "Rest assured I will respect your need for sleep. You will have to get more of it to remain healthy."

She slid her arms around his waist and sent him a sly grin. "Actually, I am not that tired, nor am I fragile."

No, she was not, and he realized he had known that all along. "Well then, Mrs. Edwards, let us away to our borrowed bed."

"That sounds like a very good plan, Mr. Edwards."

They made love once during the night, and again in the morning. As the first light of dawn streamed through the slightly parted curtains, Nasira rested her cheek on Sebastian's chest and listened to the strong beat of his heart as she basked in the afterglow of re-markable lovemaking…and much-needed hope for their future together.

Sebastian's steady strokes on her back threatened to lull her to sleep, but she awoke completely when he shifted slightly. "You know what I like best about your pregnancy?" he asked.

"I know what I like best," she murmured. "I can avoid tight clothing for nine months."

"You would look good in a gunny sack, Nasira. I personally enjoy not having to wear another bloody raincoat."

She shifted onto her back and stretched her arms above her head. "What do you mean? We are not in London, Sebastian. Today you will not need a rain-coat. The forecast calls for an abundance of sunshine."

He chuckled. "I meant raincoat as in *condoms*. I've had enough of those annoying rubber ducks to last a lifetime. Sheer torture, I tell you."

The description made her smile. "The reference to a bath toy presents quite a grand visual."

He rolled to his side, bent his elbow for support and propped his jaw on his palm. "What time do we have to be at the wedding?"

"Noon. I have to assist Violet with her dress."

He lowered the sheet, baring Nasira's torso, and laid his cheek beneath her breasts. "I'm certain she has several ladies-in-waiting who will come to her aid."

"Perhaps, but I would like to be a part of the process."

Using a fingertip, he drew circles around her belly. "Then you should definitely get some rest."

"How can I rest with you touching me this way?"

"I am trying to connect with our child."

And that proclamation moved Nasira in unexpected and wonderful ways. "Do you wish for a boy or a girl?"

His hand came to a stop on her belly. "I'm still getting use to the fatherhood idea. I haven't had time to consider the gender."

She stroked his hair. "I personally have no preference, although I could see you with a daughter. She would have you wrapped around her finger in an instant."

"That would mean she's exactly like her mother." He pressed a kiss on her belly then rose up slightly and began to speak softly, sincerely. "Hello there, baby Edwards. This is your old dad. I wanted to introduce myself even though some might believe I've taken total leave of my senses, talking to a tadpole who undoubtedly won't remember this conversation."

He sent Nasira a grin before giving his consideration back to his unborn child. "In the future, beyond your toddler years, you're most likely going to be frustrated with me, and perhaps during your teens, you're going to despise me. At times I might be strict, but you never need to doubt how much I love you, and how much I love this wonderful woman who is currently giving you a safe haven in which to grow. But whatever you decide to become, be it a businessman or a butler, please know I will always be proud of you, and I promise I will always forgive your faults."

Overwhelmed by the sweetness of his words, Nasira battled tears. This time, tears of joy. Of blessed relief. "You will be an amazing father."

He returned to her side and kissed her cheek. "I will be the best father I can be."

"Sebastian, my love, I know in my soul you will be the very best."

Nasira had finally been granted her heart's desire—the gift of a precious baby and the love a good man. She felt as if she were the most fortunate woman in the world. And before she drifted off again, she wished that same good fortune on Rafe and Violet on this day when their life together would truly begin....

"With the power vested in me by the great State of Texas, I now pronounce you husband and wife. Now give that little gal a kiss."

Nothing was more boring than sitting through a wedding, especially when the man presiding over the nuptials was clearly a repressed comedian. Yet Sebastian admittedly enjoyed Nasira squeezing his hand during the vows. And he reluctantly acknowledged that Violet and Rafe's pledge to each other had been rather moving at times.

Bloody hell. He had turned into a lovesick sap. But he wouldn't want it any other way.

After the bride and groom vacated the makeshift altar, Sebastian took his wife by the hand and led her through the hordes of humanity. He had no idea so many people resided in this spot-in-the-road town of Royal.

"I'm going to congratulate Violet and Rafe," Nasira said when they managed to find a small space to stand without bumping into guests. "Are you coming with me?"

Sebastian peered out over the crowd and noticed the lengthy reception line near the white tent. He also spotted one man he needed to speak with out of his wife's earshot. "If you don't mind, I believe I'll find a waiter and get a drink. I'll catch up with you in a bit."

She brushed a kiss across his cheek. "All right, but please hurry. I do not want anyone to assume I put you on a plane to London without me."

He frowned. "Why would anyone assume that?"

"This is a very small town, Sebastian. Gossip travels at the speed of lightning, according to Violet."

Nothing he hadn't encountered in the jolly old town of London. "I'll be along briefly."

After Nasira disappeared in the sea of people, Sebastian set out for Mac McCallum, who was standing near the bar bedecked in white bunting. He could now kill two birds with one stone.

As soon as he reached the drink station, he addressed the bartender, tip in hand. "I need a scotch, neat. The best scotch you have, actually."

The man poured the drink and set it before him. "It's free."

Did he think he was so socially inept that he didn't understand the concept of an open bar? "I realize that," he said as he tossed the fifty-dollar bill on the counter. "This is a tip."

"Thanks a heap, mister."

"You're most welcome, barkeep."

He grabbed the drink, approached Mac and looked around before he began asking questions. Realizing the coast was crystal clear, he addressed the cowboy. "Did you make the arrangements?" he asked in a lowered voice.

"Yeah, I did. Delivered the funds personally."

"What timeline should I expect?"

Mac swiped a hand over his jaw. "You're going completely custom, so I estimate at least a year, maybe a bit longer."

That would allow enough time to finalize the deal before the birth of their child. Odd that only a few weeks ago, he would not allow himself to believe he could continue the Edwards legacy. "I appreciate your help. And by the way, who are all these people?"

Mac leaned back against the bar. "Most are Texas Cattleman's Club members, old and new, and their significant others. The man over there is Ben Rassad, Darin Shakir's cousin. And that guy over there is Gavin McNeal."

"I met the former sheriff at the festival a few weeks ago."

"Yeah, he's part of the old guard. The man standing near him is the new Texas Cattleman's Club president, Case Baxter and his wife, Mellie. I'm surprised he bothered to show up, but I guess he's decided to bury the hatchet. And right over there is the current sheriff, Nathan Battle."

Sebastian sensed a story coming on. "Does this Baxter fellow have a problem with the bride and groom?"

Mac set his empty beer aside and straightened. "It's a long story, but Case was very angry with Rafe for secretly trying to buy up the town, including Mellie's land where the club sits. But all's been settled now that Rafe decided not to get revenge on me for his assumption I defiled your wife a long time ago, and as you probably know, that led to Rafe's torture and confinement by your deceased father-in-law."

The unbelievable story, laid out in such a manner, reeked of a made-for-TV movie plot. And although he now knew the details, and that Mac had no designs on Nasira, he still wasn't pleased with the man using *defiled* and *his wife* in the same sentence. "Regardless, I'm glad the situation has been resolved."

He was also glad to see his spouse weaving through the masses, heading his way. When she arrived, he slipped his arm around her slender waist. "Did you give the happy couple my regards?"

"Unfortunately I could not reach them. Fortunately we have time to visit with them before our flight departs tonight." She turned her smile on Mac. "I spoke with Andrea a few moments ago. I believe she is searching for you."

The man's expression lit up like a livewire. "She's probably wondering about the documents I left her yesterday. You folks enjoy the rest of the day, and have a safe flight."

Nasira laughed as soon as Mac left the immediate premises. "Did you notice how quickly he left when I mentioned his assistant's name?"

"I did. Obviously she is very efficient."

She frowned. "She is very attractive, and Mac is completely smitten. I would not be surprised to learn they are the next couple to wed in Royal."

Honestly, Sebastian didn't care about anyone other than the woman standing next to him, looking stunning in her coral chiffon gown and matching heels. He crooked his finger in invitation. "I would greatly appreciate some alone time with my wife."

She took a moment to survey the frantic scene. "That could be difficult to come by unless I borrow a cattle prod to clear the crowd."

Cattle prod? Obviously his wife had resided in Texas long enough to adopt the classic cowboy colloquialisms. "I don't see anyone milling about that massive statue of the woman Gavin McNeal mentioned at the fair."

Nasira peered off into the distance. "Oh, yes, the statue of Jess Golden, his wife's distant relative. If we hurry, perhaps we might steal some privacy, although we will have ample alone time on the plane."

He liked the sound of that, yet he refused to wait until they boarded the jet to let her in on his secret plan. He

felt like an impetuous schoolboy on Christmas Eve as
he guided her toward the legendary figure from Texas
Cattleman's Club's past. Once they arrived, he gave his
beautiful bride a kiss and as an added bonus, a pat on
her shapely bottom.

"I spoke with Mac earlier today," he began, "and he
told me that at one time, the Texas Cattleman's Club
members engaged in missions bordering on espionage.
Apparently it was quite the rage back then."

She favored him with an endearing smile. "You cannot believe everything you hear, although I admit, I have
heard the same. However, clearly times have changed."

He looked lovingly at Nasira and in that moment recognized the value of family and love. "I'd personally
like to believe that men of honor still have the capacity
to come to the rescue of their fair maidens."

She touched his face with reverence. "They do. After
all, you have rescued me from a life without a child,
fathered by the man I love with all my heart and soul."

"You have done the same for me. I want nothing
more than to have you as the mother of our children,
my love. And to reward you for your efforts, I have a
gift to present you."

Her sunny expression melted into a frown. "You have
already given me the best gift I could have ever wished
for. Our baby-to-be."

She had given him more than he could express. "This
will be something we can all enjoy as a family."

"Is it bigger than a music box?"

"Much bigger."

"Where is it?"

"It is being built as of tomorrow."

She looked entirely confused. "Sebastian, I have the Bentley. I do not need another car."

"It's not a car, sweetheart. It's a house."

She appeared unimpressed. "We already own two houses."

"And we shall have three, only this one is a vacation home and will not be located in the UK."

"Tahiti?"

"No. Royal."

Worried that he might have permanently rendered her speechless, he waited for her shock to subside. "Why? Where?"

"In the gated golf community of Pine Valley. I selected a lot and I met with the architect after you left me to return to Rafe's. It's a place we can call home when we return next year on holiday."

Her eyes brightened. "Oh, Sebastian, that would be marvelous. By that time, we will have our baby and we can introduce him or her to its new cousin."

Knowing he had pleased her pleased Sebastian greatly. "I vow to make this home as extravagant as you like."

She wrapped her arms around his neck and held him tightly for a time. "My dear sweet love, my home is anywhere you are."

This incredible woman, his wife, the mother of his child, had changed him in ways he had never believed possible. "And I promise you this day, beneath this historic statue and this symbol of bygone days, I will be there for you and our children through good times and bad."

She pulled away and stared at him. "Children?"

"Certainly. At least five. However, you do realize that will require quite a bit of practice, beginning tonight in the sleeping quarters on the plane."

"I am already pregnant, Sebastian."

"My dear, practice does make perfect."

As they rejoined the celebrants and sought out the bride and groom, Sebastian Edwards realized that perfection was in his reach. He had a remarkable wife, the promise of a bright future and a love he had resisted out of fear. He had learned to forgive when forgiveness had not come easily for him, yet he had his lovely bride to thank for that. The moment he returned home, he would seek out his father and afford him the benevolence Nasira had taught him, before it was too late to mend their relationship.

Ten years ago, the confirmed bachelor and billionaire had entered into a convenient marriage with an exotic stranger. He had done so to produce the requisite heir but had abandoned that plan and refused to entertain the idea of having children when she'd miscarried. For her part, Nasira had married to escape a life dictated by her father's belief she wasn't worthy to choose her own mate. Never in a million years would Sebastian have believed this arrangement would result in undeniable, unconditional love.

Life was good, and he predicted it would only grow better with each passing day. Forgiveness was his for the taking, and love would forever be the constant that ruled his life. Not business. Not gold. Only Nasira.

Always Nasira.

* * * * *

## "Don't forget why we planned this outing."

Jean-Pierre's words were softly spoken, a gentle rumble between them while they stood so close.

"To show any nearby press that we're spending time together. That there is no bad blood between us."

"We are going to have to do better than demonstrate a lack of enmity. We need to show we're more than just friends, Tatiana. We're building a story so we can introduce our son to the world." He lowered his head closer to hers, his lips brushing her hair as he spoke into her ear. "But if you leap away every time I touch you, no one is going to buy it."

The warmth of his body next to hers awakened every nerve ending. He smelled good, like spices and fresh air. She closed her eyes for just a moment, breathing him in. She lifted her palms to his chest, touching him on instinct. And while she might tell herself that touch maintained a few inches of space between them, she knew better.

Having her hands on him was a simple pleasure too good to deny herself after the tumultuous last weeks.

"Agreed."

\* \* \*

**Secret Baby Scandal**
is part of the Bayou Billionaires series—
secrets and scandal are a Cajun family
legacy for the Reynaud brothers!

# SECRET BABY SCANDAL

BY
JOANNE ROCK

First Published in Great Britain 2016
By Mills & Boon, an imprint of HarperCollins*Publishers*
1 London Bridge Street, London, SE1 9GF

© 2016 by Joanne Rock

ISBN: 978-0-263-91860-1

51-0516

Our policy is to use papers that are natural, renewable and recyclable products and made from wood grown in sustainable forests. The logging and manufacturing processes conform to the legal environmental regulations of the country of origin.

Printed and bound in Spain
by CPI, Barcelona

Three-time RITA® Award nominee **Joanne Rock** has penned over sixty stories for Mills & Boon. An optimist by nature and perpetual seeker of silver linings, Joanne finds romance fits her life outlook perfectly—love is worth fighting for. A former Golden Heart® Award recipient, she has won numerous awards for her stories. Learn more about Joanne's imaginative Muse by visiting her website www.joannerock.com or follow @joannerock6 on Twitter.

To the Desire authors and editors
who made me feel so welcome in this series
long before my first book hit the shelves.
Thank you!

# One

"Good game, Reynaud." The beat writer who covered the New York Gladiators waited with a microphone in hand as starting quarterback, Jean-Pierre Reynaud, stepped into the interview room at the Coliseum Sports Complex.

Jean-Pierre was prepared for the reporter's questions as he settled into a canvas director's chair in the small, glassed-in booth after his third straight win at home. Just outside the interview room, thousands of fans lingered in the Coliseum's Coaches Club, staying after the game to see the players take turns answering questions for the media. Here, fans could relax and have a drink at the bar while the traffic thinned out after the Sunday night matchup versus Philadelphia.

After clipping the small microphone onto his jacket lapel with his right hand, which not too long ago had thrown the game-winning pass, Jean-Pierre gave the crowd a quick wave. The high ticket prices for the exclusive Coaches Club didn't prevent the fans here from bringing glittery signs or asking for autographs, but team security made sure these kinds of events went smoothly. Jean-Pierre would give an interview and roll out of here in less than thirty minutes, which would leave enough time to catch a private plane to New Orleans tonight. He needed to take care of some Reynaud family business, for one thing.

And for another? He planned to discreetly scout his brother's team, the New Orleans Hurricanes, before the much touted brother-against-brother football showdown in week twelve of the regular season. Of the four Reynaud siblings, Jean-Pierre's eldest brother, Gervais, owned the Hurricanes. The next oldest, Dempsey, coached the Hurricanes. And Henri Reynaud, known league-wide as the Bayou Bomber, ran the Hurricanes' offense from the quarterback position, slinging record-setting pass yardage with an arm destined for hall-of-fame greatness.

Living up to that legacy? No big deal. Right?

Damn.

As the youngest member of Louisiana's wealthiest family and co-owner of the Reynaud Shipping empire, Jean-Pierre had inherited his love of the game from his father and his grandfather, the same as his brothers. But he was the player the New Orleans papers liked to call "the Louisiana Turncoat" for daring to forge a career outside his home state—and outside of his family's sphere of influence. But since no NFL club had ever successfully split the starting QB job between two players, and Jean-Pierre wasn't the kind of man to play in a brother's shadow, he didn't care what the Big Easy sports pundits had to say about that. When the Gladiators made him an offer, he'd taken it gladly…once he'd recovered from the shock, of course. Gladiators head coach Jack Doucet had been an enemy of the Reynauds after a football-related falling-out between their families. Jack had been the second in command back on a Texas team that Jean-Pierre's grandfather had owned, and not only had the split been acrimonious, but it had also severed Jean-Pierre's brief prep-school romance with Jack's daughter when they moved across the country.

So yeah, it had been a surprise when Jack's team had offered Jean-Pierre a contract with the Gladiators.

New York was a big enough stage to prove himself worthy of the family's football legacy, but there was no room for failure. No NFL team sat in a brighter spotlight—the Gladiators doled out the highest number of press passes to media members. And if Jean-Pierre didn't hold their interest? He lost ink—and fans—to the second NFL club in New York, the one he got stuck sharing a stadium with on the weekends. He'd learned to play the press as well as he played his position on the field, was unwilling to lose the traction he'd gained since arriving in the Big Apple.

"Are you ready?" a New York sports radio personality asked him as the number of interviewers around him multiplied.

Jean-Pierre nodded, shoving his still-damp hair off his forehead before straightening his tie. The fast showers after a game barely took the steam off him. His muscles remained hot long afterward, especially since he did the interviews in suit and tie. His silk jacket weighed on his shoulders like a stack of wool blankets after two hours on the field dodging hits from the fastest D-line in the game.

Around him, the room quieted. The doors had been secured. Waiting for the first question to be fired his way, he peered past the reporters to the fans in the Coaches Club. All around the space, huge televisions that normally broadcast the game were now filled with the feed from the interview room. Jean-Pierre's gaze roamed over to where the team owner sat, holding court at one end of the bar with a handful of minor celebrities and a few of the first-year players.

And just when he needed his focus most, that's when he glimpsed *her.*

The head coach's daughter, Tatiana Doucet.

Infuriating. Sexy. And completely off-limits.

Their impulsive one-night stand last year had wrecked any chance they might have had at recovering their friendship. But dammit all, just looking at her still set his body on fire in a way that tripled any heat lingering from his time on the field.

He tugged at his tie and took in the sight of her, unable to tear his eyes away.

Tall and lean, she wore one of those dresses that showed off mile-long legs. Even though the rest of the dress was modest—splashes of colors highlighted with sequins, neckline up to her throat, sleeves that hit her wrist—the acres of bare skin from the middle of her thigh that trailed south were enough to stop traffic. She wore a silk scarf around her hair like a headband, no doubt to hold back the riot of dark brown curls that brushed her shoulders. Curls he remembered plunging his hands into during the best sex of his life. She stood at the back of the room, hovering close to an exit as if she wanted to be ready to run at first sight of him.

He understood that feeling well.

The punch to his chest from just *seeing* her was so strong he missed the first question in the interview, the words a warble of background noise in his head. How long had it been since she'd shown up at any Gladiators event?

Not since last season. Jean-Pierre hadn't laid eyes on her since that ill-advised night they'd spent tearing off each other's clothes.

Ignoring the aggravating rush of air though his lungs at spotting the woman he'd once cared about—a woman who'd since traded her soul for the sake of her job as a trial attorney—Jean-Pierre focused on the man holding the microphone.

"Run that question by me again?" He hitched the heel of his shoe on the metal bar of the director's chair and tried to get comfortable and relax into the interview the way he always did, even though his pulse hammered hard and his temperature spiked.

A low rumble of laughter from the journalists told Jean-Pierre he'd missed something. The throng crowded him, the handheld mics pushing closer while the boom mic overhead lowered a fraction. The sudden tension in the air was thick and palpable.

"No doubt it's a question you can't prepare for." The reporter from Gladiators TV, a popular app for mobile users, grinned at him. "But I have to ask what you think of Tatiana Doucet's remark to me just a minute ago, that she wouldn't bet against the Bayou Bomber playing in his home state when you match up against your brother's team in week twelve?"

The words sunk in. Hard. They damn near knocked him back in his chair.

Tatiana had said that? Implying she *would* bet against the Gladiators, the team her father coached? Or, more precisely, she would bet against Jean-Pierre.

Her father was going to have a conniption over that remark. Not just because of the suggestion that anyone in his family would bet on a game in any way, which was strictly forbidden. Jack Doucet would also spit nails over the fact that his own daughter was generating media hype in favor of an opponent.

Jean-Pierre didn't spare a glance to see the head coach's

reaction in real time out in the Coaches Club, however. He'd been giving interviews too long to get caught flat-footed twice in a row. He wasn't about to let the media play him over a thoughtless remark Tatiana must have uttered with no regard to who might overhear. Hell no. Instead, he spouted the first scrap of damage control his brain had to offer.

"My guess is that Miss Doucet would like to fire up the Gladiators and help us play our best, even if that means putting a little good-natured ribbing into the mix." He flashed his most careless grin in a performance worthy of an Academy Award given the way she'd just kicked his teeth in.

Ten reporters asked questions at the same time, the cacophony making it hard to hear what anyone was saying. They ended up deferring to the *New York Post* reporter, a cantankerous older guy who scared off any journalist who hadn't been around since the typewriter era.

"C'mon, Reynaud," he growled, a sour expression on his face while he took notes in longhand. "Her words don't sound playful to me. When even the coach's daughter doesn't believe in you—"

"Hey. You can stop right there." Jean-Pierre cut the guy off, unwilling to let him stir the pot with that line of questioning. "Tatiana and I went to school together and I know her well. I guarantee she was joking." He sensed the unrest in the room despite his reassurances. This remark was the kind of thing that overshadowed games. Teams. Whole freaking seasons. And he was not going to allow one superficial remark to steal the spotlight from the Gladiators' hard work.

So he lied through his teeth.

"In fact," he continued, never allowing that fake smile to falter, "Tatiana will be going with me to New Orleans as a special guest of the Reynaud family during the bye week. She can't wait to visit Bayou country again."

He glanced outside the glass to where she'd been standing earlier, but she had disappeared. No doubt she hadn't wanted to field follow-up questions. Or answer to her father.

Or see him? Yes, that bothered him more than it should. But he couldn't deny he missed her.

When they were teenagers, Tatiana had spent two years at a prep school half an hour away from the Reynaud family compound. Consequently, she'd visited his house on the shore of Lake Pontchartrain plenty of times when they were younger.

The beat of silence following Jean-Pierre's announcement might have been laughable if he hadn't needed the time to brace himself for round two of the questions that didn't have a damn thing to do with the game he'd just played. But he'd set them all back on their heels for a second.

"A guest of the *family* or of yours?"

One reporter barely finished speaking before the next question.

"Does it bother you that she prosecuted your old teammate in a sexual harassment suit last winter?"

"Is she invited to your brother's wedding?"

Reporters were talking over each other again, firing off questions left and right, but this time Jean-Pierre could pick out a few of them. He had no intention of discussing the weeks he and Tatiana had sat on opposite sides of a tense courtroom while she used all her talents as an attorney to win a civil suit against one of his old friends. As for the wedding, Gervais planned to marry a foreign princess in New Orleans during the team's bye week—the week neither the Gladiators nor the Hurricanes played.

But since Gervais and his fiancée had done all they could to keep the details private, that question would go unanswered, too. Still, Jean-Pierre didn't mind letting the press assume Tatiana was his guest for that event.

For that matter, he would have to make sure she was his real date for his brother's nuptials. No way would the media interest in them die without serious effort from both of them. Their fiery past would have to take a backseat because he couldn't let her derail his career.

She knew the politics of this world well enough to understand a comment like hers simply couldn't stand. She would have to help put out the fire she'd started. God only knew why she'd done it since she was normally as cautious in her personal life as she was in the courtroom.

"Any questions you would like to ask me about the game?" Jean-Pierre asked, figuring he'd given them enough to refute Tatiana's earlier remark.

His gaze slid to the Coaches Club and he noticed that both Jack and his daughter had disappeared. No doubt Tatiana's father was giving her hell somewhere privately. But then, her old man had always put football before family. He was an okay guy to play for once they'd gotten past the old Reynaud-Doucet rift, but that sure didn't make him a good father.

Jean-Pierre fielded a few more interview questions, quickly outlining his decision-making for a couple of passes that he'd thrown and discussing a controversial pass-interference call. Then he was on his feet and unclipping the mic for the next player, the Gladiators' Pro-Bowl star safety, Tevon Alvarez.

"That was some serious grace under pressure, dude," Tevon muttered in Jean-Pierre's ear as he clapped him on the shoulder. "You're my idol with the hacks."

"I'm used to facing the meanest defensive ends in the

NFL every week," he told him. "The hacks aren't nearly as scary."

Jean-Pierre stepped into the private tunnel leading toward the players' lounge, but midway through, he doubled back toward the Coaches Club. He'd approach it from the private entrance, close to where the Gladiators administration kept a couple of offices.

Because there wasn't a chance in hell he was leaving this stadium without talking to Tatiana first. She might have successfully ducked him since last winter, but with her remark to the media tonight, she'd put herself right back in his world. Now he planned to keep her there for however long it took for this new scandal to die down.

In her professional life, Tatiana Doucet had often been praised for her cool head and ability to organize her thoughts into a reasoned, intelligent argument. So it seemed unfair that on the day when she needed to make the most important and *private* announcement of her life, she'd wound up nervously babbling to a reporter, of all people. In public.

Standing outside the New York Gladiators postgame press event, Tatiana folded a cocktail napkin into her palm and mopped it across her forehead. What had she been thinking to spout such an offhand comment to a stranger across from her at the ice-cream-sundae bar? She hadn't seen the reporter's press pass—he must have taken it off. Although clearly he hadn't turned off his recorder. Looking back, it seemed obvious the guy had been baiting her to make a comment about the upcoming Hurricanes game.

And she'd played right into his hands because she'd been nervous about seeing Jean-Pierre. She'd accidentally given a sound bite that would be all the New York sports media talked about for weeks. Her father would strangle her when he found her. But so far, she'd eluded him. The subterranean hallways of the Coliseum were narrow and echoed, making it easy to stay one step ahead of a coach charging around like an angry bull.

But while she'd put off a confrontation with her dad, she couldn't afford to delay the conversation she needed to have with another man who would have every reason to be angry with her.

Gladiators starting quarterback, Jean-Pierre Reynaud.

She hadn't stayed in the Coaches Club long enough to hear how Jean-Pierre responded to the reporter who'd blindsided him with her remark. She'd turned on her heels and booked out of there. But somehow, she needed to find Jean-Pierre before she left tonight. Her private announcement was for his ears only.

She'd justified staying away from him after their one night together last winter, since their parting had been as passionate as the sex, although not nearly as fulfilling. They had a tumultuous history, considering their prepschool romance that had failed thanks to their families' well-documented enmity. Then, after meeting up years later, they'd been on opposite sides of a prominent sexual harassment case she'd prosecuted a year ago against Jean-Pierre's former teammate. Jean-Pierre had been in the courtroom almost every day after practice until she'd won a verdict against the retired football player. She'd been flush with the professional victory until a coldly furious Jean-Pierre confronted her to inform her she'd ruined an innocent man's reputation.

Even now, she didn't understand how their argument had turned into the most passionate encounter she'd ever experienced, but she sure understood his icy parting words the next morning.

*That mistake will never be repeated.*

She'd been cooking him breakfast at the time and hoping for…what? That they might have a shot at understanding each other even though their romantic history had proved them incompatible before they were twenty years old? Stubborn pride and embarrassment at her foolishness had kept her mouth shut for months. But tonight, she needed to set aside her old hurts and face him once and for all.

The sooner she got this over with, the better, since she needed to head home. Standing on the narrow threshold of a closed door in a deserted corridor of offices, Tatiana debated where to find her quarry. Surely he wouldn't have lingered around the Coaches Club. Maybe she could ask the security guard outside the players' lounge where Jean-Pierre was. Or would she be better off staking out his car in the parking garage? That way she could be sure she wouldn't miss him.

Darting back the way she came, she turned a corner and nearly plowed right into none other than Jean-Pierre himself.

"Oh!" With a yelp of surprise, she gripped his forearm to stay upright.

"Shh," Jean-Pierre warned her, tucking her under his arm and pressing a finger to her lips. "There's a camera crew just down that hallway." He nodded to the ramp just ahead on his right.

Tatiana tensed at his touch. His scent. His maleness. She'd spent so long avoiding him, but in spite of all logic, he affected her. At six-three, and at this close range, he had to peer down at her, his brown eyes flecked with hints of gold and green. She'd fallen for him hard back in prep school, a young love that had only felt more poignant after they'd been torn apart by their families' sudden rift. They'd both moved on, of course, two thousand miles of separation proving as effective a deterrent as the well-publicized feud. But when he'd joined the Gladiators and she'd seen him at the occasional party, she'd been as drawn to him as ever. It had been an attraction that hadn't been reciprocated, judging by his cold words about her court case last winter. She still didn't understand how that terse confrontation in the courtroom had turned so heated.

Now, heart hammering, she simply nodded, knowing they needed to avoid the press. Heaven forbid the media were to overhear what she had to tell Jean-Pierre.

He frowned down at her, not moving.

"What?" she whispered, shaky and off balance as she peered up into his shadowed face.

"We could let them find us," he suggested, his gaze roving over her as he seemed to weigh the idea. "They could photograph us kissing."

The mention of kissing should not have sent a bolt of lightning through her. Especially when Jean-Pierre seemed to be mulling over the idea with the same attention he might give a playbook. Dispassionate. Assessing.

"Are you insane?" Her whisper notched up an octave as she grabbed his sleeve and tugged him in the other direction.

Not that he moved.

"It would end the speculation that we're enemies," he said. They stood facing each other in silence for a moment until she could hear the echo of footsteps in the northern corridor.

"We *are* enemies," she reminded him, tugging his arm with more urgency. "Just because you and my father patched things up enough for you to play in New York doesn't mean the Reynauds and Doucets suddenly became friends. When your grandfather fired my father from his old director-of-personnel position with the Mustangs, it might as well have been an act of war."

Her father had moved the whole family across the country, pulling her out of school and demanding an end to her relationship with Jean-Pierre. And if her father hadn't been adamant enough, her mother had been downright immovable on the subject. Seventeen at the time, Tatiana had fallen in line and put Jean-Pierre in her past…right up until that day he'd approached her after court and her old feelings had spun out of control for one passionate night.

"You think I don't remember?" He fell into step beside her now, guiding her deeper into the private areas of the stadium. "But I'd call us casualties of that battle, not enemies. And either way, I would have preferred to lock down any mentions of bad blood to the media."

He nodded to one of the guards outside the locker rooms as they passed a secured area.

"I realize that." Her heart hummed along at high speed even as she warned herself to be coolheaded. To ignore the feel of his hand on her waist when he ushered her through the heavy steel door that led to the parking garage. "I'm out of practice dealing with the media or I never would have been so flippant with a stranger. Obviously, I know better. I apologize."

His terse nod gave away nothing.

"I'm parked over here." He hit the fob on his key chain and the lights on a nearby gray Aston Martin coupe flashed twice. "I can give you a ride home and we'll…talk."

She wondered at that meaningful pause. Was he still stewing about her comment to the reporter? Regardless, she needed to do some talking of her own.

"Thank you." The clamminess that she'd felt on her skin earlier returned. Her time to tell him was running out. "I took a car service to the game so I appreciate the ride."

She'd timed her arrival so that she wouldn't set foot in the stadium until a few minutes before the game ended, hoping to avoid her father and spend as little time away from home as possible.

The tail end of the silk scarf she'd tied around her head caught on one of the sequins of her dress and she struggled to untangle it as she walked to his car. She was hot, tired and out of sorts, so it was no surprise that she popped a whole row of sequins off. They bounced around the floor of the parking garage while Jean-Pierre held open the door of his sports car.

It wasn't fair that he looked impeccable in a custom Hugo Boss suit while her life frayed at the seams. With an impatient swipe, she slid the scarf off her hair and lowered herself into the leather seat.

When he came around to the driver's side, he wasted no time putting the car into Reverse and heading out the exit. Game traffic had thinned out by now, putting them on the highway in no time. At this rate, in ten more minutes they'd be at her front door. Her stomach tightened at how fast her time was running out to make her cool, calm announcement. If she could even remember that speech she'd practiced in her mind a thousand times. She toyed with the fringe on the edges of her silk scarf, watching the play of pink, green and blue threads over her fingers.

"You didn't hear my answers in that interview, did you?" Jean-Pierre said suddenly, diverting her thoughts.

"No, I'm afraid not." She seized on the reprieve with both hands. "I ditched the Coaches Club the second I recognized that reporter's face on the big screen over the bar. I knew he was about to corner you with what I'd just told him, so I left before my father could blow a gasket and blast me in front of five thousand fans."

She studied Jean-Pierre's expression in the dashboard

lights, his chiseled profile deep in five-o'clock shadow and a fresh scrape visible on his right cheekbone. He'd been lucky today. She'd spent enough time in her father's world to see the toll that football could take on the strongest men.

"I told the media you were joking." He glanced at her as they neared signs for the Lincoln Tunnel.

"Of course I was. I thought I was talking to a Gladiators fan and I was just messing around." She knew from experience she didn't need to stroke this man's ego, but she also didn't like the idea that he might think she'd been in earnest. "Obviously you and Henri are supremely well-matched. If you played ten games, I'd give you each five."

"Very generous of you." He downshifted as traffic slowed in a sea of brake lights. "And probably accurate given our stats in backyard games. But back to the interview. I not only told the reporter you were joking, I also assured him you were going to be my guest for the bye week and that you couldn't wait to return to Louisiana for a visit."

He said it so tonelessly that she hoped she'd misheard. Surely he wouldn't have done that. He didn't even *like* her anymore. He'd made sure she knew as much when he'd walked out of her home the last time.

"No. You. Didn't." The words were a soft scrape of air, her voice vanishing as they entered the tunnel, the regular intervals of fluorescent light flashing through the car and making her dizzy.

"Oh, yes, I most certainly did. What would you have suggested I say, Tatiana?" His grip on the wheel tightened for a moment before he loosened his hold again. He removed one hand from the wheel altogether and flexed his knuckles, as if forcing himself to relax. Or maybe he was nursing an injury.

And, oh, God, how could he have just told the whole world they were going to be spending a week together?

"I just—" She swallowed hard. Tried to channel her inner lawyer and come up with a quietly reasoned argument. But all the arguments that came to mind were conversational dynamite. "That can't happen," she said lamely.

"And yet, we'll have to make a good show of it since your comment could cause the kind of media uproar that steals focus away from a team. I can't afford that distraction right now." He lifted a hand to his tie and loosened the knot, looking for all the world like a dissolute playboy with his unshaven jaw in his sexy car.

But looks were deceiving, and nothing about this man was dissolute or inclined to play. It didn't matter that his weekly contests were labeled "games," Jean-Pierre Reynaud was one of the most serious and hardworking men she'd ever met. He was relentless in achieving what he wanted, in fact. So she understood immediately that he wouldn't back down on the good show for the media now that he'd promised it.

"You don't understand—" she began, only to be cut short.

"It might be you who doesn't understand." He steered off the exit toward 42nd Street and she wished she could turn back the clock on this evening to make the outcome different. To give her more time. She took in his tight jaw, his tense shoulders. "I didn't have time to consult you for a plan. You put me on the spot in front of my team, the league, the media and the fans."

"You're right. That part, I do understand." Her breasts ached beneath her dress, the need to return home a sudden, biological need. Thankfully, all the lights on 10th Avenue went green and they surged through one after the other as they headed north.

"Excellent. You are already invited to my brother's wedding." He resumed laying out the calm, controlled plan that she knew would never happen. "We can attend the ceremony together and then you will stay in New Orleans until the Gladiators game against the Hurricanes the week after. I'll have to commute back and forth for practices, but I'll be around enough to ensure we're photographed together. We can put a quick end to the old rumors about our families. And about us."

Only a Reynaud would seriously contemplate "commuting" between New York and New Orleans. She would have laughed if she hadn't been so upset, rapidly bordering on panicked. But she'd certainly learned how to deal with unexpected consequences. Now, Jean-Pierre would have to learn, too.

"Fine," she agreed rather than waste her breath arguing, already knowing whatever plans he made now were about to be blown up anyhow. "You may not want me in New Orleans with you once you hear what I have to say." She gritted her teeth as they hit Central Park West and neared her building. The ache in her chest shifted painfully. "Would you come in with me so we can continue this discussion inside?"

"Of course. We have a lot of plans to make." He pulled in alongside the valet and handed over his keys.

On the elevator, she realized she had effectively put off her important announcement so long that very soon no words would be necessary and she would lose her window to tell Jean-Pierre herself. She wasn't proud of that. But she was tired, aching and uncomfortable. And didn't he bear half the blame for this impossible situation?

Yet, as soon as the elevator stopped on her floor and the doors slid open, she knew she couldn't let him find out this way.

"We do have a lot of plans to make." She spun to face him, the words spilling out fast. "But not the kind you think."

"I don't understand." His jaw flexed, his gaze narrowing.

She drew in a deep breath.

"Remember that night last winter?" She didn't wait for his reply, as she heard a long, high-pitched wail from inside her apartment. "I should have told you sooner, but you walked out the next day and said it was a mistake. Talking was all but impossible after a parting like that and then, well—" She shook her head, impatient with herself and the excuses that didn't matter now, with her baby crying on the other side of her front door. "Come and meet your son, Jean-Pierre."

# Two

S on?

Jean-Pierre had taken hits from the toughest, strongest, meanest players in the NFL. Afterward, as he lay in the grass with his ears ringing and his vision blurred, he would struggle to snap out of the slow-motion fog that felt kind of like being underwater.

That was exactly how he felt walking into Tatiana's apartment, her words slowly permeating his consciousness along with the cry of an infant. Dazed, confused and trying to stand up straight despite the floor shifting under his feet, Jean-Pierre stood in her foyer and waited for her to return from wherever she'd disappeared.

"Mr. Reynaud?" An older woman in a simple gray dress stepped into the living area to his right. "Miss Doucet asked if you wouldn't mind joining her in the family room. It's just past the staircase on the left." She pointed the way and then went about her business, picking up a few things in the living room.

A bright blue blanket. A baby bottle.

Seeing that bottle was like the second hit when you were already down.

At the same time, it was enough to make the mental fog evaporate and get his feet moving.

Fast.

He needed answers now. Hell, he needed answers months ago. Tatiana had done a whole lot more than throw his career into a tailspin tonight with her unguarded remark to a member of the press. She'd been hiding the biggest possible secret that was going to bind their lives together forever.

"Tatiana?" Her name was a sharp bark on his lips as he entered the spacious suite overlooking Central Park.

Framed playbills lined the walls along with photos of Tatiana and her family. Tatiana with her father at her graduation from Columbia. The Doucets outside of a downtown skyscraper with the brass name plaque of her prestigious law firm. Every picture was a reminder of the life he might have had with her if her family hadn't turned her against him.

A blaze crackled in a fireplace on the far side of the living area. And beside it, in that warm glow of flickering light, he spotted her on the dark leather love seat, cradling a tiny bundle of blankets to her breast. Tatiana's dark brown curls shielded her body as much as the blanket, the firelight making the skin of one shoulder glow where she'd unfastened her dress to feed the baby.

Her baby.

His…son.

Something shifted inside Jean-Pierre, his whole world tipping on its axis as everything changed irreversibly.

"I am sorry," she said softly, her hand shifting to cover a tiny foot kicking free of the cotton bundle. "I left New

York in my sixth month so that no one would find out. I wanted you to be the first to know."

He had moved deeper into the room, drawn to the sight of woman and child, trying like hell to focus on them and what they meant for him. To him. But his brain was scrambling to catch up on nearly a year's worth of living in mere moments.

"What about your family?" Had he been playing games for Jack Doucet's team while the guy kept this news hidden from him? If so, it was going to blow the Doucet-Reynaud feud wide-open again, because Jean-Pierre could not deal with that kind of duplicity. Lowering himself to the chair across from her, he sat with his back to the view of Central Park at night, his eyes on the only thing that mattered. He needed Tatiana to keep talking. To explain why he had no knowledge of this development in their lives.

"They only know I took an extended vacation. I couldn't tell them before I told you."

The tone she used suggested that was the only sensible approach, when in fact, none of this made sense to him. Who kept this kind of news from their family? Jean-Pierre might not be as close to his brothers as he once was, but damn straight they wouldn't keep something like this from each other. He'd told her how much a secret like this had hurt his own family—had hurt his half brother. "I think I'm going to need you to spell this out for me more thoroughly."

"I had so many things to organize," she continued. "I needed a good midwife. And at first I requested a leave from my job. But then I realized I needed to change my role with the law practice so that I'd be doing legal research and writing briefs instead of taking cases to trial." Her eyes were bright and worried as they flashed up to his.

At least she seemed to understand how thin her reasons sounded. But then, she'd always placed a higher priority on appearances than him. The framed photos on the walls around her sure never showed a single misstep in her perfect life. He wouldn't be surprised if the pregnancy had thrown her into a panic trying to find a way to tell her parents.

"Where did you go when you left New York?" He knew he needed to process this fast. To move past the shock of what she was telling him and start being a support to her and this new reality. But the truth of the situation was like waves at high tide, thrashing him over and over.

She'd had months to come to terms with this. He had minutes. And he didn't dare make a mistake.

"The Caribbean. Saint Thomas has a good hospital in case I needed one. I rented a villa on the beach." Her voice wavered. "I was trying to be discreet. To keep this out of the press and away from the old family drama until I spoke to you and we could figure out how to handle the future. But just when I had everything set and was ready to call you, I went into labor three weeks early."

Now that knocked the wind out of his rising anger.

"Is he okay? Are you?" A stab of fear jabbed Jean-Pierre hard, outweighing every other emotion. His brother's wife, Fiona, had lost a baby. He understood the danger.

"We're fine. Thirty-seven weeks is within normal range. César was six pounds and fourteen ounces."

The pain in his chest eased, a small sliver of the tension giving way to an unexpected tenderness.

"César," he repeated, gaze shifting to the squirming blanket and restless tiny foot.

"For your great-grandfather and for my—"

"Grandfather," he interrupted, knowing they both had Césars in their family trees. He remembered the roots of the Doucet family almost as well as his own. He'd been a guest at their home when he'd dated Tatiana, before his grandfather Leon had fired Jack from the Texas Mustangs after two seasons of poorly performing teams.

An old bitterness that would have to take a backseat now.

"Our son is five weeks old. We just flew in from Saint Thomas two days ago. His nanny, Lucinda, made the trip with me. She watched him tonight while I went to find you."

That must have been the woman he'd seen earlier.

"May I see him?" Jean-Pierre didn't want to interrupt a feeding, but the urgency of the infant's small suckling sounds had slowed from when he'd first entered the room.

"Of course." Tatiana shifted the bundle in her arms. She lifted the baby upright, her dress falling closed. "Here's a cloth." She nodded to a square of white cotton folded beside her on the love seat. "For your shoulder if you want to—"

She trailed off as he took the baby, who was possibly quieted by Jean-Pierre's sure grip. At least half the Gladiators had kids, so he'd handled plenty during private team events. But holding this one...

"He has the Reynaud eyes." They were brown and flecked with green. The tiny hands were covered by the sleeves of his shirt, the fabric folded over them. But the boy's color was good—pink and healthy. A thatch of dark hair, spiky but soft, stood on end as if he'd been caught in a wind tunnel.

"I was only with you last year, no one else," Tatiana said softly, her dark curls brushing Jean-Pierre's shoulder as she leaned closer to look down at the infant. "He is yours."

"No question." He trusted this implicitly. He might not be happy with her decision to keep the news of her pregnancy to herself—and he was shoving aside a whole lot of unhappiness about that, in fact—yet he knew her well enough to know that she was careful with relationships.

"May I?" She reached for César. "Just to finish the feeding?"

Wordlessly, he passed the baby back to her. He watched as she slipped her dress off her other shoulder, vaguely aware that many women preferred privacy for such a moment. But he'd been denied too much time already, so he didn't take his eyes off her as she cradled the tiny body to her swollen breast and helped him to find the dark pink nipple.

"You look so…" *Beautiful*, he thought. But the moment was too intimate already with them sitting almost shoulder-to-shoulder, her curls still clinging to the sleeve of his jacket. "At ease with him."

He envied that, he realized.

"I've had more time with him." She bit her lip, perhaps guessing how that statement might sting. When she turned to face him, her eyes shone with unshed tears. "No one warned me what an emotional time this would be." She lifted a shaky hand to first one eye and then the other. "I knew pregnancy hormones could make women emotional, but I didn't count on feeling so different after giving birth. You know I'm not the kind of person to make unguarded comments to the media, and yet tonight I was so nervous about seeing you and telling you, that I just blurted that remark with zero thought."

As troubling as that seemed to be for Tatiana, it explained a whole lot of things as far as he was concerned.

"Having lived through puberty, I can assure you that I understand hormones are a powerful force of nature."

She gave a watery chuckle. "I've made a good living on being rational. Logical. It's like I'm operating on a whole new kind of software."

She gestured to the handful of baby items strewn on the coffee table—a half-open diaper bag with the contents spilling out, a stack of newspapers and some folded sheets. Not a mess by any stretch, but for a woman who liked to show a perfect face to the world, the scene probably bordered on chaos.

"Maybe that's why biology let men off the hook during pregnancy. So we can be the logical ones." He forced a grin, trying to keep things light since it wasn't going to do either of them any good to have a big confrontation about the ethics of keeping him in the dark about the pregnancy.

She'd been nervous to tell him. And he had to take some blame for that given the way he'd left things between them last winter.

"*You're* going to be the voice of reason?" She arched an eyebrow, her voice steady and full of attitude.

That was more like it.

"Definitely."

"Don't forget I was in your backyard the summer you decided it was a good idea to jump off a second-story deck into your family's pool." A smile transformed her features as she shifted her gaze down to the baby in her arms.

And it damn near took his breath away. No wonder she'd looked so good tonight. She had that new-mother glow.

"A minor sprain was a small price to pay for the serious rotation I got on that dive." He needed her smiling. Relaxed.

Trusting him.

Because he'd been formulating plans from the moment he understood the magnitude of the secret she'd been keeping.

"Nevertheless, I think I'll keep my own counsel even while I'm under the influence of my hormones."

"Fair enough. But because you're a reasonable woman, I know you're going to agree with me on this first order of business." He reached to touch her arm where she cradled their son, needing a connection with her when he made his appeal.

"We need to tell our families." Her gaze met his, the firelight reflected in their depths.

She was a beautiful woman. An intelligent, hardworking woman. And there was undeniable chemistry between them or this situation wouldn't have arisen in the first place.

"That's the second order of business." They'd take care of that soon enough. "First, we need to get married."

There was a unique brand of hurt in hearing a man you once cared about offer a sham marriage when he no longer cared about you.

Tatiana breathed through that hurt now, telling herself she could not afford to be any more emotional tonight than she already had been. But heaven help her, how could she not feel vulnerable when her arms were full of the precious baby they'd created, César's soft breath warming her breast as he began to nod off after his feeding? She was exposed in every possible way, and maybe just for a moment she'd allowed herself to sink into the warmth of Jean-Pierre beside her as they'd marveled together at their tiny shared miracle.

Carefully, she lifted the baby to her shoulder and tucked her breast back into her dress. Patting his back, she took comfort in the ritual, grounding herself in the actions of a new mother. She needed to be strong for her son, no matter that Jean-Pierre's halfhearted suggestion called to old feelings inside her. She would tamp down those emotions right now.

"The last time we met, you told me in no uncertain terms that the mistake of us being together would never be repeated." Grateful her voice didn't quaver while uttering those damning words that had caused her no end of grief these past months, she straightened to face him. "Let's not fool ourselves into thinking we can take a relationship from that level of animosity to marriage, no matter how cold-bloodedly we approach our goals. You may be a master strategist on the football field, but César and I are not components of an offense to be moved around at your will."

Jean-Pierre cocked an eyebrow. "So I assume that's a *no* to my proposal?"

Swallowing hard, she nodded. "Most definitely."

"I'm going to ask again."

"And I'm going to ask you to leave if you don't respect my wishes," she said firmly, praying he wouldn't roll out his old charm, which could too easily whittle away her shaky resistance.

"Fair enough then. For now. Because I very much want to stay. May I take him?" Jean-Pierre offered, already reaching to lift César from her shoulder. "You must be exhausted."

She wanted to argue since it comforted her to feel the baby's warm body against hers, but she was indeed tired. And she couldn't begrudge César's father this time with him. Not when he'd been denied five weeks of his life already.

"Thank you." She straightened the spit cloth that he'd tossed over his suit jacket, trying not to notice the attractive vision this powerful man made while holding his son— their child—with such tenderness. "While it's tempting to hold him all the time, I'm learning to rest more often. I was so tired the whole first week."

"I wish I'd been there to help you," he said simply. "Parenting is a team sport." He patted the baby twice, elicited the necessary burp, then tucked the infant in the crook of his arm as securely as he carried a football for a first down. "That's why I stand by the marriage offer. I don't call that cold-blooded. I call it keeping your eye on the end zone. It would benefit our son for us to work together."

"I don't think a child gains anything from parents who aren't happy and yet force themselves to be together. We'd be better off trying to figure out how to effectively co-parent." Feeling rumpled and flustered, she fastened her dress. What woman wanted to field a marriage proposal over the head of a newborn, her breasts sore and her body bone-weary from the physical odyssey of a first pregnancy?

She knew it was foolish to care, but she could only imagine how she looked right now. And yes, she wished she could have met Jean-Pierre in one of her sleek Stella McCartney dresses, but they were all still too small for her postpartum body to fit into.

"I'm not sure your father is going to think much of a plan to co-parent from separate homes." He wrapped a dangling swath of blanket around the baby's foot.

"My father also parented his football players more than his own daughter, so I'm not accepting advice on the subject from Jack Doucet." She loved her father, but she'd witnessed the way he indulged the elite athletes, giving them preferential treatment. As a teen, it had hurt to see him spend more time with them, showing up at a college prospect's house on the weekend to establish a relationship while blowing off Tatiana's debate championship—or any other noteworthy accomplishment.

Although, even as she said it, she realized that Jean-Pierre might bear more of her father's disappointment than she would. But she'd learned long ago she couldn't make decisions to please other people. She relied on herself and no one else.

"Of course." He agreed more easily than she'd expected.

"This is a lot for both of us to take in right now. We'll talk tomorrow. I can put him to bed for you if you want to get some sleep." He laid a hand over hers, a tender gesture that stirred all those emotions she couldn't control lately.

But no matter how kindly he offered help now, she couldn't forget that he'd walked away from her last time. Underneath the civil politeness, he was still the same athlete who'd spent weeks fuming silently at her while she'd methodically proved his former teammate guilty of sexual harassment. Afterward, he had continued to defend the man. If not for the spike of attraction that had never been too far beneath the surface with them, she and Jean-Pierre didn't have anything in common.

Except now they shared responsibility for this precious life they'd created.

"I have a night nurse. She can take him. She knows his routine." She glanced into Jean-Pierre's eyes quickly. "I'm sorry. You can do it soon, but please, can we keep things simple for tonight? We have so much to sort through."

Sliding her hand out from under his, Tatiana reached to take the baby, more exhausted now than she had been after eighteen hours of labor. She hadn't known how stressful speaking to Jean-Pierre would be.

But now that he finally knew the truth, some of that weight had been shifted off her shoulders.

"I'm sure the night nurse is great." He didn't hand over the sleeping infant. "But since I have lost weeks I'll never recover with him, I would appreciate being able to put him in his bed for the night."

The cool words didn't hide his judgment of her—he blamed her for not coming to him sooner about the pregnancy.

"Follow me." Too weary to argue, she rose to her feet, gladly leaving behind the gorgeous Louboutin heels. The shoes that once brought her so much joy were now instruments of torture.

She led the way up the curving staircase of her apartment, a prewar building with plenty of amenities for children that she would be taking advantage of now that she could share the news of her baby with the world.

"Should you be climbing so many stairs?" He was beside her suddenly, his hand on her lower back.

It was a warm touch despite his frustration with her.

"Stairs are fine. I didn't have a C-section so I'm in good shape." Figuratively speaking. Her actual shape still leaned toward the soft side.

"I hope you are taking care of yourself." His touch fell away as they arrived on the second floor and she pointed the way to César's room.

The night nurse greeted her as they entered the nursery, but discreetly retreated to her own bedroom across the hall.

"I am. I'm looking forward to bringing him out in the stroller for walks once we speak to my family. The fresh air will be good for both of us." Leaning into the antique crib she'd bought online and had shipped to the house before she'd even returned from the Caribbean, Tatiana slid aside the blue baby blanket. It went with the aquatic theme of the room.

She'd need major amounts of fresh air after speaking to her father. He'd always set the bar so damn high for her. Even when she was soaring at the top of her class or making junior partner ahead of schedule at her firm, she felt the pressure of his expectations. Now? She couldn't even imagine telling him that his first grandson was a Reynaud.

"We can see your parents first thing in the morning. But I would like to leave for New Orleans shortly afterward." He bent into the crib and laid César beside a stuffed baby whale.

One broad shoulder brushed the starfish mobile as he straightened, setting off a few gentle musical notes.

"You're going there to tell your family?" She knew his parents, Theo and Alessandra Reynaud, had been divorced for years and weren't even full-time residents of Louisiana anymore. Alessandra worked in Hollywood. Theo globe-hopped, content to live off his family's money. But Jean-Pierre's grandfather, Leon, still acted as the Reynaud patriarch in the public eye.

Leon, who had fired Tatiana's father from the Mustangs and created the Doucet-Reynaud rift. Her stomach clenched at the thought of facing him.

"My family can wait." Jean-Pierre stared down at her in the soft blue glow of the nursery's night-light, his strong male presence radiating warmth and making her realize how close they stood. "We need to go there together to fulfill the promise I made in a televised interview this evening. I told the world you were going to be a guest of the Reynauds before the Gladiators-Hurricanes game."

The words didn't make sense at first. He couldn't be serious about them simply pretending to be dating.

"I don't understand. Now you must see that's impossible." She gestured to the crib, where César clutched a handful of blanket. "I can't leave New York."

"We are a family now, Tatiana, whether you want to be or not." His voice suggested a patience that his body language did not. He loomed over her, tense and unyielding. "It makes more sense than ever that you come to Louisiana with me while we work out some logistics of parenting."

Her gaze slipped back down to César, peaceful and unaware of the tension between his parents. She knew that Jean-Pierre was right. They had to find some way to raise their child together even though there would be no wedding. No pretend romance to mask the animosity between them.

Maybe, given some time, she could negotiate a peaceful future for her son in the same way she argued court cases. She would find a way to get on top of her runaway pregnancy hormones and the mixed feelings she still had for Jean-Pierre—hurt, resentment, attraction. A potent mix.

"I'll need a private room," she said finally, tilting her chin up and laying the groundwork for this very dicey compromise. "I will go with you, but I can't perform a charade for the media or our families."

"Meaning you won't pretend to like the father of your child?" One heavy eyebrow arched as he watched her.

Her heartbeat quickened for no discernible reason. They were drawing boundaries, weren't they? That was a good thing.

"Meaning there will be no maneuvering each other by implying an engagement or imminent wedding that we both know will not happen."

"Deal." His agreement was quick and easy, catching her off guard. He took her hand in his. "You have my word."

His touch sparked memories of another time they'd been face-to-face like this—arguing heatedly about her court case. He'd touched her to emphasize a point, perhaps. And somewhere in that moment, the chemistry of the contact had shifted, turning heated. Making it impossible to pull their hands off of each other. She felt the weight of that moment now, along with the possibility that it could happen again if she wasn't careful. It was there, in her fluttering pulse. In her rapid breathing.

She hovered there, on that razor's edge between tension and attraction, understanding too late how easy it would be to slide into that dangerous terrain.

"Sleep well then." He lifted her hand to his lips. Brushed

a brief kiss along the backs of her fingers as though it was the most natural thing in the world. "I'll pick you up in the morning so we can speak to your father together. And make no mistake, I will be there by your side."

She nodded, her mouth dry, her skin tingling where he'd kissed her. She watched Jean-Pierre turn to leave and show himself out, her emotions tangled, knotted and taut. She had thought telling him about their child would be the most difficult thing she'd ever have to do. But now, feeling the way her body still responded to him, she knew that resisting the lure of a Reynaud man would be a challenge beyond anything she'd imagined.

# Three

Between NFL games, Jean-Pierre had a week to strategize. He studied his opponent, searching for weaknesses and ways to exploit them. He developed a game plan and made adjustments right up until the moment when he took the field to execute it.

With Tatiana, he didn't have a week for anything.

He'd had twelve intense hours to get his head around fatherhood before facing her family with news that had obviously blindsided them. Twelve hours to figure out his game plan, when his whole world was off balance. And while they'd delivered the news to the Doucets in their living room half an hour ago and it had gone as smoothly as could be expected, Jean-Pierre now braced himself for whatever his coach wanted to say to him privately. In a room nearby, the women took turns holding César while he watched Jack Doucet shut the door behind him and turn on him.

"You bastard." Red-faced, his coach stared him down with a fury he no longer hid. A defensive end in his college days, Jack had softened in his coaching years, a rounded gut and flushed face attesting to the comfortable life of a man who didn't deny himself any pleasures.

But right now, with the look in the older man's eye, Jean-Pierre didn't doubt for a second the guy would deliver one hell of a hit if he decided to come after him.

"She didn't tell me," Jean-Pierre reminded him, remembering the time the coach had hurled a helmet across the locker room into a rookie's head for missing his play cue. "I didn't know until last night and I'm here now—"

"Don't bullshit me. A man always knows there's a chance." Jack's fists clenched at his sides, his chin jutting closer. "That's my daughter we're talking about."

"And that's my son." Jean-Pierre kept his voice quiet, recognizing the imperative of keeping a lid on this conversation with the women in the other room. "And since we both want to protect our families, I suggest we figure out how to have this discussion without upsetting anyone on the other side of that door." His heart slugged hard in his chest.

He did not want a brawl to commemorate this day. That wasn't the kind of start he needed with Tatiana.

"As much as I'd like to plant my fist in your jaw, even if it cost you a game, Reynaud, you have a point." The older man spun on his heel and turned to the bar. He poured himself a measure of Irish whiskey from a bottle centered on a silver serving tray.

Jean-Pierre hoped the whiskey cooled him off. He edged back a step, waiting to resume their conversation once Jack had a hold of himself.

All around the study were framed news clippings and photographs from Jack's career as a head coach in New

York. The most prominent photos were of the team's two division championships and a Super Bowl win four years ago. There were no photos from Jack's years as Leon Reynaud's second in command for the Mustangs, even though the two of them had taken the team to new heights, developing a fast style of offense copied throughout the league and setting records in passing that still stood today.

Jack had severed all ties with Leon and the Reynauds until he needed a strong quarterback to lead the Gladiators. Even then, the head coach hadn't done much to make Jean-Pierre feel welcome in New York. They'd simply worked toward their common goal to make the Gladiators a powerhouse team again.

"You've got a hell of a lot of nerve." Jack slammed the whiskey glass on the desk as he turned to face him. "I brought you to New York to give you a chance to step out of the family shadow. To make your own mark on this game. And this is how you repay me?" He gripped the neck of the whiskey bottle tighter, his voice low.

"Now I'd like to return the favor and ask that you don't try to bullshit me. You didn't bring me here out of the kindness of your heart. You brought me here to win games," he said evenly. "I've done that and more."

Jack remained silent as he scrubbed a hand through thinning hair.

"I've played my part for you," Jean-Pierre continued. "A little too damn well now that I think about it. It's one thing for you to ask me to win games, but it was another to expect me to stay away from Tatiana."

He'd backed off ten years ago when she had sided with her family and told him they were through. But all those old feelings hadn't just evaporated because Jack Doucet told his daughter not to see him anymore. They'd been festering somewhere inside them both, only to implode that day in the courtroom when he'd confronted her after the case.

"I should have never brought you to the Gladiators," Jack muttered, pouring himself a third shot.

"Beyond the winning record, I've provided the locker-room stability you need to keep a team of aging veterans and wild rookies on the same page each week. If you're unhappy with my performance, I'm happy to revisit our terms at contract time." Knowing he wasn't going to smooth over this problem today, he wondered how soon he could reasonably walk out of the Doucet household with Tatiana and his son.

His son.

He still couldn't think about the magnitude of that news without the words reverberating through him long afterward. But he needed to move past the awe of it fast in order to protect César's future. He had so much to organize, so many plans to put in place. Not the least of which was convincing Tatiana to stay with him.

It was a feat that he'd never achieve while her father remained furious with him. But dammit, he needed to ensure César had the kind of stability his own life had lacked. Theo's illegitimate son—Jean-Pierre's half brother, Dempsey—had suffered the consequences of their father's choices his whole life. Jean-Pierre didn't want that for César.

"I don't care if you set the record for completions this season." The older man raised his voice, scaring off a heavy gray tabby cat that had been snoozing on the leather chair behind the desk. The animal took cover behind a red drapery and peered down into the expansive view of Central Park. "I want my daughter happy and my grandson to have a name."

"He has my name. My protection. All the resources my

family can possibly give him." He'd been up most of the night working out details with his lawyer to ensure paperwork was already in motion.

"Let me be clearer." Jack shook a finger too damn close to Jean-Pierre's face. "I want my grandson to have a name that isn't Reynaud."

"Nevertheless, I will do everything possible to ensure Tatiana is taken care of as well. You know as well as I do that being a Reynaud ensures she'll never want for anything."

"Meaning you will marry her?" Appearing to mull this over, Jack strode over to the tabby cat, picked it up and stroked the animal's broad head.

"She asked me not to pressure her about that and I will do as she requests."

"But you will see that it happens." The coach met his gaze over the cat's head.

It was a directive, not a question. Maybe Jean-Pierre would have resisted more if he hadn't been on the same page with the man.

"That's my intent. Yes. But I'm curious. You wouldn't protest a union between families? Despite the rift?" He remembered a time when the Doucets had taken away Tatiana's car as a punishment for driving to see him.

That was a long time ago, but Jack held the kind of grudges that grew deeper with age.

"You've given me little choice."

"I have two weeks with her in New Orleans and even she won't back out of that." He wouldn't break his agreement with Tatiana by implying a union she might not agree to. But he also couldn't afford putting more pressure on the Gladiators by ticking off his coach further. "I hope that attending my brother's wedding will make her reconsider marriage."

"I'm not so sure about that plan. She ought to keep the child secret longer down there," her father mused. "Old Leon must have the family compound locked down like Fort Knox with a foreign princess on the grounds."

"It's secure. There will be no media unless Tatiana chooses to speak with reporters." He hadn't really considered that option—keeping César a secret from the press for a while longer. But maybe Jack had a point. There would be pressure enough on them with the media interest already brewing. "I won't be budging on that."

"Good." Jack set down the cat on a wingback chair. "By the time I see an announcement about my grandson in the papers, it will coincide with news of your marriage."

He didn't argue with Jack. But as he stood to exit the study with him, he couldn't help but remind him of one important fact.

"It has to be her idea to get married since she's already put her foot down on the subject." He understood that much about her. She was a strong-minded woman and she didn't budge once she made up her mind. He'd seen it in the courtroom last year.

"And so it will be." Jack opened up the door and gestured for Jean-Pierre to go ahead of him. "Because if it's not, you can start looking for a new team. I can guarantee that if I'm not happy with you, son, I'll do everything in my power to bury your career."

"I've missed this place." Tatiana stared out the window of the chauffeur-driven luxury SUV that had met them at the private airport just outside of New Orleans.

Spanish moss dripped from live oak trees on either side of the private driveway leading into the Reynaud estate on Lake Pontchartrain in an exclusive section of Metairie, Louisiana, west of the city. Pontoon boats were moored in the shallow waters while long docks stretched into the low-lying mist that had settled on the surface. The green of the gardens was rich and verdant, the ground so fertile that a team of gardeners was needed to hold back the wild undergrowth that could take over land like this in just a few short weeks' time.

She knew because her family's yard had been like that, full of kudzu back when her father had been with the Texas football team. The Doucets didn't have the same level of wealth as the Reynauds and even now, the apartments on Central Park West were relatively new luxuries. Back when Tatiana had attended prep school nearby, her mother had taken a condo in Baton Rouge while her father remained in East Texas for his job with the Mustangs.

Jean-Pierre sat beside her while César napped in his car seat in the bench-row seat ahead of them. The trip had been smooth, from the car service in New York to the quick private flight to the spacious SUV with a Reynaud family driver to load their luggage. She wished she knew what exactly had transpired between Jean-Pierre and her father when they left to speak privately, but she'd only learned that her father suggested they keep news of César out of the press for as long as possible, an approach that made sense while they figured out how to share custody.

After leaving her parents' home, Jean-Pierre had assured her that he would immediately outfit a nursery in Louisiana for César, so she hadn't brought much for him. The baby's night nurse would fly to New Orleans later, but until then, local staff had been retained to help Lucinda.

Tatiana had to admit, Jean-Pierre had made things as easy as possible for her. And while she'd guessed he would probably step up and be supportive of their child, a small part of her had feared otherwise. That he would be too angry at being shut out of César's birth to treat her with so much thoughtfulness. She'd hardly slept the night before, wondering how today would be with him, not to mention all of his family.

"I miss this city every time I'm away," he confided to her now. Leaning forward to look at the lake with her, Jean-Pierre was a warm, vital presence in the vehicle.

The tinted windows ensured their privacy as they rounded the first bend. She spotted a Greek revival mansion that hadn't been there before.

"Wow." She marveled at how well the new home complemented the existing one where Jean-Pierre had grown up, a home she'd visited as a teen even before they dated since her father had worked with Leon Reynaud. "Did Gervais build this for his soon-to-be bride?"

Speculation about Gervais and Princess Erika's wedding had filled the tabloids for weeks. Tatiana had devoured the articles during those uncomfortable last weeks of pregnancy when she had done little more than read and wait.

"No. Dempsey had this built when he took over as head coach of the Hurricanes. Gervais and Erika are in the original home." Jean-Pierre pointed to the mansion, which was almost double the size of the Greek revival house, on the other side of the street. "Henri and I share time in the big Italianate monstrosity that Leon purchased for guests when we were young. You remember it?"

"The abandoned house where you wanted to celebrate my seventeenth birthday?" Her skin warmed at the memory. She'd had such a crush on him back then, she would have followed him anywhere. Even into a house that had been fenced off and marked with construction-zone signs.

But he'd just started attending the same school as she and they'd been spending more time together. Their families had been friends for years—before the big rift—so they'd had an easy relationship marked by meetings at football games or summer homes. But once Jean-Pierre had enrolled in her school, things shifted between them. She couldn't keep her eyes off him.

That weekend at the Reynauds' house—her birthday weekend—had moved things out of the friend zone. He'd kissed her that night and everything had changed.

"You have to admit I made you one hell of a birthday cake." His gaze lingered on her. Was he thinking about that kiss, too?

"Or your family chef did." She refused to be charmed by old memories. There were too many unhappy newer ones.

"But how do you think he knew to make a raspberry almond torte with purple frosting?"

"I was in a serious purple phase."

She had all but melted at his feet when he brought it out with seventeen lit wooden matches in place of the candles he'd forgotten. They'd eaten it on the dock outside the boathouse, and she'd informed him that at seventeen, she was officially old enough to be his girlfriend.

The night had only gotten more romantic after he fed her that first piece of cake.

He'd been eighteen, worldly beyond any other boy she knew, and wary of dating someone younger. But she'd been persistent.

"Not much has changed." He gave the hem of her skirt a light tug for emphasis, the lavender silk edged with darker plum fringe.

Through the fringe, the back of one knuckle grazed her bare knee and sent a jolt of adrenaline buzzing up her thigh. She bit the inside of her cheek.

"I've only just returned to bright colors, though. For years, I draped myself in navy and beige when I went in front of a jury." She'd grown tired of the conservative wardrobe her career dictated, but she hadn't realized how much she'd reined in her fashion creativity until her more recent wardrobe choices had all been bright colors, sequins, feathers and fringe.

"Anything to win a case," he remarked dryly, no doubt thinking of the civil suit she'd won against his friend.

"I hope you don't expect me to apologize for being good at my job." They might as well address it since it had been the source of their last argument, the reason he'd walked out on her and said their time together had been a mistake. "It's not up to me to determine right from wrong. That's a jury's job. I'm simply paid to win. Just like you are."

She tucked her phone into her purse as the vehicle stopped in front of the stucco Italianate mansion that had been updated and whitewashed since the last time she'd been here. Their driver, a former Hurricanes' player named Evan, opened the back door for them and began to bring their bags inside.

"You didn't use to believe in winning at any cost." He didn't move to exit the vehicle.

"That was before I realized that if you don't fight for yourself, no one else is going to fight for you." She reached into the car seat to unbuckle César, but Jean-Pierre took over the task.

"Let me." He lifted the baby in one arm and stepped out into the sunlight to help her exit the SUV. He held onto her arm even after she stood by his side. "Do you really think I didn't fight for you all those years ago?"

She didn't need to ask what he was talking about. She'd been hurt when he hadn't tried harder to see her despite their families' dictate that they stay away from each other.

"It's ancient history now." She wasn't about to admit how much that breakup had stung.

Especially not now, when she needed to shape a future

for herself and her son. The less she looked back at the past, the better.

"I hope so. We've got a whole future ahead of us to plan." His hand found the small of her back as she stepped up onto the stone landing of the front steps. "Together."

His touch set off the familiar awareness that he'd always inspired. And how potent it felt now as they moved toward the threshold of this home with their son in his arms.

She'd be staying for two weeks inside a home where Jean-Pierre had almost seduced her ten years ago. How resistant would she be here, of all places, when they shared so much history? Lucky for her, she had César to remind her of her priorities. She wouldn't allow herself to be trapped in a loveless marriage. Children didn't thrive in that kind of stilted environment.

"I'm sure we'll figure out an equitable arrangement." Her familiarity with legal settlements had already prompted her to draw up some possible scenarios for sharing custody, but she wanted to wait a few days to raise the topic for discussion.

Give him some time to see she genuinely wanted what was best for their child.

"His happiness will be our highest priority." Jean-Pierre shifted César in his arms and the baby made a soft cooing sound. "Welcome back, Tatiana. If there's anything I can do to make your stay here more comfortable, I hope you'll let me know."

"Thank you." She felt the warm Louisiana breeze tousle her curls. Camellias and roses all around the front entrance beckoned her toward the open door. "It looks so much different."

"I should hope so. You've been gone a long time." He followed her into the cool foyer, where pale tile floors and heavy, dark furnishings gave the place a Mediterranean feel.

A courtyard ahead of them made her realize the house was built around a wide space that was open to the sunlight. Terra-cotta floors and some kind of potted citrus trees imparted a warmth to the home she hadn't expected. Brightly patterned pillows decorated carved wooden benches while a water feature in the center gurgled softly.

"It's very inviting." She could picture herself here, surrounded by sunlight and flowers.

"Fiona, Henri's wife, did some decorating when they married. But Henri and Fiona will be staying at their home in the Garden District all during the wedding festivities. So we'll have this whole place to ourselves." He gestured toward the steps and she followed him up the gently rounded staircase.

"I may need a map to navigate." She peered over the thick banister down into the foyer, noting the tapestry that bore a Reynaud family shield from the days of the Crusades. Jean-Pierre had written a paper on the meaning of the heraldry in high school and she'd proofread it for him before he turned it in.

"Hardly. Your father's house in the Hamptons is bigger than this." He pointed to a room on the left side of the main corridor upstairs and led her into a nursery decorated in gray, blue and yellow. A stuffed giraffe almost as tall as the ceiling stood in one corner, watching over the crib. A carved fireplace covered with a cream-colored grate took up the opposite wall.

While Jean-Pierre lay the still snoozing baby in the crib, she marveled at all the special details in place for the room's tiny occupant. Besides the beautiful décor, the open closet held extra blankets, diapers, towels and clothes.

A discreet changing station had been built in to the gray cabinetry.

"Your staff must have worked all night to decorate." She couldn't imagine how they'd created the beautiful space so quickly. "Are you sure we'll be able to keep César a secret if—"

"The staff here is carefully screened and sign confidentiality agreements before working with the family. But in this case, I didn't need to ask for extra help. Henri and Fiona had already installed the basics for a nursery before…" He straightened from the crib. "Fiona lost a pregnancy and they had a difficult stretch. Her experience makes me all the more grateful you and César are both healthy and thriving."

The concern in his eyes told her how deeply he meant it. The emotion she glimpsed touched her, even as her heart ached for his brother and sister-in-law.

"I can't imagine how hard that must have been." She leaned into the crib to kiss her son's soft baby hair. The mattress was raised to the highest setting inside the wooden rails since he was too young to sit up on his own.

"Thankfully, she's well now. There's a video monitoring system if you'd like to keep an eye on him." He pointed to a handheld device broadcasting a color image of the crib. "The camera is inside the giraffe's mouth. You can also program your phone to pick up the feed if that's easier for you."

"That would be great." She hugged her arms around herself, feeling oddly adrift without César to hold now that she'd handed off some of his care to Jean-Pierre. "I will rest easier knowing I can check on him without even leaving my room."

"I can introduce you to the relief caregiver later, to help out when Lucinda needs a break. I'll show you to your room first. You must be exhausted with so much travel in the last week."

Not to mention the stress of telling him about their child.

But she didn't remind him of that.

"Thank you. I would appreciate it." She tucked the nursery monitor in her bag and followed him through the wide hallway to a room two doors down.

"I thought you'd prefer to be close to César, although if the room isn't to your liking, there are several other options." He switched on a chandelier, even though daylight still shone in through the floor-to-ceiling windows on the exterior wall.

At first, she thought he'd brought her into a family room by mistake. But it was actually the sitting area of a spacious guest suite. Beyond the couches and wet bar of the living space, two steps led into the bedroom, the area divided by a low wall with two red marble pillars. A king-size bed was tucked into a corner beside an exit to a private terrace overlooking the lake. A fireplace had been built into one wall, and a ceiling fan turned languidly over the bed. The ceilings had to be at least fifteen feet high.

"The Reynauds live well," she said finally, setting her bag on one of the long, forest green couches. "I'm sure this room will be more than adequate."

"Good." He nodded, satisfied. "I told Evan to put your luggage in the closet, but I can send someone up to unpack for you."

"That's not necessary." She'd forgotten the level of wealth in his family. The Reynauds didn't just have homes around the globe. They had well-staffed homes. Private planes. A global shipping empire.

For her father, football was a lucrative career. For the Reynauds, it was a passion and a pastime, the income a small facet of a net worth she couldn't fully appreciate. And while that was all very nice for them, she wasn't sure how she felt about having her son raised to think this was how people lived.

"As you wish." He nodded and backed up a step. "Dinner is at seven thirty if you'd like to rest before then. The caregiver can oversee César's next feeding if Lucinda needs to unpack."

"No." She wouldn't hand over her son to a woman she hadn't even met yet. "I'll just keep the monitor close by." She retrieved it from her bag.

"But you'll join me for dinner?" he asked. He did not demand. "I've asked my family to give us some privacy until we settle in, so it will be just us tonight."

She appreciated that for a lot of reasons, not the least of which was needing to steel herself for a reunion with a family she hadn't acknowledged in a decade. A family that had been kind to her, whose kindness she'd repaid by turning her back on them when her father told her to.

But she was also glad for the way Jean-Pierre seemed to understand she needed some time and space to make her own decision about their future together. She was grateful for that right now when she was beginning to feel overwhelmed by this life of privilege.

"Dinner sounds nice." Maybe after a shower and a change of clothes she'd feel less vulnerable, more ready to stake her claim for a future independent of Reynaud influence. "I look forward to it."

She said it as a polite social nicety. But something flared in his eyes at the words, a heated interest she didn't miss. That he could feel attracted to her now—when she was bone-weary and still recovering from pregnancy—caught her by surprise. It amazed her even more to realize his interest stirred her own.

Where would he be sleeping? And what a crazy thought that was on more than one level. The doctor hadn't even cleared her for sex yet. If she was even planning on having sex with Jean-Pierre again. Which she wasn't.

"As do I." His gaze roamed over her, warming every place it rested. "Until then, you should feel safe to walk the grounds if you wish. Between the extra security on staff for the wedding and the usual precautions around the property, you won't have to worry about any unwelcome interruptions from the media. Just be careful near the lake or on the decks overlooking the water. Telephoto lenses from boats or nearby properties would be able to capture images at that distance."

"I'll keep that in mind." She would keep her blinds closed as well, as much as she'd prefer the water view. "The longer we can protect César's privacy, the better. Although some photos of you and me here together might help quiet the rumors I created back in New York."

"If you feel up for a boat ride tomorrow, I'll take you out on the lake." His gaze held hers. "Just like old times."

A half smile teased his mouth as he reached for the door. A shared memory flashed between them. He used to take her out on the boat to be alone with her—away from his family. They would anchor near a quiet cove and steal belowdecks. She would try to tempt him enough to forget the restraints he'd always put on their relationship, always knowing she was safe with him. But there were times that they'd pushed the boundaries...

Just thinking about those trips warmed her skin. The urge to kiss him flared hot even though they stood on opposite sides of the room. She licked her lips instead, suddenly nervous.

"I'm sorry you have to spend your time staging photo opportunities for the press to cover up my mistake with that reporter." She had never understood how he could rattle her so easily when she felt sure of herself with the rest of the world.

His hand fell away from the door but he didn't advance toward her.

"Even if it hadn't been for that comment to the reporter, we would need to be together this week anyway." The hint of a smile had vanished, his expression serious. "You and César are my highest priorities now."

Jean-Pierre would bear his responsibilities because he had to, not because he wanted to. She nodded, understanding better than he realized.

As he left her alone to rest and unpack, Tatiana knew it would be a stretch to appear in photos with him as if they were still old friends. The truth was that they were so much more than that. Enemies, lovers, parents. A combustible combination with attraction simmering just below the surface.

It would take a whole lot of focus just to keep it from boiling over.

# Four

"Tatiana?"

A man's voice awoke her later that night, the sultry drawl of a Cajun accent lingering in her ear. Confused about the time and her whereabouts, she struggled to orient herself. A strange coverlet pressed into her cheek, the pale piping making a ridge along her jaw. Moonlight streamed in through a door near her bed where she'd forgotten to close the blinds. She lay atop the duvet, still fully clothed.

"Jean-Pierre?" The voice sounded so close to her, but she didn't see him in the moonlit room.

Had she been dreaming of him?

"I'm in César's room," the voice returned softly, the sound coming through the nursery monitor, which rested on the bed nearby. "I wasn't sure if you heard him cry, but I think he's hungry if you still want to feed him."

Waking faster now, she realized it must be late. Her breasts were swollen to aching.

"Yes. I'm coming." She scrambled off the bed, wishing she'd changed into something more comfortable. She was a wrinkled mess in her traveling clothes. She must have slept right through dinner.

"Don't hurry. We're fine." The gentleness in Jean-Pierre's tone slipped right past her boundaries, making her smile. Of course, the warmth and kindness were intended for his son. He was speaking as much to César as to her. "It's a nice night if you want to sit outside. I've got a fire going."

"I'd like that." Her eye went to the door; she could see a blaze in one of the fire pits. She hurried anyway, thinking maybe she had time to slide into fresh clothes after all.

"I'll stop by the kitchen to grab you something to eat. You must be hungry," he said as she slid out of her dress and into a pair of knit pajama pants and a matching button-up top that made nursing easier.

Hearing him while she was mostly naked roused a whole host of feelings she wasn't ready to deal with.

"I'm on my way." She grabbed a throw blanket off the end of the bed for good measure. The more barriers between her and Jean-Pierre, the better.

She had to remind herself that he only saw her as a responsibility. A duty to be handled, the way he competently managed every other task and obstacle life had thrown his way.

Steeling herself with that chilling reminder, she ventured out onto the second-floor veranda.

The cool breeze carried the scent of wood smoke and ginger. The gardens here were heavy with flowers even though it was November. Camellias bloomed all around, along with a golden flower on nearby trees she didn't recognize. But the fragrant ginger came from dense plantings of white flowers lining the paths around the pool. She'd noticed it earlier as she was falling asleep, the Louisiana breezes taking her back to childhood and happier times when her father had worked with Leon Reynaud and the families had spring holidays here after the football season ended.

"Someone misses you," Jean-Pierre called to her from a spot by the fire.

Rounding a hedgerow on the far side of the pool, she spotted the Adirondack chairs pulled up to a round fire pit surrounded by a low wall of flat rocks. A glider swing with a seat as big as a full-size bed anchored the space, draped in breezy white gauze threaded with a few fairy lights overhead. The cushion in the swing was draped in colorful blankets, as if someone had dragged half the contents of the linen closet outdoors.

"I think I see my seat." She hugged the blanket she was carrying like a shawl, tightening it around her as she stepped into the firelight.

Jean-Pierre rose from one of the chairs. César was wide-eyed in his arms, their son's tiny face only half visible behind his father's shoulder. Even in his casual clothes, Jean-Pierre looked crisp and pressed while she felt rumpled and tired from the long nap she hadn't meant to take.

The stress of the last weeks must have caught up to her.

"I didn't know how cold it might be when I first came out here, so I loaded up on the blankets." He followed her as she made herself comfortable in the glider swing, the cushion so thick a small child could use it as a trampoline.

"You were trying to lure me outside?" She covered her legs with one of the extrasoft wooly throws even though the fire warmed the area just fine.

The blaze crackled as a log shifted.

"I thought the view out here would be nicer than in the nursery." He dragged another pillow over from the other end of the swing and tucked it between her hip and the arm of the swing. "The whole reason Leon bought this property was for the view. If not for the lake, we'd be in the Garden District."

"It would be tougher to create a Reynaud compound in a city where families hold on to their houses for centuries." She loved the Garden District, but she guessed it would be difficult to find homes close together up for sale at the same time.

Here, the Reynauds had three homes and plenty of lake frontage.

"Leon was smart to think about privacy." Jean-Pierre didn't hand her the baby yet, instead gesturing toward a server holding a small tray that Tatiana hadn't noticed. "It's easier to keep the media at bay here."

The young woman flicked open a silver stand with one hand and settled the tray on top of it with the other, never so much as wobbling the full urn of ice water or the pot of tea wrapped in a bright red cozy. The food was hidden beneath gleaming domes that she didn't take off before hurrying away.

"This is what you meant when you said you were going to stop by the kitchen for something to eat?" Tatiana reached for César as soon as the server left.

"I might be new to child-rearing, but I figured it was best not to juggle the pot of tea while carrying a newborn." He passed the baby over, carefully supporting his head until she had him secured.

Already, the baby arched and squirmed, making small hungry sounds until she settled him to her breast. He latched on with the fierceness of an experienced eater.

"Here." Jean-Pierre folded one of the extra blankets and tucked it under her arm where the baby's head rested. "Does that help?"

"Definitely." She'd never been so comfortable while nursing, in fact. "This is an incredible setup. I wish all the nighttime feedings had been this easy."

His jaw flexed, the muscle working as he leaned over to pull the lids off the food trays. "All future feedings can be."

"Although this week, you have a light schedule with football. Normally, you'd be working." She kept her focus on the fruit-and-cheese board he'd revealed, not wanting to launch into an argument with him. But she refused to let him paint a false picture of the role he could play in any kind of family life.

She picked up a slice of kiwi and popped it into her mouth.

"I don't work at this hour." He used a pair of tongs to transfer select pieces of fruit and cheese to a smaller plate.

"But if you're on the road, that's as good as working since you wouldn't be at home," the lawyer in her pointed out, unable to resist.

He set the painted china dish on the glider cushion near César's feet, putting it in easy reach. His arm brushed hers, a warm, solid weight that had her wondering what it would be like to lean on him. Into him.

She took a piece of crusty bread and bit into it.

"Other players' families travel with them to have more time together." He loaded a second plate for himself, pulling items from another tray of cold meats.

Seeing him balance salmon and chicken on the too-small plate made her remember how careful he was about what he ate. Other players—big, heavy lineman or younger men new to the league—might see their job as a ticket to eat as much as they wanted. But even as a teen, Jean-Pierre had made a study of nutrition and workouts, turning his body into a lean, muscular machine uniquely adapted for the quarterback role. He swore the good diet and fitness regimen minimized injuries and would keep him playing longer.

Yet another way he opted to forego pleasure for obligation, dutifully doing the right thing.

"Maybe some families sacrifice one spouse's career for the sake of the other's." She helped herself to a strawberry, grateful her job didn't call for her to choke down extra protein at all hours of the day. "But I'm not sure how happy that makes everyone in the long run. Not to mention the hardship on the children. That's a lot of moving around."

"Did you mind being on the road during the season as a kid?" Finished loading up his plate, he tugged an Adirondack chair closer to the glider and sat down.

"Loaded question." During the football season, she was able to spend more time with her father, but that came with its own set of challenges. She stared into the flames as she stroked the soft tuft of hair on César's head. His suckling had slowed, reminding her she should move him to the other side to nurse.

"You loved it and so did I. What's loaded about that?"

"We were overprivileged, with way too much freedom." She didn't want to raise her son like that. "Our parents didn't keep track of us half the time and we could have gotten into all kinds of trouble."

"But we didn't. And we learned self-sufficiency."

Lifting up César, she laid him against her shoulder and patted his back.

"Having kids learn through trial by fire isn't my idea of good parenting." Even though she got the most time with her father during football season, he still seemed happiest with her when she amused herself all day and stayed out of his hair so he could focus on his duties with the Texas team.

If that meant she made a game of seeing how long she

could leave the hotel without anyone noticing she was gone, her father praised her—days later, of course—for how "good" she'd been during the week.

"But you can be an effective parent whether you're at home or not. My point is, kids are adaptable. They don't need to be in the same house day in and day out to feel a sense of stability. That comes from family, not a place." He worked methodically through his food and through his argument.

The lawyer in her should appreciate the well-reasoned views, at least. But it frustrated her that this man, of all people, didn't understand her better than that.

He'd been a part of her past. He'd seen her father in action.

"All the more reason why it's important to build a functional, loving family and not a group bound by duty alone." She shifted the baby to the other side and Jean-Pierre reached to reorganize her plate, her pillow and the prop under César's head.

"Being dutiful means being committed. Some people would think that's a good thing in a family relationship. Devotion and commitment are important components of stability." He even tugged the blanket back over her toes after it had gotten tangled from all the movement.

She had to appreciate his thoughtfulness. But his carefully scripted sense of family? It sounded like a pale imitation of the kind of loving relationship she'd once dreamed about.

"I'm sure César will benefit from those qualities." There was a cool breeze carrying the dampness of the lake, so she wrapped the baby blanket tighter around him. "I'm anxious to work out a way to co-parent, too, believe me. But it's been a long day and maybe we should table the rest of this discussion until tomorrow when I'm more clearheaded."

"You mean after you've had time to prepare your opening arguments?" He rose from his seat and paced the patio around the fire pit, one hand shoved in his pocket.

"No." She shook her head, wearier than ever despite the nap. "After I've caught up on some rest. I didn't expect motherhood to be so exhausting and I think the added stress of knowing we needed to work out so much between us had been weighing on me more than I realized. Now, it's like all the stress of the last few months has just drained me."

He quit pacing.

"Of course." His nod was sympathetic. Dutiful. "May I take him from you? I'd appreciate the chance to put him back in his crib and tuck him in for the night."

Ah, that wasn't just duty, though. She could hear the emotion behind the words, no matter how drily they were delivered.

"Certainly. Thank you." She wished, just for a moment, that he was tucking her in, too. Blinking fast, she ignored the wayward thought and passed César to his father. Jean-Pierre took him in one arm. With his other hand, he reached toward her, gently pulling her blouse back into place over her half-bared breast.

Her eyes flew to his. Held.

"Thank you, Tatiana, for taking good care of him." Jean-Pierre covered the baby's back with his broad hand and patted gently. "I hope we can learn to be friends again somehow. For his sake, we will need to trust each other."

"We will." She had to believe that. She loved her newborn son. There was no other option than to find a way through this mess she'd made in not letting Jean-Pierre know sooner. "Tonight was a start for the three of us. Having you with me allowed me to catch up on some much-needed rest. Tomorrow, we'll figure out our next steps."

"A boat ride is good for clearing the head." He extended a hand to her. "Can I walk you back to your room?"

"If you don't mind, I think I'll watch the stars a little longer and have a cup of the tea." She needed to give herself a mental pep talk before his family descended on them tomorrow. Before that boat ride that he'd promised.

The excursion wouldn't include César, so she wouldn't have her son's warm weight in her arms, reminding her to tread carefully with Jean-Pierre.

"I'll be glad to know you're down here enjoying some quiet time." He brushed a touch along her cheek, stirring her curls and her awareness. "We could make one hell of a team, Tatiana."

For a moment, she wanted to tell him that their time to figure that out had passed. That they'd had a chance to be together long ago and lost it. Twice. First when they caved to family pressure to split up. Again when they settled a heated disagreement with sex instead of talking.

But she couldn't end the night on a sad note. He was trying, after all. And he would make a great father for César. But after the way he'd walked out on her ten months ago, he simply would never be more than that to her.

"Care to tell me why I have to read the papers to find out my kid brother is in town?"

Straightening from his work on the midsize power yacht he'd towed out of the boathouse, Jean-Pierre squinted into the morning sunlight to see Dempsey on the dock.

As the New Orleans Hurricanes head coach, Dempsey was the public face of the team owned by their older brother, Gervais. All too soon, they'd be standing on opposite sides of the football field inside the Zephyr Dome, pitted against each other in the matchup that had both the local and national sports media talking.

"You knew damn well I'd be coming down here to steal a firsthand look at your playbook." Jean-Pierre strode across the bow toward the back of the boat as Dempsey stepped aboard. "Good to see you, bro." He threw a few air punches at him by way of greeting.

Dempsey clapped him on the shoulder. "You're supposed to be here for a wedding, not work."

"That, too." Jean-Pierre returned to fixing the trim on a fishing-rod holder that had snapped while the boat was in storage. "Have a seat. Tell me what's new."

"How about *you* tell *me*? Sounds like this thing with Tatiana Doucet is new." Dempsey slid into the captain's seat and went to work checking the electrical components for him, systematically flipping switches and looking below the bridge area at the wiring.

Dempsey was good like that. Technically his half brother, Dempsey had been raised until he was thirteen without knowing who his real father was, so he didn't have the same upbringing as the rest of the Reynauds. For thirteen years he'd taken care of his drug-addicted mother, getting by on a meal or two a day. And while he lived a far more extravagant lifestyle now, he'd never really shaken that complete self-reliance. And his ability to fix things with his own two hands was legendary.

Although right now, Jean-Pierre sincerely hoped he wasn't the target for his brother's next fix-it-up project.

"You can't blame me for trying to spin a story for the press after she threw me under the bus with that comment about not betting against Henri for our matchup." He understood now why she'd said it. She'd been nervous about seeing him and overtired from caring for a newborn.

It still stung that she'd said it. The way it still stung that she hadn't told him she was pregnant months ago.

He twisted a nut tighter with his vise grips, his teeth grinding in frustration.

"I get it. I've been known to use the media to my advantage in the past." Dempsey thumbed through the open tool kit on the deck and pulled out a volt meter. "When I didn't want Adelaide to quit her job as my personal assistant, I announced our engagement."

Jean-Pierre put down the vise grips and stared at his brother. "Seriously? I thought you two were crazy about each other."

"That came later." Dempsey used the volt meter to test the battery and tossed it back in the tool kit. "And it wasn't easy for her that I put her on the spot like that."

"It worked, though. You're engaged for real now, aren't you?" He wondered how well he knew his brother after all.

"Damn straight. But I can tell you it wasn't as easy as me saying it was so. Women expect a lot more than that."

And men expected to be informed of impending fatherhood. But clearly he and Tatiana were making this up as they went along.

"I know smoothing things out with Tatiana isn't going to be easy, either." He debated how much to say on the subject and then decided to go for broke. "She left town this summer and I didn't know why until two nights ago. She gave birth to our son without telling anyone. Not even her family."

Dempsey's eyes widened for a split second before he could school his features. "You weren't there with her when your boy was born?"

Jean-Pierre tensed at the accusation in his brother's tone.

"I didn't even know about him. She never told me she was pregnant." Jean-Pierre could hear the frustration in his own voice; he sure hadn't expected to have to defend himself to his own family.

"You weren't in a relationship?"

"Correct."

"You're damn well in one now." His brother got to his feet.

He forced himself to stay levelheaded about this and not engage. But Dempsey looked twitchy and judgmental, a combination that didn't sit real well with him right now.

"I need more time to convince her of that." His gaze moved to the second-floor veranda, where her bedroom doors opened onto a private patio. There'd been no movement outside yet, but he'd spoken to the nanny before he left the house and showed her around the place so she knew where to find anything she needed.

"Do I need to remind you why it's important that you do?" Dempsey's voice lowered, but it didn't soften. He'd adopted his steely coaching persona, so it was a face Jean-Pierre recognized from the field.

"Hell no." He understood Dempsey's take on this would be different. The guy had grown up not knowing his father or half brothers. "I'm not Dad. I would never ignore my obligation to my son."

"Then why is Gervais beating you to the altar next weekend?"

"What part of 'I just found out two days ago' did you not understand?" Frustration simmered at the implication he hadn't done enough.

"The part that had my college-educated brother failing to make use of the local justice of the peace." Dempsey made a show of checking his watch. "The clerk's office is open right now."

"It's Saturday." Jean-Pierre had a good plan for using the boat ride to provide a photo opportunity for any media looking for a story. The watercraft rocked gently beneath his feet.

"And lucky for you, I happen to know they have Saturday hours. One of my star players got his girlfriend pregnant last year and I looked it up when I gave my guy the same talk I'm giving you now."

Jean-Pierre shook his head. He normally appreciated Dempsey's down-to-earth take on things, but he couldn't see a way to twist Tatiana's arm to get married. He respected her too much to push her hard when she had been through so much on her own in the last weeks. She'd even admitted she was at an emotionally vulnerable place right now. What kind of man would he be to try and capitalize on that?

"You can spare me the rest of the talk since I already popped the question. The bride said no, for the record. Until I can close that particular deal, I would appreciate some help from the family to show her how welcoming the Reynauds can be."

"You know you don't have to ask. But it's only a matter of time before someone from the press spots her with the baby and then what? The media spotlight you're in now is going to be nothing compared to the juicy news that a player knocked up the coach's daughter."

Jean-Pierre's head snapped up.

"That's my future wife you're talking about."

"That's the spirit." Dempsey clapped him on the shoulder. "The sooner you make it so, the better." He climbed out of the boat and up onto the dock. "One more thing. I forgot the whole reason I came over here."

"What's up?" Jean-Pierre shoved the remaining tools in the tool kit and tucked it into a storage bin on the port side.

"Gervais and Erika are concerned about a media circus if they hold the wedding here as planned. They're going to assemble guests here and then fly them to the private island off Galveston."

The Texas branch of the family was deeply involved in the shipping and cruise business. The island off Galveston was a self-sustaining working ranch and an optional stop on many of their cruise itineraries. Guests could ride horseback on the gulf beaches or take part in one of the farm-to-table feasts that made use of the organically grown vegetables. Jean-Pierre hadn't visited his Texas cousins in years due to a family rift. His grandfather Leon had publicly cut his oldest son, Christophe, out of his will long ago, but since Uncle Christophe still retained his title as a vice president of global operations, he was very much a part of the family business along with his oldest son, Colton.

"Is Kimberly still running the ranch on the island?" She was the youngest of Uncle Christophe's large family, a sweet-natured girl Jean-Pierre remembered fondly from visits to the ranch when they were kids.

"Yes. But Gervais called Colton directly to make sure the island would be available that day. Apparently they're bumping a scheduled cruise from the stop to ensure Gervais and Princess Erika will have total privacy."

"Thanks for the heads-up. I'll let Tatiana know we'll be on the move." He'd been concerned about the extra press attention the wedding would bring to the family. "The additional security will make things easier for her."

Dempsey hesitated.

"What is it?" Jean-Pierre saw movement up by the house and spotted Tatiana on the patio.

He lifted a hand to wave to her.

"Have you read today's headlines about the two of you?" Dempsey reached into his pocket and pulled out a phone.

"I checked in yesterday long enough to assure myself the story about her coming down here with me read roughly as expected." He'd seen her misquoted in a few places, but for the most part, the story ran as Coach's Daughter Bets Against Home Team, or some variation of the basic theme.

Just what he'd anticipated and not the end of the world given the way he'd downplayed it.

"Today they're rehashing that whole court case she won against your friend Marcus Caruthers." Dempsey flipped his phone around to show him the story, complete with sketches from the courtroom showing Tatiana interviewing Marcus on the stand.

The case—which Jean-Pierre considered to be completely unfounded—against one of the game's best running backs had put Marcus out of a contract. Jean-Pierre had done his best to support his friend despite the torrent of bad press he'd received after inflammatory claims of sexual harassment, but the judgment Tatiana had won against him effectively ended his career. The article included quotes Jean-Pierre had given the media at the time, quotes that were now used to suggest a feud between him and Tatiana—one that started with the old family rift and ended with the court battle.

"Marcus didn't deserve this." He thrust the phone back at his brother. "Not then and not now."

"Her client lied. No doubt. But that's not her fault." Dempsey jammed the device back in the pocket of his cargo shorts. "But you must have reached the same conclusion or else you wouldn't be sharing the parenting duties now." He flashed a grin as he backed up a step. "Don't forget about that clerk's office. It's open for four more hours today."

Jean-Pierre gave him a thumbs-up, the most he could manage with the new weight crushing his chest. The truth was, he hadn't come close to making peace with Tatiana for raining hell on his friend's career and personal life. She'd done her job with ruthless precision, winning a judgment for a woman who'd perjured herself, although Tatiana hadn't seen it that way.

He'd been trying not to think about that case in his rush to wrap his head around becoming a father. But maybe today they needed to address the issue that had pushed them both to the boiling point last winter. He'd walked away from her after an unforgettable night—that's how upset he'd been. He'd told her he wouldn't ever make the same mistake, words that had obviously wounded her deeply since she hadn't come to him about her pregnancy sooner.

As he watched her stride down the dock in a fluttery crimson-colored bathing-suit cover-up, he wondered if she'd forgiven him for the things he'd said. It hardly seemed possible since he wasn't sure he'd forgiven her, either. Hopeful mood sinking, he stepped up onto the dock to greet her. He'd face the situation the way he faced any football matchup—grind it out until he got the outcome he sought.

Lucky for him, a victory with this vibrant, sensual woman promised far more satisfying rewards.

# Five

To the woman Tatiana had been before her pregnancy, making her way down the dock in a bathing suit just five and a half weeks after giving birth would have been out of the question. But as much as she wished she fit into the sleek black one-piece a bit more easily, she also couldn't deny a certain relief that she had higher priorities now than how good she looked in swimwear. Her body had given her César. And since she loved to swim, she'd made a special appointment with her midwife after she returned to New York to make sure she was safe to go in the water. The laps in her building's heated pool had relaxed her.

If she was a little worse for wear in a bathing suit, so what? She'd figure out what to do with the extra curves next time she went shopping.

Until then thank goodness for cover-ups. The gauzy crimson-paisley tunic felt breezy and pretty as she strode down the wooden planks toward the boat. Right now, she intended to make the most of this break while her son napped under the watchful eye of the nanny.

She could see one of Jean-Pierre's brothers just stepping off the watercraft and she braced herself as he headed toward her.

There was a look to the Reynaud men, making it tricky to tell who was who from a distance. They were all tall with athletic builds. Television didn't do professional athletes justice; because they were viewed in context and next to one another, they all looked a similar size. But when a football player stood next to a regular person, it was impossible not to appreciate the way they were built on a whole different scale.

As the man drew closer, she recognized Dempsey, Jean-Pierre's half brother, from his square jaw and the cleft in his chin, traits he must have inherited from his mother. But his dark hair and brown eyes with hints of green were straight-up Reynaud features.

"Hello, Dempsey." She greeted him with a smile despite the nervous butterflies in her stomach.

How would this family view her after the way she'd kept Jean-Pierre in the dark about his son? In particular, how would this man view her, given he'd been kept from his father as a child?

"Tatiana." He opened his arms and surprised her with a quick embrace. "I'm so glad you're here. I know my brother is anxious to spend time alone with you, but I hope you'll have dinner with the family tonight." A half grin lifted his lips. "That is, if you're up for a reunion with all of us at once. Gervais has a hell of a chef working for him, so we could meet at his place. His fiancée, Erika, wants to see us all so she can share some new details about their wedding."

Tatiana's stomach clenched. A meal with all the Reynauds at once? Nothing like trial by fire. Still, she was heartened by Dempsey's warm reception. The sun seemed to shine a little brighter, glistening off the lightly rolling waves lapping the dock moorings.

"Thank you. That sounds great." She was genuinely curious to meet the women who'd captured the hearts of Jean-Pierre's brothers. The press had plenty to say about each of the three women, but the press wasn't known for being honest. "We'll be there as long as your brother delivers us back here in one piece before dinnertime. I seem to remember he drives a boat like he's eluding the Coast Guard."

Dempsey threw his head back and laughed.

"Some things never change. But I've never seen him lose a passenger yet. I'll let Gervais and Erika know to expect two more." He paused. "Or might that be three?"

Her knees wobbled as a bout of light-headedness shook her. "He told you?"

If so, who else knew? She understood the news needed to be relayed to his family as soon as possible. And truly, she didn't feel any need to be at Jean-Pierre's side when he told them. It had been difficult enough confronting her parents and feeling the weight of their expectations on her shoulders. But even now, she didn't feel emotionally prepared for the fallout this baby would bring.

"He did. And I couldn't be happier for you both. I know the rest of the family will feel the same way." He said it with a steely conviction that suggested he was determined to make it so.

Perhaps he would make a good ally for her son, who'd also been born without the legal protection of her marriage to his father.

"I'm not sure I should come to the big dinner just yet after all because—"

"Whatever you think is best. But don't forget we're

his family. We protect our own." Dempsey lifted a hand to give her shoulder a light squeeze before he set off at a brisk pace down the dock.

Leaving her alone and shaken. The Reynauds protected their own. She believed that. But she couldn't miss the way the words sounded like a proprietary claim. Like the Reynauds had a stake in her son and wouldn't forget it. The resources of this family were beyond imagining. She could never afford a power struggle with such a wealthy, well-connected clan.

Hearing her name called from the water shook her from her thoughts, giving her a welcome distraction from her fears. She looked up to see Jean-Pierre standing on the bow of his yacht peering her way. She didn't need to see his expression to recognize the curiosity and concern in his body language. And didn't that remind her how well she knew him even if they hadn't done more than exchange social niceties for years? Well, except a year ago when they'd exchanged a little more than niceties.

She hurried toward him, telling herself not to be rattled. Not to fall into the trap of thinking she needed his strong arms around her to steady her. Too bad for her, she'd dreamed about sinking into his arms all night long. That and a whole lot more.

"Everything okay?" He straddled the dock and the boat to help her aboard, his sure hand gripping her forearm.

For a moment, their bodies brushed against each other enticingly. The warmth of his thigh tantalized her, evoking a memory of being naked with him while he lay above her…

"Fine," she blurted, leaping back from the contact so fast she had to catch herself against the captain's chair. "Just fine."

His eyes searched hers.

"I hope my brother didn't upset you." He took her by the shoulders and steadied her, his fingers stirring more of the sensual memories she'd tried hard to forget these last months. "We agreed to tell our families about César before we figure out how to go to the press."

"Of course. I'm not upset." She had to keep herself in check or he would see the hunger she was feeling.

His hands stilled on her arms and he studied her for so long she wondered if he recognized what she was feeling. Was her reaction to him more obvious than she realized?

"Don't forget why we planned this outing." His words were softly spoken, a gentle rumble between them while they stood so close.

"To show any press lurking nearby that we're spending time together. That there is no bad blood between us." Although that had honestly been the last thing on her mind after the conversation with Dempsey. Not to mention the upsetting phone call from her father before she'd even rolled out of bed this morning.

A call in which he'd upbraided her for keeping him in the dark about his grandson. Browbeat her for information about when she was going to return to her practice as a trial lawyer instead of the research work she'd taken on recently. Appearances mattered to Jack Doucet and apparently a behind-the-scenes job wasn't good enough for his daughter.

"We are going to have to do better than just demonstrate a lack of enmity. We need to show we're more than just friends, Tatiana. We're building a story so we can introduce César to the world." He lowered his head closer to hers, his lips brushing her hair as he spoke into her ear. "But if you leap away every time I touch you, no one is going to buy it."

The warmth of his body next to hers awakened every

nerve ending. He smelled good, like spices and fresh air. She closed her eyes for just a moment, breathing him in. She lifted her palms to his chest, touching him on instinct. And while she might tell herself that touch maintained a few inches of space between them, she knew better. Having her hands on him was a simple pleasure too good to deny herself after the tumultuous last weeks.

"Agreed." Standing there with him on the lightly rocking deck, she understood the value of what he was suggesting. Pretending a romance between them would only benefit their son.

"Seriously?" He tipped up her chin and the warm sun bathed her cheeks.

"Yes. Your plan makes sense." As worried as she'd been about the reactions of their families to the baby news, she was even more concerned about the way it would play in the press. She'd worked too hard cultivating her career and her professional reputation to be portrayed as a superstar athlete's baby mama.

His dark gaze searched hers. "I'm not used to wrangling an agreement out of the hard-nosed attorney so easily."

"Maybe motherhood has softened my edge." She fought the urge to turn her cheek more firmly into his touch. "It's probably just as well I left litigation behind to focus on legal research."

Releasing her, he frowned. "You're sharp and talented no matter what aspect of the law you're practicing."

She missed his touch even as she felt grateful for the reprieve from the sensual attraction. She watched him untie a cleat hitch on the stern and climb over the bow to follow his lead on the other cleat.

"Thank you." She wasn't accustomed to praise for her work from the people in her life. Usually, her colleagues were a better source of encouragement than her parents.

And, of all people, Jean-Pierre had reason to resent her skills as a lawyer. He'd made it abundantly clear he didn't agree with her efforts to win a judgment against his friend Marcus.

But as they set off onto the lake for the day, she tried to put that behind her to focus on the future. It all started with a believable story, just as he'd said.

She hoped it didn't matter that the romance they were building was strictly for show.

An hour into their boating expedition, Jean-Pierre found the cove he'd been looking for.

He didn't know if Tatiana would even recognize it after so many years, but he was pulling out all the stops to remind her of their past together—a time when they'd been happy. He wasn't ready to talk about her case against Marcus or the way the media was quickly resurrecting that story. He hoped she didn't know about that.

She certainly hadn't mentioned anything about seeing the day's headlines. Instead, they'd focused on having a fun outing with the grim determination of two high achievers. Tatiana had always succeeded at anything she tried thanks to a need to please the people around her—namely her father. As for Jean-Pierre, he'd usually met his goals by refusing to accept any outcome but the one he chose. So they'd both adopted their game faces, mindful of the fact that they were probably being followed by the telephoto lenses of enterprising journalists along the shore.

None of it sat well with him. He craved one real moment with her. Some kind of honest interaction not dictated by what they wanted the cameras to see.

"I can't believe you brought me here." She peered over her shoulder at him from where she lay sunbathing on a deck lounger. She'd slathered on sunscreen, willfully ignoring his repeated offers to help apply it to her back.

The need to touch her grew with every second he spent in her company, but he was trying to play his hand carefully, biding his time until she couldn't resist the current between them any more than he could.

"You remember it?" He pressed the button to lower the anchor on the thirty-six-foot sport yacht.

She shifted positions on the bright yellow towel draped over the lounger.

"We went skinny-dipping here." She arched a dark eyebrow at him.

He noticed how her glossy brown curls had escaped the knot she'd twisted at the back of her head. Everything about her was lusher than he remembered. Her hair had gotten longer and thicker, the curls even more riotous than they'd been ten months ago. And her curves...

He couldn't even think about the eye-popping differences in her figure without facing the uncomfortable physical consequences. He should have noticed right away when he'd seen her at the Coliseum, but she'd been wearing some kind of loose dress that had hidden everything but her mile-long legs. Today, however, in a sleek black one-piece bathing suit, her hourglass shape was the kind that screen sirens had made famous in another era. Extravagant breasts. Generous hips.

He needed to remember she was still recovering from childbirth. But his brain wasn't working on all cylinders right now.

"Did we?" He didn't dare step out from behind the bridge until he had himself under control from just thinking about her, his body's reaction impossible to hide. "It was too dark for me to get a good look that night, so I was never sure if you really took it all off."

"You know perfectly well you copped a feel underwater," she retorted. "Don't pretend."

"I told you that was a fish." He thumped a hand to his chest in mock indignation. "I completely respected your 'no touching' boundaries." He grinned at the memory.

"You had a squirrely brand of ethics even then, Mr. Reynaud." She propped big sunglasses on top of her head and rose to stand at the starboard rail. "It seems funny that mystery fish chose to brush against my left breast."

"If it had been me, I wouldn't have settled for just one." He tried not to think about his odds of touching her this afternoon, although the area around the cove was still secluded, making it a perfect stop for privacy. This section of the lakeshore was no more populated now than it had been ten years ago. Would they get a chance to replay the memory?

"That may be the most convincing argument you've made yet relating to that old disagreement." She turned from the rail to watch him, the sun burnishing her hair in a way that showed subtle streaks of copper. "But since you probably didn't bring me here to skinny-dip, I can't help but wonder what we're doing in this spot."

"We're in the public eye often enough. I thought you'd appreciate some private time." He pointed to her bathing suit. "You seem dressed for a swim even though no native would dream of getting in the water this time of year."

He'd used the fish-finder system to double-check the water nearby and knew there were no rocks or obstacles in the lake. It was deep enough to jump and safe to swim.

"I've been doing laps in gym pools for two weeks with the doctor's okay. And after spending years in New York, this feels like summer weather to me." She tipped her head up to the sun. "And don't try to tell me you wouldn't go in the water. I've seen you jump overboard in January."

"I'll always wade a little if the fish are biting." Focused so narrowly on football, he hadn't been fly-fishing in years. But he'd liked it as a kid, finding comfort in the quietness of the ritual when the rest of his life was so frenetic.

"Was I the only one who thought there might be a swim involved today?" She scraped back some of the loose strands of her hair and tucked them into the knot at the back of her head.

"The air temperature hasn't hit eighty in weeks so there's no telling how cold the water is." He made a show of peering overboard and shivering.

"Guess you're not as warm-blooded as me." She marched the length of the boat toward the swim platform at the back.

He was actually heating up just fine watching her in action, but he kept that to himself.

"Probably not, but I don't think it would be right to let you go all alone." He stalked toward her as she tossed aside her sunglasses. "My camp counselors taught me to use the buddy system when swimming."

She shook her head, a smile curving her lips right before she jumped in with a splash.

And a yelp.

She shrieked about how cold it was, but given how fired up she made him, that could only be a good thing as far as he was concerned. Stripping off his shirt and sliding out of his shoes, he stepped down to the platform to see for himself.

He aimed his jump to land a few feet from Tatiana. She swam with sure strokes through the dark water, her skin pale beneath the surface. He caught her around the ankle for a moment, relishing the feel of her silky soft skin. Allowing her to wriggle free, he treaded water and watched her cavort around in the waves.

"I thought it was too cold for you." She paused when she saw he'd stopped moving. Her long dark lashes had turned into spiky fringes around her bottle green eyes.

"I was afraid there might be more fish out to get you." He hadn't been kidding about the buddy system.

Not to mention, this was the mother of his child. He had every reason to protect her.

"I think I felt one around my ankle a minute ago." She seemed more relaxed out here.

"Did you ever miss it here?" He swam closer, drawn to her when she smiled and teased like the woman he'd once known.

Her smile faded.

"If I did, I wasn't allowed to show it." She shrugged, sending ripples out through the water near her. "I learned to love New York."

And she'd left him in the dust the same way she'd ditched the Big Easy.

"Remember that time I went to visit you during spring break after you moved to New York and you wouldn't see me?" He'd defied his older brothers and caught a commercial flight to Manhattan. Pounded on her family's door until her father threatened to call the cops.

"Of course. You said you wouldn't leave until you saw me." She held herself very still. "My father eventually made me come out of my room to tell you to go home."

"I understood that you were seventeen and had to do what they said. I didn't expect you to jump into a cab with me and run away to Spain or something." Even though he'd proposed just that at one point. But that was mostly because one of her father's favorite players was harassing her and Jack let the guy get away with it. "I just hoped you'd use the chance to tell your dad he didn't always know what was best for you."

Jean-Pierre had been angry at the time that she'd knuckled under so easily. But he hadn't understood how important it was to her to be accepted. To earn her father's approval. Maybe he still didn't get it.

Then again, his parents had never expected much from him or any of their sons. His dad had been a player all his life, and not just on the football field. Hence their half brother Dempsey, who was so close in age to Gervais it had been the last straw for his mother. She'd left the family shortly after Theo had moved Dempsey into their home.

Jean-Pierre had worked too damn hard to differentiate himself from his father to ever be viewed as some kind of womanizer.

"I learned to decide what was best for me eventually." She swam by him toward the boat. "At least, I hope I did."

Water sluiced off her as she hauled herself up the ladder and into the boat. Not finished with this conversation, Jean-Pierre followed her. He'd waited too long to talk to her after that time she'd told him she didn't ever want to see him again. And then, ten years later when he'd been so angry about the court case that he confronted her, the feelings had been so strong and so convoluted he didn't know what they'd acted on that night. Passion? Resentment? Anger? A toxic mix of all three?

And yet…not toxic. She'd conceived that night, and he wanted to understand what had happened between them so they could provide a healthy environment for a child in the future.

"I forgot a towel," she called over her shoulder. "Do you have extras?"

"I do." He pulled one out of the warming drawer beneath a bench seat. "But do you want to sit in the front deck hot tub for a few minutes to warm up?"

He tossed her the towel and toed aside the leather cover

of the small tub built into the bow. Steam wafted up, surrounding them both in a soft white mist.

Her eyes went wide as she snuggled deeper into the towel. "I can't believe there was a hot tub under there." She came closer to see for herself. "I thought that covered up a holding tank for fish or something."

"Hardly." He folded the leather cover in half and pulled it the rest of the way off. "I'm not eighteen anymore, Tatiana. I allow myself a few creature comforts these days."

She bit her lip and unfastened the hair tie that had held her curls. "I don't want to stay out too much longer. I need to feed César soon."

Still, he would bet money she was tempted. And seeing her shift her weight uncertainly from one long, sleek leg to the other had him feeling damn tempted, too.

"I can get us back home in about half the time I took to travel out here. How about we get in the tub just long enough to warm up?" He went with the reasonable approach. But then, remembering what she'd said about runaway emotions since giving birth, he tried another appeal. "Besides, you've been so focused on caring for César that it doesn't seem like you've made much time to relax and recover. You won't be much good to him if you wear yourself out."

Her gaze flipped up to meet his for a moment before she dipped her toes in the steaming pool. He reached over to the side of a deck box and switched on the air jets. The motor hummed as bubbles erupted on the surface of the water, sending even more steam into the air.

"Maybe for a few minutes," she agreed, slipping out of the towel and stepping down into the hot tub.

He shifted closer to steady her arm, following her into the swirl of frothy water.

The purr of contentment she made as she settled into a

seat beside him stirred him as quickly as a physical touch, the sound reverberating down his spine to remind him how much he wanted her. How much he wanted to inspire that same moan of satisfaction from her.

"Feel good?" Being around her had always revved him high and this day with her was testing his every last restraint.

He allowed his gaze to roam over her the way his hands wanted to, which was easier to do with her eyes closed and her head tipped back against a neck pillow. Her loosened hair floated around her shoulders. She was like a mermaid dragging him down to his doom. High, full breasts showed above the surface, in easy reach of his mouth. And at this rate, he felt as if the temperature in the hot tub had been cranked a few degrees higher.

"Feels amazing." She still didn't open her eyes. "My body has been through the wringer these last weeks. And not just from childbirth. Even carrying him around…that sounds silly, I know." She straightened and glanced over at him. "He's only nine pounds. But still, I'm not used to the position and I get all kinked up."

She rolled her shoulders and then her neck.

He tightened his self-restraint, until it felt like an iron vise.

"Turn around." He caught one shoulder in his hand and guided her so that her back was to him. "I'm good at this."

"That's really not necessary," she protested, but when he got both hands on those trapezius muscles, all objections ceased. "Ooh."

She melted beneath his touch. And while he would have liked it to be even more intimate, it satisfied the hell out of him that he could give her this pleasure.

"Relax," he urged her, shifting their positions so she sat between his legs. "This is going to help."

He felt her tense for a moment as her hip grazed the inside of his thigh beneath the water. But then, as he worked his fingertips deeper into the deltoid muscles, she went limp again, her head lolling forward while he massaged her back and neck.

The bubbles rushed toward her skin and burst in an endless cycle of movement from the jets.

"I had no idea you possessed this skill." Her voice hummed through his fingertips, the sound a vibration he could feel as he worked a kink from her left side. "I've paid big bucks for professional massages that haven't felt this good."

"Working with trainers really increased my awareness of the muscle groups. I wouldn't have maintained a career for this long without good sports therapy." He tried to focus on the conversation and not how good she felt. How soft and supple beneath his hands.

And how good she smelled.

Even after the swim in the lake followed by the chlorinated spa tub, a fragrant hint of lemons clung to her skin and hair. He breathed deep, inhaling her scent as he molded her body with his touch.

"You get a lot of massages?" She tilted her head from side to side slowly before she turned to peer back at him.

"Yes, but not many of the kind that feel good. I tend to get the deep-tissue stuff that leaves bruises."

"Ouch." She winced in sympathy. "I'm sure I wouldn't like that."

"I don't always like it, either, but it can really help alleviate muscle strains."

"Like your triceps last season?"

"Exactly. I injured my arm when I hyperextended—hey. How did you know about that?" He paused, looking over her shoulder to see her face.

The movement of the boat in the waves sloshed a little water out of the tub to spill on the deck.

"I might have been paying attention to some of your games." She spun around to face him, her hair fanning out in the water as she whirled. "That felt great by the way. Thank you."

"I like touching you," he said simply, surprised that she'd followed his career. "I always have."

One dark curl clung damply to her neck, snagging his eye. He slid a finger beneath it, barely brushing her skin, intending to relocate the strands behind her back. But that was before he felt the leap of her pulse in her throat. A quick, erratic rhythm that he could almost see in the tender column of her neck.

He didn't want to press her. But his hand didn't seem to be taking instruction from his brain. He laid his palm against her damp skin to get a better feel of that thready, anxious beat. Her eyes closed on contact, her head tipping back in a way that brought her lips within kissing range.

Sensual hunger washed over him like a rogue wave. He slid his fingers around the base of her neck and steered her mouth to his. Warning bells blared in his head that he couldn't let things get out of control like last time. He knew that. So with every bit of willpower he possessed, he kissed her gently. Softly, but with a lingering lick along her lower lip. And a nip at the end because she had the most lush, inviting lips he'd ever tasted.

But then, he let her go. Even though it cost him dearly, he untangled his hand from her hair and released her. Sitting back in the tub with wide eyes, her lips parted slightly, she looked as surprised as he felt.

There would be time enough for more, when she was ready. For now, he had to let her come to him so that whatever happened next was her choice. It was a good plan.

Smart. Logical. And it didn't do a damn thing to ease a body on fire for her. Taking deep breaths as he willed his urges into submission, he knew he wouldn't be climbing out of that hot tub anytime soon.

# Six

"I can't believe you convinced me to bring César to this dinner party." Flustered in every way possible, Tatiana navigated the whitewashed stone walkway in kitten heels, holding tight to Jean-Pierre's arm out of stress more than a need for balance.

They strode side by side up a pathway from his home to his brother's residence, a huge mansion on the hill that she'd visited many times as a teen. First with her father, when he'd spend time with Leon Reynaud during the spring months to plan for their team, and later on her own when she'd dated Jean-Pierre for those brief months in prep school.

Now, Gervais, the owner of the New Orleans Hurricanes and Jean-Pierre's oldest brother, made the big house his own along with his soon-to-be wife, Princess Erika Mitras. No doubt the home would be different than Tatiana remembered. Normally, she would look forward to a visit like this, but tonight there was so much stress riding on her shoulders she couldn't work up the energy to be excited to meet royalty. Jean-Pierre was getting under her skin, for one thing. Her whole body still hummed from their too brief encounter on his boat, her every nerve ending now sensually attuned to his touch. But worse than that, she was starting to feel more than just attracted to him. His care and concern over her well-being made her question what she knew about him. Made her rethink all the reasons she was fighting her attraction.

And on top of everything else, he wanted to bring their newborn with them tonight. Not the reveal she had in mind.

"It's funny you think that, because I don't see you holding César." Jean-Pierre wrapped his arm around her waist to steady her and she couldn't think of a single good reason to pull away.

The kiss on the boat had shifted something between them, forcing her to admit they had a whole lot of unfinished business.

"I know." Her heart beat faster, her nerves twitching as they neared the huge Greek revival mansion. Out front, a black Range Rover was parked grille-to-grille across from a Ferrari. "But Lucinda will be bringing him shortly. And it seems like a lot to bombard your brothers with at once—telling them you have a son and then actually having them meet a baby."

"Not just any baby." His voice held a note of unmistakable pride. "Our son. And the first thing my brothers will ask once we tell them about César is when they can meet him. Trust me. They would feel slighted if we didn't introduce them to their nephew."

She peered up at him in the gray, single-breasted suit that he wore exceedingly well. The white dress shirt, open at the neck and worn with no tie, was his nod to a more casual gathering, but the man looked good enough to touch, to eat. She could see the lines of the comb through his hair, still damp from the shower he'd taken when they returned from the boat, and her fingers ached to smooth over them.

"I'll let you take the conversational lead then." She had enough worries just thinking about how to address a princess and how to assure the rest of the Reynaud brothers that she didn't hold a grudge against them the way her father did.

"Of course." He squeezed her gently, his grip tightening around her waist and drawing her closer. "And don't be so tense or I'll have no choice but to give you more massages."

A tingle of pleasure went through her, her whole body warming with a sensual promise she shouldn't be feeling. Then again, she wasn't even cleared for intimacy from her doctor, so it wasn't as though anything would happen. Maybe she shouldn't be fighting this so hard—the massage, the kisses, all of which she couldn't deny wanting.

"That might not be such a bad thing," she admitted softly as they climbed the steps toward the front entrance, camellias in bloom in urns near the entrance.

"I want to take care of you." With just two fingers, he stroked her hip, a small gesture with an incredible impact she felt through the thin layers of her jade-colored dress. "In whatever way you'll let me."

Her mind went in all kinds of seductive directions. He'd taken care of her with exquisite care in their explosive night together. For that matter, back when they were dating, she'd been a virgin, but even then Jean-Pierre had taught her memorable lessons about other ways to find satisfaction. He'd taken good care of her then, too, even if they'd refrained from ever having sex.

Until the night they'd made César. They had been long

past virginity days, but they'd still had a first time together. Their only time?

Tongue-tied, she smoothed back her loose hair and tried to recover.

"You're blushing," he said in her ear, the soft whisper almost a caress in itself. "And it's killing me."

She braved a look at him then, only to find he was watching her with the same hunger she was feeling. If they hadn't been headed to a family dinner party, she might have dragged him back to his house. But just then, he pressed the doorbell.

"Welcome home, Mr. Reynaud." An attractive gray-haired woman in a pressed black uniform stood aside to let them enter. "Won't you come in?"

Tatiana's stomach muscles clenched as they stepped into the echoing foyer. She took in the white marble floors and walls covered in hand-painted murals depicting a fox hunt. An impressive banister wrapped around a huge staircase with a landing that looked big enough for a cocktail party.

"They're outside," the servant informed them, gesturing for them to go through a room on the left. "We're serving cocktails by the fire."

The woman hurried ahead to open a second set of doors, but Jean-Pierre shook his head.

"I know the way. Thank you." After dismissing the help, he returned his attention to Tatiana as they walked through an opulent dining room surrounded by silk curtains and set aglow by the light of a breathtaking chandelier. Fresh flowers dotted the table at regular intervals.

Nerves tightening with every step, she smoothed a hand over her hair. She'd left it loose after her shower, but now she wished she'd gone with a more polished style.

"You look beautiful." Jean-Pierre's voice startled her, mostly because he seemed to have read her mind.

No. He guessed she was nervous because she was fidgeting with her hair like a preteen. She should have worn one of her navy court suits that gave her the mental armor for battle, clothes that reminded her she was smart and well prepared for her job.

"Thank you." She appreciated his thoughtfulness even as she resented him for seeing that vulnerability. She needed to work out a plan for co-parenting with him, not rely on him for muscle massages and emotional support. This was the same man who'd walked out on her after the most passionate encounter of her life. "I'll be fine. I'm ready."

Nodding, he seemed to accept her at her word. He led her out of the dining room and into a more casual family space with an entertainment bar and Palladian windows overlooking the pool and grounds. A slow Cajun love song drifted on the breeze, the accordion and fiddle pouring out a heartfelt zydeco tune. Torches were lit at regular intervals around the pool in addition to landscape lighting that highlighted ornamental plantings and statues. To one side of the pool, she thought she spied an outdoor kitchen. But the hearth area was unmistakable, a fire already ablaze in the stone surround. Built-in stone seating was covered with thick cushions protected by a pergola, where another wrought-iron chandelier hung, this one more casual.

She couldn't see the faces of the people out there, but she heard their laughter, saw the movement of a couple slow-dancing to one side of the pool.

"They don't bite," Jean-Pierre promised, waiting for her while she took it all in.

"You forget I met Henri before he was fully domesticated." She had always liked the Reynaud brothers. When they were younger, she loved to see them wrestle and play, always in competition with each other, from sports to board games to who could eat their cereal faster.

Sometimes, when her father would spend a week with Leon to plot and plan a strategy for trades, she would roam free with the boys on their big ranch in Texas, or else they'd stay here. The best part of the Louisiana house had always been the lake. Before they were old enough to take out boats, they'd still built sand castles or tried to dam a little waterway that ran into Pontchartrain. She hadn't needed to worry about appearances with them back when Jack Doucet had viewed Leon Reynaud as a trusted friend. It was only afterward that her father had warned her never to reveal the financial hardship brought on by the rift. That part was in the past, but the resentment hadn't faded.

"He channels the fierce side into game days now." He paused at the screen door leading out onto the patio. "Although you'd never know he had a fierce side lately to look at him with Fiona." He pointed to the couple she'd seen dancing by the pool.

The two moved as one, the woman's long black skirt wrapping around the man's thigh when he turned her, their steps synched to a private beat. Just looking at them made Tatiana's heart ache. There'd been a time she'd longed for that kind of romance in her life. Now, her heart was full of love for César and she was glad for it. But a mother's all-consuming tenderness for her child was a far cry from the emotional bond so obviously shared by the dancers.

Everyone on the pool patio looked happy, in fact. The two couples seated near the fireplace spoke animatedly. An extravagant blonde held court with a story that required both hands to tell. Tatiana almost hated to interrupt them. It would have been awkward enough setting foot in the Reynaud home after the way Leon had fired her father. And her dad had reciprocated, bashing the family's lauded football savvy in the press, calling Leon a micro-managing control freak who couldn't share the spotlight with anyone who knew more than him. The quotes came to mind easily even now. But that wasn't all; tonight she had to get reacquainted with the family at the same time she introduced them to them to the child she'd kept secret.

"Here we go." Jean-Pierre palmed the small of her back, guiding her through the door out into the night air.

The scent of burning firewood wafted on the breeze, mingling with the chlorine tinge of the pool. Six sets of eyes turned toward them as they strode closer.

"It's the prodigal son returned," Jean-Pierre called to them. "I'm back on the bayou and ready for a wedding."

Tatiana couldn't process who shouted what, but he was greeted with a chorus of male taunts with every step.

"I hope you can find a tie before the wedding."

"I thought I was the prodigal son?"

"Technically, we're not on the bayou, dude."

But despite the ribbing, his brothers descended on him, giving him a variety of punches, backslaps and compli-cated handshakes that looked more fit for the gridiron than cocktail hour. They were an absurdly good-looking fam-ily with their tall, athletic builds, dark hair and dark eyes. Their mother had passed along their coloring while their father had donated his size and strength. Would César look like them as he grew up?

Tatiana was only too glad to fade into the background for the moment, but she could feel the keen eye of her host-ess and the other women even before Gervais separated himself from the men.

"Tatiana." His nod was reserved as he extended a hand. He had always been the most refined of the brothers, aware of his role as head of the family even as a teen. Tonight, he was dressed like a man worthy of a princess, his flawless silk suit custom-tailored to fit his wide shoulders. "It's good to see you again."

"Is that any way to greet my biggest fan?" Henri elbowed past Dempsey and Gervais, his slim-cut jacket a smooth fit over a dark T-shirt. He pulled her in for a hug. "Welcome back to Cajun country, darlin', and thank you kindly for single-handedly increasing my odds of winning next week's Hurricanes versus Gladiators matchup, according to the latest Vegas line."

Henri cut a glance at his brother, clearly angling to aggravate Jean-Pierre. Before he could respond, however, Dempsey pulled Henri away and stood beside her, his gray jacket as crisp as the gray linen shirt beneath it. His white-and-gray-striped tie was pinned into place with a silver football tac.

"Don't mind Henri," Dempsey warned. "He's had locker-room manners for so long we don't know if we can fix him."

"You *all* flunk the manners class," the platinum-haired beauty informed them from her seat beside the fire. Only now was it evident the woman was pregnant, the empire waist of her dress settling on a baby bump. "Some of us have not been introduced to our guest."

Jean-Pierre escorted Tatiana over to Gervais's fiancée, who must not have been quite as frightening as she sounded since none of the Reynauds appeared chastened in the least.

"Erika, my apologies. Thank you for having us. Please meet Tatiana Doucet." His hand was steady on her spine, a warmth that gave her courage.

Because no matter how the family responded to her now, they were bound to behave differently once they found out about the son she'd kept a secret from Jean-Pierre. That is, if they didn't know already. Would Dempsey have mentioned it? But looking into the cool blue gaze of her hostess, Tatiana couldn't glean a guess one way or the other. Which was rare for her since she'd always been good at sizing up a jury.

"A pleasure to meet you." Her fingers closed around Tatiana's, a collection of delicate silver rings pressing against her skin. But Tatiana's gaze was all for the impressive sparkler on the woman's left hand; it seemed to throw rainbows of reflected firelight into the dark evening. "We have all been curious who Jean-Pierre would bring to the wedding. You can imagine our surprise when we heard his date announced in a press interview rather than an RSVP."

Henri's wife, Fiona, a woman Tatiana had only seen in photographs online, came to stand beside Erika. A petite brunette with a ponytail almost to her waist flanked the princess's other side.

Tatiana took a moment to formulate a response, but the woman with the ponytail leaped into the momentary silence.

"Actually, Dempsey announced our engagement in a postgame conference, so I wasn't at all surprised." She thrust out her hand. "I'm Adelaide."

"So nice to meet you." Tatiana remembered reading that Dempsey had proposed to his longtime personal assistant, a friend from his childhood.

"I'm Fiona, Henri's wife," the other woman said, shaking Tatiana's hand. "And I'm thrilled to have finally evened out the gender gap at family events, so you are most welcome, Tatiana."

"Thank you. I'm grateful for the chance to reconnect with the Reynauds." Her gaze slid over the faces of each brother as they crowded closer to their respective women. She really had missed their friendship even though she'd never been as close to the others as she'd been to Jean-

Pierre. "I didn't realize until recently what a mistake it's been to allow my father's quarrels to become my own."

"There is a family dispute?" Erika frowned, turning her crystalline-blue gaze to Gervais. "I thought the problem stemmed from the court case—" She must have sensed the sudden tension in the group because she cut herself off midsentence. "Forgive me. I have been away from diplomacy for too long and my skills are rusty."

Tatiana's cheeks heated as the blaze in the fireplace flared high.

"There is nothing to forgive. Long after my father argued with Leon, I added fuel to an old fire by taking a case that pitted me against a well-known football player who is a friend to this family." She hadn't known the connection at the time—not until the case had gone to trial.

She swallowed hard, feeling the convivial atmosphere fading. Even easygoing Henri wouldn't meet her eyes.

"But the case is done," Jean-Pierre reminded her—and everyone else—while a server moved silently around the patio setting up trays and glasses. "And I've never held her father's choices against her. So I thought it was well past time for her to return to New Orleans."

Uncomfortable as she was about subterfuge, she shifted slightly closer to him, grateful for his support among people who respected Marcus Caruthers, the player whose career she'd effectively ended.

No, she reminded herself. The man who had effectively ended his own career by firing an assistant after she'd complained about sexual harassment in the workplace. Tatiana steeled her spine again; she needed to recover her lawyerly disposition even more than she needed her prebaby body.

"Actually, Jean-Pierre is being kind. He came to my rescue after I made a very offhanded remark to a man I didn't realize was a reporter." She'd been a babbling, nervous wreck before she had finally confronted Jean-Pierre about their son. She needed to be careful she didn't become a babbling nervous wreck all over again. Cursing postpartum hormones, she turned to Erika, feeling as if she owed her hostess an explanation. "So I was as surprised as anyone that he invited me to be his guest for the week. It was quick thinking on his part to deflect interest from my comment, and I'm truly grateful he did since I didn't mean it and because it gave me the chance to reconnect with all the Reynauds."

A beat of silence followed. Beside her, she sensed Jean-Pierre's tension in the way he held himself. For her part, however, she felt relieved to share the truth.

The family shared uneasy glances. What had she said?

"We had hoped you were a couple," Adelaide explained, perhaps seeing her confusion. "Photographs from your boat ride today are already appearing online, so we hoped—"

"Let's have a toast," Gervais proposed, coming to Adelaide's rescue. He waved forward a server who'd been setting up a small outdoor bar. "It's time we celebrated your return, no matter how unorthodox the circumstances."

The young man tending the bar brought a tray full of glasses in one hand and two distinctive black bottles of champagne in the other. Another server, a woman dressed in a tuxedo shirt and pants that matched the man's, joined him to help him pop the tops and quickly pour champagne for everyone but Erika, who was given a fresh glass of seltzer. Tatiana decided a small, social sip of champagne would not derail her nursing.

Gervais didn't miss a beat, raising his cut-crystal flute as soon as it was placed in his hand. Everyone else followed suit and waited for his toast. Tatiana could hear the waves of the lake against the shore nearby in the quiet.

"To Jean-Pierre and Tatiana, reunited after too long."

Grateful for the way the eldest Reynaud smoothed over the strained moment, she relaxed for the first time since she'd walked in the front door. But before she could lift her glass to her lips, the maid who'd admitted them reappeared at Jean-Pierre's side.

"Excuse me." She spoke in soft tones that Tatiana could overhear. "I believe the guest you invited is here, sir."

"Of course. Hold that thought, Gervais." Jean-Pierre strode toward the back of the patio, where Lucinda was standing at the door, a small bundle in her arms.

All at once, Tatiana remembered that the biggest hurdle of the night still awaited them.

And while the timing felt a bit awkward to her, Jean-Pierre grinned, as if a big reveal had been his intention all along.

Her knees turned to water as she stood alone with the rest of the family. All eyes turned to Jean-Pierre as he escorted Lucinda into the firelight with her precious charge cradled in her arms.

A collective gasp sounded. Tatiana could feel the shock travel from one Reynaud to the next, like Sunday football fans performing the wave around a crowded stadium.

"When Tatiana said she was glad to reconnect, she didn't mention the reason we are happiest to be together." He stared at her in the shifting shadows from the burning torches all around the party, his expression full of paternal pride.

"Meet our son, César."

# Seven

Somehow, the zydeco music continued playing on Gervais Reynaud's expansive patio and pool deck. The servers poured more champagne and Gervais offered a toast to César Reynaud, the first of the next generation. People helped themselves to hors d'oeuvres while conversation slowly recovered.

Tatiana sat on a far ottoman, nibbling on a grits-and-gumbo crostini topped with a tiny shrimp skewer. She knew it was delicious, as it incorporated all the flavors of the famed Cajun stew. But she barely registered the taste.

Everyone offered congratulations. Of course they did.

She'd murmured polite acknowledgments and enough commentary to be social, but as the focus shifted fully to the baby, she was able to clear her head long enough to take a much-needed deep breath and calm down. Because all the while Jean-Pierre showed off his firstborn, she seethed at the way her son's introduction to his family had been tainted by half-truths.

Since the Reynauds had been given no explanation for why Tatiana and Jean-Pierre had kept their baby news quiet, she knew without question his family would blame her for keeping César a secret. Surely they all believed that if Jean-Pierre knew about the baby before now, he would have told them. And, no doubt, he would have.

So even as they passed around the sleeping newborn in his cream-colored footie with a velour shawl collar, they must have guessed that Tatiana had been the one keeping secrets.

But what Jean-Pierre had failed to share with them was her reason for not including him in their son's birth. He had called their union a mistake. He'd walked out on her the morning after their one-night stand, making it clear that he'd only been on board for one night.

What was she supposed to do when that first pregnancy test had come back positive? How could she share such incredible, life-changing news with a man who might view their son as…another mistake? She swallowed hard, reminding herself that her fear had passed. Seeing Jean-Pierre hold César so tenderly now, and hearing the obvious pride in his voice as he talked about their son, it was almost inconceivable that she'd once feared early on that Jean-Pierre might have suggested she terminate her pregnancy.

But with the way they'd parted, she had most certainly feared the worst.

"Excuse me," she said to no one in particular, backing away from the crowd around César. She needed a moment to herself, the ugly thoughts spinning so fast she felt dizzy. "I'll be right back."

Hurrying inside the house, she rushed through the beautifully appointed spaces, passing a server on the way who told her where to find a powder room.

"Tatiana?" She heard Jean-Pierre's voice and quick footsteps behind her, and slowed down before she could reach her destination.

She ducked into a nearby doorway, a den she had noticed vaguely when she'd first arrived tonight. The powder-room visit would wait since she didn't want to have this conversation over the sink. Here, leather club chairs and a small bar flanked a darkened fireplace, while books and football memorabilia lined the walls. A banker's desk lamp glowed softly over a masculine expanse of polished oak.

"Are you all right?" He followed her into the den, taking her hands in both of his. "We don't need to stay for dinner if you don't feel up to it. Everyone will understand you're tired from the travel and still recovering from having a baby."

Had she felt a warm connection to him earlier today on the boat? It was difficult to remember now with her stomach in knots.

"I will not let your family think even worse of me than they already do. I don't want them to assume I'm ignoring them." She allowed him to draw her down to a buttery soft leather settee, but then withdrew her hands from his. "I am staying for dinner."

"No one thinks poorly of you." Tipping his head to one side, he considered her. "And I guarantee everyone out there is sympathetic to the fact that you gave birth less than six weeks ago."

"Are they?" She folded her arms across breasts that felt more functional than attractive lately. She ached to hold her child already. Sharing him with this large, charismatic family was tougher than she'd expected.

Not that she should care about that right now. But this man had always called to her on the most fundamental level; not even her anger with him could diminish that. As they'd discovered last winter.

"Of course they are." Seated beside her, he stared at her as if she'd lost her grip on reality. "In case you haven't noticed, Erika is very pregnant with twins. Gervais can't be there for her enough, doing everything in his power to make her life easier so her strength goes toward nurturing their children. Do you honestly think anyone would begrudge you recovery time after delivering my child?"

"Our. Our child." She did feel exhausted suddenly, but she didn't know if it had to do with postpartum tiredness or the stress of negotiating her role in parenting with this man. "I am not here to hand him over to you, Jean-Pierre, or to your family, so don't get in the habit of claiming him as yours alone."

"Of course. My God, of course I know that. I would never deny our child his mother." Even in the darkened room, his gaze burned with a tangle of emotions she couldn't interpret. "Tatiana, I understand this isn't easy on you, but I thought it best to come straight to the point with my family."

Unlike the way she'd done in telling him about their child? She couldn't help but note how differently they'd shared the news.

"But we both wanted to tell our families and now those closest to us know the truth," he continued. "Next, we can focus on carefully unveiling the story we want to share with the media."

"You know what?" She smoothed nervous hands over the short silk skirt of her dress. The brush of the fabric against her skin was the most sensual touch she'd felt on her legs in months. "I disagree that our families learned the whole truth. All your brothers have found out is that I kept your son a secret from you."

"I never said that." His jaw flexed, the shadows falling across his face in the dim room.

She sprang up from her seat, unwilling to sit so close to him with this restless anger churning in her blood.

"Maybe. But by not saying anything to explain our belated revelation, you allow them to think the worst of me and that starts us out badly when our families already have issues."

"And what would you have me say?" He rose from the settee as well, but he moved in the opposite direction from her. They faced off on either side of the study, backs to the walls of books. "Because I'm fairly unclear on why I got scratched from your contact list while you gave birth to *our* child by yourself."

"Then let me be very clear." Frustration simmered and her patience snapped. "The last words you said to me before I found out I was pregnant was that you would never repeat the mistake of being with me."

"That's not fair."

"You asked. And while it might not feel fair to you, it didn't feel fair to me that you could hold me in contempt for doing my job in the courtroom." She braced her back against the bookshelves, needing the support of something—anything—in her life right now. "After we…had sex that night, I foolishly assumed you realized that you were wrong to find fault with me for winning my case. I woke up happy. Did you even know I was making you breakfast when you stormed out of that room? I had the concierge find me fresh eggs and a pan so I could make them myself in that tiny kitchen."

She hadn't meant to share all that, dammit. It was far too revealing.

For a moment, he didn't speak. When he did, he cursed softly.

"I didn't hold the verdict against you." He pounded his fist gently against the bookshelf closest to him. "I just thought you might want to know what I'd seen as Marcus's friend. His assistant was—is—an untrustworthy woman."

"I can't choose the clients my firm takes on, and I won't argue that with you again." She'd heard as much as she wanted to hear of his side during the case. "When I thought we'd put that behind us, I was all the more hurt to discover you regretted being with me."

"So you didn't tell me about César to punish me?" The gaze he leveled at her made her wonder how they'd ever find common ground to raise their son.

Some of the fight leaked out of her and she raked a hand through her hair.

"I didn't tell you because I couldn't bear to hear that having César was a mistake."

Two hours later, Jean-Pierre walked out of the most uncomfortable meal of his life. Knowing what Tatiana thought of him—that he'd been denied the early weeks of his son's life because she assumed he was the worst sort of human being—had made it damn near impossible to choke down food and pretend everything was all right in his world.

He'd quietly walked back to his home with Tatiana, making sure she was safely inside before he left again. After their exchange in the den, she'd had little to say to him anyhow, and their quick stroll back to his house had been devoid of conversation save an agreement to speak again tomorrow when cooler heads prevailed.

Before then, he needed a plan for how to proceed with her, something he wasn't going to accomplish until he could blow off some steam.

He headed to the three-bay garage on one side of the house and hit the button for the closest door. The reinforced steel retracted silently to reveal the BMW M6 he kept registered in Louisiana. The silver Gran Coupé wasn't as flashy as the Aston Martin he used in Manhattan, but it would get him to the Hurricanes' training complex in a hurry. Slipping into the driver's seat, he nailed the accelerator and left the family compound behind.

Perhaps it was a conflict of interest for him to work out in a competing team's training facility before he faced them. But he wouldn't be anywhere near the players' areas. And hell, he was one of the family.

Twenty minutes later, when he parked in the owner's spot with the assurance that Gervais wouldn't show up for work for at least six more hours, Jean-Pierre took the private elevator to the gym for the front office personnel. He was a Reynaud, dammit. He had a key. He'd invested personally in building the facility, as well as the Zephyr Dome downtown. And he'd never needed a workout as much as he did now.

Helping himself to Dempsey's locker—helpfully labeled with a brass nameplate—he found workout clothes and changed into black mesh shorts and a T-shirt. He ran the track. Ran the bleachers, ran the treadmill. And when that didn't manage to pound the thoughts out of his head, he hit the weights. He dragged a set of heavy chains from the wall and draped them around his waist while he did pull-ups. He did waist-high box jumps from a standing position with an eighty-pound-weight vest. If it hadn't been a bye week, he wouldn't have been able to trash his body so thoroughly, but he had time to recover before the game against the Hurricanes.

And sweating out the sound of Tatiana's damning words had become a critical mission.

*I didn't tell you because I couldn't bear to hear that having César was a mistake.*

Drenched with sweat and so exhausted he feared the

next jump would sprain an ankle, he unhooked the chains and finally slogged to the showers. Only then did it occur to him what he needed to do to move forward with Tatiana.

She didn't trust him now any more than she had when she first found out she was expecting their child. He had to change that. Luckily, no matter what she said about the effects of postpartum hormones, she was a lawyer and a deeply rational woman. She would appreciate a well-thought-out campaign to win her over. Well-reasoned arguments for why they should stay together.

He would dismantle her defenses as thoroughly as he deconstructed his opponents on the field. While he couldn't study game film of Tatiana, he had past encounters to teach him. He could use that to understand her better. To draw on what she liked and didn't like to become the man she couldn't refuse.

And then? Game over.

He would be announcing their marriage at the same time he introduced César to the media and then they could both put this chapter of their lives behind them. It was the perfect game plan.

Provided he could persuade her to agree.

# Eight

Even when angry, Tatiana dreamed about him.

Perversely, that made her even madder, distracting her all morning when she'd had errands to run outside the house. How could she go to bed so upset with Jean-Pierre and yet dream about his touch all night long?

She'd awoken on edge and cranky even though César had slept through the night for the first time ever. She'd almost missed her morning doctor's appointment, a checkup she'd scheduled with a local obstetrician to be sure she was healing. An appointment that had given her clearance for intimacy at a time when she knew that was highly unlikely to happen since Jean-Pierre hadn't even wanted to sleep in the same house as her the night before.

Now, changing into fresh clothes after the morning's outing, she wished she'd had the option to hop in a luxury sports car the night before and disappear the way Jean-Pierre had.

From the patio outside her suite, she'd watched him roar off, the tension evident in his every movement. She hadn't heard him come home, but he'd texted her, asking to join him at Gervais's house today to help with some kind of wedding crisis. She couldn't begin to guess what that meant, but once she'd eaten a light meal and fed and snuggled with César, she put on a crochet knit minidress with bright stripes around the skirt and headed outside to see what was happening. The temperature had dropped overnight so that the air was milder this afternoon, but still comfortable enough that she didn't need a sweater.

Her phone rang before she reached Gervais's house. Checking the display, she spotted her father's cell phone number.

She took a deep breath before she answered. "Hello, Dad," she said as she wound through the manicured gardens of a side yard between the Reynaud homes.

She kept her tone light, praying he would reciprocate. She couldn't handle any more tension right now.

"Are you reading the headlines?" he barked, not bothering to ask her how she'd been.

Which reminded her of why she couldn't bind herself to Jean-Pierre, another man who focused on himself and to hell with her needs. Sure, he'd caught her off guard with his careful treatment of her and the thoughtful massage, but how much of that kindness was to serve his own ends? She needed to be wary.

"I've been fairly consumed with motherhood," she reminded her father, wondering why she'd struggled for so long to win approval from a man who cared more about how his family appeared to the rest of the world than how they felt.

"Well, you've done a good job keeping that under wraps," he admitted. The sounds of the city were amplified in the background—squealing air brakes and honking horns. He must be in the car between meetings. "And the photos of your boat outing are a nice touch, much as it still galls me to see you with a Reynaud."

"You liked this family well enough once." She lowered her voice even though there was no one around as she sidled around a low brick dividing wall laden with thick green vines. "And you raised me to like them, too."

"A little too damn well," he snapped. "But that could work to my advantage. Maybe you can tell me the location of this big royal wedding. Because if you can give me something I can sell to the press and one-up Leon, you could be forgiven for hobnobbing with the Reynauds."

She gasped, hoping he wasn't serious, not even remotely. "I'm appalled. You've got to be kidding. For pity's sake, Dad—"

"Oh, stop it. I really am only kidding. Mostly." In the background of the call, she could hear the running commentary of a football game announcer. No doubt her father was watching game film while his driver navigated traffic. "I'm checking in to see if you can make an announcement to the press that will shut them up about the Marcus Caruthers case. That angle of your relationship with Jean-Pierre is getting a lot of coverage and it's not good for an NFL coach to have his daughter trying cases against players."

Her blood boiled as she paused beside a rose-covered arbor. She tipped her head against the painted wood frame and hoped the scent of roses would calm her. Her father had been even more furious with her than Jean-Pierre had been over that case, insisting that he'd lose his coaching position for allowing his daughter to argue a harassment suit against a player. She'd called BS on that one. Since Marcus didn't play for the Gladiators, there was no conflict of interest. Tatiana had become all the more adamant to take the case as her father became more insistent that she didn't. And after growing up in a house where superstar athletes had always been more important than his daughter, she'd been determined to win the judgment.

Perhaps she'd resisted Jean-Pierre's protests of Marcus's innocence because of that. But bottom line, it had been her job to argue for her client. Yanking a rose off the vine-covered arbor, she charged up the flagstone path toward the house.

"We've had this argument. At length." She stopped in Gervais's driveway to finish her call since she couldn't enter the house while discussing a hot-button topic. "The case is over."

"Not in the eyes of the press, it's not," her father growled at her, his voice forcing her to turn down the volume on her phone. "This is a story all over again, Tatiana, and you can't just bury your head in the sand and pretend it doesn't exist. You stirred the pot by baiting Jean-Pierre with that comment to a reporter. Now you've got to deal with the fallout, and you need to do it before you introduce my grandson to the world."

He was right about that much.

And possibly the part about burying her head in the sand, too. She closed her eyes, willing her heart rate to slow down. She inhaled the scent of the rose she still held crushed in one palm.

"I'll read the headlines and look into a plan of action," she assured him. "I'll do what I can to take care of this. But, Dad?"

"I'm listening."

"If you do anything to detract from this wedding, or in any way upset the Reynauds, you will be alienating me and your grandson, too." Her voice vibrated as she said the words. It was a sign of nervousness but she hoped it came across as an indication of how thoroughly she meant it.

She'd tried to please an impossible taskmaster for too long. Somehow, being a mother gave her fresh perspective on that relationship. And maybe gave her a bit more backbone as well.

"Dammit, honey, I told you I was teasing," he grumbled while a siren wailed on his end of the phone. "Call your mother soon, won't you?"

A deep sigh escaped her as she thought of how easily her mother had always let Dad steamroller them both, never taking Tatiana's side when they disagreed. She loved her mother, but she had vowed to be stronger than that for César. "Of course."

Disconnecting the call, she felt relieved to have drawn a line in the sand with her father. But the news he'd delivered still sucked some of the life out of her on a day that had already started out badly. Reminding herself Marcus Caruthers had been tried in front of a jury of his peers, she shoved the thoughts out of her head to focus on whatever wedding crisis Gervais and Erika were facing. If she'd met the couple under different circumstances, she would have truly enjoyed her evening with them the night before.

Pressing the doorbell, Tatiana barely had time to toss aside the crushed rose before the door swung open. A different maid greeted her in the entryway today. But she was no less efficient. With a smile and gesture, the woman guided Tatiana inside. Tatiana followed her across the marble floors in the opposite direction from the night before.

Her high heels echoed in the wide-open corridors as they passed a library and a feminine-looking office space in the front of the house. Reaching a closed door at the far end, Tatiana could hear music from within—a '70s disco tune. Two female voices were harmonizing the chorus. So far, it didn't sound like a crisis.

The maid knocked briefly on the door and then opened it to admit her to a dimly lit home theater room with deep blue walls and rich, burgundy trim. Wide leather seats faced a screen showing Hurricanes game film, though the sound was turned off. And instead of Gervais and the rest of the family sitting in the chairs, she found all seven of them—including Jean-Pierre—seated on the floor in the open space between the seats and the screen, surrounded by boxes of small wine bottles, stacks of labels and pots of brightly colored paints on a drop cloth.

Someone turned the music down as she neared the group.

Jean-Pierre rose to greet her while the others called out hellos. For the most part, however, they remained focused on their task. Which seemed to be painting labels.

She turned questioningly toward Jean-Pierre, whose presence reminded her in vivid detail of the dreams she'd had about him the night before. Dreams where he'd peeled off all her clothing with slow, tantalizing touches, kissing each inch as he unveiled her...

"Thank you for coming." If he noticed that she felt flustered, he didn't say anything about it. Tucking a hand under her arm, he led her toward the group seated on the floor, the warmth of his hand on her bare skin sending a delicious shiver through her. "Gervais and Erika had a setback with their wedding plans last night and we're helping them out in here because the media room is the most secure room in the house and there seems to have been a privacy breach from someone on staff here."

Tatiana stiffened since her father had only recently suggested she betray the family's privacy. But she knew he would never choose revenge over his own daughter. He might be a self-centered man, but he loved her in his own way.

Erika stopped in midsong to interject. "We're not sure about the breach."

Fiona continued to hum along and paint from where she sat, crossed-legged, on Henri's lap.

Henri reclined against a chair and used Fiona's back as his painting surface, his tongue tucked into his cheek as he gave the project intense concentration. The couple, she realized, never seemed to stop touching each other, which said a lot for their marriage considering they were far from newlyweds.

"It could have been a coincidence," Gervais continued, looking up from his work, which involved centering the dried labels on the wine bottles.

They were wedding favors, she realized, with a personalized message on each bottle for their guests.

"Our wedding planner is ill after traveling to Singapore last week for an event." Erika leaned back from her work, tossing her head so that her thick blond hair almost grazed the floor when she arched her spine to stretch out a kink.

Gervais reached to rub her back for her while Jean-Pierre cleared a spot on the floor for Tatiana to sit. Not an easy task when she'd worn a minidress, but Adelaide seemed to sense her dilemma and handed her a giant pillow.

"For your lap," she whispered as she leaned over.

Gratefully, Tatiana used the pillow to cover her legs.

"The wedding planner obtained the wine for us, but she had a difficult time of it even though we purposely ordered from Gervais's Uncle Michael, who has a vineyard on the West Coast." Erika recounted the tale with her lovely accent that sounded a bit like Swedish; her tiny island country sat off the Finnish coast. "Apparently, there is another family feud that I did not know about." She raised an eyebrow at Gervais.

"I didn't know where you sourced the wine, but I regret the stress it has caused." He spoke to his pregnant bride with a gentleness that made Tatiana's heart feel hollow by comparison.

She glanced at Jean-Pierre beside her, wondering where he'd spent the night after leaving her alone. He looked even more exhausted than she felt, with shadows under his eyes and his face still sporting yesterday's growth of beard. She wondered what it would feel like to run her fingers across his darkened jaw, to kiss the strong column of his neck.

"It is all right. I come from a large family myself. I understand the inevitable disputes." Erika brushed her fingers along Gervais's face in the way Tatiana had just been daydreaming of touching Jean-Pierre.

Did these women know how fortunate they were to have found love that would sustain their hearts as well as their physical needs? Amid so much romance, Tatiana almost found it difficult to breathe. She, of all of them, should have worked out her relationship before she had a child. She regretted for César's sake that she'd failed.

"So your wedding planner obtained the bottles but they didn't come with labels?" Tatiana asked, wanting to help and needing a task before her thoughts drove her mad with wanting and frustration.

"My wedding planner would have helped me with the messages for each bottle. She's very good at this kind of thing and she set aside the next two days to paint the labels personally since the shipment was late and she knows we cannot trust many outsiders with wedding details."

"But then she got ill." Tatiana began to see the problem.

"We have not subcontracted many of the responsibilities for the wedding since the press has been relentless in trying to figure out our plans," Erika continued. "And I really wanted the date and our names on these, so I could hardly ask a local artist to do this without risking helicopter flyovers during my vows." She straightened from her brief break and went back to painting a daisy on a label. "This, I will not have."

Beside her, Jean-Pierre passed her a list of guests' names.

"The rest of us are just filling in the standard information," he explained, showing her several templates. "The whole point is to make each one unique, so you can be creative."

Seeing these men—two of them superstars in the NFL and the other two the power behind the Hurricanes' success—all giving their undivided attention to the preparation of personalized wedding favors would have tugged at her emotions even if she hadn't been vulnerable to bouts of sentimentality lately. The idea of these brothers, who had always been so strong-willed and competitive, all pulling together to provide a happy day for a pregnant princess really got to her.

There was no doubt about it, she wished she'd been able to establish herself within a supportive family situation before the birth of her son. He deserved to have come into the world with this kind of love all around him, as opposed to alone on a Caribbean island with only his mother to welcome him.

She peered around at the work of each of the Reynaud men. She noted the neat black lines on Jean-Pierre's labels, no surprise since he tended to be methodical in football, too, clinically picking apart defenses. Henri chose bold colors and took more chances in his artwork, the same way he did on the field when he chose the long, risky passes that sometimes paid off and sometimes backfired. Dempsey created geometric grid borders, choosing established patterns but filling them in with unexpected colors, which seemed to coincide with an upbringing where he'd had to make up the rules himself since his drug-addicted birth mother had never provided boundaries or safety. And Gervais, the oldest, was probably the most stern and serious of the four, yet his labels were the most unique and fully imagined. One of his starry sky backgrounds suggested he had real artistic talent.

Jean-Pierre dragged over a few pots of watercolors for her while the rest of the family went back to painting and talking, or singing along to the music that someone had turned back up. Adelaide rose from her seat on the other side of Tatiana to grab a bottle of water from a cooler, leaving Jean-Pierre and Tatiana in a bubble of privacy.

"I'm sorry about last night." He sketched his label letters in pencil, using a ruler to be sure of the spacing. "I wish I'd had the presence of mind to talk things through with you then, but I hope we can correct that later today."

Surprised, she picked up her first blank label and thought about what she would create. What would her patterns and colors say about her? She knew one thing. She was done coloring in the lines and making safe choices to please the people around her. Now that she was a mother, she understood that she didn't want her child to have a role model who played it safe all the time. She dipped a brush into a pot of bright orange paint.

"A discussion would probably be wise." She knew without question that he wanted what was best for César. Jean-Pierre's love for his child had been evident almost immediately in the tender way he held him. After seeing the way he behaved with his son, she wondered how she could have doubted him during her pregnancy. But she'd had her reasons at the time. She could only move forward now. "My father called this morning to alert me to the media's renewed interest in the Caruthers case. I didn't realize it had come back to life, but I do want to think about how to deflect interest away from that if at all possible."

"Good." Setting aside his pencil, he watched her for a long moment as she painted a starburst border on her first label. "I want to do whatever it takes to find some common ground this week. I am fully committed."

Something in his tone made her pause. She moved the brush away from the label so as not to spoil her work.

One look into Jean-Pierre's dark eyes told her he meant it. There was a depth of sincerity there that she would guess he didn't let many people see. She herself hadn't seen it in years. But she remembered that expression from long, long ago.

And it had much the same effect on her now that it'd had then. Her heart fluttered. Sped up. Made her breathless.

"That sounds..." Her voice hitched and she cleared her throat, trying to banish runaway thoughts of what it might be like to have this man fully committed to her. Even just for the rest of the week. Even for just one more night. "That is, I agree."

She licked her lips and went back to the label, blinking away the chemistry that had always hit her so hard with him.

"Need some cold water?" Adelaide asked her, suddenly appearing beside her with an extra bottle from the cooler.

*You have no idea,* she thought.

"Thank you." She took it gratefully, hoping that she could turn down the temperature of her heated skin with a drink. But no such luck.

His low chuckle suggested he hadn't missed her reaction.

Having Jean-Pierre working silently beside her called to her senses, making her wish she could climb into his lap the way Fiona did with Henri. Or that he would steal a kiss when he thought no one was looking, the way she'd seen Dempsey do with Adelaide.

But the most she could hope for—and all that Jean-Pierre really wanted—was to find some kind of mental common ground where they could agree on how to raise César together in a way that would help their son to thrive.

She wanted that, too. And yet…how nice it would have been to have something more. Some sense that he would throw logic and caution to the wind and take a chance on a deeper connection than carefully agreed on terms for parenting.

"Before I forget," Gervais said suddenly, turning down the music again. "I've chartered two flights on Saturday for wedding guests who arrive here thinking the wedding is still taking place in Louisiana. But the family will relocate to the island early to settle in before the ceremony. Leon and his nurse will leave in the morning, so he'll meet us there. Can everyone else be ready to depart tomorrow evening?"

While the group fine-tuned travel arrangements, Jean-Pierre's gaze connected with hers. Perhaps he sensed her apprehension at seeing Leon again. The Reynaud family patriarch had been the one to fire her father and turn her life upside down, effectively ending the young romance she'd apparently never gotten over.

"Will your grandfather keep César a secret from the press?" she ventured aloud to Jean-Pierre, unsure how much longer they would be able to keep their son out of the media storm swirling around the Reynauds lately.

"We should probably talk about that." He slid a hand onto her knee beneath the pillow on her lap. But his expression was serious. He seemed to be touching her to steady her more than anything. "Leon has Alzheimer's and can't keep a secret of any kind. He's been blurting out information from the past and nothing's sacred with him because he can't remember what to keep quiet about."

"I'm sorry to hear that," she said quickly, genuinely saddened to learn of his health problems. She couldn't stop herself from touching Jean-Pierre's hand lightly. "I know this must hurt you. I wish César could have the chance to know him better before...well. It's just such a tragic disease. I'm not sure what to say or how to handle things. It could complicate the announcement about César."

"I know." Jean-Pierre's thumb shifted on the inside of her knee, a tiny movement that sent a bolt of awareness through her whole body. "All the more reason we need a plan for how to reveal him to the press so we control the story."

"Right." She agreed wholeheartedly.

The problem was, neither of them seemed to have any idea what that story might be. Because the only thing she understood for certain about her relationship with Jean-Pierre right now was that she couldn't go on denying the chemistry that all but set her on fire every time he was near.

Besides, she'd been to see a local doctor this morning and obtained her official six-week clearance for intimacy. Just thinking about it made her stomach flutter with nerves—and excitement. She couldn't deny she still wanted Jean-Pierre.

Even thinking about his grandfather's illness made her realize what a short window of time she had here to make some life-altering decisions. This could well be her last chance to indulge in this tenacious attraction.

Maybe, in this frustrating search for common ground, they needed to revisit the one place they'd always found it—in each other's arms.

# Nine

Jean-Pierre checked his watch at seven o'clock the next evening as the limo dropped him and Tatiana, as well as César and his nanny, off at the private airport close to the family compound. The party of four had arrived early to give Tatiana a little extra time to settle the baby. She had delayed the morning feeding so he could nurse during takeoff. She hoped to ease César's transition into the air since small children often felt the effects of the change in air pressure as pain in the ears. Apparently, the act of suckling relieved that pressure. That she'd researched this before the flight impressed Jean-Pierre, giving him yet another reason to admire her parenting.

He'd begun to think that the best way to convince her to say yes to his marriage proposal was to demonstrate his value to her as a father. But beyond naming the child heir to a fortune, he was still looking for ways to make his potential contributions more apparent.

Now, he passed a fussing César into Lucinda's arms while he helped Tatiana from the vehicle. Their driver had already taken charge of the luggage, so they were able to board after an exchange of pleasantries with the pilot, a man who'd flown Jean-Pierre back and forth to New York on numerous occasions.

He hoped the man proved as trustworthy as he'd always thought him to be because allowing him to observe Tatiana and César in Jean-Pierre's company amounted to giving him one hell of a valuable headline. But after considerable discussion the day before, he and Tatiana had agreed it would be best to bring César to Texas with them. She was breast-feeding almost exclusively, for one thing. And for another, Jean-Pierre found he didn't want to lose any time with his son after missing those early weeks of the child's life. Besides, if he was going to prove his value to Tatiana as a father, it would help to keep his son close at hand and learn more about this little life they'd made together.

Even if the boy's presence made it a challenge to get time with her alone.

"Where should we sit?" she asked as they boarded the empty plane.

The Gulfstream had been designed for business more than pleasure, but there were a few different seat configurations to choose from. Jean-Pierre pointed to seats in the back.

"It will be most private back here." He escorted her to two seats positioned side by side. "There's a privacy screen that's meant for sleeping, but I can lower that for you, too."

Lucinda passed César back to him before taking another chair on the opposite side of the plane and withdrawing a book from her bag.

Peering down at his son's wriggling form, his tiny mouth seeking food as his head turned this way and that,

Jean-Pierre experienced a rush of protectiveness so fierce it damn near floored him.

"I'm ready," he heard Tatiana say behind him, reminding him he had a role to play, too. "I don't want the baby to have to wait much longer. And we should be taking off soon."

Would he be able to continue playing football at the level he maintained now? Somehow he didn't think his focus would ever be the same again. Traveling across the country with Tatiana and César in tow wouldn't allow him to spend the same amount of time on his game preparation, which some sportswriters suggested was actually his strongest asset as an athlete. His mental game. What Henri had always managed through God-given talent and instinct, Jean-Pierre manufactured through sheer will and study.

"Jean-Pierre?" Tatiana called to him. "I can take him."

Turning to see her with her simple sundress already sliding off one creamy shoulder, his thoughts shifted from his son to the boy's mother so fast he felt dizzy.

She'd brought a soft purple cashmere sweater to rest on her shoulders. The line of pearl buttons followed her curves in a way that made his mouth go dry.

Lowering himself to sit beside her, he tugged down the privacy screen beside his seat, shrouding them in relative intimacy. His eyes never left her body—so beautiful, but so much more than that—as she reached to take César and cradle him to her breast.

Speechless at the sight of her, Jean-Pierre couldn't wait to get to Texas so they could be alone. To lay claim to her as his in a way he hadn't been able to the only time they'd shared a bed. Being with her now would be so much different than it had been ten months ago.

"We're sharing a room on the island," he announced in the hands-down worse segue of his life.

Of course, if she could have followed his thoughts, it would have made perfect sense.

"I understand." She brushed a dark curl away from her face, revealing an earring with a simple diamond stud in her ear. "I know the ranch is not a hotel. I'm just glad to have a place to stay."

The fact that she hadn't protested the arrangement encouraged him. Since their blowup the first night at Gervais's, they both seemed to tread a bit more cautiously. And, perhaps, respectfully. They had too much at stake to risk alienating one another.

"Lucinda will share a room with César next door, but you might speak with her about the importance of remaining within her quarters as much as possible for security purposes." He worried about what a leak to the press might do at this stage of their relationship. "We have weathered enough media scrutiny and conjecture for one week."

Outside the plane, he could hear the others arriving and more luggage being stowed beneath the passenger cabin. As the first of their party boarded, he could hear the nanny explaining to someone—Fiona, he thought—that Tatiana was feeding César.

That would save him from having to greet his family for now. He'd far rather watch Tatiana nurse his son. He leaned closer to brush her hair from her shoulder, out of the way of César's clutching hand. The boy seemed to meet his gaze over the high curve of Tatiana's breast. Jean-Pierre gave the baby one of his fingers to grip instead.

The action had been instinctual, sure. But as soon as he did it, he realized how the movement put his palm mere inches from Tatiana's other breast. Still tucked safely in her dress, the soft curve called to him anyhow. This close to her, he caught the scent of her fragrance, something clean and lemony that made him hunger to find its source.

Behind an ear? Along the slender column of her neck?

"Jean-Pierre?" she whispered suddenly, her voice containing an unexpected hint of urgency while his family found seats scattered around the luxury jet.

"What is it? Do you need anything?" Had she forgotten some necessity back at the house? Even now the door was closing to the passenger cabin, the pilot warning them to strap in for the flight.

"No. It's not—" She bit her lip, her green gaze sliding higher to meet his. He could see the heat there. The hunger. "You shouldn't look at me like that in public places."

Understanding dawned. And with it came a need so strong he debated carrying her off the plane and finding the nearest hotel room. He might have done it, too, if not for César.

In fact he had done something just like that nearly a year ago when they'd created their child.

"The flight is blessedly short. And we have a good excuse for retreating directly to our suite since we have an infant to care for." And then another thought occurred to him. "Although we need to wait until you see a physician—"

"I did. Yesterday morning before we worked on the wine-bottle labels. That's why I was late to Gervais's house." She lowered her window shade as the plane began to taxi toward the short runway.

"You saw a local doctor?" He pried his finger from the baby's grip, regretting not being there with her for that visit. She must have gone out while he'd been recovering from the midnight workout at the Hurricanes' training facility. "Is everything…okay?"

The barest hint of a smile teased her lips. "I'm cleared to resume normal activity, if that's what you mean."

He sure as hell couldn't miss what she implied.

Heat scorched its way up his spine as the plane fired faster. His pulse kicked up speed, too, not just because of the green light she'd received from an obstetrician, but also from the green light he spied in her eyes.

For him.

"I care about more than that, Tatiana." He cradled her cheek in his hand as the aircraft lifted off. "I am so grateful you are healthy and that you did a beautiful thing in delivering our son. But I'd be lying if I said I wasn't extremely interested in touching you. Everywhere."

Her slow swallow intrigued him. She cleared her throat and then asked, "How long did you say the flight lasts?"

The flight went as quickly as Jean-Pierre had said it would. But the pilot couldn't land on the island so they needed to ferry over from Galveston. Or, rather, the pilot could have landed on the Reynauds' private island off the Texas gulf coast, but Gervais hadn't wanted to draw that kind of attention to the wedding destination since the family's every movement was being scrutinized. Bodyguards traveled with them now. Decoy limos had left the family compound at intervals all day to confuse the members of the media who'd set up camp outside the gates to the houses on Lake Pontchartrain.

A Reynaud wedding garnered attention. A Reynaud wedding to a royal made for a media circus.

So the trip to the island was purposely a bit longer than necessary to throw story seekers off their scent, which was a good thing for César's sake as well as protecting the wedding secret. The private ferry ride from Galveston to the island went smoothly enough. As they reached the dock on the western side of the land mass, Tatiana wished it was daylight so she could appreciate the lay of the land.

She hugged the rail of the boat while the others began

debarking. Lucinda held César, who was fast asleep. But Tatiana didn't feel even the smallest bit tired after her electrifying conversation with the man standing next to her. Her body still hummed with anticipation from just a few simple words.

He'd said he wanted to touch her. Everywhere.

His eyes had communicated his desires far more explicitly, however. And all the pent-up hunger she felt coursed through her tenfold.

If they salvaged nothing else from their relationship, they would have César. And they would have tonight.

"Ready?" Jean-Pierre asked, extending a hand. The lights from the dock behind him cast his features in shadow, but made him appear all the larger.

If any paparazzi surprised them, she thought she would be able to hide behind his broad shoulders easily.

"Very." She laid her palm against his for a moment before interlacing their fingers, locking them together.

"I'll introduce you to my cousin Kimberly, then I'll see about getting you and César both settled for the night."

She wanted to press herself into him and kiss him, then and there. Remind him that she didn't want to be settled. That what she wanted was to have his arms around her, sifting through her hair and parting the zipper on her dress. She wanted to take chances and throw caution to the humid Texas wind.

"That sounds good." Realistically, she knew she didn't have to wait much longer to touch him. But she didn't know how she'd make it through much more social chitchat. To distract herself from the kiss she wanted, she asked him about his relatives. "Tell me about the Texas Reynauds. How come I never met any of your cousins when I visited your family at the big ranch?"

Memories of the endless spread of hill country returned.

There had been long afternoons of hiking trails or horse-back riding, nighttime picnics under the stars, and the heady pleasure of being the only girl with four handsome older boys to keep her entertained. Before they'd grown older and started to pursue their own interests, leaving her to Jean-Pierre's care, her ten-year-old self had been a little in love with them all.

"My grandfather, Leon, did a great job stepping in to raise my brothers and me after our parents divorced. But the reason Leon worked hard to get it right with us is because he screwed up his own sons so thoroughly. His words, not mine, by the way." Jean-Pierre's gaze followed Lucinda, his sharp eyes missing nothing as she stepped into a waiting golf cart with César and they sped off toward the looming ranch house in the distance.

Gervais commandeered a small luxury bus for the rest of them while giving instructions for the luggage. Tatiana admired that no matter how wealthy and powerful the man was, he still oversaw details himself, taking no chances with his pregnant wife or his family.

"Leon blames himself for his sons' shortcomings? Keep in mind, I don't know anything about your uncles and I've only met your father a few times." She'd only spoken to Theo Reynaud once, at a long-ago birthday party for one of the boys. The man had touched down by helicopter, stayed long enough to have a few drinks and departed with his latest girlfriend within the hour.

Tatiana had been decidedly unimpressed.

Following Jean-Pierre toward the waiting vehicle, she noticed Adelaide tucked under Dempsey's arm as they sat on a bench on the dock, her eyes closed as she tipped her head against his chest. Fiona and Henri were quiet, too, talking softly in the back of the bus when Tatiana entered with Jean-Pierre. So it didn't feel rude to continue their own conversation while the family boarded.

"Leon thought it would make his sons tougher to pit them against each other." Jean-Pierre slid into a leather captain's chair midway up one aisle of the bus. He reached up to turn off the reading lamp above the seat, plunging them into darkness before he tugged her closer, wrapping an arm around her waist. "He started rivalries when they were young, pushing them to outdo one another on the football field and on the ranch since he was based in Texas back then. Once, a bull-riding contest between them nearly killed my Uncle Michael."

"That's awful." She relaxed against him, her cheek pressed to the hard muscle of his chest, his body warming her.

She felt the slow thud of his heartbeat beneath her ear and she couldn't resist laying her hand on him, feeling the hard ridges of muscles in his abdomen beneath the thin cotton of his shirt.

He responded by stroking her hair away from her face. A gentle gesture that might appear sweet to a casual observer, but the sensual heat it roused was enough to set her on fire.

"Eventually, Christophe, Michael and my father cut all personal ties and moved to different states. But since the shipping empire is still a family business, they are bound together professionally." He nodded to Gervais as his brother boarded with his fiancée. The couple took the front seat behind the driver and signaled him to begin the short trip to the main house while Jean-Pierre wound up his family primer for her. "Kimberly, who we'll meet when we get to the house, is one of Christophe's daughters. She doesn't get along with her father, either, but she deals with him well enough that he lets her run this place. The island ranch is a self-sustaining subsidiary of the main ranching operation and also a stop on many of our cruise ships' Gulf of Mexico itineraries."

Tatiana lifted her head from her comfortable position to peer up at him. "You're such a successful athlete, I forget that you have a whole other side to you as an heir to the family's business."

"It's a lot to keep up with since the company interests are so diverse, but considering the short career of an NFL athlete, I know that the business will keep me employed long after football is done with me."

The luxury bus hit a pothole and pitched enough to one side that she fell against him again. Not that she minded. And from the way his eyes glittered in the dim lights outlining the walkway on the floor, she'd guess he didn't mind, either.

"You're only a year older than me," she teased, smoothing a hand along his shoulder and upper arm to grip his biceps. "I think you've got a few years left in your arm."

"If I'm lucky," he said, in all seriousness. "Injuries can happen at any time in the game. I don't count on a paycheck from the Gladiators or any other team, but no matter what my future is in football, rest assured our son will be well provided for. Always."

"I don't want to think about you being hurt." She closed her eyes tight, knowing he spoke the truth. She'd been around football long enough to understand the dangers, to see young, vital men halted in their athletic careers because of irreversible damage that decreased their speed or mobility.

"I'm a realist. I account for as many possibilities as I can foresee, and that's a skill that has served me well." His hand slid beneath the collar of her cashmere sweater to massage the bare skin of her shoulder. "But I can honestly say César was an outcome I never accounted for and I should have. I'm sorry about that, Tatiana."

The soft words, spoken into her hair as the bus slowed to a stop, caught her off guard. She hadn't expected him to apologize for not checking in with her after that explosive encounter ten and a half months ago, but she appreciated the thought nevertheless.

"We were careful at the time. You had no reason to suspect—"

"It's always a possibility." The brusque statement left no room for argument. "I should have called afterward, when I'd cooled down…" She sensed a hesitation. As if he didn't want to confide whatever he was thinking.

And he didn't.

Instead, he straightened, bringing her with him. As they followed his brothers and their significant others from the vehicle, Tatiana shoved aside her troubled thoughts so she could meet their hostess.

The Tides Ranch was a massive complex with a central hacienda-style adobe main house that glowed a bronze shade of pink in the landscape lights. Native plantings on terraced beds hinted at the ranch's self-sustaining practices, as did the solar panels on the roofs, evident even in the dark from the way they glinted in the moonlight. Although Tatiana had read that the ranch housed some of the owner's family year-round, the front entrance had the feel of a hotel, complete with a staffed front desk, since the island received a high number of annual visitors thanks to being a stop for cruise ships.

Warm mesquite wood furnishings and Saltillo tile floors enhanced the Southwest appeal of the house. Exposed beam ceilings and bright woven rugs drew her eye toward a large entertaining space, a family room that looked as though it would hold sixty people easily.

"Welcome to the Tides." A willowy blonde with cool gray eyes appeared in the reception area as they entered, opening her arms to Gervais and each of the Reynaud brothers in turn, then greeting the women briefly. "I can't tell you how thrilled I am to host a wedding this weekend instead of our usual tourists," she said, squeezing Erika's hand warmly. "Not that we don't appreciate all our visitors, of course. But it will be fun to take our level of entertaining up a notch. As a foreign princess, your options for wedding sites must have been limitless."

Tatiana knew how tired Erika was by that time, having recently survived her own narcoleptic second trimester. And she hadn't even been pregnant with twins. But looking at the bride-to-be, you'd never guess she had fallen asleep on Gervais's shoulder on the short bus trip from the dock to the ranch house.

"Come on." Jean-Pierre spoke into her ear, tugging her away from the conversation. "I grabbed our key from the desk. Kimberly knows about the baby. She'll understand."

He tossed a brief "good night and thank you" over his shoulder as he pulled Tatiana toward the back of the main building. Her kitten heels clicked on the Saltillo tiles, her hand warm in his as he drew her up a short staircase decorated with Spanish tile mosaic. They walked out into a breezeway open to the elements, cloister-style. He paused outside a dark wooden door decorated with a blue-and-yellow tile motif that matched the card on the old-fashioned key he carried.

Hearing it click into place in the lock made her temperature spike, the sound an audible reminder of what was to come with the utter privacy behind that door.

"Should I check on César?" she asked, peering around the corridor as if she could guess what room he might be in.

"Why don't you let me. I'll give you some privacy to

get settled while I make sure Lucinda has the baby's bags and we have ours." He pushed open the door and held it for her. "I'll get a baby monitor, too, so we can hear him tonight if he needs to be fed."

"Okay." She nodded, a nervous laugh escaping. "Is it strange to plan for baby care the second time we ever share a…um, romantic evening?"

"No." He drew her into the room with him, letting the door fall shut behind them. A small wrought-iron chandelier in the foyer area flickered to life on a dim setting as they entered. He stood, centered under that chandelier, and reeled her toward him. Closer. Closer. Until she was toe-to-toe with him. Breasts-to-chest. "It seems like everything I've wanted since I first saw you holding our son that night in New York is about to come true." His hands clamped her forearms, holding her still. His voice dipped lower as he tipped her chin up with one finger. "It feels perfect."

Nervousness faded. Her pulse hammered faster as sensations skidded along her spine, tension coiling deep within her.

When his mouth finally brushed hers, she thought she'd faint from the sheer pleasure of it. The warm slide of his lips was a sensual treat for a woman who'd had little enough romantic attention in the last year. The bay-rum-and-sandalwood scent of his aftershave teased her nose, calling her to taste his skin, but Jean-Pierre had taken full command of the kiss by then.

Her head spun as he raised his hand to either side of her face, bracketing her jaw and tilting her chin to just the right angle. Her knees wobbled, her body seized with the need to melt into him. A moan simmered up her throat but didn't escape, his kiss consuming it. His fingers sifted into her hair, sending tantalizing warmth along the base of her scalp even as shivers tingled along her nerve endings.

She would have fallen into him completely if he hadn't pulled away just then. As he glanced down at her, his breath came fast, his chest moving up and down as though he'd been sprinting.

"Hold that thought." He kissed her hard on the lips, like a warrior leaving to do battle instead of a new father retrieving a nursery monitor. But feeling the way she did, she could completely appreciate where he was coming from because pulling away from that kiss took a whole lot of grit and resolve, almost more than she could manage right now. "I'll be right back."

As he strode out of their suite, she hoped he would hurry.

If this trip was the only time they had together, she wanted it to be perfect.

# Ten

He only left the room for fifteen minutes to tuck in César.

Jean-Pierre kissed his sleeping son's head, ensured the baby and his nanny had everything they needed and then double-checked the status of their bags. Because he didn't want someone knocking on his door in half an hour to deliver them, he waited just long enough to secure the luggage personally and have it brought up with him. Impatient as hell, he tipped the young man generously to make sure they weren't disturbed until he called downstairs, but he put in an advance order with the kitchen to have a few of Tatiana's favorites ready upon request later.

After a deep bracing breath, he opened the door to the bedroom he would be sharing with Tatiana.

The air left his lungs twice as fast.

Considering how briefly he'd left the room, he was surprised at the transformation when he returned. Not that he'd devoted even two seconds checking out the décor when they'd arrived. He'd been too busy trying not to devour Tatiana whole.

But when he'd been in the suite before, there hadn't been any seductive Spanish guitar music gently playing from hidden speakers. And he wouldn't have missed candlelight flickering through the open archway that led to the bedroom. The warm golden glow was the only thing that illuminated the space, though a smaller candle burned on top of the wet bar close to the entrance. The windows had been thrown open—though the heavy wooden blinds remaining closed—so that a fresh gulf breeze drifted through the slats, gently stirring the sheer white curtains draping the corners of a wrought-iron four-poster bed.

He could see the bed now as he was drawn deeper into the suite to see what other surprises the night—and Tatiana—had in store.

"I hope you don't mind the candles." Tatiana emerged from behind a decorative screen made of colorful serapes that had been stretched to fit tall, rectangular frames.

Her feet were bare, her beautiful dark hair loose around her shoulders as she brushed it, one slow seductive sweep at a time. She wore a white linen nightgown that bared her shoulders and just covered her knees. He'd seen her wear something just like it once before, when he'd thrown stones at her bedroom window as a teenager to get her attention and she'd opened the sash to lean out.

He couldn't decide if seeing her this way was like seeing his teenage fantasy come to life.

Or like taking a bride to his bed.

Both thoughts rattled him, but for far different reasons. "Tatiana?"

"You have to ask?" She laughed softly, setting aside the silver-backed hairbrush, although she didn't step any closer. "I can switch on a real light if you need one. It's just that candlelight is a postpartum woman's best friend. More flattering, you know?" she rambled, obviously nervous. "My body has been through a lot since the last time you saw it."

Ruthlessly, he tamped down his own lust to dial into what she was saying.

"You look so damn beautiful I can't even find words," he said and meant it. Every. Damn. Word.

He took a step toward her, the movement so carefully measured he probably looked like a robot.

But it was that, or risk a diving tackle that would get them both horizontal as fast as possible and…yeah. Not happening. He needed to remember she'd had a baby recently. And yes, he wanted to savor every moment of being with her again.

Another step brought him close enough to touch her. He skimmed a light caress up her arms, circling around the tops of her shoulders and slipping his thumbs just barely under the wide straps of the nightgown until a shiver ran through her.

"Thank you for understanding." She lifted her palms to his chest and smoothed them down the front of his shirt. She hesitated at the bottom, but soon she walked two fingers beneath the fabric to hook into the waistband of his trousers. "It's hard to think about being with you when you work so hard to hone and refine your body every day for football and I just—"

"You used yours for the most important thing in the world. No comparison." He wasn't even listening to that line of discussion. His touch fell to her belly through the soft linen. "If we'd been together while César grew inside you, I would have told you every day how amazing you were to do that. And I am certain you were every bit as beautiful."

Her lips curved in a smile, bringing a sparkle to her green eyes.

"But since we weren't together during those months—" she arched up on her toes to whisper in his ear "—I've had a long time to miss your touch."

A groan vibrated through him, the hunger tougher to restrain when she said things like that. Especially now that her palm raked over his abs and around to the small of his back, and delectable breasts pressed against his chest.

Seized by the need to lie with her, he plucked her off her feet and cradled her in his arms, carrying her to the high bed. He climbed onto the soft down mattress, the feather stuffing flattening under his knees as he shifted his weight to make her more comfortable.

He wanted to take his time. To square the pillow beneath her head and smooth her hair from her shoulders. To breathe kisses along her collarbone and up the creamy arch of her neck. But she was already making quick work of the buttons on his shirt, skimming the fabric off his shoulders until he had no choice but to ease it to the floor beside the bed.

"We have to go slow," he reminded her. "Be careful."

"I can't go slow." She shook her head, sending dark curls wriggling on the pale sheets. "I need you. I need this."

"I don't want to hurt you." Grinding his teeth as she pressed a kiss along his jaw, he hoped he had the fortitude to ensure he was careful with her.

Six weeks ago she'd delivered a baby. And although she looked more beautiful than ever, and she'd kissed him with enough heat to scorch the sheets, he would make damn sure he took care of her.

"You won't hurt me." She twisted her leg so that her foot stroked up his calf, the movement causing her thigh to shift against his, her hips cradling the hard length of him against her softness.

"Tatiana." He had to close his eyes against another heated rush of longing. Hunger.

"Please," she whispered in his ear, nipping the lobe before she licked it with a deft swipe of her tongue. "For a little while, I just want to be a woman and not a mother."

Her confession called to the most elemental need and he tunneled his hands beneath the nightgown to touch her naked body. Hips, waist, breasts. He reacquainted himself with her curves in long, possessive strokes over her skin.

The touch unleashed something in her, a reserve that she was only too glad to set aside, her kisses growing more fevered.

Rolling her on top of him, he skimmed the gown up and off of her, her dark hair falling all around him and veiling their kiss in curls. He cupped her breasts, heavier than they'd been the last time, but the tips tightened just the way he remembered.

With the lemony scent of her hair in his nose and the golden glow of candlelight flickering over her creamy skin, he could have explored her body all night long. But he didn't want to wear her out. Instead, he flipped her to her back on the thick feather bed and proceeded to give her what she'd asked for.

Because it would be his intense pleasure to make her feel like a woman.

"Jean-Pierre?" Tatiana blinked up at him as he stretched out over her, his powerful body making her feel tiny beneath him despite the extra weight the pregnancy had left behind.

Shirtless, he was a mouthwatering sight. But the fact that his mouth trailed kisses lower and lower down her newly curvier body made her self-conscious no matter what he spouted about her beauty. Her stretch marks looked like white vines had a stranglehold on her hips.

"Too late to change your mind," he warned her, his breath fanning over her belly as he spoke. "I'm on a mission."

His tongue swirled into the hollow of her navel, sending pleasurable shivers across her skin along with a rush of heat between her legs. Even seeing his strong shoulders pinning her thighs to the bed was enough to hurtle her affection-starved body toward release.

"I didn't know you would embrace the task so, er... wholeheartedly." She'd had visions of the missionary position. Lovely, fulfilling visions where she could simply close her eyes and lose herself in the feel of all that male strength around and inside her. "Did I mention I'm feeling self-conscious?"

He trailed kisses to one hip and then the other, peering up at her with dark eyes as he licked her. Thoroughly.

"For a little while tonight, you're not a mother." He parroted her words, punctuating them with a kiss on the waistband of her simple cotton bikini panties. "You're a sexy, tantalizing woman." His teeth latched onto the elastic enough to edge them lower on her hip, before his hands slid them off completely. "My woman."

The kiss centered between her thighs was her undoing.

A gasp caught in her throat, the feel of his mouth administering wicked pleasure an experience too good to be tainted with hesitation. Her eyes slid closed, her body melting at his touch. His kiss.

She lost herself utterly, her brain latching on to the sensation of his fingers gripping her hips and his mouth teasing a response from her body faster than she would have imagined possible.

Her release hit her hard, coming in wave after wave of

pleasure. He cupped her with his palm, capturing her release and helping her to ride out each heady spasm.

By the time she dared to slide open her eyes, he was already off the bed and undressing the rest of the way. Grateful she hadn't missed the sight of him naked, she savored the burnished gold of his muscles in the candlelight, his back tapering to narrow hips and strong thighs.

Reaching a languid hand out to touch him, she met his dark gaze and shivered anew. The satisfaction that weighted her limbs and curled in her belly was a release he hadn't found yet—a release he'd delayed for her sake. Even as she appreciated his restraint, she wanted desperately to distract him from his methodical seduction. He deserved the kind of passion that had taken hold of them ten and a half months ago like a fever in their blood.

Infused with new purpose, she levered herself up on an elbow and then to her knees, shuffling over to the edge of the bed where he stood. The glitter of frank male interest in his eyes gratified her, his gaze traveling all over her more generous curves in a way that gave her as much confidence as she could have ever wanted. She twined her arms around his neck and aligned their bodies again, her breasts molding to the hard planes of his pectorals.

With a growl of approval, he banded his arms around her, fitting them together tighter. Harder. Her heart rate sped up as the kiss became more demanding, his fingers spearing into her hair to cup the back of her head, angling her to receive the lush thrust of his tongue.

Lowering her to the bed, he followed her down, one hard thigh claiming the space between hers. He took a condom from the nightstand; he must have left it there when he shed his clothes.

"I've got it." Peering out of the corner of her eye, she took the condom from him. "I don't want you to stop touching me for even a second." Fingers fumbling, she opened the foil package and reached to roll the condom into place.

"Wait." He manacled her wrist with an immovable grip, surprising her. "Your touch could be the end of me." Releasing his hold, he took the condom back. "Let me."

Touched to learn she could affect him like that—this man who had groupies, for pity's sake—she caressed his bristle-roughened jaw and peered into his eyes once he had the protection in place.

Tenderness for him, for all that they'd shared, filled her chest. There'd been a time when she'd been certain she'd lose her virginity to him. A time when she'd dreamed of it in detail—repeatedly.

"Are you okay?" His question brought her back to the moment. Unwilling to let her runaway emotions spoil this, she brushed his dark hair from his forehead.

"I'll be better with you inside me," she told him honestly, needing more of the fulfillment only he could bring.

His gaze narrowed, becoming heavy-lidded with sensual focus. Lowering his mouth to her breast, he teased one tight peak with slow, circling kisses while his fingers dipped between her thighs to play in the slick heat he found there.

Her throaty moan must have encouraged him because he wasted no time positioning himself between her legs. He whispered seductive encouragement in her ear, cradling her close as he entered her. But she felt too good to go slow and, arching her hips, took more of him.

He exercised that iron grip again, holding her there for a long moment, but whether it was for his sake or her own, she couldn't say. All she knew was that it felt perfect, sharing her body with him and sharing this undeniable heat and chemistry that had never really died between them.

Eventually, he moved within her, finding a rhythm that

drove them both to the brink and beyond. As she hurtled toward release, she felt him find his, the hot surge of him inside her driving her higher.

The moment went on and on as they clutched each other in the big feather bed, clinging until every last wave of pleasure had been exhausted. Only then did they fall into each other's arms in the candlelight, allowing the cool gulf breeze to soothe their overheated bodies.

They didn't speak much, but the way he stroked his hand up and down her spine made her feel cherished even if he would never say such a thing. Here, in this bed, there was a connection they'd never been able to form anywhere else.

For now, she didn't want to jinx it. Didn't want to wake up and find that they were back to being at odds again. So with her head tucked against Jean-Pierre's chest, she closed her eyes and wished the night didn't have to end.

# Eleven

Two days later, Tatiana was as nervous as a bride and it wasn't even *her* wedding.

The Mitras royal family had arrived at the Tides Ranch the day before, to much fanfare since even the employees of the Reynaud family—who'd seen plenty of celebrities come and go at their elite homes all over the world—were not immune to the draw of royalty. Despite confidentiality agreements and strict rules governing their conduct, everyone from ranch hands to caterers had cell phones out to record the procession of platinum-haired princesses and their elegant parents.

A king and queen.

Tatiana had watched from her suite's private balcony the day before. Curled in Jean-Pierre's lap while César snoozed in a bassinet nearby, she'd been tempted to snap some photos herself.

She had refrained then, but she'd given in to the impulse

to capture a few candids the morning of the wedding while she assisted with last-minute preparations. She'd been helping Jean-Pierre's cousin Kimberly thread bright red hibiscus flowers into a graceful willow arch that would frame the bride and groom during their vows when she'd noticed one of the island's luxury buses rumbling past with wedding guests newly flown in. Unlike the Reynauds, these newest arrivals had landed directly on the island's runway since Gervais and Erika had decided they didn't need the same kind of privacy safeguards this close to the event.

It was too late now. No paparazzi photographer would have the resources to follow the Reynaud private planes before the ceremony began.

"I can't imagine marrying royalty," Kimberly remarked as she dragged over another bucket of hibiscus blooms.

Tatiana had noticed in their short stay that the woman was a hands-on manager of the property, as comfortable greeting guests and riding horses as she was feeding the goats that provided natural weed control on the self-sustaining eco-island. Tatiana admired her commitment to this being an environmentally friendly ranch, right down to the solar-powered cell-phone tower.

"Really?" She stepped back and took a photo of their handiwork to see how it looked on camera. "I always think of the Reynauds as a sort of American royalty, between the wealth, the global connections and the fame."

Kimberly laughed while Tatiana studied her photos and made adjustments.

"Seriously?" The other woman shook her head, peering over Tatiana's shoulder to see how the arch looked on the screen. "I guess the Texas Reynauds are less famous because we don't play football. And since I spend most of my time negotiating with stubborn goats as opposed to negotiating big business deals, I guess I don't see myself as more than a rancher's daughter." Squinting at the thumbnail images on Tatiana's phone, Kimberly pointed to one. "Can I see the rest of your pictures? Some of those Hurricane players are so cute."

"Sure." She passed the device to Jean-Pierre's cousin and straightened a few of the chairs set up for the outdoor ceremony. "But you are far too modest, Kimberly. Anyone can see you make an incredible contribution to the family's cruise ship business by having the Tides as a featured stop on the itineraries. You keep the tourist dollars coming, plus you have an opportunity to educate a huge number of people on the advantages of eco-farming. That must be fulfilling."

"My father doesn't see it that way." Kimberly lowered herself to one of the folding chairs decorated with a length of ice-blue tulle. "He doesn't care about the dollars that funnel into the cruise ship business. He just sees the Tides as a sorry excuse for a ranch compared to the five-thousand-acre spread he oversees."

Tatiana rolled her eyes sympathetically. "That I can empathize with. My father is more interested in my contribution to my law firm's billable hours than my happiness." With a pang, she realized how little he'd said to her about the birth of her son. And while she realized it had been a shock to him at the time, she would have appreciated a call or a note since then.

One that wasn't focused on her plans to keep César hidden from the media for a little while longer.

"Tatiana?" Kimberly seemed to be enlarging one of the images as she stared at it. "Can you take a look at this?"

"Sure." She sat down on the closest chair. Already dressed for the wedding, she rearranged her skirts around her. Her lemon-colored princess-cut gown was strapless and highlighted with tiny yellow sequins in a subtle sunburst pattern. It looked as if a sun glowed from the area of her waist. "Did you find a cute player you want to dance with?"

"I thought I recognized this woman, actually." She pointed to a figure under one of the rookie Hurricane players' arms. "Not all of the guests' names were on my list since many of the wedding attendees were bringing a plus-one that might not be a wife."

Her gaze settled on the person in question. A female a bit blurred from having the photo stretched as large as possible. But Tatiana had captured her as she exited the limo and strode toward the Tides' main building. She must have missed seeing the woman at the time of the photo, her eye focusing on someone or something else in the excitement of the new arrivals.

Yet she recognized her former client very well. Blair Jones was the woman she'd helped sue Marcus Caruthers for sexual harassment. And now, here was Blair, attending a Reynaud wedding with another football player when the Reynaud brothers had every reason to resent and dislike her. Worry and suspicion joined forces, making Tatiana fear what her presence meant.

"Blair Jones." Tatiana confirmed the woman's identity aloud. "You probably recognized her from her sexual harassment case against—"

"Marcus." Kimberly frowned, touching the edge of the phone lightly. "I had a crush on him when I was a teen. I got his autograph his rookie year when his team came to town to play the Mustangs. I never believed for a second he was guilty."

Tatiana wondered if she knew about her connection to Blair, but decided to leave well enough alone for now. She wanted to confront Blair before the ceremony and find out what the woman's intentions were. Her lawyer instincts told her she wasn't going to like the answer.

"You're not the only one," Tatiana remarked lightly, tucking her phone into her sequined yellow purse. "Would you excuse me while I go find Jean-Pierre before the wedding starts?"

Striding up the long aisle of carpet that had been rolled out on the sand, Tatiana did plan to seek out Jean-Pierre. She needed to warn him that Blair had somehow wrangled her way into the private family event. But first, she would try to find the woman herself, because every inch of her feminine intuition screamed that something was amiss. She didn't want her son—or her tentative relationship with Jean-Pierre—to be caught in the cross fire of whatever scandal was stirring around that woman.

"I've brought you a little something, boys." Leon Reynaud stood on the threshold of the Tides Ranch library that Gervais had opted to use as a gathering place for his groomsmen.

Jean-Pierre bounced a tennis ball on a huge piece of cypress wood fashioned into a desk at the back corner of the room. He'd been distracted with thoughts of Tatiana all morning, thinking about what Dempsey had said to him back in New Orleans.

*So why is Gervais beating you to the altar?*

It bothered Jean-Pierre that he hadn't managed to change that state of affairs. That he'd had a son born out of wedlock while Gervais was moving heaven and earth to ensure he put a ring on Erika's finger before his twins arrived. Now, with their vows just minutes away, he knew there would be no trip to any clerk's office with Tatiana before then. With that heavy weight of failure on his shoul-

ders, he was only too glad to quit bouncing the tennis ball
to see what Leon had to say.

"You're looking mighty sharp, Gramps," he called over
his brothers' heads.

Dempsey and Gervais were taking turns remarking
on how badly Henri's bow-tie-tying skills sucked, which
was more a game of who could come up with better in-
sults than anything, since Henri wore Tom Ford as well as
anyone in the room. In matching silk tuxes, the Reynaud
men cleaned up quite nicely.

"Same to you, son," Leon called, waving an impatient
hand at the others to quiet them. "And the tie just needs a
woman's touch, Henri," their grandfather muttered to the
beleaguered Hurricanes starting quarterback. "If you got
laid more, your tie would look just fine."

Gramps waggled shaggy white eyebrows and the four
of them howled with laughter. Henri's laugh was loudest
of all, since he tended to disappear in coat closets at the
drop of a hat with his wife lately. He didn't seem to be suf-
fering in that department.

But even better than Leon's perfectly timed insult was
the fact that he looked so clear-eyed today. The old man
was on his game despite the Alzheimer's and that pleased
Jean-Pierre to no end. Their grandfather hadn't given them
the most traditional upbringing once he'd stepped in to
take charge with the unruly foursome, but he understood
boys. He'd always been able to break the tension with a
laugh. And despite his shortcomings, that showed a level
of caring that would help Jean-Pierre be a better father.

When the room had quieted enough to hear him again,
Leon set a wooden box on the desk beside Jean-Pierre. He
opened it to reveal the dark Scotch whiskey inside.

"I'm not staying, you know. I've got a nursemaid hovering by the door even now, ready to box my ears if I enjoy

the free bar at this shindig." He pointed a crooked finger at the archway where a placid, middle-aged woman checked her hair in a mirror. "But I wanted you all to enjoy a toast on me."

They crowded around the bottle—a sixty-two-year-old reserve blend—just as they had when Gramps brought a fifties-era Harley-Davidson bike to the ranch to give them a lesson in engine rebuilding. The motorcycle had been in crates when he bought the relic, but by the end of the summer they'd taken turns seeing how fast it would go on the private ranch roads.

No doubt it was the wedding making Jean-Pierre sentimental today as he thought about the past. And about how much he wished Tatiana would make things permanent between them so they could be a real family. Because even though that summer rebuilding the bike had been fun, he wanted a different kind of family for César.

"Thank you, *Grand-père*." Gervais clapped the older man on the shoulder. "I hope you'll stay for the toast even if you won't have a drink."

"No, I'm feeling my age and want to step out while I'm still fresh." He shook his head while Dempsey found glasses in a bar cabinet and Henri opened the bottle. "This is a day for the young. Enjoy it, boys. I'm proud of you all."

Jean-Pierre was heartbroken to see Leon's eyes mist over. But then their grandfather stalked out of the room toward his nurse, taking her arm like an old-time suitor on a first date.

Gervais wasted no time pouring the Scotch, the dark amber liquid fragrant in a room grown more somber.

"To Leon." Gervais lifted his glass.

They all nodded agreement, their glasses raised. But they had a family tradition of toasting around the horn, so they all added one.

"To the groom," Jean-Pierre offered.

"To fatherhood," Dempsey added, shooting a meaningful look at both Jean-Pierre and Gervais.

"To family," Henri added, bringing his glass in for the clink.

Jean-Pierre downed his fast, never having been a hardcore whiskey drinker. But this was smooth and rich, without the burn of a cheaper blend.

Outside the library, he could see the wedding guests filling in the seats down by the beach. He hadn't seen Tatiana since early that morning and he wanted to find her soon to be sure he sat near her after his brief part in the ceremony.

He wondered if she'd been looking for him since he'd lost track of the passing hours in the library.

"Gentlemen?" The minister stepped into the room, a friend of Gervais's from Louisiana. "We'll need to take our places outside. It's time."

As they filed out, Dempsey hung back to walk with him.

"Today is the day. You know that, right?" Dempsey tugged his elbow to slow him down.

"It seems like a good evening for a sunset wedding," he agreed pleasantly.

"It's a good night for a proposal," Dempsey asserted with the authority of a lifetime matchmaker. Too bad he was just a nosy football coach who actually had no idea when the right time to propose might be.

"We'll see." Jean-Pierre had been thinking about it, in fact. There was a boathouse on the Tides Ranch that reminded him of the one where he'd taken Tatiana to fool around back when they'd been dating.

That had significance, right? He wanted to show her he was trying. That he cared about how she felt and what she thought. Yet he also knew time was of the essence. He wanted to be married when they introduced César to the press and the longer they waited to the tie the knot, the greater the risk of discovery. And once the press knew about the baby, wouldn't she be less likely to say yes? As it stood now, Jean-Pierre suspected that she felt at least some social pressure to marry.

But once the news was out and she weathered that storm, what if she decided she didn't need to wed?

"You have a ring, right?" Dempsey asked.

"Since when are you the local ambassador of marriage?" He'd actually had a ring at the ready all week, but he wanted to find the right moment. As he exited the side stairs of the main ranch house, Jean-Pierre searched the wedding guests for a sign of Tatiana.

He'd seen the yellow gown she planned to wear hanging in a clear plastic garment bag, but had left before she'd dressed. When he'd seen her last, she'd been backed up against the white tile wall of the shower stall, her cheeks suffused with red from what they'd shared under the hot rush of water.

"I'm looking out for you, and you know it. You're rolling the dice with your reputation and hers, too. By not tackling this head-on, you're juicing up the press to get more and more inventive with headlines." His older brother straightened his tie as he hit the carpet. "Do you see Adelaide?"

Despite Dempsey's hard-edged veneer, he loved his former personal assistant with a passion he never bothered to disguise. He wasn't the kind to drag her into coat closets, but his eyes followed where she went.

"Dude." Jean-Pierre grabbed his brother's arm before he could leave. "How did you know it was the right time to ask Adelaide to marry you? That she'd say yes?"

"You think I knew she'd say yes?" Dempsey shook his head, as disappointed as if Jean-Pierre was a rookie who didn't understand a play. "Brother, you have to go all in even when you don't have any idea. Put yourself on the line. Or I promise you, she'll never say yes."

Without a single word of encouragement, his brother spun on his heel and melted into the crowd to find Adelaide, leaving Jean-Pierre just as clueless as before.

So it wasn't exactly ideal timing that Tatiana found him then, her dark curls spilling over one bare shoulder in a side-swept hairstyle that exposed the smooth skin of her neck. As always, she looked good enough to eat.

But he didn't have any idea how to tell her he wanted more from her than that. That he wanted to be a husband to her. A father to their son. He knew that without question.

"Blair Jones is here," she blurted suddenly, her words a hushed hiss of sound. Her expression, he realized, was venomous.

"Your client? The same Blair who lied about Marcus under oath?" He'd told her as much from the very beginning of the case, but Tatiana had explained to him—repeatedly—the rules of her job as Blair's attorney.

Now, however, she didn't appear as calmly accepting about Blair Jones as she had last winter.

"The same." Tatiana wrapped her hand around his forearm and turned him away from the crowd milling around the beach seating. A small chamber orchestra played, alternating zydeco music with classical selections from Erika's homeland. "And would you believe, she just admitted to me in private that she did exactly that? Lied under oath about Marcus?"

Jean-Pierre thought he might have spotted steam wafting up from her ears. Her cheeks were definitely red again, but not in the good way they'd been this morning in the shower. She was livid, he realized.

"I can't say I'm surprised," he admitted. "I thought as much all along."

Up front by the flower-covered archway, his brothers waved him over.

"Well, I'm reporting her to the judge," she growled, her eyes snapping emerald fire. The sea breeze lifted a few curls to blow them across her cheek. "I've been used by a greedy liar who doesn't care whose reputation she ruins." She bit her lip and arched up to speak more quietly close to his cheek. "But I'm also terrified she'll find out about César and run to the press for a lucrative payday."

Alarms blared in Jean-Pierre's head as he held up a finger to signal to his brothers that he'd be with them in a moment. After all the toasts about family, he didn't want to let them down today.

"Do you have any reason to believe she knows about our son?" They'd been so careful he didn't think that was possible. But then again, this woman—a menace to the football community for reasons he couldn't begin to guess—was now circulating among their closest friends and family.

Who knew what she might hear this weekend?

"No." Tatiana shook her head, biting her lip, rubbing her arms in a nervous shiver. "But I'm scared. And I have a bad feeling about her. I'm sure she was unhappy with me when I told her I was going to report her for perjury. Attorney-client privilege doesn't apply in this instance since I am no longer her lawyer and I wasn't acting as her lawyer when she spoke to me."

"You told her that?" His insides sank with foreboding.

"I was angry." Her eyes glistened. "I unknowingly helped her ruin an innocent man's reputation."

Jean-Pierre hauled her into a hug as the chamber orchestra finished their song. There were no words to make this better. The guilt in her eyes spoke volumes. It hadn't been her fault she'd believed her client and done her job. He saw that now and wished he could have been more levelheaded then. He held her tighter, pressing a kiss to her temple.

"The wedding is about to begin." He kissed her cheek. "We'll figure it out. Save me a seat and we'll talk afterward."

He didn't like walking away from her when she was so upset. But he had a duty to perform.

His sixth sense niggled in the back of his mind even as he reached the floral archway to wait with Gervais for his bride. Already he knew it was going to be a bad day for a marriage proposal of his own. He just hoped his proposal was the only thing ruined on a day that should be the happiest of his brother's life.

# Twelve

The wedding reception was truly magical.

After the sunset beachside vows, guests were ushered into a hacienda pavilion built in the style of traditional Spanish colonial architecture. The tile floors and sun-bleached stone walls supported high arches looking out over the water. A dark tile roof protected them from the sun, while the ever-present solar panels collected the energy to keep the generators running. The chamber musicians had given up their spot to a popular country band and already the foreign princesses were dancing with dashing husbands in various hues of military dress and ornamentation. A few of the younger football players joined them, two-stepping circles around the more formal waltzes of their royal counterparts.

Greenery bedecked every archway and long ropes of ivy decorated the exposed beams overhead. The effect was like having a party in a secret garden. Erika had told Tatiana earlier that they'd purchased the flowers and greens back when they hoped to have the event on Lake Pontchartrain, but if the princess minded exchanging her vows on a beach and having her reception in a hacienda instead, no one would have ever guessed. She danced with Gervais long before any formal introduction of the couple, and Tatiana couldn't help but admire a bride who didn't stand on ceremony.

If a woman only had one wedding in her life, she deserved to have fun during every moment of it. That was one of many reasons Tatiana was on the lookout for her former client while Jean-Pierre consulted with Henri and Dempsey in a far corner of the pavilion. She didn't want more scandal to dim Erika's enjoyment of her day.

"I recognize this young woman all grown up." The male voice close to Tatiana's elbow surprised her. "Care to dance?"

She turned to find Leon Reynaud, the man who had fired her father. Leon had been formidable well into his seventies, but his age had caught up to him a bit. His shoulders had thinned and he'd lost some of the impressive height that had been a genetic gift to his football-playing grandsons. Wispy white hair and overgrown white eyebrows didn't detract from the elegance of his appearance, however. She took in the crisp black tuxedo and starched French cuffs turned back from gnarled fingers as he offered his arm.

"I'd love to, sir, but I'm waiting to speak to your grandson. And are you sure you remember me?" She would be surprised if he knew her. He'd never paid her much attention when she'd visited their home in the past since he'd usually been closeted with her father in business meetings the whole time.

"You're the daughter of the infamous Jack Doucet, if I

don't miss my guess. I fired him." He said it with a jovial air, loud enough to turn heads of people nearby. Perhaps he didn't realize how devastating it had been for her father and her whole family at the time—and for years afterward.

They didn't have the resources that the Reynauds did, and losing a lucrative job over a petty grievance between friends had shaken the Doucet family to its foundation.

This week, especially, she'd found herself wondering what might have become of her relationship with Jean-Pierre if they hadn't been separated so acrimoniously back then.

"You have a good memory." She had changed a lot since she was seventeen. Especially in the last few months. Plus, she'd thought the older man suffered from Alzheimer's.

"You should tell my nurse," he grumbled, pointing toward a middle-aged woman in a pressed gray uniform standing a few feet away and taking photos of the table arrangements. "She doesn't think I can remember anything."

"Your nurse?" She studied the woman more closely and realized now the older man was confused after all. "That can't be her. I recognize that woman from Gervais's house. She's on the housekeeping staff."

Leon's eyes bulged. "Confound it, woman!" He turned on the housekeeper and gripped her arm. "I knew you weren't my health-care worker."

His raised voice attracted more turned heads even though the band continued to play. Jean-Pierre was by Tatiana's side almost instantly, while Henri and Dempsey attempted to take their grandfather aside.

"What's wrong?" Jean-Pierre asked, slipping an arm around her shoulders, the muscles hard and firm against her.

She pointed to the maid who darted out of the pavilion the moment Leon released his hold.

"That woman." Tatiana pointed her out, a sinking feeling in her gut. "Leon thought it was his caregiver, but I know she was the same woman who greeted us the night we had dinner at your brother's home. I just said I didn't think that could be his nurse and—"

"Who in the hell was she?" Leon was shouting now, loud enough to pull Gervais away from his new bride.

"Gramps, what's wrong?" He tried, like his brothers, to usher the agitated man aside, but the more they tried to move him, the more belligerent he became.

"You all sent me to a strange place with a woman I didn't even know and tried to convince me she was my nurse." Leon scoffed as if the word left a bad taste. "She's a harlot and a liar. She told me I missed seeing Jean-Pierre's son, but I know damn well Jean-Pierre isn't a father yet."

Tatiana froze.

Everyone close to her seemed to turn stone-still as well. Jean-Pierre looked to her helplessly while his brothers looked at him, all of them waiting for someone to say something. To announce whatever story it was that they wanted to use.

Now was the time, while a whole pavilion full of wedding guests listened. Including Blair Jones, who would surely have reason to want to spread the gossip with malicious glee after Tatiana had threatened to turn her in for perjury.

Tatiana shook her head at Jean-Pierre. She had no idea what to say. If she'd had a good cover story for César, she would have given it out months ago instead of running off to the Caribbean to give birth privately.

"Come on, Gramps." Dempsey slung an arm around his grandfather as some of the fight seemed to slip out of Leon. "Let's step away to figure out what's going on and let Gervais have his wedding, okay?"

"Sure," Leon said agreeably, although his expression remained troubled. "You're a good boy, Theo. Always were my favorite."

Tatiana's heart squeezed painfully in her chest as she listened to him say words destined to hurt his other children—and knowing she'd also lost her window to admit the truth. That she and Jean-Pierre had a child together. End of story.

Wasn't it? But if so, why had they waited so long to reveal it, missed so many opportunities and flirted with disaster this way? It was as if they'd set themselves up for failure.

She looked at Jean-Pierre, the man who'd come back into her life to help her discover the truth about her lying client. She hadn't listened to him then, and their argument had turned into something beautiful and complicated. A night she would never regret.

But these last days, she'd hoped they were moving toward that common ground they'd shared long ago when they were teenagers. He'd taken her to his bed with all the passion she'd once dreamed of and more. But he still hadn't claimed to love her. And she knew him well enough to know he'd never speak those words if he didn't mean them. She could hardly believe he'd simply overlooked them…

"Tatiana." He hooked his arm around her now, guiding her from the pavilion and out into the clear, warm night. He purposely walked her past Kimberly and stopped, interrupting the woman's phone call. "Kimberly, I'd owe you a favor forever if you would cut the power to that cell tower as fast as possible."

"Seriously?" She frowned.

"We've got leaks all over the place and I want to sit on a story to let the bride and groom have their day." His hand gripped Tatiana's waist gently, his fingers grazing her hip.

"I do love being off the grid." Kimberly grinned, stabbing a few buttons on her phone. "And I don't mind going incognito for however long you like. Although, I've got to warn you, if my father finds out we're disconnected, he'll be on the first boat out here."

"I just need to buy some time," Jean-Pierre assured her while the country band turned up their amps and the fiddle player kicked into high gear.

"Done." She flipped her phone toward him so he could see. "Look close because I'll lose the image as soon as I shut down that tower." She showed him a picture of a cell tower disguised as a pine tree on the screen, then hit a button.

The image vanished. Thanking her, he continued toward a section of the island Tatiana hadn't seen before. It wasn't the dock where their ferry had parked, but it was a pier of some sort. And, she could see by the moonlight, a boathouse.

"Where are we going?" She had worn low heels for the wedding, but there'd been carpet on the beach. Now, she tugged the shoes off and left them on a planter incorporated into the landscaping.

"I thought about taking you to the boathouse on Lake Pontchartrain. But there wasn't enough time, so this is going to have to do." He slid off his shoes, too, and left them by hers.

"We used to fool around in the boathouse." She'd fallen in love with him there.

Of course, that was a long time ago and she'd buried all those feelings. Did he know they were breaking through all the barriers she'd put around them? That the past and present had mingled in her mind and heart, helping her to see the old hints of the boy she'd loved along with the more reserved man she'd carefully avoided ever since he'd come to New York two years ago to play for the Gladiators?

"It remains my fondest teenage memory." He held her hand as they walked out onto the pier and then up the steps of a simple boathouse with a deck on the flat roof.

Jean-Pierre led her past a small shed containing extra lifesaving gear and utilitarian jackets to the front railing that looked out over the gulf.

She wanted to ask him more about that. To hear why he remembered those days fondly, too. She'd always suspected his heart hardened toward her when she'd told him to leave and not come back—a directive given by her father, but one that she meant since his family had hurt hers irreparably.

Only by being the best in her class had they afforded Columbia. Only by being the best in her job had she afforded her apartment, and even then, she'd been fortunate to have a connection in the law firm who knew the building owner. But she didn't want to win cases at the expense of the truth. She never would have taken that case if she'd known that Blair Jones lied through her teeth.

"Who do you think that woman was who posed as Leon's nurse?" She felt as if she had too many puzzle pieces that she couldn't fit together. And maybe she was avoiding thinking about what mattered most. One benefit of having the truth come out about César would be she didn't have to hide him any longer. She wasn't going to live for the sake of keeping up appearances anymore.

"Someone looking for a payout by obtaining unauthorized pictures of the event." Jean-Pierre shrugged. "You said she was taking photographs, so I assume she planned to sell out the family and offer wedding photos to the highest tabloid bidder."

"But doesn't Leon have a real caregiver? Do you think the nurse made the trip?" She felt worried about him after seeing the way he'd veered from clarity to confusion and back again. It must be frightening to lose your grip on your memories.

"We'll find out," Jean-Pierre promised her, taking her hands in both of his. "She might have made a deal to split the payday with the nurse, or just paid the woman outright. It's very difficult to find loyal employees, especially when scandal draws us into the headlines and the price for a story goes sky-high. Once interest in us dies down, the staff will go back to honoring those confidentiality agreements they all signed."

"It's my fault that interest really ramped up right before the wedding. I'm so sorry. I never meant for any of this to spill over into Gervais and Erika's special day."

"Erika is tough. She would probably be the first to say it's not a royal wedding without a tabloid crasher." Jean-Pierre tried to smile, but she could tell the turn of events troubled him, too.

"What should we do next?" She shivered as the breeze turned cooler.

A wave splashed against the boathouse with a little extra force, enough to cause a fine spray of mist on her skin.

"I hope we will do what I've wanted all along." He withdrew a ring box from the breast pocket of his tuxedo jacket.

Her heart stilled. Her mouth went dry.

Jean-Pierre, the father of her child, got down on one knee in the moonlight. She could hardly process what was happening. She'd expected a game plan. A strategy for coming up with a story. Not a heartfelt proposal.

Hope stirred within. Maybe their time together had cracked open his heart and made him realize he loved her after all.

That their common ground could be so much more beautiful than just co-parenting according to a contract.

"Tatiana." He looked up at her, his eyes as dark as the

water below, his expression inscrutable. "You and César are more important to me than anything in the world."

In her old fantasies of this moment—the ones she'd dreamed up a decade ago—he'd led his speech with "I love you and I can't live without you." But she recognized that she wasn't speaking to her eighteen-year-old boyfriend, dammit. Jean-Pierre was a formidable man. A world-renowned athlete. A business tycoon with interests all over the globe.

For him to say she was the most important thing in his world—along with their baby—was saying a great deal.

"When I look at you holding our son in your arms, I want to give you the world. To make sure that nothing ever hurts you. To keep you safe forever." He kissed the back of her left hand and then the left ring finger. "Nothing would bring me more happiness than if you would be my wife."

Her heart pounded so loudly she wondered if she'd missed that he also wanted to give her his heart. But maybe he included that when he said he'd give her the world? Worry made her heart beat crazily as he opened up the ring box and withdrew a magnificent diamond, a huge, sparkling pear-shaped central stone with two smaller stones to either side. There was an elegant simplicity about it, but her longstanding interest in appearances told her that it was at least eight carats. If she was still a woman who cared about those things, that ring would have dazzled her.

It still dazzled her.

But had she missed hearing the one thing her heart most craved?

She swallowed hard.

"Jean-Pierre." She savored his name on her lips. How many times had she stenciled it on notebooks or in her diary once upon a time, adding his last name to her first? "You know how nervous I can get. And I hope to remember this moment always." After all they'd shared the last few days, after the way he'd made love to her, surely that had nudged his heart into a more tender place toward her? "Do you…love me?"

It had cost her so much to ask. And she had her answer instantly. It was there, in the fleeting panic in his dark eyes.

The hesitation that told her this was the last question he wanted to field during a proposal of marriage.

"Never mind." She rushed to fill that moment of silence, thrusting his ring back in his palm. "I'm being overly sentimental, I know. You didn't expect that from me with all my lawyerly practicality, did you?" She shook her head, babbling and unable to stop herself since her eyes burned and she couldn't bear for him to see her cry. Damn these postpartum hormones still having their way with her. "And so foolish of me, too, since you had no problem walking away from me after we were together last winter. I mean, who walks away if they have an ounce of tenderness in their hearts?"

"Please, listen." He was on his feet, tucking the ring box in his pocket again.

"No. I don't think I will." She held up her hands defensively. "I don't think I can. I was listening very hard a moment ago, and when I didn't hear what I hoped to, I had to ask about it, embarrassing us both." She headed for the stairs, needing to put space between them. "Now, I'm going to return to my room and we can figure out how to co-parent when I'm not completely mortified over needing footnotes to explain my marriage proposals."

He chased her down, capturing her before she could descend the wooden steps.

"You're the only woman to ever break my heart, Tatiana. The. Only." His face was inches from hers, his grip unshakable. "I put everything on the line to come to New

York at eighteen and see you. To tell you all the things I have a hard time saying now. Leon made sure my life was hell afterward since I left without his knowledge or permission and he was furious that I would dare to step foot in Jack Doucet's house. But none of that mattered to me because you wouldn't even speak to me."

She spun to face him, her yellow dress swishing around her legs. "I was just seventeen years old, for heaven's sake. My father made me say that."

He thrust his fingers through his hair in exasperation. "I realize that now. Do you think it mattered to me then?" He set her aside gently and shook his head, as if the memory was something he didn't want to think about. "I became a much different person after that, and I know you did, too. It was no fault of yours or mine. But you, of all people, should understand that I don't think I can fall in love in a week these days. I turned off that switch a long time ago."

"You've never been in love? Ever." She didn't believe him. "If you've never been in love, then how do you know what a broken heart is?"

"I'm twenty-eight years old, and call it a cop-out—but I'm married to the game."

"You can't be serious." It added insult to injury that he would use that for an excuse not to get close to someone.

His fierce expression never wavered. "It takes all my time. All my brainpower. Every ounce of my physical energy. Normally, I'm training for hours every day. This week I've sacrificed workout after workout trying to show you how much I want to be a part of César's life. And yours. I wish that was good enough for you, because I'm offering you more than I've ever wanted to share with anyone else."

"So I should be thrilled that I rate higher than your free weights this week?" She wanted to throttle him. To make him see how ridiculous that sounded. To make him stop breaking *her* heart.

"I hoped you would be happy to sleep in my arms at night and give us more time to fall in love." The sincerity in his eyes hit home, finding a place in her heart.

Why hadn't he said this before? Or did he only go to this argument as his plan B? She didn't want to be his checkdown because he couldn't complete the long pass. She wouldn't be his safe option.

"Marriage is forever for me. I won't gamble on a maybe." She knew he'd said all he could say. That he'd dug as deep as he could for her.

But no matter how much she wanted it to be enough, she knew she would always feel as if she'd settled. As if she'd been too concerned about appearances and married the father of her son to quiet any gossip.

"I respect that." He shook his head, his proud shoulders falling just a little. "But I'm not going to lie. It hurts like hell to think I won't be with you and César every day."

She couldn't agree more on the hurt-like-hell part. But they'd reached an impasse. And no matter how valiantly Jean-Pierre fought to keep a lid on the news of their son's existence, the story was going to come out all too soon.

And despite what she'd hoped, there wouldn't be any wedding news attached to it. Unable to return to someone else's happy event, she descended the boathouse stairs and headed toward the main house, knowing all that remained for her here was to pack her bags.

# Thirteen

*Good game, Reynaud,* Jean-Pierre thought to himself—heavy on the sarcasm—as yet another poorly thrown pass got picked off in practice the week after Gervais's wedding.

Back in New York at the Gladiators' training facility, Jean-Pierre finished up his last practice before the game against the Hurricanes two days from now. The team would fly to New Orleans in the morning and have a meal together the night before the brother-against-brother matchup the media had been hyping for weeks.

His ill-fated reunion with the coach's daughter had only revved the hype to a fever pitch, putting the game in the public eye in a way that went far beyond the interest of football fans. Since news of their son had hit the papers the day after Gervais's wedding, the press had mobbed the Gladiators' practice field during the sanctioned media times, making it impossible to duck their questions. While Jack Doucet—who'd barely spoken to him this week, pre-

ferring to glare darkly at him—had texted him a reminder
that he did not need to discuss his personal life in the interviews, the questions were nonstop.

*Will you live in the same state as your son? What are
Tatiana's plans now?* As if he flipping knew. As if she
cared about him enough to tell him. Her law firm had sent
him an efficient packet of options for possible co-parenting agreements, but he'd been too disheartened to wade
through the legalese.

"Get your head in the game!" the quarterback coach
shouted at him across the field as if Jean-Pierre was a distracted JV player and not one of the league's elite.

Actually, with how he'd been playing all week in practice, the JV comparison felt kind of accurate.

The coach's whistle trilled from the sidelines, calling
an end to the day's team workout. Jean-Pierre would still
prepare for hours with the offensive coordinator, with the
quarterback coach and then on his own to be sure he understood the game plan and his opponent. But whereas
at another time he might enjoy the challenge of going up
against Henri and really pitting their strengths against each
other, this week he felt as though someone had put a fist
in his chest and stolen his heart. No doubt this was what
heartbreak felt like.

The ache was so literal it was ridiculous.

And how ass-backward was it of him to realize what all
that hurt was about now that it was killing him. He loved
Tatiana. He was just too blind to recognize that feeling for
what it was. He'd spent so much time living in his head,
methodically moving through his life, that he'd forgotten
how messy and painful emotions could be. You couldn't
control them the way you could manage a game plan or
manipulate a play.

"Reynaud!" The shout didn't surprise him. Someone

or another had been chewing his ass all week for his piss-poor efforts on the field.

Turning, he was surprised to see Jack Doucet himself storming toward him. He noticed most of the rest of the team had already headed indoors to shower up and head home. Actually, now that he thought about it, some of them would be talking to the press since there was a scheduled media hour after this practice.

More time to face the firing squad about his shortcomings as a man. He hadn't even managed to communicate how much he loved the mother of his firstborn. Thinking about that made him welcome whatever diatribe Jack Doucet had in store for him.

"Yes, sir?" Jean Pierre lifted a towel from the metal bench along the sidelines, swiping the sweat from his face and hair. The team had practiced outdoors in the November cold, but the sharp gray wind didn't penetrate a helmet.

"What the hell do you think you're doing, boy?" The coach slammed his clipboard onto the bench with enough force to make the metal ring. "You've got the eyes of the whole football nation on you, and you're lumbering through this week like a homesick rookie."

A kind assessment, in Jean-Pierre's opinion. He nodded, knowing the coach wasn't close to finished.

"As your coach, I'm so furious with you I want to start your backup." He pointed a finger in his face. "But as the grandfather of your son, I'm going to ignore all that for the sake of my daughter and ask you what you're going to do to fix this mess you made with her?"

Surprised at the question, which bordered on warm and fuzzy from a coach with a legendary temper, Jean-Pierre lifted a wary gaze to Tatiana's father. The older man glared at him, but there were lines on his brow that suggested he was worried more than he was angry. Concern etched his features.

With nothing left to lose, Jean-Pierre told him the truth.

"She needed me to tell her I loved her. And I, like the cerebral half-ass that I am, hadn't worked all that out in my head yet." Remembering the look in her eyes gutted him. "In other words, when the game was on the line, I choked."

"Who looks for love in their head?" The coach's face screwed up as though he'd gulped down grapefruit juice. "You figure that out in your heart, Reynaud."

"Not my area of expertise, sir." He looped the sweaty towel around his neck and scooped up his helmet to head indoors.

The coach held up a hand to stop him. "You didn't answer my question. How are you going to fix this?"

The pain in Jean-Pierre's chest tightened into a knot.

"I proposed twice." He'd put a lot of thought and effort into the second go-round, thinking about what he'd say and studying diamond choices. Hell, he'd even taken her to a boathouse roof, a nod to their past he was sure she would appreciate. But he'd been focusing on the peripherals and not the only thing that mattered to her. "Your daughter isn't a woman to give unlimited chances."

Jack Doucet shook his head. "My daughter is a woman who deserves to know she's worthy of love. So even if she sends your ass to the showers for a third time, I suggest you inform her about what's in here." He jabbed his finger into Jean-Pierre's chest protector with enough force to send him back a step.

Before he could answer, the coach turned on his heel and barreled away. He was only a few yards away when he called over his shoulder.

"And get your head in the damn game while you're at it."

Easier said than done.

Dropping to the bench on the sidelines, he reached into his bag, where he'd stashed his water bottle and headphones. Finding his phone, he gritted his teeth and pulled up Tatiana's contact information. Her image filled his screen for a moment, her dark curls and pretty smile so beautiful that he couldn't breathe.

Maybe the people who are slow to love are the ones who love the most, he texted fast, knowing he needed to say it before he second-guessed himself. By the time they've finished studying all the angles and assessing the situation, they are heart-deep. Please see me after the game on Sunday.

He wasn't surprised when there was no reply.

But he would honor his coach's suggestion because it was a good one. Tatiana deserved to know how he felt, even if she'd already closed her heart to him forever.

Tatiana caused a stir in the Zephyr Dome when she arrived at the Hurricanes' home field in New Orleans on Sunday. The tabloid coverage of her romance with Jean-Pierre had spilled into the mainstream media so that she'd become a recognizable face in this particular crowd. Although she'd had a security guard escort her to her seat—a measure taken by a stadium staffer who'd quickly realized she was starting a mob scene in the concession area—Tatiana had been approached by one fan after another before the game. She'd obtained box seats in the first row closest to the field, so they were excellent seats. But seeing the attention she received, an usher had requested that she move to the Hurricane owner's private box—an invitation she knew was a sought-after commodity even among celebrities. Yet she felt too awkward to sit with Jean-Pierre's family after the way she'd left the Tides Ranch during Erika's wedding.

She was only here because Jean-Pierre had sent her a text asking to see her.

Pulling her phone from her purse shortly before half-time, she double-checked the message that had landed in her in-box on Friday.

Maybe the people who are slow to love are the ones who love the most. By the time they've finished studying all the angles and assessing the situation, they are heart-deep. Please see me after the game on Sunday.

She'd reread the words so many times she could have recited them in her sleep. She probably *had* the last two nights, in fact. But seeing them on the screen of her phone, with Jean-Pierre's name at the top, reminded her that he had been the author of those cryptic lines.

Not that she'd come to the game with any illusions about his feelings. But he'd asked to see her. And since he had yet to return any of the paperwork outlining their custody arrangement for César, she thought seeing him would facilitate that necessary step. It was all very logical and practical, just like him.

Except how did he know that those who were slow to love might love in any special way? The question had replayed over and over in her thoughts ever since the text had arrived.

Now, as the whistle blew signaling the end of the first half of the game, the teams on the field relaxed and strode toward their respective sidelines before heading into the locker room. The music in the stadium increased in volume and many fans stood to seek refreshments in the concession area or wait in long lines at the bathrooms. Tatiana stayed in her seat, wondering if she was crazy for being here. She'd convinced her mother to fly down and babysit

César for her during the game. It had been hard watching Henri and Jean-Pierre face off, but they were tied going into the half.

Fourteen to fourteen.

"Look, Ms. Doucet!" A fan wearing black and gold Hurricanes' colors and team gear on every part of her body turned in her seat next to her and gripped Tatiana's knee. "You're on the big screen!"

Following where the woman pointed with her eyes, Tatiana spied an image of herself on the jumbo board over the football field. She tried to smile since the fans were cheering for her even though she'd worn a Gladiators jersey, but she saw that her pretend smile looked more like a grimace.

As the electronic screen switched over to highlights from the game, the fans cheered for other things and Tatiana allowed her attention to return to the field. The players vacated the sidelines and the cheerleaders took up positions. Automatically, her gaze sought out Jean-Pierre, only to see him still on the sidelines, scanning the bleachers.

He shielded his eyes from the sun since the retractable dome was open today. Close to where he stood, fans pointed him downfield.

In her direction.

Heart in her throat, she watched the highly unorthodox interaction. Her father would be furious if his quarterback didn't get into the locker room pronto. The team made adjustments during halftime and Jean-Pierre would have a key role to play. Except now the fans were all in an uproar because he was jogging alongside the high wall of the bleachers.

Toward her.

"Tatiana!" he shouted, lifting a hand to give a wave.

Helmet removed, he was sweaty and his face had a

smudge on one cheek, as if someone's cleat had landed on his face. But his dark eyes were locked on her; he was oblivious to the fans, who were going berserk to have him this close. It didn't matter that he played for the opposing side. He was a Reynaud. One of the game's elite.

And he only had eyes for her.

Standing, she leaned over the rail, not even caring that all the eyes of section A-101 were following their every movement.

"Hi," she said, perplexed. It wasn't like Jean-Pierre to pull unorthodox moves. That had always been Henri's claim to fame. "What are you doing?"

He leaped up to grip the metal railing in front of her and the fans shouted and crowded her. She hadn't realized half of section A-101 had left their seats to get closer to the action. Jean-Pierre hoisted himself higher and fans reached over as if to pull him into the stands.

She feared a riot or a stampede, but Jean-Pierre just shook off the help with a grin that she recognized as his public face, the disarming charm that all the Reynauds employed with ease when they needed it.

"I've got this!" he called to the fans. "Just here to see this beautiful lady."

Female fans swooned. She could honestly hear the collective sigh.

"Jean-Pierre?" She wondered if this was a publicity stunt, but that would be so out of character for him. "What's going on?"

"I love you." His muscles flexed as he held himself there like a gymnast on the high bar. "I needed to tell you in person, not in a text. But I couldn't wait another minute."

She'd fallen off the swings once as a girl and it had felt just like this. Like the wind was knocked out of her. Like she couldn't figure out quite what had happened.

"I don't understand."

"Your father will be losing his mind in the locker room any minute." Jean-Pierre glanced down the sidelines at the runway that led into the visiting team's locker room. "I have to go. But don't leave afterward, okay? I want to tell you better than this. I just…" He shook his head. "Damn, Tatiana. I don't expect anything from you. I just want you to listen."

Before she could reply, he kissed her hard on the cheek and then dropped out of sight. As he hit the ground with a thud, the crowd went wild.

The whole, entire stadium.

Because the jumbo screen was trained on Jean-Pierre even now, following the sideline antics with an up close view for everyone to see.

As he jogged toward the runway, helmet in hand, she wondered if he knew he'd just declared his love for her in front of the whole world. Then, remembering this was Jean-Pierre, the most methodical, analytical, cautious QB in the game of football, she realized of course he knew what he'd done. He'd given her a moment that was unexpected, unscripted and from the heart.

She couldn't have asked for more proof that he'd handed her his whole heart.

The total stranger in the Hurricanes gear next to her opened her arms to her, sharing a phenomenal game moment in the way fans do. It was crazy. And yet, she allowed herself to be hugged, congratulated and feted by all of section A-101, who were beside themselves with being part of a famous love story.

When they'd finally freed her shortly before the second half started, she allowed the usher to escort her out of the box and up the stairs. She definitely needed to talk to Jean-Pierre for real. Without an audience.

But now, she had every reason in the world to hope this really was the start of a famous love story. The emphasis, at last, on *love*.

Waiting in the wives' lounge on the same corridor as the visiting team's locker room, Tatiana could watch game highlights from the brother-versus-brother showdown. The Gladiators had lost even though Jean-Pierre had set a new career high for pass yardage. He'd played an incredible game, but the Gladiators came up short after Henri marched his team down the field with forty-five seconds left to put them in field-goal range, beating his brother by three points.

The game had been epic, to steal an overblown adjective from the excited sportscasters whose coverage she now watched. Almost epic enough to overshadow Jean-Pierre's halftime declaration of love, but not quite. She'd seen footage of his leap up to the stands at least five times while she waited for him to emerge. Only a handful of other women waited with her since the press interviews were still going on. Contractually, the players had to stay for a certain amount of time afterward to field questions.

Unless they were injured.

And in one of the kindest things her father had ever done for her, he texted her after the game to let her know that Jean-Pierre was being seen by a team doctor for a possible concussion. She'd been around the game—and her wily dad—long enough to interpret the text as his shorthand for saying that he'd officially excused his quarterback from press interviews. In other words, the coach had sprung his star early for her sake by supplying the media with the only legitimate excuse for not attending.

When the door opened and Jean-Pierre's large frame filled it, his dark hair still damp from his shower and his attire a standard issue team T-shirt, he didn't look like the bayou billionaire who'd escorted her to his brother's wedding last week or introduced her to foreign royalty. He looked like her high school boyfriend after a rough practice, a bit banged up and bruised with a scrape over one eye. But his eyes definitely lit up at the sight of her.

"You're here. I hoped you would be, but I wasn't sure." Shouldering a duffel bag, he gestured toward the exit on the other side of the lounge. "Do you mind if we find some-place else to talk?"

"Sure." She hugged her arms around herself, feeling as nervous as a girl waiting to be asked to the prom—even though she was pretty sure the boy she liked now liked her back. "How long before you have to be ready for the team flight back to New York?"

"It leaves at seven." He held the door for her that led out into a quiet hallway. "But the coach knows I might need further evaluation from a local doctor, so I'm able to fly back tomorrow if necessary."

She couldn't quite smother a laugh. "My father must really want us to have time to talk."

"He made that very clear." He strode toward a side exit and nodded at the door. "My brothers sent a limo for me. It's in the home team lot. If you want we could sit in there."

"Okay. My mother has César, so I don't need to worry about him." As she followed Jean-Pierre through the maze of corridors beneath the Zephyr Dome, she was glad to be with someone who knew the lay of the land. She was just glad to be near Jean-Pierre, period. She couldn't wait to sit beside him and look in his eyes. Find out what on earth was going through that mind of his. "I hope Dad didn't pressure you to—"

"Absolutely not." He steered her toward a limo nearby.

"He floored me, actually, by giving me the best advice of my life."

"My father?" She hurried to keep pace with his long strides.

A driver exited the limo and took Jean-Pierre's bag before tipping his cap at Tatiana. While the chauffer stored the item, Jean Pierre opened the back door to the vehicle. They got in and he locked it from inside. Then he used a remote to lock the privacy window.

White roses filled a vase beside a bottle of champagne in an ice bucket. The black leather bench seats let them sit close to one another while, up front, the driver fired the engine to life. She had no idea where they were going and she didn't care. All her attention was focused on the man beside her.

"Your dad surprised me. He didn't say anything when I first got back to New York, but by Friday, he stormed over and demanded to know what was going on between us since I'd been screwing up every way possible in practice."

"I didn't tell my parents anything when I got back. I was too upset to talk about it and they respected that." Her eyes scanned his face and it was all she could do not to lift her fingers to the scrape above his eyebrow. But she wanted to hear more, to find out what had gone on with him since she left the Tides Ranch.

"I was very blunt when I told him how I'd messed up with you. How I hadn't recognized what I was feeling because I was so busy thinking it all through."

"You do like to analyze things." She remembered his mathematically drawn wine labels, his lettering perfectly spaced.

"Right. And he said you don't find love in your head. You find it in your heart."

That did not compute for Tatiana. "I can't imagine my father saying anything like that."

"Picture the words infused with more cursing while he yells them at me."

She fell against Jean-Pierre as the limo took a hard turn exiting the parking garage. The feel of his muscular body against hers made her want to curl up and stay there. With an effort, she straightened and met his gaze evenly.

"That I can envision." She refused to ask him again about love. She'd been mortified enough for one lifetime on that score.

"But by then I already knew the truth. That I love you like crazy. I could tell because when you left the ranch it was like you'd ripped my heart out and took it with you."

She'd felt that way, too. As if she'd left her heart on the island with him. Still, she waited.

He took her shoulders in his hands and squared her to face him on the seat.

"I am in pain without you. I love you and I'm sure of it. This love will never go away." He stroked the outside of her arms, sliding his fingers along the silky sleeves of the Gladiators jersey she'd worn to the game. "I understand if you don't trust me enough to take another chance with me. But your father was right when he told me that you deserved to know how I feel."

If the "I love you" part hadn't hit her heart like an arrow, straight and true, then the last part would have sealed the deal. He didn't expect anything from her in return. He just wanted her to know.

Tears sprang to her eyes and her throat closed up with too many emotions to name.

"I love you, too." Her words were a harsh whisper, the only sound she could make over the burn in her throat. "So much."

He folded her in his strong arms and she leaned into him. Home at last.

He held her tight, with a fierceness that told her how much he'd missed her. How much he'd hurt without her. She understood this reserved man so much better than she'd given herself credit for. She'd fallen in love with him a long time ago, and no matter what he said about being a different man now, she saw her old love inside the new one.

"Let's not be apart anymore." She levered back to look up at him, realizing they'd left the stadium and were on the highway that led west toward Lake Pontchartrain.

"I'd give anything to take you home with me." He stroked a thumb along her cheek and tipped her face up to his. "Forever."

When his kiss brushed her lips, she twined her arms around his neck and he pulled her into his lap. Tomorrow was soon enough to get married. For tonight, no matter the scandal, she was going to go home with Jean-Pierre Reynaud, the man who'd always had her heart.

\* \* \* \* \*

# MILLS & BOON®

## *Desire*™

PASSIONATE AND DRAMATIC LOVE STORIES

---

## A sneak peek at next month's titles...

### In stores from 5th May 2016:

- **Redeeming the Billionaire SEAL** – Lauren Canan *and*
  **A Pregnancy Scandal** – Kat Cantrell

- **A Bride for the Boss** – Maureen Child *and*
  **The Boss and His Cowgirl** – Silver James

- **Arranged Marriage, Bedroom Secrets** – Yvonne Lindsay
  *and* **Trapped with the Maverick Millionaire** – Joss Wood

---

Available at WHSmith, Tesco, Asda, Eason, Amazon and Apple

*Just can't wait?*
Buy our books online a month before they hit the shops!
**visit www.millsandboon.co.uk**

**These books are also available in eBook format!**